one is evil

A BOBBY GRECO NOVEL

Check out **Upcoming Releases** on www.jeffbuick.com
for all the details, and be sure to sign up for
Jeff's newsletter so you never miss a new title.

other titles by

JEFF BUICK

Bobby Greco series

No End of Bad Guys—September 2019

https://www.jeffbuick.com/books/no-end-of-bad-guys/

Curtis Westcott series

A Killing Game—December 2019

https://www.jeffbuick.com/books/a-killing-game/

AJ Costa series

Size Four—TBD

https://www.jeffbuick.com/books/size-four/

Stand-alone titles

The Krubera Conspiracy—March 2020

https://www.jeffbuick.com/books/the-krubera-conspiracy/

Bloodline—TBD

https://www.jeffbuick.com/books/bloodline/

The Art of Deceit—TBD

https://www.jeffbuick.com/books/the-art-of-deceit/

The Reluctant Truth—TBD

https://www.jeffbuick.com/books/the-reluctant-truth/

Published by Novel Words Inc. and Jeff Buick
www.jeffbuick.com

Cover and interior design by Lance Buckley
www.lancebuckley.com

ISBN—13: 978-1-9995334-3-4

To Danielle!

one is evil

Here's a new series for you

A BOBBY GRECO NOVEL

Nov 2022

JEFF BUICK

NOVEL WORDS INC.

Dedicated to

Celia Rushford

The love of my life.

three months before

She heard him coming up from behind, moving fast, and lengthened her strides on the wet cobblestones. Her long legs were pumping hard, her breath coming in short gasps as she rounded the corner. One foot almost slid out from under her and she had to break pace to keep from falling. He caught up to her.

And passed, his arms tight to his lean body, his breathing deep and rhythmic. He started to pull away and she doubled down until she matched his speed, the stone buildings flying by. They rounded a long sweeping curve and she caught a glimpse of the Eiffel Tower, lit up and sparkling against the dark sky. A lone car glided past, its headlights casting yellow beams that cut through the grey streetscape.

This was her Paris, the one she had known since childhood, before the rest of the world had invaded her space. Early morning, without the onslaught of people and vehicles, was the only time left when the city was still as it had been. Her Paris still existed, but only for those willing to get up at four in the morning.

Only two more blocks. She was pacing him now, waiting for the exact moment to make her move. They passed the final crossroad and she drove her legs ahead, sprinting flat out, her eyes focused on nothing but the road. One misstep and she would go down in a heap.

Ahead, the iron gates sensed her cell phone and started opening. She willed an extra sliver of speed out of her aching body and pulled ahead by a couple of feet, then cut hard into the courtyard. A fountain was directly ahead, and she slid on the wet stones as she tried to stop, her shin hitting the edge. She went down on her side and lay on the ground, staring up at him.

"I beat you," she gasped.

"Don't look so smug." He grabbed a towel from the pile sitting on the fountain and wiped the sweat from his face. "You're twenty-five years younger than me." He picked up another one and threw it to her.

"And you're a man. Men are stronger, and faster. Supposedly."

He ran his hands across the top of his head and slicked back his jet-black hair. His deep brown eyes were hard to read in the low light. "Did you bruise your leg, Monique?"

She glanced down. "I don't think so."

"Good. No more risks. We can't have you hurt. Not now."

Monique jackknifed to a sitting position and stared at him with eager eyes.

"Soon." He smiled. "Get cleaned up and meet me in the main salon."

When she had left he entered the house and made his way up to the master bedroom and into the en suite bath. The shower was hot and the stinging water invigorated his skin. He dried off and slipped into a pair of jeans and a short-sleeve shirt, then sat on the edge of the bed. The woman rolled over and slowly opened an eye.

"You should get up," he said. "Monique will be waiting. She's excited."

She managed a nod. "I'll be down in a bit, Armand."

He leaned over and kissed her on the forehead.

The clouds had cleared and the first rays of sunlight were streaming through the massive bank of windows overlooking the street when Monique arrived. Her jeans were snug, not tight, and there was a subtle grace to her steps as she sauntered across the room and stretched her lanky frame out on the sofa. Armand Cortez watched her with a critical eye. Every nuance—how she walked, talked, smiled and laughed—was crucial. Never more so than now.

"Well?" Monique said.

"Let's wait for your mother."

Sylvia Dupres didn't rush getting ready. It was almost an hour before she swept into the room, dressed in Dior and Jimmy Choo. A classic beauty, it was difficult, impossible perhaps, to pin an age on her. Her wavy, brown hair still hung past her shoulders, and people often mistook her and Monique for sisters. She sat on the couch beside Armand, who lit a cigarette and handed it to her. It dangled precariously from her slender fingers as she surveyed her daughter.

"No second chances, Monique, this is once in a lifetime," Sylvia said. "You can't let your guard down, even for a moment."

Monique's lips slowly curled into a knowing smile, and in that moment Armand knew she was ready. She would pull it off, Monique had too much of her mother in her to fail. By all appearances, both women were understanding and compassionate. Yet under the surface, they were calculating and cold, driven by money and power. He was the only person they couldn't manipulate—he knew them too well.

"It's time," Cortez said.

Monique jumped off the sofa, ran across the room and threw her arms around his neck, then looked at her mother. "I won't disappoint."

When Sylvia Dupres answered, there was little warmth to her voice. "No, you won't."

chapter one

Ryan Chamberlain's Gulfstream circled over central Florida and touched down on the tarmac at Orlando's Executive Airport. The plane taxied to a private hangar and after a few minutes the plane door opened and Ryan's assistant appeared in the opening.

"Welcome back. How was your flight?"

"Fine, and very safe." Ryan glanced over at his traveling companion, an FBI agent with a military bearing. "They haven't let me out of their sight since I left the Pentagon."

"Is that it?" Shawn Falstaff asked, motioning at Ryan's leather briefcase.

Ryan nodded. "All there, the signed contracts and the hard drive."

"Jesus, we really have it," Shawn said, taking a slight step back. He adjusted his wire-rim glasses and glanced at his watch. "Your department heads will be in the boardroom tomorrow morning at eight."

"Good." Ryan stood, his tall frame barely fitting under the cabin roof. "Are you riding with us?" he asked the agent.

The man had an earpiece attached to a coiled wire in one ear and he listened for a moment, then shook his head. "I'll be in the car behind you."

Ryan and Shawn moved through the small, executive terminal with a group of four agents trailing behind them. They slid into the rear of a waiting car and the chauffeur headed for Synergy, the Fortune 500 company Ryan had spent his career building. Two black Lincoln Navigators pulled in behind them.

"Serious looking guys," Shawn said, peering out the back window.

Ryan nodded slowly. "Well, there's some seriously bad missile technology in my briefcase." He glanced over at Shawn and added, "Don't look so worried, it's encrypted. One of those FBI guys needs to be there when we download it into the mainframe."

Ryan dialed a number on his cell. When a woman's voice came on, he said, "Hi, we just landed."

"Everything go okay in D.C.?" In the background were the sounds of a television and kids' voices.

"It did. Shawn and I are headed to the office, then I'll be home."

"Deal," she said. "See you in a while. Love you."

"Love you too." He killed the line.

Ryan slipped the phone into his pocket and turned to his assistant. "Let's head straight to The Fort. I don't want to stop at my office."

"Late for dinner are you?" Shawn asked with a straight face.

"Funny guy."

The Fort, its nickname from Fort Knox in Kentucky, was the most secure spot on the Synergy compound. In the heart of the building was a stand-alone mainframe computer. Other than its connection to the power grid and a handful of cables snaking off to high-security terminals inside the building, the computer had no links to the outside world or the Internet. The chance of anyone hacking the system was pretty much zero.

Outside the car window, palm trees and manicured boulevards slipped past as dusk settled in. Ryan glanced at the briefcase sitting on the seat between them. The Joint-Air-to-Surface Standoff Missile had been a staple of the American weaponry arsenal for years, yet no one had come close to replicating its technology. Now his firm had been tasked with making it faster, more powerful, and invisible. He shuddered slightly at the impact a stealth version of JASSM would have on the balance of power if a country like North Korea or Iraq got their hands on it. They could attack neighboring countries and it would be impossible to prove who had launched the missile. He willed himself to relax, Synergy was building a game changer and he needed to get that clear in his head.

"Seriously, about dinner, what's up at the Blackwell's?" Shawn asked, then added when Ryan shot him a glance. "It's in your calendar."

"Their annual garden party. Alexis and I actually enjoy going. He's a good man."

Shawn grinned. "That, and a huge influence on the appropriations committee."

Ryan nodded, staring at the clouds rolling in from the fringe of the hurricane pummeling Cuba and heading for Key West. What was its name? Lorraine. The twelfth storm of the season and it was only late September. It had been a bad year for the islands. They hardly needed another hurricane.

He snapped back to the present as the car pulled up to the gates of the Synergy complex. "Yeah, Blackwell is in our corner. He had a lot of pull on us getting the JASSM contract."

Shawn handled things with the security guards, including getting the two Navigators through the main gate. Ten minutes later they were inside and on the short drive to The Fort.

"Things will be tighter at the gate in a few days," Shawn said. "The new retina scanners are almost live."

"Good. That will be better than the old card access system."

"Way more secure," Shawn beamed. "And we tightened up everyone's security clearances."

"Excellent." Ryan slipped out of the car, the briefcase in his hand. "It's unnerving, having this technology on site."

The FBI agents fell in behind them as they entered the building and passed through the security checkpoint, first swiping their cards through a reader, then entering a PIN. The night guard scrutinized their photos on his monitor as they went by, and once inside it was a three-minute walk to the standalone mainframe in the heart of the building. Security outside the computer room was heightened, with two guards personally inspecting their ID's and watching as they placed their right index fingers on a glass panel beside the door. The program confirmed all their identities and the door opened with a swish, but only the FBI agent who had accompanied Ryan on the Gulfstream was allowed in the room. One Synergy guard watched the hallway for potential threats, while the other kept an eye on the three remaining FBI agents and the bank of CCTV screens at the security station.

Inside the bunker, the only sound was the low hissing of ventilation fans hidden somewhere in the dropped ceiling. The mainframe sat alone under a bank of fluorescent lights, cut off from the world. The master set of plans for Synergy's new design would be kept in this room, eliminating the chance of a working prototype being leaked to an unauthorized person. Pieces of the design could be locked in Ryan's office safe for short periods, but never the entire missile specs at one time.

Embedded in one of the concrete walls was a massive safe where the specs would be stored. There were only six people who could open the door, Ryan and Shawn being two of them. Ryan swiped his card, then placed his finger on the glass. Once he passed the usual two-step authentication, a command appeared on the screen asking him to stand in front of a camera set off to one side of the safe. It snapped a picture of his face, then compared it to the one on file, using thousands of markers to ensure it was the same person. The green light lit up and the five-minute delay started to count down.

"Impressive," the FBI agent said.

Shawn nodded. "Next time you're here, we'll have another level of security. Retina scans will be a baseline authentication procedure for every employee entering the complex."

Ryan and Shawn spent the five-minute delay checking their phones and answering emails. Shawn pulled on the handle when the light on the door panel turned to green and it opened with no resistance. Inside, the safe was lined with metal shelves, all stacked with well-ordered piles of documents. Ryan removed the hard drive from his briefcase and set it on one of the shelves, then backed out and closed the door. The light turned red and the bolts slid into place.

"We're done here," Ryan said to the agent. "I'm heading home, unless there's something else you need me to do."

"No, we're good. Keep in mind I have to be here when you transfer any data from the portable hard drive to the mainframe."

"Right," Ryan said. "Shawn will be in touch."

The agent continued. "The only approved locations to store the specs are here, or in the vault in your office. No more than three of the individual components can be in your office vault at any given time." The man locked eyes with Ryan for longer than necessary. "Are you clear on the rules?"

"I am," Ryan nodded.

He and Shawn escorted the agents back to the entrance and saw them off. The security personnel didn't ask for ID as he left the compound and that bothered him. The retina scans would be a great addition, but Synergy was only as secure as its weakest link. He made a mental note to have his head of security tighten things up across the board.

Rush hour was long over and Ryan kept to just over the speed limit, pulling into the driveway of his Winter Park home at twenty minutes past seven. Alexis met him at the door, threw her arms around his neck and kissed him on the lips. She pushed her body against his and they held each other close for a minute, then grudgingly parted. He couldn't help smiling. He loved everything about her, especially her green, cat-like eyes that sparkled when she felt sexy.

Ryan ran his finger along the soft, tanned skin of her cheek and she gave him a hint of a smile. "What a day," he said.

She grabbed his hand and pulled him into the house. "You're home now and that's what matters."

He followed, like a glider behind the tow plane. "You know, you're pretty sexy for a physics geek."

She squeezed his fingers a touch too tight. "That's why you married me." They reached the kitchen and she let go, but her eyes still had that look.

"Hi, dad." Zach's voice shot through the room like a blast of ice water. "Had a good trip, huh?"

"Hi, kid." Ryan tussled the youngster's hair.

"Hey, don't damage the merchandise." Zach pulled back and smoothed out his hair. "I have an image, you know."

"Yeah, okay. Got it." He slipped his arm around Zach's shoulder. "I heard something about a seriously good mark in science. Any truth to that?"

"One hundred percent," he shot back. "That's tough to beat."

"No kidding. What was the test?"

"We had to dissect a frog and label all the parts. Easy-peasey. I like that stuff."

Ryan rolled his eyes. "Our son, the thirteen-year-old coroner."

"Yeah, that sounds cool." Zach eyes grew larger. "People would be easier, the parts are bigger."

Alexis shuddered and gave Zach one of her patented mom-looks, then turned to Ryan. "Do you want to change before we head out?" When he shook his head, she said, "We should probably get going."

"Sure."

Alexis yelled at the hallway. "Patricia, come and say hi to your dad before we leave."

Patricia poked her head around the corner and came running. Ryan scooped her up and gave her exactly the right amount of attention for a nine-year-old who hadn't seen her father for a couple of days, which included a piggyback around the house and hanging her upside down until she squealed. He gave her a final hug and she scurried off to watch television after promising to behave for her older brother. Zach followed them out to the car, his head nodding like a bobblehead as they went over the rules, then he raced back into the house.

They slipped into the car and Alexis put her hand on Ryan's arm before he could back out of the driveway. "Is the JASSM technology actually in the safe at Synergy?"

"It is." He raked his hand through his hair. "Hard to wrap your head around, isn't it?"

"Pretty scary stuff."

"That's an understatement." He was quiet for a minute, then said, "It's a first strike weapon, Alexis." He put the car in drive and stepped on the gas. "If the wrong people got their hands on this thing..."

Alexis sensed there was more on his mind and she waited.

"Do you know how long a person has to live from the time they see the incoming missile?"

"No idea."

"Less than two seconds." He shook his head. "Not very long, is it?"

"Hardly long enough to stick your head between your legs and kiss your ass goodbye," Alexis said.

He glanced over at her, but she wasn't smiling.

chapter two

The narrow road that wound from the street to the Blackwell mansion was bordered by swaying palms, their trunks wrapped in strands of glittering lights. The warm air felt humid and the sky was threatening, but so far the rain was holding off. Ryan rounded the final curve and a sleek bungalow with shades of Frank Lloyd Wright came into view. Every light was on and it shone like a crown jewel.

"I love this house," Alexis said as they pulled up to the valet.

"I know." Ryan handed over the car keys, took the numbered tag, and they headed for the front door. "Hey, what are the Blackwell kids up to?" he asked.

Since she had given up working, Alexis had become the hub for their social lives. Between Orlando and Washington D.C., they had a wealth of connections and she handled the steady flow of invites they received, delicately declining or enthusiastically accepting. She also kept up on the minutiae of people's lives, and knew who was doing what.

"Their daughter just got accepted to Harvard," she said, grabbing at her hair which was blowing every direction in the wind.

"Good to know. What's her name?"

"Emily."

Ryan motioned toward a man and a woman near the front entrance, both with earpieces and watching the new arrivals. "Check it out. Secret service."

"I think I recognize the woman," Alexis said, still clutching her hair.

"Seriously?" Ryan said as they entered the house. "Dark suit, no smile—they all look the same."

"No, I think it's her." They stood in the foyer for a few seconds getting their bearings. "You ready for this?" she asked and he nodded.

Senator Ernst Blackwell was an icon in Washington, sitting on the appropriations committee responsible for both the Patriot and Joint-Air-to-Surface Standoff Missiles, and lifelong friends with General Mark MacIntyre, the chair of the Joint Chiefs. Without his influence, Synergy wouldn't be working on the stealth version of the missile. That was one reason Ryan and Alexis were going to the Blackwell's party. The other reason was because they liked Ernst and Alice Blackwell.

The party was in the garden and people were standing in groups around the pool and on the trimmed lawn, chatting and laughing. They were barely through the patio door when Debbie Mayther, a longtime friend, approached them. The three of them shifted to a quiet spot by the cabana and she turned to Alexis.

"Ready for tomorrow night?" Her face was alive and excited.

"You bet," Alexis said. She glanced at Ryan, who looked puzzled. "I'm playing with Debbie in the club championship. I was going to tell you, but you were in Washington."

"My doubles partner is laid up with a pulled muscle," Debbie said, and put her arm around Alexis. Few women could make Alexis look small, and Debbie was one of them. "Lucky me."

Ryan saw the competitive edge creep into his wife's eyes. Thirty-five and she was still all in for the challenge. "You two are going to kick some serious butt."

"Damn straight." Debbie gave Alexis a big hug and headed back into the crowd around the pool.

"What time do you play?" Ryan asked, helping himself to an appetizer as a waiter passed by with a tray.

"Six. Are you going to come and watch?"

Ryan grinned. "Wouldn't miss it. I love watching you play. So do the kids. You're a really good player."

"Back in the day, maybe," she said, watching Debbie work her way through the throng.

"Oh, my," Alexis said as an elderly woman materialized out of the crowd and headed directly toward them. She was early eighties with a heavy head of white hair, swept back from her face and tucked under a bright red hat.

Alexis lit up and she whispered to Ryan. "See, I told you I recognized that Secret Service woman."

"Auntie Laura," Alexis said, gently grasping the woman's hand.

"Alexis." Laura Neilson gave her a substantial hug. "And Ryan. What a delightful surprise."

"Oh my gosh. What brings you to Orlando?" Alexis asked, her hand still in the woman's grasp.

"Popped in for a few days and ran into Ernst and Alice." She finally let go of Alexis. "Don't you look wonderful."

"Thank you," Alexis said.

"Let's have a photo," Laura said as she spied a newspaper photographer heading their way.

The photographer walked a bit faster as she saw them crowding together for her. She framed them against the background and shot a handful of pictures. "Thank you," she said, asking Ryan and Alexis to jot down their names so she got the spelling correct. She didn't bother asking Laura Neilson.

When they were alone again, Ryan asked, "How is William?"

"Keeping his head above water, I think. I seldom see him these days. Mostly, I keep up with what he's doing by watching CNN."

Ryan shook his head. "Well, he's a busy man."

"I suppose." Laura turned back to Alexis. "I hear Zach is going to try hockey this winter, and Patricia is back in dance classes."

"All true," Alexis said. "Very good."

Laura Neilson winked. "I'm connected."

Alexis felt a tap on her shoulder and turned. Two people were hovering behind her with wide smiles. The man was at least six-four, with huge shoulders, a barrel chest, and a clean-shaven face. The woman was large-boned and tall, with wide hips and shoulders.

Alexis gasped. "Mom. Dad. I didn't know you were in Orlando."

"It's Ernst and Alice's party," Percy Rothchild said, giving his daughter a bear hug. "Not a chance we'd miss it."

"How long are you staying?" Alexis asked.

"We'll be heading back home tomorrow," Etonia said as she gave Laura Neilson a warm smile.

The conversation revolved around everything from Alexis and Ryan's children to the current state of affairs in Washington and how things were going at Synergy. It was public knowledge that his firm had won the contract to work on the missile, and he gave his father-in-law the standard pitch about what a massive opportunity it was and how focused his team was on the work. Nothing more. Nothing that could be considered confidential. After ten minutes, Percy cut away to work the room, leaving Ryan with the women.

With another few minutes of conversation under his belt, Ryan spied a new arrival he needed to speak with, and made his excuses.

"Not to worry," Laura replied. "We three ladies will find a soft spot to sit and catch up on things." They headed to a nearby couch under the watchful eye of her secret service detail, and when they were tucked in with fresh drinks, Laura said to Alexis, "Now, tell me everything. I have nothing but time."

An hour later, Mrs. Neilson declared herself tired and headed for the door after giving both Alexis and Etonia long, sincere hugs. Alexis and her mom stayed sequestered on the couch, away from the crowds, and caught up on the latest news in each other's lives. Eventually, Percy joined them and finally Ryan finished making the rounds and sat down with his in-laws.

"So how is retirement?" Ryan asked Percy. "Travelling, getting out on the boat, sleeping in?"

"None of the above," Percy stated with a good degree of firmness. "Etonia is keeping me busier than ever. I don't have five minutes to rub together."

His wife gave him a look. "Hardly. Percy does what he wants."

The evening wore on, with the four of them staying put as others stopped by to visit. The vice president made a quick appearance late in the evening and took a couple of minutes to chat before being whisked away by his handlers. It was pushing eleven o'clock when Percy and Etonia called it a night.

Once the Rothchilds had departed, Ryan and Alexis made their way to the bar. "Laura Neilson. She really likes you."

Alexis brightened. "I think she does. We go back a long way."

"Spending all those summers together when you were growing up," Ryan said.

"A bit of luck, that. My parents buying the beach house next door to the Neilson's."

"Then their son goes on to become president."

"Who would have thought?" she said.

They reached the front of the line and ordered drinks, soda for Ryan, who was driving. "What was he like, back then? Before he got into politics."

Alexis considered the question, then said, "I was just a kid, and he was older. I'm not sure."

"Right, but you knew him personally, away from the cameras."

She gave it some serious thought, then said, "He was warm, and very approachable. He seemed to care about the people around him. He'd come and sit on the dock with us and joke around. Water fights and everyone getting thrown in the ocean. He was fun."

"Fun? Warm? Those don't sound like words used to describe a politician."

"Well, he really was."

They were leaving the bar with drinks in hand when the crowd parted, and a man headed directly for them, like a bear coming out of the forest. He was Ryan's height but almost twice his girth, and his strides were long and determined. Senator Ernst Blackwell had spotted them.

"Ryan, Alexis." He shook Ryan's hand and gave Alexis a long hug. "How is my favorite young couple?"

"Busy," Alexis said. "At least I am. Ryan heads to the office every day and puts his feet on his desk. I have the kids."

Blackwell laughed, a full-bodied roar. He winked at her from under a thick eyebrow. "He turned me down for a round of golf the other day, so he must be doing something over there at Synergy."

Alexis looked skeptical. "I'm not so sure."

They talked for a few minutes, mostly about Emily and her upcoming stint at Harvard, then Blackwell said, "Alexis, can I have Ryan for a bit?"

"Of course." She hugged him and wandered off in search of a good conversation.

Blackwell's stony face was all business. "JASSM. What's happening?"

"I brought the specs back from D.C. today and put them under lock and key in the vault."

"This is the one that's going to put you on top, Ryan."

"I know, and believe me when I say how much your confidence in us has helped. I know you pushed for us to get the contract."

Blackwell nodded. "My neck is on the line, but that's not what is important. Staying on schedule and delivering a stealth version of the missile is the key. The missile is already a hell of a weapon, but if you can make it invisible..."

"I understand the gravity of what we're doing."

"Do you?" Blackwell asked. "If the new design fell into the wrong hands..." He hesitated for a moment. "They could launch a missile against any number of countries and there would be no way of tracing it back to its origin. One of these missiles, with a rogue hand on the trigger, could start a war."

Ryan swallowed hard. "I *do* understand, senator."

Blackwell stared at him for a good fifteen seconds, then said, "Okay, fix the thing, make it invisible, and keep the technology secure. Don't fucking lose it, Ryan."

No one had ever accused Ernst Blackwell of being subtle.

chapter three

The screen at the front of the room came to life. It flashed an FBI warning that promised a lengthy jail term if the viewer discussed the Joint Air-to-Surface Standoff Missile with any non-classified person. Then sky and clouds appeared on the screen and moments later the back of a JASSM missile appeared, flying at a high rate of speed, a slight vapor trail behind it. Twenty seconds into the footage the missile changed course and plunged earthward. The F/A-18F fighter that was filming it followed.

It was almost possible to feel the g-forces as the fighter dove in sync with the missile. The ground was approaching at an alarming rate and at the last possible second the fighter pulled up while the camera swiveled and locked on the missile. Then it hit. A puff of dirt, hardly noticeable, plumed thirty feet into the air. Nothing for three seconds, then the earth came apart. Dirt and rocks spewed over two hundred feet into the air and littered a five-hundred-yard-wide area when it came plunging back down. A huge crater, almost one hundred feet across, scarred the earth where the missile had hit. Then the screen went black. White lettering rolled across.

Target:Subterranean bunker
Target depth:150 feet below surface
Percentage destroyed:100%

"That," Ryan Chamberlain said to the room of stunned faces, "is what we're building.

The lights came on and he stood quietly for a minute, letting the words sink in. He made eye contact individually with all sixteen people in the room, gauging their reactions. They ranged from fear to excitement and almost everything in between.

"We have a tough deadline ahead of us. The time frames are short, security is tight, and a lot of important eyes at the Pentagon and in Washington are watching. They've put their trust in our team," he said, holding up a thick document that listed all the team members, "and this project could make or break our standing with the military. We need this one."

A few heads were nodding, but mostly there were a lot of serious expressions, and a palpable nervousness filled the room. Ryan continued by addressing specific personnel individually. Cameron Nelson appeared to be the most enthusiastic, so Ryan started with him.

"Dr. Nelson, your team will head up the GPS systems. They were thought to be jam resistant, but have been proven otherwise. They *must* be jam resistant."

"They will be," Nelson said.

"And hopefully on schedule, Cam." Ryan's tone sucked a bit of the seriousness out of the room.

"Oh, well, that changes things." There was a spattering of laughter and the mood lightened somewhat.

Ryan continued. "Dr. Anderson, you and your team are tasked with autonomous terminal guidance."

She shifted around in her chair, looking a bit uncomfortable, then said, "We're on it."

Ryan continued doling out the assignments. "Mr. Holden and his group get inertial measurement and inertial guidance."

Holden, a stern looking man, simply nodded.

"Dr. Childers gets the plum." He stared directly at her. "Figuring out the stealth technology is all yours. You get to make our missile completely invisible. You'll be working closely with both the body design and engine teams. No vapor trail, no signature to even the most sensitive monitoring systems."

June Childers couldn't mask her emotions and cracked a small smile. "Oh, we'll make it invisible all right."

"That's a bit ironic," Ryan said to the entire room. "All this time and expertise so no one can see our work."

That drew a response—heads were nodding and a feeling of determination began to flow through the room. The session ran for a little over two hours, then the team headed out to pass along the objectives and deadlines to their staff. Ryan returned to his office, satisfied with how the meeting had gone. When he arrived, Shawn Falstaff was waiting.

"I met with our chief of security this morning," Shawn said. "He's ready to go with the retinal scans."

Chamberlain slid in behind his desk, opened his email and gave it a quick look. "Good timing on that."

"He wants to bring you up to speed."

"Okay, when?" Ryan asked, still studying his screen.

"How's four-thirty this afternoon? You have two meetings before that, but they shouldn't run over."

Ryan trusted his EA to know how long meetings were going to last, and said, "Okay, I'll squeeze him in. But it can't run more than half an hour. I need to be at the club by six. Alexis is playing in a tournament."

"I thought she was finished with competitive sports, what with her knee and all."

"You know Alexis. Never say never." He closed his email program and signed off his computer.

Falstaff laughed. "Yeah, I know Alexis."

Ryan smiled. "Maybe I should send her some flowers."

"You should, and consider it done." Falstaff keyed in a quick reminder on his phone.

Ryan stood up. "Okay, let's get the JASSM specs onto the mainframe."

Falstaff headed for the door, grinning. "I'll get your FBI buddy."

The agent was right outside Ryan's door and the three of them made their way to the Fort. Once they were through security and into the room that housed the mainframe, Ryan removed the hard drive from the safe and under the watchful eye of the FBI man attached it to the computer. An icon for the external drive appeared on the screen, and when he opened it a program classified as TOP SECRET showed up in bold caps. He waited thirty seconds as the software loaded, then entered his username. The program requested a nine-digit code, cautioning him that failure to enter the correct code on the first try would result in the hard drive incinerating. He carefully typed the digits one at a time from memory. A message appeared on the screen, requesting the decryption algorithm that would unscramble the data on the drive.

He glanced at the agent. "I think this is where you come in."

The man stepped over to Ryan. "I need to verify your identity, then I can authorize the decryption key for the download to your mainframe." He opened his briefcase and withdrew a rectangular box about eighteen inches long by ten wide and three deep. He flipped open the top cover and touched the power switch. A soft green light flowed out and the FBI agent placed it on a nearby desk. "Could you place your fingertips on the screen, please. Right hand first. Wait for this light to flash." He pointed to a small red light on the upper right corner. "When it flashes, switch hands."

Ryan put his fingertips on the screen and held them tight to the glass for fifteen seconds. The red light blinked and he switched hands, setting his left fingertips firmly on the glass. Another few seconds and the light blinked again.

"Thank you. The decryption software is working on the files now. It will tell you when it's done, and then you can transfer the file clusters to your department heads."

After a few minutes a menu appeared on the screen, and Ryan initiated the file transfers. He downloaded the guidance systems to Alan Holden's terminal, then the stealth software to June Childers. He continued until the entire system had been sent to the correct addresses inside his company. The FBI man watched as Ryan closed the file and reinstalled the encryption software.

When he had finished, the agent nodded. "If you need to open the master file again, give me at least two hours notice. I'm staying in Orlando, but I have to set up the file transfers through Quantico. There's no other way."

"Okay. I don't think we'll need the hard drive again." Ryan placed it in the safe and closed it. "The departments should have what they need. Thanks for waiting until I was ready."

"Not a problem. It's all part of the job, sir."

Shawn Falstaff watched him leave. "Cheery type."

Ryan sat on the edge of the desk and stared at the mainframe. Washington had been adamant about the security protocol. He couldn't open the master file for the new missile without having his identity verified, and when he closed the file it must be re-encrypted. No exceptions.

He looked Shawn in the eyes. "Think about what he's protecting."

"The missile," Shawn said.

Ryan shook his head. "The world."

chapter four

Fernando's was a dingy hole in the wall, tucked into a dead-end street in Eatonville. The bar catered to bikers, winos, and prostitutes and needed no advertising to draw in clientele. A single neon sign flickered *Open*, and two Harleys were parked on the cracked asphalt next to the door. It was almost three in the morning and most of the motley crowd had left for the night. Chad Sommers wiped the bar for the last time and flicked a switch. The open sign faded to black.

"Finish your beer, Tiny," Chad snapped at a burly leather-wrapped biker. "It's closing time. I want to go home."

The man raised his left hand and extended his middle finger. "Fuck you, Chad. I drink at my own speed."

"Then drink the fucking thing on your bike. I want to close. I'm tired and this dump doesn't pay me after three."

Tiny checked his watch. It was six minutes to three. "You're still on the clock." He took a small sip of beer.

Chad Sommers gritted his teeth and kept his mouth shut. No one talked to the bikers like he did. They put up with him because he looked the other way, but Chad knew even *he* had to watch his tongue with Tiny and his crew, or he'd be taking a trip to the local emergency room. Or the morgue. He certainly wasn't any sort of physical match for them—at five-eight and one-sixty he was an appetizer. Another biker came out of the restroom, zipping up. He motioned to Tiny and they left together. Three minutes to three. Chad retrieved the empty beer bottle and gave the table a quick wipe, then switched off the lights.

The room was dark except for thin shafts of light stealing through cracks in the shutters. Chad sat at the bar and waited, acutely aware of every sound. His hands were shaking slightly and he pushed his palms against the table. His brain was alive with fast-firing thoughts and he sucked in a few deep breaths to try and calm himself. After five minutes in the dark he slipped behind the bar and poured some scotch into a tumbler. He took a long hit, grimacing from the burn as it went down, then returned to the table, fidgeting with the glass as he nursed the remainder of the drink. At three-twenty a car pulled up to the building and a man came in through the front door.

"Chad?"

"Yeah Andy, I'm here." His voice sounded tinny and too high. "Come on in."

"It's dark in here. Turn on some lights."

"No. We're closed. That'll attract the cops if they drive by. Leave the door open a touch. That'll be enough light."

The man grunted something under his breath as he made his way into the bar and sat down next to Chad. He reached into his pocket and slid a small packet onto the table. "Here's your tester."

Chad concentrated on keeping his hands from shaking as he opened the packet. There was white powder inside. He licked his finger, touched the powder, then set it on his tongue. Cocaine. He nodded. "Can I put some up the nose?"

"Do whatever the fuck you want with it. It's yours. The same shit you get tomorrow night. All four and a half pounds of it."

"You're sure it hasn't been stepped on any more?"

The dealer leaned forward into the beam of light. His breath was hot and smelled of garlic. "You don't trust me, Chad?"

"Not a problem. Of course I trust you." Chad felt beads of sweat forming under his arms and dripping onto his shirt.

"Good." Andy leaned back, his face partially disappearing into the shadows. "I wouldn't want to sell two kilos of product to someone who doesn't trust me."

Chad snorted a line up each nostril and gave the thumbs up. "Yeah, it's perfect. We're on for tomorrow."

"Ten o'clock, the warehouse at the west end of Pine Street. See you there."

"Yeah. See you there." Chad watched the dealer leave and breathed a heavy sigh. He waited for ten minutes, more than enough time to ensure Andy was gone and not returning, then made his way to the bar and picked up the phone. He dialed carefully and a voice answered.

"It's going down tomorrow night at ten. West end of Pine Street in Taft, the warehouse on the right side of the road. You can't miss it." There were muted words over the line and Chad nodded. "Yeah, I know, I know. I already got the blanks and the gun. Wait 'til you yell *police*, point and fire twice." The voice spoke again and Chad responded. "Yeah, you just remember to take care of Andy, or he'll come looking for me." Chad hung up, downed another shot of Scotch and left the bar.

It was on. He'd give Orlando Vice a mid-level drug dealer who had put two people in the morgue, and he got to keep a kilo of high-grade cocaine. What a hell of a deal.

chapter five

The City of Orlando projects a carefully cultivated image to the world. Universal Studios, Splendid China, Disney and a raft of top-rated golf courses. Nothing but the best family entertainment money can buy. Under the glossy surface, though, is another city, and it isn't pretty. Enough so that the brass at the Orlando Police Department organized a special department for just that purpose.

The Violent Crime Section consisted of three specific units. Homicide dealt with the cases that produced a dead body. Robbery covered home invasions, car-jackings, extortion, bribery and simple robberies, and lastly, Assault and Battery took care of the beatings that didn't quite kill the victim.

Bobby Greco worked Homicide.

But on Tuesday, September 30, Detective Greco was on loan to the Drug Enforcement Division. Someone at headquarters had decided that inter-departmental cooperation would teach some of the old dogs a few new tricks. Stacey Daniels, his lieutenant and the woman who ran his department, figured the whole thing was a waste of time, but since Bobby's partner was on vacation he drew the short straw and it went ahead anyway. Greco was assigned to the non-uniform section of DED and teamed up with Darren Ross and Patrick Sorrenson. The vice cops were both veterans and visibly amused when Greco showed up at their precinct looking for them.

"Here to babysit us, Bobby?" Ross asked after they introduced themselves. "We sure need some babysitting down here in vice." Sorrenson, who was standing back a few feet, snorted a weird sort of laugh.

Greco shrugged. "You knew I was coming. What have you got lined up?"

While Bobby was American, born and raised in Orlando for all of his thirty-six years, he was still immensely proud of his Italian heritage and had the olive complexion common to Italians living on the Mediterranean. His hair was dark brown, not black, with a mind of its own, and Bobby constantly looked like he'd just showered and forgot to run a comb through the tangles.

Sorrenson stepped forward a couple of feet. "We've got a tip on some bag of shit who's picking up some coke. Nothing special."

Bobby didn't need to hear another word from Sorrenson—he already couldn't stand the guy. His breath held a hint of whiskey and his eyes moved too fast and wandered, never staying in contact. Bobby made a mental note not to turn his back on Sorrenson during the bust.

Ross glanced at the wall clock, it was almost six. "The deal goes down at ten in a warehouse at the west end of Pine Street. It's in Taft, south of Florida Mall. You know it?"

Bobby nodded. "It's west of Orlando International." He didn't mind Darren Ross. The guy looked like a vice cop—hair a touch too long, blue jeans and t-shirt. And he looked you in the eye. Nothing like his partner.

"You guys want to get something to eat?" Bobby asked.

Sorrenson answered. "Yeah, Italian okay? I know a place."

I'm Italian, you idiot. "Sure, that's fine."

Sorrenson pointed at the lockup area of the precinct. "You want to check out the guns now or after dinner?"

Bobby shrugged. "We've got four hours. Get 'em later maybe."

"Later's good."

Ryan steered into the parking lot of Heathrow Country Club, hitting the speed bumps a little too fast. Zach and Patricia both bounced off the seat far enough that their belts snapped them back, and they were giggling as he nabbed a spot near the front entrance. They jumped out and raced into the club, the thump of a ball hitting a racquet growing louder as they neared the court. The match was already underway, and the stands, which held about three hundred, were about half full. Alexis glanced up as they entered and gave them a quick nod as they took their seats.

Ryan looked at the scoreboard. He'd missed the first game, and Alexis and Debbie's opponents had saved serve. One game to zero, Chamberlain and Mayther serving. Alexis bounced the ball twice, her trademark, then tossed it up and drilled it. It touched the tape on the centerline and zipped through for an ace. 15-love.

"Mom nailed the ball," Zach said proudly. "That other lady couldn't even touch it."

"Yeah, she's pulled that one on me a few times," Ryan said quietly. "The only problem is, once the other player knows you can hit the center line, they stay closer to the middle. Just watch."

Alexis showed no mercy, going to second serve only once. The returns were weak and easy to put away. They went 40-love, then game. The set was tied, and after a couple of volleys Alexis and Debbie were on the verge of breaking serve. Their opponents placed a strong cross-court forehand to Alexis's backhand. She doubled up her grip on the racquet, left over right and fired a rocket back across the net. No return. Game Chamberlain/Mayther. Things started to fall apart for the other team, and Alexis's side took the first set 6-4.

The second set was painful to watch. Alexis and Debbie were relentless, mixing hard driving shots with topspin lobs and chips. The set was mercifully short, with Chamberlain/Mayther winning 6-2. Game, set and match. Alexis and her partner were through to the second round.

Ryan got the kids some food from the deli while they waited for Alexis to change, and they were just finishing when she showed up.

"You were awesome, Mom," Zach said as they drove home.

Alexis laughed. "Debbie carried me, Zach. I was the weak link. We got lucky tonight. That's what happens when you hit thirty-five and don't practice much. Why, I'll bet even your dad could beat me now I'm so out of shape."

Patricia and Zach both squealed with laughter as Ryan screwed up his face in indignation. He didn't argue—she was probably correct.

"What's that?" Alexis pointed to a small metal box wedged in the console between the bucket seats. It looked like a digital camera.

Ryan slowed for a red light, then picked it up and pointed it at her. "Smile," he said and pushed a button. A green light flashed through the vehicle, then he set the camera back on the console.

"Cool," Zach said, grabbing it and giving it the once over.

"What is it?" Alexis asked.

"It's a handheld retina scanner. I met with our security team this afternoon and they lent it to me. It can scan a retina in milliseconds from up to eight feet. We'll be able to use it to identify employees as they come in the main gate. Our security is pretty much airtight."

"Did you just scan my retina?" Alexis asked.

"I did."

"From that distance? Impossible."

He took the camera back from Zach and gave it a gentle pat. "Totally possible. The green light freezes your pupil and keeps it from dilating while an infra-red beam scans the back of the eye. Presto. Retinal scans in less than five hundred milliseconds."

"So that thing has a usable picture of my retina on it?"

Ryan nodded. "It should, if I pushed the right button. I'll find out tomorrow when I take it to the office and download the picture."

"All employees will be scanned?"

"Everyone."

"Makes sense," she said, still looking at the small box. "Having JASSM on site is a bit scary."

"Yeah," he said. "Scary is a good word."

"Choose your poison." Darren Ross pointed to a line of shotguns behind the weapons counter. Bobby Greco leaned on the scratched metal countertop and looked over the selection. Mostly Berettas, dated and well used. He scanned the guns until he saw the one he wanted.

"Is that a Remington 700?" he asked the counter cop. The guy nodded. "Can I see it?" Bobby took the gun and tilted it, checking out the different angles. It was an EtronX System with an electrical pulse to ignite the primers. Bobby looked hopeful. "Can I take this one?"

"Sure, just don't break it. They're expensive." The munitions constable slid a pen and some paperwork Bobby's way. "Push hard, you're making three copies."

"Shit, I can't believe we're still doing stuff on paper," Bobby said.

"Budgets," the cop behind the desk said. "Never any money to modernize."

Bobby filled out the forms, shouldered the gun and left the precinct with Sorrenson and Ross. They piled into the vice cop's ride and headed for the light industrial area west of Orlando International. Bobby sat in the back, listening to the radio chatter as they drove and catching the evening activity. He didn't like leaving his car behind, but the orders from HQ were specific. Ride with the guys, spend a shift with them, and learn why a vice problem sometimes becomes a homicide problem. What a load of crap.

Bobby watched the city slide by as they continued south from Lake Lola Park district. Strip malls, with fresh-looking stucco and brick trim. Quiet residential streets with kids playing under the palms. Lush green parks with winding paths and still, blue water everywhere you looked. It was beautiful—like a Disney postcard. Unless you knew what Bobby Greco knew.

The strip malls housed small businesses laundering money for the drug lords in Miami, and the quiet streets were lined with homes that could become a crime scene in the blink of an eye. He'd tagged a lot of bodies on those pristine avenues. The parks, they were hunting grounds for the sick predators who preyed on kids and women, and what better place to dump a body than in the nearest lake.

Orlando was gorgeous—or not. It all depended on how you looked at it.

Night had overtaken the city and streetlights illuminated the roads as Ross pulled off the 527 onto Pine. He turned onto a side street, drove two blocks farther down and parked. He checked his watch. Nine-twenty. Forty minutes until the buy went down. They settled in, idly chatting about sports and women. Bobby put in his two cents, but didn't feel like part of the group. This wasn't his territory.

At quarter to ten, Sorrenson gave the word and Ross started the car. They pulled slowly onto the street running parallel to Pine, lights off. Ross hugged the right side of the road as they drove west, toward the warehouse.

"The warehouse is single story, except in the front office where there's a mezzanine," Sorrenson explained to Bobby. Tires crunched on bits of gravel as they crept along the quiet street. "The parking lot is off the front, and there's a man-door about twenty feet down the side of the building. The buy is going down in the office area. We'll go in through the door off the parking lot. You can go in through rear of the building. You're there to watch the back in case they run, but don't worry, they won't get by us."

"You seem to know a lot about how things are going down," Greco said, pumping cartridges into the Remington.

"Wiretaps," Darren Ross said, his eyes glued to the road. They reached the end of Cypress and all three men craned their necks to the left, looking one block down to Pine. The warehouse was dark, with no trace of light on either the main floor or the mezzanine-level offices. "You wouldn't believe the stuff we get off wiretaps. These guys are so fucking stupid they lay down every detail for us on their cell phones. Dumb asses."

"Pull into that lot." Sorrenson pointed to the other side of the street. Ross let the car glide noiselessly across the road and rolled up behind a Dumpster. He cut the ignition and turned to Greco, waiting in the back seat.

"Remember, the deal's going down out front. We'll take care of it. You're there in case they run." He glanced at his watch. "Six minutes."

"Yeah, I got it. In through the door at the back."

The three men exited the car, quietly closing the doors. Bobby split off from the vice cops and moved fast through the salvage yard that bordered the warehouse. Most of the discarded equipment was from old conveyors and boilers and it was easy to slip in and out of sight as he ran. Bobby reached the warehouse in less than three minutes and hugged the side of the building as he searched for a way in. The ground beside the building was covered with grass, and he moved quickly without making any noise. He found the door and checked his watch. One minute. Bobby took a few deep breaths and then pulled on the handle. It was unlocked. That struck him as strange—why would the back door of a warehouse be open after hours? His sixth sense, the one that had kept him alive so many times over the past twelve years, started to tingle. He released the safety on the Remington and slipped inside.

The warehouse was dark, but not completely black. There was one low-wattage bulb burning about halfway between Bobby and the front of the building and he moved slowly toward it, his eyes scanning the shadows. Rows of heavy metallic shelving were bolted to the floor, and Bobby crept forward, one section at a time. He could hear voices now, coming from directly ahead. Something was wrong. This wasn't going down like Sorrenson and Ross had said it would. The dealers were in the back of the building, not up front.

Bobby reached the end of the shelving and peered around the corner. There were two men standing in the soft glow of an exit sign, and their voices were discernable now. One was young and thin, with stringy blond hair, and the other was larger and meaner looking. Bobby figured the kid to be the buyer. He stayed still and listened.

"Yeah, it's from the same batch as the stuff you tried in the bar last night. Don't be fucking with me, Chad, just show me the money."

Chad let out a nervous chuckle. "Show me the money. Jerry Maguire. Funny, Andy."

"What the fuck you talking about? Who's Jerry Maguire?"

"No, it's nothing, Andy. Just a movie is all. Here." He bent down and picked up the gym bag by his feet. It looked heavy. "It's all there. Twenties and fifties."

Andy unzipped the bag and peered inside. He took out one stack of bills and flipped through it. He replaced the wad and closed the zipper. "I'm not worried, Chad. I know where to find you if it's not right. See ya." He turned to leave, toward the exit sign.

Bobby had a split second to make a decision. Sorrenson and Ross were wrong. The deal was done and the dealer was going to walk.

He jumped from behind the shelf, pumped the shotgun and yelled, "Orlando PD. Stop right where you are. Hands up."

The dealer stopped and turned. He dropped the bag and slowly raised his hands. The kid did the exact opposite. He pulled out a revolver, aimed and pulled the trigger. Two quick shots boomed through the warehouse, and Bobby threw himself to the ground. He rolled hard to his right and came up firing, the Remington deadly from inside twenty-five feet. The shotgun blast hit the kid in the chest and threw him back ten feet into a shelf, his shirt covered in pellet marks and blood. The revolver slipped from his hand and clattered to the floor. He tried to breath, but there was only a gurgle.

"Don't you fucking move," Bobby yelled at the dealer. He kept the shotgun on him as he approached and leaned over the kid.

"Who the fuck are you?" the boy managed. Then he died.

chapter six

Zach spilled his orange juice on the kitchen floor and Patricia started laughing. Their mother failed to see the humor.

"C'mon, Zach, you're old enough to drink your juice without dumping it all over the place," Alexis said. Some days being the adult in the room was tough. "Now finish your breakfast and brush your teeth. You have five minutes before it's time to leave for school."

"Okay, mom." He giggled as he dug into his cereal. "Sorry."

The phone rang as Alexis wiped up the spill. She checked the caller ID and saw it was Ryan. "Hello, sweetheart."

"Hi. How are things at home?"

"Not so great. I'm cleaning orange juice off the floor right now."

"That's no fun. Do you have another match at the club today?" he asked.

"No, not until tomorrow," she said, straightening up for a moment. "We have a second-round bye, so our next game is Thursday at two in the afternoon."

"I can't make it. I'm in meetings all day Thursday."

"Don't worry. If we get through you can come and watch the quarter-finals."

"Sounds like a plan. I have to run, talk to you later."

"Later."

As Alexis got back to wiping up the mess, her cell went off again. This time her parents' number came up. "Hi, mom," she said.

"Alexis, good morning love. Wasn't that fun last night? You and Ryan both looked fantastic."

You wouldn't say that if you could see me right now, she thought, the dirty dishrag hanging from her hand. "It was a fun night. I'm glad you and dad could make it down, but hey, you should have called and let us know you'd be there."

"We wouldn't have missed it. And all my favorite people were going to be there. How could I say no?"

"You knew Auntie Laura was coming?" Alexis asked.

"Of course. She called a few days ago and we haven't seen each other for ages."

Alexis smiled to herself, she should have known. Her mom and Laura were tight, and their families so entwined that Alexis had no memory of life without the Neilsons. "She's so kind. She makes me feel special. And she's always buying birthday presents for the kids."

"And Christmas," Etonia laughed. "She's never missed a Christmas."

"No, she hasn't. The kids love it when her package arrives." Alexis perched on a stool at the kitchen island and threw the rag in the sink. Her parents might be retired, but they were still busy, and very connected. How many people were on first name basis with the family of the president? "She's so down to earth. It's hard to believe her son is the president."

"Don't kid yourself." Etonia's voice took on an edge. "Laura can be tough when she needs to be. William didn't get to be president without her and Percy."

"No, I suppose not," Alexis said.

"Are you coming to visit soon? We'd love to see you."

"Ryan is swamped at the office these days, so I'm not sure he can make it. If we *did* come, it would likely just be me and the kids."

"Wonderful," Etonia said. "We'll set it up as soon as you give us some dates. Your father will be so happy."

Zach and Patricia piled noisily down the stairs, ready for school, and Alexis ended the conversation with her mom. She set the phone down, thinking back to her old life, the fast-paced one where she went to the office and spent her day with all the other geeky engineers. Some days she really missed it.

Bobby Greco poured himself a stale coffee and added some sugar. He tasted it, added more sugar, then dumped it in the sink and started over. Christ, was it too much to ask for a decent cup of coffee. He'd been up all night, filling out reports and dealing with a couple of Internal Affairs guys who looked more like accountants than cops. Now his boss, Lieutenant Stacey Daniels, was coming in. Bobby sat waiting, exhausted, on a bench outside the interview room at police headquarters, watching the uniforms mill about, shuffling paper from desk to desk. Bobby focused on one particular cop, tracking his movements about the huge bullpen. Answer the phone, move paper. Check the printer, move paper. Open a file, move paper to another file. Shit, the guy was an office worker, not a cop.

Stacey Daniels pushed her way through the front door and a few heads turned. At almost five-eleven and sporting short, spikey hair that suited her to a tee, she had that effect on men—and women. She spotted Bobby and angled his way, motioning for him to join her. They ducked into a private cubicle away from the noise. Stacey was on his side, he knew that, but this one was going to stretch her loyalty. She leaned over the desk, her voice just loud enough for Bobby to hear.

"What the hell happened last night, Bobby? It's really hitting the fan."

"No shit. Internal Affairs is all over me." Bobby was starting to get a bad feeling about things. He ran a hand through his tangle of hair. "Sorrenson and Ross had word on a drug deal going down around ten in a warehouse on Taft."

"I heard that much. What else?"

"We picked up some weapons at the station and I grabbed a Remington shotgun. We got there a few minutes early, sat and waited, and then about five to ten we moved in. The vice guys went in through the front office where the deal was supposed to be happening, and I covered the back of the building."

"So you were there to make sure they didn't leg it out the back door."

"Yeah, but the deal went down in the rear of the warehouse, not up front." He paused for a moment and had a sip of coffee.

"What then?" Stacey asked.

"The buy was done. The dealer had the cash and was heading for the exit. If I didn't move on him, he was gone."

"Where were Sorrenson and Ross at this time?"

"Still up front, I guess. I don't know."

"Okay, keep going."

"It was pretty dark, and I was behind a row of shelves. I stepped out, identified myself as Orlando PD and pumped the shotgun. The dealer dropped the money and raised his hands. The kid went for his gun and banged off two rounds."

"He fired at you? You're sure about that?"

"Fuck, LT. It's not hard to remember a perp pointing a gun at you and pulling the trigger. Yeah, I'm sure."

"Okay, okay." Stacey held her hands out to settle her detective. "Then what?"

"I rolled and came up firing. One shot to the chest. He lasted about thirty seconds."

Stacey Daniels waited a long moment, then said, "The other guy, the dealer, his name is Andy Rogers. He says the kid was unarmed. That you fired without cause."

"That's bullshit," Bobby exploded. "No fucking way. The kid fired twice. The gun was lying on the ground next to him."

Stacey stared into her detective's eyes for a few seconds. "There's no gun, Bobby."

"What? What are you saying?"

"No one found a gun anywhere near the kid. Rogers is adamant you killed Chad Sommers in cold blood."

Bobby sat silent, stunned. He wanted to scream at the top of his lungs that this was bullshit. He wanted to stand up and walk out of police headquarters and go back to his precinct, sit at his desk and get working on his homicide files. He wanted some sleep. He wanted this whole thing to go away. But now, with Stacey sitting across the desk and staring at him, he knew it wasn't that simple.

"You've got my side of the story, LT. What's the other?"

Stacey took a deep breath. "Sorrenson and Ross came running from the front of the warehouse when they heard the shotgun blast. They found you standing over Sommers, the shotgun trained on Rogers. Sorrenson covered Rogers and Ross got you to back away from the body. He said you needed to cool down. A couple of uniforms were on the scene in under seven minutes. They didn't find a gun."

"Then someone moved it. It was lying next to Sommers, maybe two feet to his right."

Stacey shook her head. "Sorrenson didn't leave the scene until the uniforms arrived."

"Then Sorrenson has the gun." Bobby leaned forward, his eyes on fire. "Christ. It was a setup." He sat back in the chair and rubbed his hand across his brow. Stacey didn't speak. Finally, Bobby asked, "Is there any relationship between the kid I shot and Sorrenson and Ross?"

Stacey nodded, slowly. "He was an informant. They'd worked a few busts with him in the past year. The same MO, just different results."

Bobby let his head slump onto his chest. Sorrenson and Ross had wanted the kid out of the way. If Chad Sommers had been in bed with vice, there must have been some upside for him—a portion of the drugs on each bust, some of the cash. Whatever the relationship between vice and Sommers had been, it was buried now. Dead men don't talk. The pricks in vice had used him to take care of their problem. The information on the deal hadn't been from a wiretap, it had come from Chad Sommers. They knew the deal was going to happen in the back of the warehouse. The unlocked door, Sorrenson and Ross not showing up until the shots were fired. The missing gun. It was definitely a setup.

Bobby had an idea. "LT, everyone says I was the only one to fire. But I know Sommers took two shots at me. There should be slugs somewhere in the warehouse."

Stacey shook her head. "We figured the trajectory and went over every inch of the building where the slugs should be. Nothing."

"You're sure?"

"Positive. I spent three hours at the crime scene myself working the angle. There are no bullets, Bobby."

"Jesus Christ." Bobby yelled. He leapt from his chair and slammed his fists on the table. "That's why Sommers said that to me. Son of a bitch."

"What, Bobby?" Daniels asked.

"When I went to check on him, right after the shooting, he was still alive. He looked up at me and said, *Who the fuck are you?*. You know why he said that, LT?"

"No."

"Because he expected to see Sorrenson or Ross, not me. And when he took those two shots at me, it was for Andy Rogers' benefit. To make it look like he wasn't working with the cops. They were blanks. He shot fucking blanks at me. Now ain't that a son of a bitch."

"Without someone to back up what you're saying, Bobby, this isn't going to go your way."

Bobby sat down, knowing what Stacey said was true. "How bad is it?"

"Bad, Bobby. It's really bad."

"Shit, Stacey, this is my career."

She nodded. "That's the best you can hope for." She reached out and set her hand on his forearm and squeezed hard. "I believe what you're saying and I'm behind you. I'll do everything I can to keep you from doing time."

Bobby didn't respond, just looked past his lieutenant to the bullpen. Somehow pushing paper wasn't looking so bad anymore.

chapter seven

The Country Club of Heathrow, tucked into one of Orlando's most exclusive enclaves, has a storied past. Finding celebrities wandering the halls or professional tennis players taking part in high-profile charity matches is regular fare, and winning the Heathrow ladies club championship is no small feat.

At the tournament dinner, the Chamberlain and Mayther families sat together at the same table as speeches were given, trophies handed out, and good wine flowed. The evening went late and the kids were dozing when Ryan and Alexis drove south to Winter Park. Ryan kept glancing at his wife, a boyish grin on his face. Finally, Alexis turned sideways in the car seat to face him.

"Okay, what's with you?" she asked.

"Nothing," he said, but the grin was still pasted on. "Just that I have the most wonderful woman in the entire world as my wife. How does that song by Eric Clapton go? *My darling, you are wonderful tonight*." His voice was almost as smooth as Clapton's.

"That's the nicest thing anyone said to me tonight." She slid her hand onto the console and Ryan held it as he drove. A minute passed, then she said a bit sheepishly, "I let myself get pretty wrapped up with the tournament. How things are going at the office?"

"Things are really good right now. All eleven groups are up to speed on JASSM, and the other six Washington contracts are on schedule. It's great when everything clicks." He paused a moment, then glanced over at her. "Have you thought about coming in and working on one of the projects?"

Alexis pursed her lips and didn't answer for a while. "I don't think so, I'd just be stepping on someone's toes. If you were having trouble somewhere, then yes, but not now."

He squeezed her hand. "Okay, whatever you want. But remember, there's always an opening for a talented electrical engineer if you want it."

She kissed his hand. "Thanks."

Ryan pulled into the driveway and stopped in front of the garage. They woke the kids and trundled them inside to their beds, then Ryan returned downstairs and made two cups of coffee. He met Alexis in the family room and they talked for a while about nothing in general, then shut off the lights and headed for bed. Ryan slid under the covers and ran his fingers along the small of her neck.

"Your eyes have that sparkle," he said, a touch of hopeful in his voice.

"For good reason." She flipped on her side so they were face-to-face and kissed him. "For *very* good reason."

They made love, then lay in each other's arms for the better part of an hour, whispering occasionally, but mostly just enjoying the touch of the other's skin. Finally, Ryan drifted off, leaving Alexis alone with her thoughts.

She thought back to the tennis finals, including match point, which was won with a vicious crosscourt backhand that handcuffed both her opponents. The tournament photographer had captured the shot, her right foot firmly planted, her eye on the ball as it impacted the racquet. They had framed the photo and displayed it next to the trophy in the awards cabinet. Alexis had to admit, coming out on top was a bit of a high.

A slight noise startled her, and she snapped back to the present. She listened closely for a minute or two. There it was again, almost inaudible, but now she was sure. Zach or Patricia must be out of bed. She eased out from under the covers and slipped on her housecoat. Ryan stirred, then opened his eyes.

"What's going on? Why are you up?"

"It's one of the kids. I'll be back in a few minutes." She padded quietly across the master bedroom and closed the door behind her. Ryan rested his head on the pillow and drifted off.

He woke after a while—how much time had passed he wasn't sure. Alexis hadn't returned and he checked the alarm clock on his night table. Three-fifteen. Ryan listened but couldn't hear any sounds. The silence grew until he couldn't stay in bed any longer. He slipped on his robe and went looking for her.

She was sitting in the living room, looking out the front window at the acre of grass and trees between the house and the street. Royal palms swayed in the breeze and the moon was partially obscured by a thin layer of clouds. He sat down next to her on the couch and set his hand on her shoulder. She flinched slightly, then took his hand.

"It's beautiful with the full moon," she said quietly.

He nodded, looking out the window with her. "Are the kids okay?" he asked after a minute or two.

"Yes, fine. It was Patricia. She had to go to the bathroom. I tucked her in and she was asleep in seconds."

"Kids are lucky. They lay their heads on a pillow and *wham!* they're out cold. No worries."

"I remember that," Alexis said.

"Yeah, those were the days."

He got up and held out his hand to help her off the couch—it felt warm to his touch. Back in bed, Ryan was restless, tossing about and waiting for sleep. He could hear Alexis breathing, steady and rhythmic, but he wasn't sure if she was asleep. He finally drifted off and when he woke sunshine was pouring in through the windows. He glanced at the clock and slipped out of bed. It was already ten minutes after six.

Alexis was still asleep when he finished showering and dressing, and he pulled the door closed behind him as he left the bedroom. The kids seldom stirred before seven and the house was quiet as Ryan made some toast and poured himself a coffee. His foot hit something sticky on the tile floor and he almost spilled his coffee. He looked around, whatever it was had been wiped up, albeit not all that well. He shook his head—Zach and his orange juice. He finished his breakfast on the fly, put the plate in the dishwasher and grabbed his phone.

Traffic was light and the drive to Synergy was fast, mostly because of the Sunday traffic. When he arrived, the new security was up and working and the guard at the front gate scanned his retina and had him enter his code after swiping his ID. A green light came on and the bar rose. Ryan drove into the maze of buildings feeling a bit more at ease with having the JASSM technology on site, a legitimate concern considering the size of the sprawling complex. Administration and security, maintenance, shipping and receiving, and the employee health club all had their own standalone buildings. The remaining five housed research and development. Building Nine—The Fort—was the newest and most secure on the property.

It was an imposing structure, constructed entirely of high-density concrete. Windowless walls, embedded with lead plates, extended five levels below grade, and vibration and heat sensors monitored the twelve-inch thick concrete foundation to deter any sort of tunneling. As he drove up, Ryan recognized June Childers' white Mustang and pulled in beside it.

An armed guard at the entrance rescanned Ryan's retina, then had him set all four fingers and thumb on a glass plate. The screen flashed from red to green, and Ryan repeated the procedure with his other hand. The guard waved him through and he moved on to the solid steel inner door. Ryan entered a five-digit code on the pad, then scanned his ID card into a reader. The door cracked open without a sound and he entered the top-secret world of JASSM.

Building Nine had five distinct sections. Three were filled with computer stations for storing and analyzing the missile test data. A fourth was dedicated to building the physical prototypes, and the last section was a lab, set up exclusively for testing them. June Childers was already in her office, working on her refinements to the missile so it could operate in stealth mode. Ryan stood on the outside of the glassed-in area and watched for a few minutes as she made a tiny adjustment to one of the three prototypes. She sensed someone was watching and turned and waved. He waved back.

Childers was a handsome woman, with chiseled features and an infectious grin. She was a regular at the company gym and partook enthusiastically in whatever new workout classes the trainers came up with. She had even broken her nose in a grueling cross-fit class, but the small bump suited her. June Childers was no porcelain doll.

June set down her tool and walked over to the glass door separating the lab from the outer offices. She pushed a button and the door made a quiet hiss as it opened.

"Good morning, Ryan." She undid her lab coat and pulled off her safety glasses.

"Morning, June. Hard at it I see."

She rolled her eyes. "There are a lot more flaws in the design from Washington than we thought. I'm just trying to iron out some of the wrinkles."

The area outside the lab doubled as June's office, and the odor of warm plastic followed her as she closed the door behind her. Ryan sat in a chair and put his feet up on the edge of her desk. "Deadlines. Terrible things."

She sat down next to him. "From underneath, the missile is undetectable." She leaned in. "The problem is, it creates an airfoil that ripples the air as it travels, and that makes it visible from above. Highly sensitive satellites could pick up the trail if they were programmed to look for it."

Chamberlain got up and peered at the missile. "Well, we knew there would be some bugs. Fixing them is what we're being paid for."

"We have the expertise and the equipment for the R & D, but timing is an issue."

Ryan nodded. "Right, what are your thoughts on the deadline?"

"To be in limited production by next March, we need the bugs in both the software and hardware worked out by January. It's already mid-October. I don't know if I can fix this glitch that quickly."

"What if we went back to the design team at the Pentagon and told them we need help?"

"No way." Childers' tone was firm, non-negotiable. "Washington knew what they gave us. The Pentagon had a team of scientists working on this project for years with an unlimited budget and the US military to test their prototypes. And yet they still designed a missile with a defect that we found by testing it in a wind tunnel."

"A very advanced wind tunnel," Ryan pointed out.

She laughed. "Yes, in a very advanced wind tunnel." Her face hardened. "Ryan, I wouldn't trust these guys to tie my shoes."

"Well, at the end of the day they're our client, and the ones who will get the encrypted hard drive with all our work on it."

"Still..." she said.

He sat for a while, silent and thoughtful. Finally he said, "How much time do you need to fix the problem?"

"Two months of analysis in the lab, then another month to finalize the adjustments to the body shape. I'm pretty sure I know where the problem is, but fixing it is going to be tricky."

"Okay, I'll check and see if we can hold off production of the exterior shell until mid-January. They'll get geared up to re-mold the shape as soon as you're finished, and in the meantime we can we keep the other teams moving ahead."

"That's a good plan. I'll only be changing the exterior hull by a couple of millimeters here and there, so it should be safe to have everyone else continue working."

"All right, tentatively you have until January 15, but quicker is better."

"You bet," she said.

Ryan's phone rang and he checked the caller ID. It was coming from somewhere inside Synergy.

"Chamberlain," he said, then listened for a few seconds. "Okay, I'll be there in a couple of minutes." He killed the call and stood up. "Alexis is at the front gate," he said to June. "Her retina scan failed and they won't let her in. I'll talk with you later."

Ryan hustled for the main entrance on foot, wondering what Alexis was doing at the complex. She seldom came to Synergy, especially on the weekend when the kids were at home. Alexis was sitting in her Audi at the gate, looking anything but pleased. She got out as he approached.

"My retina scan doesn't work. It keeps coming up *no match*."

The front gate attendant looked a bit unsure what to do. It was the CEO's wife, but the new policy was specific—no exceptions. "Sorry, sir, I know this woman is Mrs. Chamberlain, but the new rules are very clear."

Worry was all over the young man's face. Ryan's firm paid the security personnel considerably more than the going rate in Orlando, and his employees valued their jobs. "This could be my fault, Chris," he told the officer. "I took a quick shot of Alexis's retina with a portable scanning unit while we were in the car. That's probably why it doesn't match. Who's in the security office today?"

"Wayne Elliot. He could re-scan her, but I'll have to insist she place her fingers on the glass. I need some sort of positive ID. Even for your wife, sir. I'm sorry, but those are the rules."

"Sure. Fingers on the glass, Alexis. You know the routine."

She settled down a bit and placed her right hand on first, then her left. Both came up as perfect matches, and she gave the security man a tight smile as she slipped back in her car. "Don't worry, you did the right thing."

"Thanks for understanding, Mrs. Chamberlain."

Ryan jumped into the passenger seat and pointed to Building Four, where security and administration were housed. The gate opened and she drove through the complex and pulled into a guest spot outside the building.

"Let's get the scan done now, Ryan. That was embarrassing."

"Sure," he said, then added. "What's up?"

"I wanted to spend some time with my husband. See how things are going." They headed into the security building and Wayne Elliot's office. "How *are* things going?"

"Oh, as usual," he said. "The Pentagon sent us technology that's full of holes. The missile leaves a ripple as it cuts through the air so a satellite could see it from above."

"So what now?"

It seemed like an odd question and he gave her a sideways look. "We fix it. June thinks she can sort it out by mid-January."

Wayne Elliot, Synergy's head of security, was waiting for them when they reached his office. Elliot had been with the company since its inception and knew both of them well. "You need your retina re-scanned, Alexis?"

"Apparently. Ryan scanned it on a portable device."

He checked his files. "Okay, that makes sense. I was wondering why we didn't have a record of you being scanned into the system." He looked over at Ryan. "Did you download the scan yourself?"

Ryan nodded. "I did."

The security chief tried to disguise it, but he looked a bit ticked off. "If you could sit here," he said to Alexis, "this will only take a second."

Alexis sat on the chair and looked directly into the machine. There was a quick flash of green light and Elliot checked the image on the screen.

"That's way better. It's much clearer than the one on file. I'll update the system and you should be fine from now on."

"Thanks," she said and wagged a finger at Ryan. "The rules apply to you too, mister."

She was smiling and Ryan started laughing. "Guilty. Won't do it again."

They retraced their steps to the building entrance and Alexis asked, "What happens if you can't get JASSM up and running by March?"

He looked grim for a moment, then perked up. "We've stayed on schedule for every government contract so far. If we're late it could change the way some people on the Hill view us."

"So, meeting the deadline, it's a concern."

He slipped his arm around her shoulder and pulled her close to him. "Hey, we'll sort it out. June Childers is working on it, and if anyone can fix the glitch, it's her." He grinned at his wife, but underneath the cheery exterior a small shadow of doubt was festering.

chapter eight

Riggs & Company had offices in Miami, Tampa and Orlando. Miami was the busiest, but since the company had originated in Orlando and Clayton Riggs lived there, it remained the headquarters. The office was a modern single-story building with fresh paint and trim, facing onto North Thompson Road. At the start of soccer season the neighborhood teams showed up looking for sponsorship, and they usually left with something. Clayton Riggs was a good corporate citizen.

He could afford to be. His company investigated insurance fraud, and business was brisk. Insurance companies hired him so they didn't get stuck paying fraudulent claims, and his cut was substantial. Turning work down because he didn't have a warm body to handle the file was his pet peeve, and he was always on the lookout for good investigators.

Bobby Greco pushed through the firm's front door, introduced himself and told the receptionist he had a two o'clock meeting with Mr. Riggs. She checked the day's schedule, nodded, and asked him to take a seat. Bobby picked an overstuffed chair in the corner and glanced around the room. Soft music played from hidden speakers and the carpet was plush underfoot. Expensive-looking paintings hung on the walls and the leather cushions felt soft and warm against his skin. It was a hell of a difference from the ratty precincts where he had spent so many years of his life. He glanced up as a fifty-something man with a quick step approached him.

"Hi, you must be Robert Greco," he said. "I'm Clayton Riggs."

"Pleased to meet you."

They shook hands and Riggs pointed to the hallway. "Let's sit in my office, shall we?"

Bobby followed him past a number of newly renovated offices. The walls in each room were covered with banks of filing cabinets and maps and all the desks had two computer screens. It was obvious that the work spaces were geared to getting things done. Riggs asked his assistant to bring coffee and veered off into his office with Bobby in tow. They sat at a round table near the window. Bobby had always liked round tables—it put people on equal footing.

It was a tiny detail, but from all Bobby's years in major crimes and homicide, those little quirks seldom escaped him. Cases were often solved, or not, on the smallest of things. A comment early on by someone who wasn't a suspect could change the entire direction of the investigation. What wrist they wore their watch on—the color of their eyes—whether it had rained that night. Tiny things that seemed so unimportant at the time, yet ended up blowing the case open. So far, he liked what he'd seen at Riggs and Company, including the man sitting opposite him. Clayton Riggs had honest, intelligent eyes, and for Bobby that had great value.

"So, you'd like to work for our company, Robert," Riggs started.

"It's Bobby. No one ever calls me Robert."

"Okay, Bobby it is. Call me Clayton." Bobby nodded and Clayton continued. "Why Riggs and Company?"

"A couple of things." Bobby sipped the coffee and raised an eyebrow. "Three now I've tasted your coffee. It's a lot better than the stuff at the station." Riggs laughed and Bobby continued. "I think my talents would lend themselves to what you do here. I'm extremely good at investigative work, can move about without being noticed, and know how to read people. I work well in a team environment and I'm a quick learner. I'll be up to speed in no time."

"Okay, counting the coffee that's two things," Riggs said. "What's the third?"

"I believe in what you're doing. Trying to cut down insurance fraud."

"Then there are four reasons. You need a job." Riggs was watching him closely now. "I read the newspaper version of what happened at the warehouse on Taft. What's your side of the story?"

"I shot a guy in the middle of a drug bust. The district attorney decided not to file charges but the department still fired me. It's pretty simple, really."

"Is it? I've found that most stories have two sides to them."

Two sides to the story indeed, Bobby thought. This one included collusion by two on-duty cops who hung him out to dry for a murder they organized. Telling that side of the story would implicate Ross and Sorrenson, and while they were complete bags of shit, it was up to a court to make that decision. And it didn't look like that was ever going to happen.

"There's another side, but I'd rather not get into it right now."

There was a lingering silence, then Riggs said, "Okay, interview's over. You've got the job."

Bobby was a little taken aback. "Just like that? You're hiring me?"

"I'm a good judge of character. I already know from your resume that you're more than qualified. I've hired a few ex-cops and it's worked well for me. You can tell me your side of what happened in the warehouse when you're ready." He stood and extended his hand. "Welcome to the team."

"Thanks," Bobby said, standing up and shaking Riggs' hand.

"There's paperwork to fill out. Jill at the front desk, she'll take care of that. But first, I'd like you to meet Jacky Foster. She used to be with Orlando PD, so you have something in common straight off the top. You'll be working with her until you're up to speed on our procedures."

"Sure, that's fine." Bobby followed him into the hall and down to a corner office similar to Riggs'. A young Asian woman, maybe thirty, sat at the desk. She looked up as they entered.

"Hi, Jacky. This is Bobby Greco. Your new apprentice."

Jacky Foster stood and stretched her hand across the cluttered desk. She was short, maybe five-two, with a wide face and black hair streaked with light brown highlights. Bobby took her hand, ready for a firm grip. She didn't disappoint.

"Clayton said to expect you about now." She glanced at a clock on her desk. "It's nice when packages show up on time."

So Riggs had known before they even met that he was going to hire him. Bobby wondered how much Clayton Riggs knew about what happened at the warehouse. Probably more than he let on. "Nice to meet you, never been an apprentice before. I'll try to be good at it."

"Yeah, you detectives. Always a problem."

So she knew his history. "Clayton said you were Orlando PD a while back," he said.

"Northwest office, on Silver Star Road. I was a patrol officer for six years. Got tired of the shifts and all that. I'm sure you can relate." She waved her hand across the mess on her desk. "How are you at paperwork?"

"I type with two fingers."

"You'll fit right in. It's October 27th today. That means we have four days to wrap up some of these cases and get the invoices to Jill. Mostly she's nice, but she turns into a wolverine if you're late with billings."

"What can I do to help?" Bobby asked as Clayton Riggs slipped out the door.

Ryan shook his head and handed the document back to Shawn Falstaff. There were grammatical errors in the text, simple things that shouldn't have made it past Rhonda's desk. Lately, he was getting irritated with even the smallest of things. It wasn't like him.

"When you mention a newspaper like the *Washington Post* in text, it should be italicized. I've marked the other mistakes."

"Of course."

"She needs to get these things right the first time, Shawn." When his executive assistant didn't leave, he asked, "Is there anything else?"

He nodded and held out a thin, sealed envelope. "This is from June Childers."

Ryan opened it as Shawn left the office. Inside was a memo from Childers on her progress with the stealth systems. She was ahead of schedule and figured to be finished all her refinements before the Christmas break. He glanced at his desk calendar. November 12. Less than six weeks. This was excellent news.

Ryan stood and strolled across his office to a whiteboard where he charted the activities of each department working on JASSM. Childers' group had been the bottleneck until today. He scanned the board, looking for anything that might keep the prototype from rolling off the production line on time. There was nothing, and he let out an audible sigh. This project was a big bag of stress.

Rhonda poked her head into his office and said, "Your wife is at the front gate. She'll be here in a few minutes."

"Thanks, Rhonda."

Alexis had taken a great deal of interest in the business lately, which both surprised and pleased him. She was usually into spending her time at home with the kids, but over the past month or so she had been intrigued by Synergy's progress on JASSM. Who could blame her, it was a game changer. She had even struck up a friendship with June Childers, to the point of occasionally going for drinks after work. When Ryan had spoken to June about it, she laughed and told him to mind his own business. Who was he to stick his nose in if they had hit it off and enjoyed each other's company? He smiled as Alexis entered the room.

"Hi, sweetheart," she said, her tone upbeat. "How are things in the top-secret world of Synergy today?"

He kissed her on the lips and she pressed close to him. He had a fleeting thought that if he pushed it, she might have sex with him right then, on his desk. He gave his head a quick shake—that would be as stupid as it was dangerous. "Actually, things are looking up. And you—how's the rash this morning?"

She glanced down at her wrist. "Fine. That was really strange, reacting to my perfume like that."

"It was. You love that brand." They broke off the hug and he waited until she had sat down in one of the chairs. "I had a memo from June Childers this morning. She's finally nailed down a date for finishing the R & D on the stealth systems."

Alexis perked up. "Good news." She thought for a second, then said, "She never said anything to me, but she's not supposed to. Right?"

"Technically, no, but you do own a good portion of this company and you do have top-level clearance. Still, it's probably best if you two don't go there."

Alexis nodded. "June and I have a decent friendship. We don't discuss business while we're out shopping or having a drink, and that's the way we want to keep it."

"Well, just so you know, she'll have a working prototype before Christmas. The bugs are out and her team are running the tests now. It's a real relief. I was starting to wonder if we'd have a decent prototype by our deadline."

Alexis stood and walked across the expansive office, running her fingers over a group of statues on a sofa table. "You never told Washington the extent of the problems."

"Why bother. There'd be no end of them trying to cover their asses. I'll mention it when we deliver the goods."

"Are we charging them more because of what we had to fix?"

He shook his head. "We'll throw in some change orders and cover our expenses, but mostly this project will make sure we're at the top of the list for future contracts. The long-range payback is worth it."

She stood next to him, looking him in the eye. "So we're good. June has made it impossible to detect."

"Totally undetectable from earth or space."

"Nasty weapon," Alexis said. The tone in her voice was a bit unsettling. It was cold, calculating. "I'm glad *we* have it, not the bad guys," she said and he relaxed. That sounded more like her.

Ryan nodded. "Things could get ugly if the wrong people got their hands on it," he said.

"Yes," she agreed. "Very ugly."

Ryan gave her a quick glance. There was that tone again.

chapter nine

The place was a dump from the outside, with garbage and kids' toys littering the front yard. The drapes were drawn and had been since early the previous evening. The only activity was a small child leaving just after eight, dressed for school. Bobby stretched and poured the last cup of coffee from his thermos. He stirred in a touch of sugar and glanced back at the house. The front door opened and a middle-aged man and woman stepped out on the stoop. Bobby set the coffee down, grabbed his phone and switched on the video.

The man was carrying a neck brace in his left hand as they walked down the sidewalk. They hopped into a twenty-year-old Chevy sitting at the curb and took off down the street. Bobby slid in behind them, his '95 Olds Cutlass blending into the working-class area of Lockhart. He kept two or three cars back, out of sight but close enough that he wouldn't lose them. Eventually Gerald Coons and his girlfriend pulled into a parking lot on Clarcona Road. Near one corner of the complex was a large, colorful sign with *Marvin Atkinson, Injury Attorney* printed on it. By the time he got out of the car, Coons was wearing the neck brace and hobbling like a lame horse. Bobby sat and waited. He had the feeling that things were going to get interesting soon. If Coons got some positive news from his lawyer, and Bobby suspected he was going to, chances were good that he and his girlfriend would head out for a few drinks. Today they would let their guard down, Bobby knew it.

The meeting with their lawyer took about an hour. Coons and the woman came walking out, slower than ever. Good news. He was really piling it on now. Bobby knew the insurance company had finally made an offer, providing Coons was really injured. And Bobby knew that inside his lying, sack-of-shit body, Coons was doing a little victory dance. The one that people who pull insurance fraud always do when they get the offer. Now he had to give them some time and space. They would screw this up.

He followed them from the lawyer's office to the grocery store. Coons was still in his neck brace as they shopped, keeping his head straight as he walked stiffly up and down the aisles. The woman kept glancing about, trying to figure out if anyone was watching. She'd never see him, not in a million years. Bobby was too good at disappearing into the background. He was just a guy picking up some groceries, and never even glanced their way. Bobby sensed they were almost finished and went through the checkout before them, then waited in his car, a full block from the store. They came out and drove in the opposite direction from where he was parked, and Bobby pulled into the traffic. Twice at red lights the woman looked back to see if anyone was following. He was far enough behind that his car never registered with her. Finally, they turned into a small country bar just south of the railroad tracks on Edgewater Drive. He waited twenty-five minutes before entering.

The bar smelled musty and country music, the twangy stuff, played on a bad sound system. Bobby's eyes adjusted to the low light and he saw them sitting in a booth, close to the stage where bands played for the evening crowd. He ordered a Budweiser and set his phone on the counter so it was focused on the couple. The waitress filled her tray and headed for their table—they were ordering double whiskeys. It wouldn't be long now.

Coons got up to take a leak, and his wife handed him the neck brace. He waved it off, and his drunken body language said it all—*Who the fuck cares? We beat them, honey. We're in the money.* Bobby kept the video rolling.

By the time Coons put away six more doubles, he had lost his lawsuit. He and the woman were dancing to bad music, his head bouncing around on his neck like a ceramic bobble-head. Any judge would throw out his claim when they saw the footage. Bobby paid his tab and left the bar, shutting off the video as he hit the bright afternoon sunlight.

His cell phone rang as he headed back to the office, and his ex-wife's name came up on the caller ID. "Hi, Jan."

"Hi, Bobby. How are things?"

"Great. What's up?"

She hesitated for a moment, then said, "I was wondering if you had something for me."

"I do. Where do you want to meet?"

"The usual Starbucks? Fifteen minutes?"

"Done, see you there." He hung up and switched routes. The office could wait.

Bobby and Janis Greco never disliked each other, they just grew apart and eventually divorced. Mostly it was his job. She couldn't get around the crazy hours and the constant negativity he brought home with him. *It's homicide, people don't kill each other on our schedule.* At a certain point there had been no saving it. Their girls, Sarah and Lizzie, both lived with Janis, but Bobby saw them whenever he wanted. It was a healthy situation, good for everyone.

Once Bobby was back on the main drag and moving along with the traffic, he called Jacky's cell.

"Hi," Jacky said. "Tell me you got something."

"The mother lode. Coons drinking, dancing, and making a total fool of himself. I'll drop in with the footage in an hour or so. I have to make a quick stop first."

"No problem, I'll see you soon." She sounded happy.

He hung up and concentrated on the road. Bobby had been with Riggs & Company for three weeks now, and he and Jacky had a great working relationship. It certainly didn't hurt that she'd spent time with Orlando PD. Although she was the senior partner, she recognized the skills he brought with him from his days in homicide and let him do his own thing. They understood each other and were exposing fraud at a record pace, and that kept Clayton Riggs happy.

Bobby pulled into the Starbucks and found a spot close to the door. His wife was at a table with her coffee, reading a year-old *People* magazine. A second cup was on the table—a venti skinny latte. He sat down, wondering why they had ever split up.

"He's dead," Bobby said, pointing to one of the celebrities on the cover. "Where did you find that?"

"On the condiment counter. Someone must have left it." She made a slight motion toward the parking lot. "Nice ride."

Bobby glanced out at the '95 Cutlass and rolled his eyes. "Company car."

She eyed him up. "So how are you doing?"

"Very well, actually." He slid his hands into his pockets like a school kid. Funny how his ex-wife could still make him feel that way. She was beautiful in a cute way, always had been, even in high school. All the jocks had tried to date Janis, but she only wanted Bobby Greco. He never understood that, or why she never thought it was a mistake marrying him. He pulled a piece of paper out of his pocket.

"For you." He handed her a check for twelve hundred dollars. "That brings us up to date on the child support. Sorry about being late last month. With not working for a bit and all..."

"It's okay." She took the check. "I'm so glad the DA decided not to file charges."

Bobby just nodded.

She looked hurt and confused for a moment. "I know whatever happened in the warehouse wasn't your fault, Bobby."

He stared at the table and when he glanced up she had tears in her eyes. "Tell you what," he said. "One of these days I'll drop by the house and we'll have a coffee. I'll tell you what actually went down."

"Yeah." She reached out and squeezed his arm. "That would be really good."

Thirty minutes later Bobby pulled into the lot behind Riggs & Company and swiped his passkey on the back door. First office on the right was Jacky's and she was still in. He smiled and held up his phone.

"Coons is screwed," he said. "He's not getting a penny."

"Clayton will like that." She motioned for him to sit. "So, how do you like it so far? I mean, working here."

He raised his eyebrows. "I like it, I really do. Much more than I thought I would. Kind of surprising, actually."

"Good. Clayton and me—and you, I think—at the end of the day, we're all after the same thing."

"And what's that?"

"Catching up with the guys who cheat."

"Yeah, get the bad guys," Bobby said, laughing.

"Don't get me wrong, the pay check is nice." She grinned. "And hell, we get to carry guns and there's a parking lot full of hot cars out back."

"Like the piece of shit I was driving today?"

"Sure, like that. We only let our top guns drive that one." She lifted her coffee cup and tipped it toward him. "Welcome to the team, Bobby."

chapter ten

Patricia stared at her mom in disbelief. "Everyone knows where the Girl Guide cookies go," she said. "We keep them there every year."

Alexis smiled at her daughter. "Okay, if you're so smart, why don't you put them away, you little rascal."

Patricia jumped off the couch in the family room and made a beeline for the kitchen. Ryan's voice stopped her dead in her tracks. "It's okay, Patricia," he said. "Let Mom do it." He turned slightly on the couch to face Alexis. "Honey?"

Alexis shook her head and gave Ryan a nasty look. "It's good for the kids to do a few things around here." She grabbed the cookies and headed for the kitchen, then stopped. "In fact, it's very good." She handed the cookies back to Patricia.

Ryan didn't say anything and Patricia took the boxes of cookies and set them on the kitchen island. She pulled a large glass bowl out from inside one of the drawers and dumped the cookies in the bowl. Then she ate one.

"Perfect. Right, dad?"

"Perfect." He checked his watch. "It's Saturday night. Your favorite program is on in three minutes." They usually streamed everything, but there was one show on a major network that she watched.

"Yay." She ran back into the family room and switched on the television.

"We should get ready for dinner," Ryan said.

"Sure." They left Patricia watching her program and headed up to the master bedroom. "What was that all about?" Alexis asked when they were alone.

"Nothing."

"Yes, it was. What's going on?"

Ryan slipped a suit off its hanger and set it on the bed. "You tell me."

He watched her for a reaction, but there was nothing. She turned and walked into her closet and he could hear her rummaging about, looking for an outfit. He pulled on his shirt and buttoned it, lost in thought. His wife had changed. She didn't remember little things, like where they kept the cookies and which Christmas ornaments went on the tree. The perfume she had worn for years now gave her a rash. And she was completely different in bed. The sparkle in her eyes was gone and while she was voracious, it felt more like casual sex than anything intimate. Like he could be anyone. Something had happened and he was going to figure out what it was.

Alexis returned from the closet with an outfit, gave him a light-hearted smile and said, "Let's get through dinner tonight at the club, and we can talk later."

"Okay. Later."

Ryan finished dressing and returned to the main floor. Zach was out with friends and the sitter was curled up with Patricia on the couch watching television. Ryan went over Patricia's routine with her while Alexis headed into the kitchen and made a quick phone call. They met in the foyer and hustled out into the warm November evening with only an hour until the annual club dinner started. Alexis drove, weaving in and out of traffic at well over the posted limit and pulled up in front of the club fashionably late. When they were thirty feet inside the front door Alexis let go of Ryan's hand.

"See you in a minute, I need to use the bathroom."

He watched her slip into the crowd, wondering how the conversation would go when they got home. He was pretty sure it was going to be heated. When she had disappeared into the sea of people, he turned his attention to the other guests in the room.

Heathrow was aglow with celebrities and socialites, but it was the politicians and the power brokers that interested Ryan. JASSM was looking like a resounding success and Ryan was on the prowl for additional contracts. He spotted Senator Blackwell and made a beeline across the crowded room.

"Ernst." Ryan extended his hand. "Great to see you." He plucked two glasses of champagne off a tray as a waiter passed by. "It's been a while since your party."

"It has." Blackwell took the delicate glass in his big mitt. "I've been in D.C. a bit too much lately for my liking, but that's all part of the job."

"I know what you mean, Florida has the weather this time of year."

"I hate snow," Blackwell boomed. He finished the drink in one gulp and leaned in. "You've done a hell of a job on the JASSM contract." He tipped the empty glass toward Ryan. "There's more on the way."

"Wonderful. We're always looking for more interesting work." Ryan tried to take the eager tone out of his voice, but wasn't entirely successful.

"You've earned it," the senator said. "I get so tired of defense contractors that come in low, then hit us for all kinds of increases and change orders. I like that you don't run Synergy that way."

Ryan nodded. "Well, it's nice to hear the effort is appreciated."

Blackwell squinted at him from under a furry eyebrow. "Those specs you received from the Pentagon were crap." The stunned look on Ryan's face said it all. "I'm impressed you managed to fix things, and I'm not the only one."

"Okay," Ryan said slowly. "But how did you know what they sent? You're with appropriations, which doesn't allow access to that information."

"I have my sources, but that's not important right now." Blackwell looked around the room. "Go and enjoy yourself. Stop yakking with a wrinkly old senator. Mingle. We'll talk later, in a week or two."

"Sure." Ryan gave Blackwell a firm handshake, still a bit taken aback about the lack of secrecy surrounding the missile's shortcomings.

Blackwell was already on the move, slapping a colleague on the back and diving into a conversation. Ryan stood by himself, thinking about the cracks in security at the Pentagon and how it could affect future projects. There was no way Blackwell should have known the military had sent them a huge turd, but he did. Going forward, he would have to be careful that if there *was* a breach it could be traced back to the origin and not dumped on Synergy. He made a mental note to have Shawn gather their security team together and tighten things even further.

He saw Alexis across the room, catching up with Reggie Stewart, her old boss from the Intel days. She caught his eye and smiled, then continued talking. He felt a tap on his arm and turned to find Alexis's doubles partner, Debbie Mayther standing there, drink in hand.

"Hi, Ryan," she said. "You look great tonight. Business going well?"

"Couldn't be better. How about you? Alexis tells me you're in line for Chief of Neurology at South Seminole. Impressive."

She laughed, almost spilling her drink. "Don't be. I've been there forever. They have to promote me eventually."

"Hardly," Ryan said. "Chief of Neurology. Congratulations."

She sobered a bit. "Well, I haven't got it yet, and there's competition. Sometimes it seems it's who you know, not your abilities."

He nodded. "Who are you up against?"

"Harold Schweitzer."

"Hmm." Ryan said. "Who's making the decision?"

"A board of seven doctors from the hospital, but the deciding vote is going to be Adam Hoskins. However he leans, the rest lean."

"He's here tonight," Ryan said. "I could put in a word."

She shrugged. "That's your call, Ryan. I would never ask."

"I know you wouldn't."

They were silent for a moment, then Debbie asked, "Ryan, is everything okay with Alexis?"

"How so?"

"I don't know. She seems different since we won the tournament. She has this overly competitive edge I've never seen."

"Alexis has always been competitive," Ryan said.

"Yes, but not like this. The last few times we've played she's been a lot more aggressive." Mayther glanced around to see if anyone else was within earshot. "She hit the ball *at* a woman we were playing against. Drilled her right in the head."

"Do you think she meant to?" Ryan asked.

"Absolutely, almost knocked her unconscious."

"I see." Ryan could have told her that he'd noticed the changes, but stayed quiet. He and Alexis were going to talk later and he wouldn't back off until he found out what was going on. He snapped back as he realized Debbie was talking to him.

"I need to check in with Darryl." She gave him a light kiss on the cheek. "Have a nice evening."

"You too." He watched her walk away, then scanned the room for Adam Hoskins. The man was at the bar refilling a cognac snifter, and he headed over.

Ryan poked Adam in the ribs as he settled into the chair next to him at the bar. "Little early for cognac, don't you think, Adam?"

"Ryan," the doctor responded cheerfully and held up his glass. "To hell with convention."

"Put like that, how can I argue?" Ryan smiled. He liked Adam, older and a lifelong friend of his father's. "Adam, do you have a couple of minutes?"

"Of course. What is it?"

Five minutes later Debbie Mayther was on the inside track for the job. Hoskins had been leaning toward voting for her based on merit, but was coming under some heavy pressure to give Schweitzer the nod. Ryan Chamberlain didn't give his backing lightly, and for Adam Hoskins it was the tipping point.

At the top of the hour people started moving into the main dining room for dinner, and ten minutes later only a handful of stragglers were left in the foyer. Ryan noticed Alexis waiting at one of the doors and they strolled into the massive dining room together. Wine glasses clinked amid hushed voices, dampened by thick carpets and fine white tablecloths. Soft lights overhead illuminated Orlando's wealthiest citizens. Ryan and Alexis said a few quick hellos as they looked for their table and when they found it they introduced themselves to the one couple at the table they didn't know, then shook hands with the others. Salads arrived and the dinner began.

Serving eight hundred people was business as usual for Heathrow, and along with the salad and entrées, the wine list was a sommelier's heaven. At six hundred dollars a plate it was hardly a bargain. Ryan selected the lamb, and he was surprised to hear Alexis ordering it as well.

"You don't like lamb," he said quietly.

"Maybe I do," she replied. He touched her hand and she recoiled, ever so slightly, then took a long drink of wine and motioned for the steward to refill her glass.

"Are you okay?" Ryan leaned over and whispered.

She smiled and looked at him out of the corner of her eye. "This conversation's over." She sat back, looking away from him and across the room.

"Sure," Ryan said, clenching his jaw. "We'll talk later."

"We'll see," she said, still gazing out over the crowd.

The appetizers were cleared and the main courses arrived. The lamb was cooked to perfection. Alexis added a touch of mint and offered it to her husband. Ryan was about halfway through his meal when he started to feel short of breath. He clutched at his chest, lightly at first, then with desperation.

"It hurts," he whispered, wide eyed. Alexis and the others at the table stared at him. "My chest hurts."

Moments later, Ryan slumped forward, his head smashing onto the table. One of the women at the table screamed, and all the heads in the room turned. No one moved for a few seconds, then someone yelled for a doctor. A woman at a nearby table leapt to her feet and raced over. A man, seated close by, was at her side in seconds.

"Rose Ambers, anesthetist," she said, one eye on Ryan as she unsnapped her purse.

"Ben Olsen, cardiologist." He was already repositioning Ryan so his trachea was extended and open. "Help me," he snapped at the men seated at the table.

Together they laid Ryan on his back on the floor. Ambers had pulled a tracheal tube from her purse, and she inserted it down Ryan's throat to clear the air passage.

"No pulse," Olsen said, starting CPR.

The two doctors worked as a team, using rhythmic pressure on his chest to kickstart the heart muscles, and took turns breathing for him through the tube. When the paramedics arrived eight minutes later, Olsen hooked Ryan up to a cardiac monitor and checked all three leads.

"Asystole," he said.

Ambers grabbed the defibrillator and held the paddles over Ryan's chest. "Clear," she yelled and Olsen backed off.

She placed the paddles on his chest and hit the button. Ryan's body jerked up, then fell back to the floor. She looked at Olsen, who was watching the monitors.

"Nothing."

"Clear." She sent another 1,000 volts through his body. The green line on the monitor remained flat. "Clear." Again, she hit him with everything the machine had. No change.

The two doctors worked on him for another five minutes, but the end result was obvious to everyone. Ryan Chamberlain was dead.

The guests had backed off as the doctors tried to save him, now they stood in stunned silence. No one moved, save for Alexis. With tears streaming down her cheeks and her body shaking, she dropped to her knees beside her husband. Olsen and Ambers moved away as Alexis grasped her husband and hugged him, her cheek on his, her lips by his ear.

"You had me figured, didn't you?" She glanced up to make sure no one was close enough to overhear, then put her lips back to his ear. "Now look what you made me do."

She closed her eyes, reveling in the adrenaline surging through her veins.

chapter eleven

Ryan Chamberlain, dead at thirty-nine.

The autopsy was conclusive, confirming the diagnosis of the doctors who had tried to save him. Chamberlain had died from cardiac eurhythmia—a massive heart attack. Pathology had determined the coronary arteries were partially blocked with cholesterol, narrowing them to dangerous levels, and although Chamberlain had appeared in good health, he was, in fact, a ticking time bomb.

Alexis kept up a good front in the six weeks following the funeral. From moment one, she made it perfectly clear that she was qualified to run Synergy. She had a decent grasp of their projects, and as an electrical engineer she was quick to understand the technical details. There were only a few rumblings and Synergy's stock rebounded when Alexis took control. She didn't need to make any major changes, and simply allowed the well-oiled machine Ryan had created to continue moving ahead.

Alexis divided her time between being the new face of Synergy, mothering Zach and Patricia and redistributing Ryan's wealth, the vast majority of which was directed to her. In early January, she finally admitted the pressure was too much. Something had to give. She made a decision that some saw as necessary, others as crass. She sent Zach and Patricia to a private school in Virginia. That alleviated some of her workload, but more importantly, it removed the two remaining people who could expose her.

January 11—the first day the Chamberlain household was without children—was a Sunday. Zach and Patricia had flown out for the beginning of a new semester, and Alexis was in good humor.

Shortly after ten in the morning, a van bearing the name of a local cleaning company pulled up to 72 Twelve Oaks. It parked in the driveway at the side of the house and a woman and man, dressed in working clothes, got out. They knocked on the door and were ushered in, but aside from *good morning*, there was no conversation. The man set his pail on the floor in the family room, lifted out the mop and removed a small handheld device. He snapped a long, thin wand into a jack on the machine and walked about, searching for changes in the electromagnetic field. No fluctuations showed up on the screen and he moved to the living room, then the formal dining room, the kitchen, library, main floor office, laundry, bathroom and finally the entrance foyer.

"Clean. No bugs on the main floor." He headed upstairs. Twenty minutes later, when he was sure there were no listening devices in the house, he packed up his gear and sat down in the kitchen. Freshly brewed coffee was waiting on the island and he helped himself.

Armand Cortez raised his cup. "Well done, Monique. Or should I say, *Alexis*."

Sylvia Dupres could barely contain her smug satisfaction. "You did it."

Monique Dupres gave her mother and then Cortez a hug, grasping him a little too tight. Their success had raised her opinion of her mentor even higher. She had become Alexis Chamberlain—wealthy, widowed and the CEO of Synergy Industries.

She spun on her heels on the tile floor, arms outstretched and a huge grin pasted on her face. "What do you think?"

"You were brilliant, Monique," Sylvia beamed.

"Alexis," she said, then laughed. "The new and improved version."

Cortez looked around the house with a discerning eye, then turned his attention to Monique. She had grown her hair to exactly the same length as her sister's. Made sure her skin was tanned and her weight identical, and had spent years training so she could play tennis at Alexis's level. Armand's men had hacked into the Chamberlain's home intelligence system, giving them ears and eyes inside the house. From that, Monique had learned her sister's routine—the way she spoke, her mannerisms, everything about her children and husband. She even had

Alexis's fingerprints burned over hers with a laser. She could not have been more committed.

"What a transformation." He smiled, his voice tinged with admiration. "You are incredible."

"Still," Sylvia interjected. "Did we have to kill him?"

Monique sat and shook her head. "He was getting suspicious. I couldn't know every detail or train my skin to wear her perfume, and of course my retinas were different from hers. There were all kinds of little things, and I sure as hell didn't know what Ryan and Alexis did in bed."

Cortez found a bottle of brandy and poured some in a glass. "Well, you managed to keep him happy enough for three months."

She smiled and shrugged. "Not bad for getting dropped into someone else's life in the middle of the night. In fact, I think I was fucking fabulous."

Cortez cocked his head slightly and asked, "And how was living the lie?"

"Never easy." She looked at her mother again. "The hardest part was dealing with the kids, and things had reached a breaking point. As I told Armand on the phone, Ryan was going to confront me when we got home."

Armand sipped his brandy. "You did right to call."

"What else could I do? He knew, Armand. We were lucky he was okay with waiting until after the dinner."

"Mmmm...." Cortez smiled again, enjoying the young woman he had spent so many years mentoring. "You know, him having a coronary in a room full of doctors probably lowered the bar on the autopsy."

Monique laughed at the irony. "It worked out pretty well."

"Getting the kids out of the house and into that school in Virginia was a good idea," Cortez said. "You're really thinking on your feet."

Monique's cheeks showed a tinge of color. Accolades from Armand were few and far between and she cherished them.

Sylvia Dupres was leaning against the kitchen counter, listening. "What about Synergy?"

Monique pointed inward at herself. "You're looking at the face of Synergy."

"You still have work to do," her mother said, stubbing out her cigarette.

Monique threw her an irritated glance. "I have access to everything. Plus, I have become good friends with June Childers. Her team ironed out the bugs in the stealth systems, and her version of the missile is flawless. She trusts me."

"Have you downloaded the technology?" Cortez asked.

"No." Monique ignored her coffee and poured herself a brandy. She lit a cigarette and continued. "I have files from nine of the eleven departments. I don't have Childers' information yet, and until I do the specs on the exterior shell are useless. I need her modifications."

"When can you get them?"

Monique shrugged again. "She's a tough one. I'll get the plans when she's ready to hand them over. Until then…"

"What if she suspects you're not Alexis Chamberlain?"

"Why would she?" Monique puffed out a bit. "No one suspects. The police never even opened a file, and I've buried my husband. My in-laws are in shock and holed up in their Miami mansion, and I pick and choose my friends and when I want to see them." She took a long drag on the cigarette and blew the smoke up toward the ceiling, then crushed it out a bit too hard in the ashtray. "I *am* Alexis Chamberlain."

The room was silent for a moment, then Cortez said, "We need Childers' design specifications or the missile is worthless. My buyer will only pay for the stealth version of the JASSM."

"I can't rush her," Monique said, unflinching.

Cortez reached out and touched her cheek. "You're so close, Monique. Now all you need to do is to get your hands on the last two files."

"I'll get them."

"Good." Cortez picked up the bucket and headed for the door where Sylvia was already waiting.

They were on the step when Monique took her mother by the arm and asked, "Where is Alexis?"

"Don't worry, she won't be showing up at the doorstep." Sylvia smiled at her daughter. "I'm glad you asked."

Monique snorted. "Alexis is dangerous, mother. Perhaps it would be better if she were—not around."

"Jesus, Monique," Sylvia Dupres interrupted. "How can you even say that? She's your sister."

She slammed the door behind her as she left.

chapter twelve

In December, Riggs & Company set a record for number of cases closed in a single month, and that boded well for the bonuses Clayton Riggs handed out at the annual company party. It was always the second Sunday in January, and on the following day the doors at Riggs & Company remained tightly locked, with all calls going directly to their answering service.

Jacky Foster wasn't going to be denied a good time. She spent most of her life on call, which meant no drinking in case she had to drive. The party was one of the few days of the year when she let her proverbial hair down. By the time Bobby arrived, Jacky was already on her sixth double whiskey sour and gave Bobby a huge hug when she saw him.

"You're the best partner I ever had," she said, pressing against him. "I wish I was single."

"You *are* single." Bobby lit a cigarette as Jacky headed out onto the dance floor. He felt a tap on his shoulder and turned. It was Clayton Riggs.

"Hi, Bobby," he said. "Glad you could make it."

"Wouldn't miss it, Clayton."

Riggs laughed. "I love these parties. Everyone has a great time."

Bobby looked around. The Miami and Tampa offices were shut down and everyone was in Orlando for two days, all expenses paid. The entire bar belonged to Riggs for the night.

"Yup, happy people," he said.

"It's partly because of these." Riggs handed Bobby an envelope. "Go ahead, open it."

"Really, Clayton? I've been with the company less than three months."

"You're part of the team, Bobby. Have been since day one. Let's just say this is in anticipation of what's to come. Now for Christ's sake, open it."

Bobby ripped open the envelope and let the check slide into his hand. He stared at the amount. Ten thousand dollars. He looked up at Clayton Riggs. The man had a wide grin pasted on his face. He was going to say something, but Clayton beat him to it.

"Merry Christmas and Happy New Year." He slapped Bobby on the shoulder and threaded through the crowd toward the stage where the DJ was spinning tunes.

Bobby Greco stood immobile for a minute, then folded the check and tucked it into his back pocket. He finished his drink and headed to the bar for a refill. What the hell, he was having a great night. He looked around for Jacky. He felt like dancing.

Monique Dupres stood alone in the kitchen of her Twelve Oaks mansion, looking out over the row of palm trees that lined the water's edge. An occasional boat floated by on the glassy surface of Lake Maitland, but mostly it was quiet and peaceful. She thought about buying a boat, something seaworthy she could keep in Miami or West Palm Beach, and decided it was a good idea. Christ, being fabulously wealthy was even better than she had dreamed. Sure, Armand and her mother had money, but they had to hide it. This was different.

Now, for the first time in her life, she was someone of influence and power. Magazine photographers scrambled to snap a picture when she showed up for an event and important politicians treated her warmly, like family. Her days of trying to look inconspicuous, of trying to hide her wealth and beauty, were gone. Respect, adoration even, was finally hers, and she wasn't about to let it go.

She loved the house Ryan and Alexis had built. It was modern and bright, with four thousand square feet on the main level and that much again upstairs. Monique strolled about the home, marveling that it was now hers. The extensive selection of books in the library, the original artwork hanging on the walls, and the manicured grounds. Furnishing the house must have cost millions. And building it—tens of millions. The place was unbelievable.

She paused as she passed a recent family portrait. They were at the ocean, the puffy clouds brilliant white against the deep blue sky, and behind them the waves tipped with foam. Ryan was in the back, Alexis in the front with the two children. They were smiling. Such a happy family.

Not any more, Monique thought. Her sister was trapped in some hellish purgatory. Ryan was dead and the children shipped off like cattle. The family was in ruins. The only issue, as Monique saw it, was that her mother was soft on Alexis. From their private conversations, she knew Armand Cortez wanted her out of the way, but Sylvia would have none of it. Alexis was her daughter and would eventually end up back in her house. Before that happened, Monique was to drain the Chamberlain fortune and deposit it in untraceable offshore accounts. Despite how lucrative the arms business had been over the years, this deal was far and away Cortez's largest. The money for the missile technology, plus the cash from the estate would easily top three or four hundred million. Given the scope of the windfall, Cortez had conceded and backed off on killing Alexis to get their plan in action.

It was completely audacious and she laughed at the thought. Kidnap Alexis, then walk right in through the front door and help herself to the JASSM files. One of the most advanced security systems in the world, and it hadn't kept them out.

Monique felt a tiny surge of nerves and poured herself a drink from the bar. She was facing a mirror and she stared at her reflection. She *was* Alexis. It amazed even her how perfect she was at impersonating her sister. There had been so many places for things to go wrong. Plucking someone out of their life and substituting an imposter, even an identical twin, was next to impossible. The wheels had almost come off a few times.

Alexis entering the Heathrow club championship had been a setback. There were too many eyes focused on her to make the swap until the tournament finished. Then, on the night of the awards dinner, they made their move. Just after three in the morning, they slipped into the house and crept upstairs into the hallway near Patricia's room and made some noise. It wasn't long before Alexis appeared to check on her daughter.

Cortez knocked her unconscious and carried her downstairs. Sylvia stripped off her nightgown and Monique slipped it on as they carried Alexis out of the house. There was blood on the floor, but Monique had cleaned it up before Ryan came downstairs. The first time he touched her, a light tap on the shoulder while she was sitting in the living room, she had flinched. She cursed herself for that. She'd rehearsed that moment a thousand times in her mind. *Don't react when he first touches you. You're his wife.* But it hadn't helped. She had still tensed.

She wondered when Ryan had first suspected things weren't right. Mostly, she faked it through the days okay, but she had no idea what her sister was like in bed. Whether she moaned, or raked her nails down his back as she reached orgasm. Or was she a cold fish, not really interested. Still, the challenge was exhilarating, and her heart started pounding when he wanted to have sex. Of all her brazen acts, that one was the ultimate.

The incident with the Girl Guide cookies had been the last straw. He was baiting her by that point. It was only a matter of time before he pieced together why her retina scan had failed, and why she didn't know the idiosyncrasies of their home life. After three months she had no choice but to call in Cortez.

Monique swept open the patio doors and walked into the garden. Surrounding her were two of the most beautiful acres in the world. Now it was all hers. She liked the feel of thick Florida grass beneath her feet, and the smell of the warm, humid air. She rubbed her fingertips together, marveling at how perfectly they had healed after the laser surgery. It had taken less than twenty minutes to burn Alexis's fingerprints over hers, and five weeks for the tiny burn marks to heal. She had become her sister.

Her fabulous sister, wealthy and wired into the highest levels of American society.

Monique padded across the lawn to the pier. She walked out to the end and stood exposed to the world. She wanted to scream at the top of her lungs how gullible everyone was. All the doctors, the police, the medical examiner, the coroner, the business associates, the friends, the family. She wanted to scream out across the lake in triumph. But she didn't. Instead she said three words, quietly, to herself.

"I did it."

Bobby could barely make it down the hallway. His head felt like it was going to explode with every step. He finally reached Clayton's office and leaned against the doorjamb. Riggs was leaning back in his chair, a wet cloth on his forehead. Slowly, almost imperceptibly, he leaned forward and opened one eye. It peered out at Bobby like a wounded Cyclops. There was a good reason Riggs & Company kept the doors closed on the Monday after the party.

"Glad you're here." Clayton grabbed his head. "Ouch."

"I'm not." Bobby sat in one of the chairs facing Clayton's desk. He took the file Clayton offered. "I thought we didn't work on Monday after the party."

"We usually don't, but I had a call from First Eastern Life this morning at eight. They want someone working on this file today. It's not going to be me, I'm going home to get some sleep."

"What is it?" Bobby asked, opening the file.

"It's all in there. Some ass at First Eastern left this file sitting on their desk until last Friday, and unless they have reason to dispute the claim, it has to be paid by midnight tonight. They want us to have a quick look. Due diligence for their underwriters."

Bobby took a quick look. "Ryan Chamberlain? Christ, he died of a heart attack in a building full of doctors. I remember reading about it in the newspaper back in late November or early December."

"That's the one." Clayton Riggs pulled himself out of his chair and pushed past Bobby on his way out the door. "I'm out of here. Pay the widow a visit and sign off on it. The contact name at First Eastern is on the bottom of the first page."

Bobby wandered through the empty offices, searching for some Advil. He checked Jacky's desk and found the equivalent of a Wal-Mart pharmacy. He took two extra-strength tablets and sat down, content to wait for them to kick in. The bonus Clayton had given him the night before was still on his mind, and he slipped his hand in his back pocket. The check was there, and it was still for ten thousand dollars. He gave it a kiss and returned it to his pocket for safekeeping, then headed for the coffee room. No one was in yet and he ground some coffee, poured in the water, then opened the file on Ryan Chamberlain while it brewed.

First Eastern Life had granted a policy on Ryan a dozen years ago, when he was still an executive with Lockheed-Martin. The initial policy had been for two million dollars. Bobby checked out the monthly payments and almost choked. Just trying to make those payments would kill him. He flipped the page. Chamberlain had taken out additional coverage after establishing Synergy Industries. Four million more, for a total policy of six million dollars. No wonder First Eastern wanted someone to look at this. The coffee was ready and he poured a cup.

Apparently, First Eastern had hired a team of doctors to try and establish that Ryan Chamberlain had lied on his medical questionnaire concerning his cholesterol levels. That's why the file had just hit Riggs' desk today—the insurance company had tried to dodge the claim by proving Chamberlain lied. They had failed and now they wanted Riggs and Company to have a look.

The Advil were working, and the coffee was kicking in. He stood and stretched, figuring he'd live. He pulled out a copy of the policy and checked the address. 72 Twelve Oaks. He took a deep breath and checked his look in the mirror on the inside of his closet door. His hair was all over the place, but that was normal. His eyes had stopped bleeding and all in all, he looked okay. He poured a second cup of coffee, left the office and lit a cigarette. It tasted awful and he threw it in the gutter next to his car.

There weren't many places where Bobby felt inadequate in his BMW. Twelve Oaks was one of them. Driving the low-end BMW around here was like walking into a formal event in blue jeans. He cruised up the street, fully expecting the Chamberlain house to occupy the prime pie lot at the end, and it did. He pulled in and crept up the curved driveway to the house. Christ, their front lawn was six times the size of his lot.

He parked in front of the house and walked up to the main door and rang the bell. A woman he assumed was the hired help opened the door and asked if she could be of assistance.

"I'm looking for Alexis Chamberlain," he said, looking past her into the cavernous foyer.

"I'm sorry, sir, Mrs. Chamberlain is out. If you would care to leave a card, I'll let her know you called."

"Sure." Bobby reached in his pocket for a card. He paused in mid-action. "I need to see her today. It's really important."

"I'm sorry." She looked like she was going to shut the door.

No one shut the door on a homicide cop, and Bobby still thought like one. "I either talk to her now, or tell her not to bother calling. I'm from the insurance company and a substantial amount money is on the table until end of business today." He turned to leave, then said, "What's your name so I can tell her who I was speaking with?"

The maid gave him a long, hard stare. "She's at Heathrow Country Club, playing tennis. You didn't hear it from me." The door closed.

Bobby drove to Heathrow from memory, ignoring the GPS on his phone. He found it easily enough and pulled into the parking lot. The place was busy and he trolled around for a few minutes looking for a stall, then cut off an Infiniti making a move on a prime spot from the other direction. He ignored the glare from the driver and walked into the club.

Reception was reluctant to let him in, but he pulled the same story on the young woman behind the desk and she caved. Alexis was on an outdoor court, near the end of the row, playing singles. He found the court and sat in the stands, watching her. As the game progressed, he realized that Alexis Chamberlain was an excellent tennis player. She shifted the velocity of her first serve, sometimes slowing it to what her opponent would expect on a second serve, other times rifling an ace down the centerline. A few times Bobby was sure the other woman had made a winning shot, but Alexis came back with a crosscourt chip or a perfectly placed deep lob and won the match 6-4, 6-3.

She toweled off and left the court, but instead of following her opponent, she turned and looked directly at him. She headed into the stands and stood in front of him.

"Can I help you?" she asked. Her voice was smooth and even, without a trace of exertion from the match.

"Quite the game," Bobby said. "Your opponent is a good player."

"She should be. She's the club pro." Her eyes probed him. "You were watching us. Is there something I can do for you?"

"Yes." Bobby stood and offered his business card. She took it and scanned the printing. "First Eastern Life wanted someone to come out and chat with you concerning the life insurance policy on your husband." He shrugged his shoulders slightly. "I'm the guy."

"My solicitor is handling the life insurance," she said. "I suggest you speak with him."

"Who'd that be, Mrs. Chamberlain?" Bobby slipped a notebook and pen from his pocket.

"Horace Vander Linden," she said and smiled. It was a nice smile with perfect teeth. "He handled all the details of Ryan's estate."

"Excellent," Bobby said. "Have you and your lawyer discussed your late husband's First Eastern life insurance policy?"

She looked mildly amused at the question. "Of course. Ryan had insurance plans with two different companies. One was for three million dollars and it has been paid out. The other was with First Eastern for five or six million. That must be the one you're referring to."

"That's the one. Two policies for a total of six million."

"Is there a problem?"

"No. No problem at all. It's standard procedure for the insurance company to have someone investigate when the policy is so large."

"Is six million a large policy?" She wiped her face gently with the towel.

"I only have a couple of standard questions, Mrs. Chamberlain," Bobby said.

"Go ahead." She sat in the chair next to Bobby.

"Was your husband in good health and spirits before his heart attack?"

"Yes. He had the usual pressures associated with running a big company like Synergy, but I didn't notice anything really unusual leading up to the attack, if that's what you mean."

"That's exactly what I mean. He seemed fine, then?"

She nodded. A drop of sweat beaded on her cheek and she used the towel to dab it away. "He was in good spirits, Mr. Greco. We had a good marriage, two healthy children, and no financial problems. He worked out regularly and had a yearly physical. We both did."

"Is there a history of high cholesterol on Ryan's side?"

"No idea. Why?'

"Problems with cholesterol are often hereditary. I'm surprised your family doctor didn't tell you."

She tilted her head slightly to one side. "I didn't know that." She stood and moved to the aisle. "Is that all?"

"Yes, I think so. First Eastern will be in touch with Mr. Vander Linden to arrange payment."

"Goodbye, then." She turned and walked down the stairs without looking back.

Bobby Greco wished he had another couple of Advil. The hangover was rearing its ugly head again. He took a few deep breaths, trying to will away the pain. It wasn't working. He sat quietly, thinking about Alexis Chamberlain. She was a knockout—beautiful, charming, intelligent and athletic. Christ, with a bad heart Ryan had been lucky to survive the sex. Bobby ran over the brief meeting in his mind a few times, from different angles. Was there anything about Alexis Chamberlain that might kick-start his sixth sense? The answer was no. He struggled to his feet, feeling like a total bag of dirt, and headed for the exit.

He passed the trophy case and spotted a photograph of her. The caption read, *Match point—Alexis Chamberlain and Debbie Mayther put it away*. He studied it for a moment. Alexis was in the foreground and playing the ball—her partner was behind her, watching. At first it was simply a shot of a rich woman with a tennis racquet. He looked closer, taking in every detail. What she was wearing, how her feet were planted on the clay, the focus in her eyes. Something was wrong. It took a few minutes, then it hit him. He had just watched her play an entire set with the club pro. She had hit the ball with incredible intensity, both women all in for the match. And every backhand shot had been one-handed.

Yet when he looked at the picture of Alexis Chamberlain putting away the match point for the club championship, she was using two hands. Something wasn't right.

Bobby strolled back to the main doors, lost in thought. When he reached his car he leaned against the hood and stared back at the building. One voice inside him was saying *Ignore it*, and another was saying *Find out why*. He wasn't sure which to listen to, and the hangover wasn't helping. He glanced around to see a car waiting to pull into his spot. He waved at the driver and jumped in. When he backed out, he was startled to see the driver was Debbie Mayther, Alexis's doubles partner. He pulled ahead a bit, put on his flashers and got out.

"Debbie Mayther?" he asked when she was out of her car.

"Yes," she said hesitantly.

Bobby offered her a business card and explained who he was and why he was at the club. "I recognized you from the photo in the trophy case."

She glanced at her watch and said, "I only have a minute."

"Did you know Ryan?" Bobby asked.

Her face softened measurably. "Yes, we were friends."

"Did you see any signs that might have indicated he wasn't well?"

She shook her head. "No."

"How would you describe his state of mind prior to his death?"

She thought about how to answer. "Ryan was under a considerable amount of stress, but he seemed to be handling it. He was a kind and compassionate person, and as far as I could tell that hadn't changed."

It wasn't hard for Bobby to figure out they had been close friends.

She asked, "Are you investigating his death?"

"Should I be?" Bobby asked.

"No, I don't think so," she answered slowly. Then she dug in her purse and pulled out a business card. "I have to run, but please call me if you need anything else."

"Thanks."

Bobby read her card. *Dr. Debbie Mayther Chief of Neurology South Seminole Hospital Longwood, Florida.*

"Holy shit," he said to himself. "*Are you investigating his death?*"

He tucked her card in his pocket, knowing he was going to find out why Alexis had used two hands on her racket.

chapter thirteen

Clayton Riggs called Bobby into his office first thing Tuesday morning and waved for him to take a seat. Clayton finished his coffee, then sat forward, leaning on his elbows and still looking terrible from the party.

"Why didn't you okay First Eastern to pay the Chamberlain claim?" he asked. His voice was gravelly, almost non-existent.

"I've got a feeling about it, that's all."

"You held up a six-million-dollar payout because you had a feeling?"

"Yeah," Bobby answered. "I thought our job was to raise red flags when we suspect something."

Riggs stared at Bobby for a full thirty seconds, then settled back into his chair. "This business goes both ways. We don't hold up legitimate claims, and on occasion a lawyer will look the other way if we get into that grey ethical area. I think we just used up all our favors with Horace Vander Linden."

"Ahh, Horace."

"Yes, Horace. He was on the phone first thing this morning wondering why First Eastern had requested a two-week extension on this file."

"And what did you tell him?" Bobby was interested now. This was going to say a lot about Riggs and what kind of boss he was.

Riggs hesitated, then said, "That when we received the file we had less than twenty-four hours to look at it. I told him one of my best investigators was on it and everything looked okay, we just needed more time." He stopped for a moment. "Tell me I wasn't shitting them. Please tell me that we're not going head-to-head with Alexis Chamberlain and Horace Vander Linden."

"Okay," Bobby said. "We're not going up against Chamberlain and her high-priced help."

"Good. Then why call First Eastern and ask for an extension?"

Bobby shrugged. "I don't know. Something I saw yesterday when I met with Alexis Chamberlain bothered me. It made me want to see the ME's report." He paused. "There *was* an autopsy, wasn't there?"

"Yes, there was an autopsy. It confirmed what the doctors who worked on him at the party said. Chamberlain died of a massive heart attack."

Bobby leaned forward. "Clayton, sometimes I get these feelings. It's sort of a sixth sense, if you know what I mean. That feeling is grinding around in my gut right now, telling me to look a little further. I promise I won't piss off Horace Vander Linden any more that I absolutely have to, but I want a few more days on it. Okay?"

Riggs was unsure. "I don't know, Bobby. These are really big toes you're treading on."

"Got my hush puppies on. Promise." He made the cub scouts sign.

"All right, but don't get our heads on a platter."

"Promise," he said again, but this time he really wasn't sure.

Monique hung up the phone and stared out the window. The guy at the club yesterday, Bobby somebody, had asked for more time to review the file. Horace Vander Linden had agreed to two weeks. Common courtesy, Horace told her. She didn't like it.

Monique went back over the encounter at the club—what he said, what she said, the body language as they spoke. Nothing stood out. She had agreed to sit down with him without an appointment, then held her position with the proper amount of distance. The longer she rolled it about in her head the more convinced she was there was nothing to it. He would quietly fade away. She would have been fine with letting the six million go, but Vander Linden had insisted that dropping the insurance claim would raise some eyebrows, his included. No matter how rich you are, he told her, you don't just walk away from six million. So she had to put up with their investigator for another two weeks.

Still, Armand should know. She dialed his number and waited. When he answered she cut right to the issue. "I had a visitor yesterday, an insurance adjuster, and he's put a hold on one of the insurance policies."

Armand's response was curt. "What did he ask you?"

"About Ryan's health, his cholesterol in particular. His questions seemed reasonable."

"Nothing to indicate he suspects anything?"

"No, nothing like that," she said.

Armand was silent for a minute, then said, "What's his name?"

Monique had Bobby's card in her hand and read off the information.

"I'll take care of it," Armand said. "Goodbye."

Monique walked to the patio doors. Outside, the wind was beginning to pick up and there were reports of a storm brewing off the coast. She didn't know the weather systems in Florida well, but she knew it wasn't hurricane season. She let herself out through the patio doors and walked into the garden, her favorite part of the house. The man who had visited her at the club was a temporary irritant. Two weeks from now he would be history and she would get on with her new life.

Armand opened his laptop and typed in *Bobby Greco*. The screen filled with news articles, and he spent the next few minutes reading them.

"Shit," he said quietly. "Ex homicide."

Armand had sidestepped many police investigations over the years and he'd learned one thing as a result. The most dangerous investigators were always the homicide cops. They knew how to follow clues and build cases. Now they had an ex-cop working an insurance claim. It was the small things like this that could cause major problems down the road. He'd seen it all too often.

Armand picked up his burner cell and called the private investigator he had put on retainer when they arrived in Orlando. It was a habit he'd developed to ensure he always had a resource at his fingertips in case something like this happened.

"Stephen Bishop."

Armand introduced himself, giving the investigator the name he was registered under at the hotel. "I need you to set up surveillance on someone."

"Of course." Bishop said. "What details do you have on them?"

Armand gave him the information from Bobby's business card. "I want to know where he goes, who he visits."

"I'll call you when I have something."

Armand hung up and closed the browser on his computer. Maybe Bobby Greco would turn out to be nothing more than an overzealous insurance adjuster.

Janis Greco opened the front door of her two-story on Gardenbrook Lane. Bobby was standing on her doorstep looking concerned.

"Hi," he said. "I went by your work, but they said you were off today. They told me one of the kids wasn't feeling well."

She moved aside and he entered. "Lizzie's running a temperature. She'll be fine. It's already dropping."

"That's good," he said. "Can I see her?"

She smiled. "Of course. Silly question."

Bobby peeked in on the younger of his two girls. She was four and a half, and very proud of being more than just four. Both of the Greco girls had inherited their father's Italian lineage, with huge brown eyes and dark hair. Their faces were soft and feminine, almost duplicates of their mother, and Bobby figured his kids were destined to break a few hearts in their day. Lizzie sat up when she saw her dad.

"Hi, Daddy," she said, grinning. "Did Mommy tell you I'm sick today?"

He sat on the side of her bed and held her hand. "Yes, she did." He put his other hand on her forehead. "You don't feel too hot," he said.

"Mommy says I'm cooling down."

Bobby laughed and gave his daughter a big hug. "Would you like me to read you a book?"

Lizzie nodded vigorously and Bobby picked up her favorite, *Brer Rabbit and the Briar Patch*. She suckered him into another one and after they finished she told him with great seriousness that she was too tired for more stories and needed her rest. As he left her room, he remembered back to when he was young and feeling under the weather—nothing could have kept him from wanting another story. He found Janis on the patio, sitting under a ceiling fan.

"It's hot for January," she said.

He sat on one of the padded deck chairs and lit a cigarette. When he blew the smoke out it floated up to the fan and dissipated. "Yeah, it is. There's a storm off the coast right now. Miami's going to take the full brunt of it later today."

"Strange weather for this time of year."

He fished in his pocket, pulled out a check and handed it to her. She opened it and stared at him.

"What's this for?"

"I got a bonus from work. Thought I'd split it with you."

"Five thousand dollars?"

"Yeah. Buy something nice for yourself for a change, not just for the girls. Spoil yourself."

"I could spoil myself with five *hundred* dollars."

"It's yours. Just take it, okay?"

She nodded and tucked it away in her shorts' pocket. "Thanks, Bobby. You didn't have to."

"Yeah, I know. That's what makes it so much fun."

He didn't have to look at Janis to know how much he still loved her. That had never faded, not even a bit. Whenever he thought of her, he still got the warm feeling that came from knowing there was a person who came before him.

"Do you like your new job?" she asked.

"Yes, I do. Clayton Riggs is a good guy, and he trusts me to get things done, so he leaves me alone. Jacky's great too. I like being teamed up with her."

"You were more of a loner when you were on the force. Are you changing on me now, Bobby Greco?"

He smiled and stood. "Not that much, Jan. I gotta run. See you later."

"Bobby?"

He turned. "Yeah?"

"You promised you'd tell me what happened in the warehouse. I'm still waiting."

He thought for a moment. "Okay." He slipped back inside the front door, leaned against the jamb and told her what had gone down in the warehouse.

Janis put her hand on his arm. "Oh, Bobby, that's awful. Sorrenson and Ross, is there any way of getting at them? Forcing out the truth?"

He shook his head. "It's done. They knew exactly what they were doing and didn't leave any loose ends." He ran his hand over hers, remembering when they were inseparable. "You know what really bugs me?"

"No."

"That they used a kid and then had him killed. He didn't deserve that."

"No, he didn't."

Bobby stood in the foyer of what had once been his house, the massive sense of loss tearing at him. "And, how this will look to the kids. Their dad is the one who killed an unarmed guy and got kicked off the police force. I worry about it, Janis. This could be really hard for them."

She wrapped her arm around his waist and pulled him close. For a moment, their bodies fit together like pieces of a puzzle. "They're fine. Of all the things you have going on in your life, that's one you don't have to worry about." She pulled away a few inches so she could look in his eyes. "Trust me, Bobby, the girls are okay."

He managed a hint of a smile. "Thanks."

Bobby slipped into his car and sat in the driveway for a couple of minutes. It felt good to tell Janis the truth, and to know she believed him. There were only so many people in his corner and she was the one who really counted. He started the car and headed for the coroner's office. There was a parking spot beside the one reserved for Dr. Cook, Chief Medical Examiner. He pulled in and locked the car. The air inside the building felt cool and he could hear the quiet hum of the air-conditioner. He walked up to the front desk and leaned over the counter.

The receptionist looked up from a desk covered with family photos. "Detective Greco."

"It's just Bobby now, Sandy. How are things?"

"Peachy."

"Kids doing well?" Bobby pointed to a photo of a young man in a hockey uniform. "Jason still looking like he might have a chance at the bigs?"

"He was drafted by Tampa Bay Lightning." She was almost glowing as she spoke. "He might be playing in the NHL by next year."

"He's one hell of a hockey player, Sandy, and you really kept his feet on the ground."

"You know me, Bobby. Not a worry there."

"Is Malcolm in today?" Bobby asked.

She pointed to a corridor leading off from the reception area. He nodded, took a visitor's tag and started down the hall. Dr. Malcolm Cook and Bobby went way back. He had visited the ME's office hundreds of times over the years, but what really tied the two men together was a mistake Cook had made three years ago. It was an oversight that would have cost him his job and his license if Bobby hadn't spotted it before it went to trial. He owed Bobby big time.

Bobby reached the cutting room and ducked in after pulling on a surgical mask and booties. The room was large, perhaps sixty feet square, and one entire wall was covered with pullout drawers where the cadavers were stored. Four stainless steel gurneys were lined up on the cold tile floor, each with a tray of surgical instruments sitting beside it.

Three were empty, but the forth was occupied. A man in scrubs and a mask was carefully sawing a cadaver's skull, encircling the head until the top popped off. Once the cut was complete he glanced toward the door.

"Bobby." He set the saw on the tray. "Come in. I'm almost finished here."

"Working up an appetite for lunch, Malcolm?"

"Sure, never heard that one before. So what's up?" He snapped off his latex gloves.

"Nothing. You heard what happened with me and the force?"

"I did. Damn shame." He motioned to the door and slid his surgical mask down under his chin. "Let's talk, this guy's not going anywhere."

Bobby grinned.

"Morgue humor," Malcolm said. "Come on, I'll buy you a coffee."

They shuffled down the hallway to the coffee room, their surgical boots making a swishing sound on the tiles. The space was well appointed, with groupings of comfortable chairs and a full kitchen. Cook poured two cups and they sat in a quiet corner.

"So, let me guess, this isn't a personal visit."

"No, it's business. I've taken a job with Riggs and Company. We investigate insurance fraud."

Cook nodded. "We've had visits from them now and then. Which case are you interested in?"

"Ryan Chamberlain."

"They gave you the big potato."

"It's pretty high profile." Bobby tried the coffee—it was excellent. "Did you work on it?"

"I did. Chamberlain died of cardiac arrest complicated by respiratory failure. Nothing criminal there."

Bobby cocked his head slightly. "Respiratory failure? That's the first I've heard that mentioned. Everyone is saying heart attack."

Malcolm took a sip of coffee, then said, "Everyone understands heart attack when we say it. They don't necessarily understand respiratory failure. So when we determine the major cause of death to be myocardial infarction, that's what we run with. Why are you asking?"

"I have to check into things for the insurance company, is all. They don't like paying out large policies without covering their bases."

"Standard procedure. What do you need from us?"

Bobby leaned in a bit and kept his voice low. "I'd like to see the autopsy report. That's it, that's all I need."

Cook nodded. "I'll get you a copy. Keep it on the QT though, okay?"

"Of course." Bobby handed him a business card. "Give me a call when it's ready and I'll pop by."

Malcolm glanced around, but no one was within earshot. "I won't be able to make a copy until the place clears out a bit."

"Tonight is fine. Thanks, Malcolm."

They got up and the coroner took Bobby's cup. He stopped, turned to Bobby and said, "What happened?"

Greco looked his friend in the eyes. This was one guy he could trust to keep quiet. "Between you and me, I was set up. A couple of douche bags in Vice wanted to get rid of an informant. They used me to do it."

"No shit."

Bobby shook his head. "No shit. And that was it for my career." He left Orlando's Chief Medical Examiner standing in the coffee room, stunned and with a disgusted look on his face.

Bobby slipped into his car and headed for Twelve Oaks. He wasn't sure why, he just needed another look around. The drive took about half an hour, and by the time he'd arrived he knew why he was there. There were service vehicles parked in front of a number of different houses, otherwise the street was quiet. He tried the landscapers first.

"Do you work on this street much?" he asked one of the workers. He was a young black man, early twenties with sharp looking eyes.

"This one and a few others in the area. Why?"

"I'm trying to figure out who's been in one of the houses over the last week." He pointed down the block at the Chamberlain house. "A necklace is missing."

The guy looked thoughtful. "The only people I've seen going in or out were from Alred's Cleaning. They showed up on Sunday, about ten or eleven in the morning. Parked in the driveway and went in through the side door."

Bobby was impressed. He'd interviewed thousands of witnesses to crimes and very few of them had that sort of recollection. "That's amazing. How can you remember it so well?"

"Because it was weird. I see cleaning people show up all the time, but they always stay for five or six hours, at least. Nobody can clean one of these places in an hour. And that's all they stayed. About one hour."

"Maybe they were just giving Mrs. Chamberlain a quote."

"No, I don't think so. The guy had a bucket with him. One bucket. How weird is that? And they were dressed like they were ready to work."

"Thanks a million," Bobby said. He pulled out a fifty and slipped it into the man's hand. "Could I get your name and phone number, just in case I need it later?"

"Sure, man." He took Bobby's pen and pad and wrote down his particulars. "Have a good one."

"One last thing. Could you describe the two of them?" He glanced at the name on the paper. Jared Conroy.

"Sure. Both white, a guy about six feet with dark hair slicked back. He had darker skin than your average white guy, though. I don't think it was just tan."

"European, maybe? Olive complexion?"

"Yeah." Jared said. "That's it. Olive complexion. Sure."

"And the other person?"

"Middle age woman, around fifty-five or so. You know," he snapped his fingers as something else occurred to him. "I think another reason I remember them so well, is that they looked rich."

"What does that mean—they *looked* rich?" Bobby asked.

"Man, I see working guys around here all the time. And I see rich people. After a while you can tell the difference, no matter how they're dressed. They were dressed down, but still, it was like they were out for an expensive lunch. Her haircut, the highlights, that stuff's not cheap. Yeah, these two looked more like they should be living here than working here."

Bobby pulled out another fifty. "Thanks, Jared."

The landscaper pocketed the cash. "No, thank *you*, man."

Bobby canvassed the remainder of the crews working the street, but came up with zero. Jared the landscaper was his best source, and a damn good one at that. He drove back to the office after a quick stop for lunch at his favorite haunt. When he arrived, Jill was in her regular spot at the front desk.

"Can you pull up some information for me?" he asked.

"Sure, Bobby." Jill gave him a wide smile. She was forty-one and single, and for some reason she always seemed to have time for anything he wanted.

"I need whatever you can get on Synergy Industries. Alexis Chamberlain is running the show now, and has been since her husband died. Find out what they're working on, how their financial picture looks, if there are any pending lawsuits against them or any of the board of directors. That kind of stuff. Whatever you can get. And find out if Alred's Cleaning had one of their work vans stolen in the last week." He gave her his best grin.

"When do you need it?"

"Yesterday." He was already on his way down the hallway, heading for Jacky's office. When he got there her door was open and he poked his head in. "Hi."

"Hey, Bobby." She had recovered from the party, but had a sheepish look. "Fun party."

"Hardly remember a thing," he lied. "It's a big fuzzy blur."

"Excellent. I wish everyone else had enough common decency to have a blackout. What's up?"

He sat in the chair opposite her and set the Chamberlain file on her desk. "Clayton laid this Ryan Chamberlain thing on me." It was the highest profile job on the firm's books and he was wondering if Jacky would be pissed that Clayton had given it to him. "I wanted your impression of the case."

She gave him a raised eyebrow, revealing a very bloodshot eye. "Rich guy died of a heart attack."

She didn't seem bothered that it had gone his way, which was good. "Nice, but I was hoping for a bit more," he said.

She literally groaned and shifted in her chair. "Well, it was big news. At least, it was a couple of months ago when he died. I read the estate was in the two hundred and fifty million range, and his company has ties to the Pentagon. Government contracts. There were some rumors floating around that Washington could pull the contracts when Chamberlain died. You know, concern about security and who'd be running the company."

"They didn't pull them, did they?"

"Not that I heard. I think his wife took over."

"So Synergy got to keep their contracts, and Alexis Chamberlain inherited the company and a quarter of a billion dollars."

"Well, when you put it that way." Jacky's eyebrow went up again.

"Yeah," Bobby said. Little red flags were starting to poke through. "When you put it that way."

Jacky opened her mouth, then hesitated. She rearranged a couple of photos on the edge of her desk. Bobby waited, figuring she had something she wanted to say.

"Clayton offered me the file, Bobby. I asked him to give it to you." She pushed the file back at him with a painted fingernail.

Bobby made a mental note that he owed Jacky one very large favor. "Why?"

"The investigation might involve linking up with Orlando PD, and I figured it would give you a chance to catch up with some of your buddies on the force."

"Thanks." Bobby said. "Thanks a lot. I've already talked with one guy I know. Not a cop, but still, it was nice to be back in touch."

"I'm busy." She grinned and waved a hand at him. "Get lost."

He headed down the hall to his own office, sorted through the pile of mail, then pulled out a whiteboard and set it on a chair facing his desk. On it he wrote two headings. *Alexis Chamberlain* on the left, *Synergy Industries* on the right. Under Alexis he printed *tennis backhand* and under that, *the cleaners*. He left Synergy blank for a few minutes, then jotted down *government contracts*. As an afterthought, he added *Ryan Chamberlain* as a third column and noted *respiratory failure* and *life insurance* under his name.

Bobby sat back and stared at the whiteboard. It helped him focus, and he'd used them at the station more times than he could remember. Right now, all kinds of ideas were flying about his head and he had to concentrate, to see only the important details and blot out the rest. He closed his eyes. A few things were bothering him, and he needed to sort them out. If Jared was right, two rich people dressed as cleaners had visited the Chamberlain house. He needed to know why. Most perplexing was the question that kept coming back to him. When the club championship was on the line, why did Alexis Chamberlain change her backhand?

chapter fourteen

The Oval Office has been the epicenter of American politics since it was built in 1909. President William Neilson was seated at his desk on Wednesday, January 14th, and barely looked up as his Chief of Staff walked briskly across the room and stood waiting, holding a single sheet of paper.

"Good morning, Derek." Neilson accepted the paper. The president was a handsome man, wore a forty-four long straight off the rack, and looked every bit the figure of power that he was. He was relaxed, comfortable behind the desk, and with good reason. Neilson's administration was running at a sixty-seven percent approval rating, damn good for the second year of a presidency.

"Good morning, Mr. President." Derek Adler summed up the contents of the bi-weekly JASSM briefing as the president perused it. "March 20th is the completion date for the stealth missile prototype. They're on schedule."

"Good news." Neilson scanned the page with a heightened interest and an underlying sense of relief. Ryan's father had been a staunch supporter since he was a young, eager Florida senator. And although at sixty-nine Franklin Chamberlain was only nine years his elder, the president looked at him as a father figure. It had been an exceptionally hard blow when Franklin's son had died of a heart attack last November.

The Joint Chiefs had immediately raised concern over JASSM being left with Synergy and recommended it be reassigned to Lockheed Martin. Understandable, with the wife taking over and running the show. To them, Alexis Chamberlain was an unknown and they would have prevailed except the president himself had stepped in. Neilson knew Alexis Chamberlain personally and threw his unwavering support behind her. JASSM remained with Synergy.

"This shows everyone," the president said, holding up the briefing, "that she is more than capable of running the firm."

"Yes, sir. Even with all the problems the Pentagon sent over, they've managed to meet their targets."

Neilson's face clouded over slightly. "Our defense contractors shouldn't be on the hook for fixing the Pentagon's mistakes. Did Synergy ever put the deficiencies in writing?"

"No, sir. All done without saying a word."

Neilson set the briefing on his desk and tapped it with his pen. "If the NSA didn't have an insider at Synergy, we'd have no idea."

"True enough," Adler said.

Neilson nodded. "I don't like complainers, Derek, never have. Chamberlain simply fixed the problem without whining for more time and money. Make sure the Joint Chiefs are aware of this."

"Of course, Mr. President."

Adler retreated from the Oval Office and closed the door behind him. Neilson reread the memo, then walked to the window and looked out over the snowy landscape. There was something calming about freshly fallen snow and he felt some of his pressures melt away. Leaving Alexis Chamberlain in charge of developing the missile was a calculated risk, but he had done it for good reason. They went way back. He had spent untold hours with Alexis and the rest of her family, and she was an impressive young woman—focused, intelligent and thoughtful. It wasn't surprising that she'd stepped into Ryan's shoes with very few ripples. In his job, he made some good decisions and some not so good ones. Letting Synergy develop the missile was one of the winners.

Neilson looked back at his desk, where a stack of files needed his attention. He sat down, adjusted his reading glasses and got back to work.

Bobby Greco added another line of text to his whiteboard. Under Alexis Chamberlain, he wrote *Who is she?* He sat back and thought about that question for a while, growing more and more interested in the answer all the time. From their brief meeting at the tennis club he saw her as a strong-willed, intelligent woman. She was also wealthy and connected. Had that come from marrying Ryan Chamberlain, or was she a mover and shaker prior to them getting together?

Bobby made his way up to Jill's desk. She had just arrived and was pulling last night's messages from the answering service. She smiled and handed him a note from Malcolm Cook. A copy of the autopsy report on Ryan Chamberlain was ready for pickup.

"Thanks, Jill," he said. "Feel like doing a bit of digging for me?"

"Sure, what do you need?"

"Alexis Chamberlain. Who was she before she married Ryan Chamberlain? What sort of upbringing did she have? Is she originally from Florida? Her education, likes, dislikes, previous boyfriends, anything you can find. And get an address for her parents."

"I'm on it," Jill said. "I'll text you when I have something."

Other employees were showing up as he headed out to pick up the autopsy report. He made it to the coroner's office in good time, and picked up the sealed package Malcolm had left at the front desk. Bobby drove straight back to the office, doctored a coffee with cream and sugar, then retreated to his office and closed the door. He adjusted his desk light slightly and started reading.

The presentation aspect of the autopsy was simple—a 39-year-old Caucasian male, admitted DOA. The subject's history was from his GP's files, and consisted of Ryan's yearly physical. Blood pressure was 116 over 92, heart rate was 63 bpm, normal body temperature and respiratory rate. No vitals were available at time of death.

Bobby started into the coroner's findings with the report on the central nervous system. Scalp and meninges were normal, no sign of internal bleeding or bruising. The brain weighed 1460 grams, no evidence of cerebral oedema, and no focal lesions identified. On slicing, infarction found in the right cerebral hemisphere. Marked atheroma of basilar artery. Circle of Willis normal. So far, so good, results consistent with a heart attack.

His endocrine system showed normal adrenal, pituitary and thyroid glands, but the respiratory system caught his interest and he zeroed in on the findings. The victim's main bronchi and trachea were congested, and lung surfaces fibrotic. Pleural plaques were found near the base of left lung and the lungs weighed approximately 500-550 grams each. Fairly normal, yet Malcolm had said a contributing factor in the cause of death was respiratory failure. He read on.

The cardiovascular system. Pericardial sac slightly abnormal, with fibrous adhesions. Heart weight 370 grams, with hypertrophy of left ventricle. Aortic, tricuspid and pulmonary valves intact. Aorta showing severe atheroma, but still patent. Bobby read carefully as the coroner described the coronary arteries. Renal artery partially congested, carotid open, and left coronary artery congested. Higher than normal cholesterol levels in renal and left coronary arteries.

Greco sat back and sipped his coffee. At the time of his yearly physical last November, Ryan Chamberlain was in excellent health. High cholesterol perhaps, but nothing serious enough to kill him. With blood pressure of 116 over 92, the blood was flowing easily from the heart into the system of arteries and veins that ran through his body. Yet he was dead, of a heart attack. Bobby sat forward and continued reading, his interest piqued.

Musculo-skeletal system intact, reticulo-endothelial system fine, with the spleen normal and weighing in at 170 grams. Gastrointestinal System all normal, including the cut sections of the liver. His mouth, esophagus, stomach and gall bladder all okay, with bile drainage in the duodenum normal. The Genito-Urinary System was a perfect ten. Kidneys, external and cut sections, okay, pelvicalyceal system, ureters, and bladder all fine. No evidence of mucosal inflammation. Even Ryan's prostate was in great condition.

Bobby flipped through the final pages and set the autopsy report on his desk. Ryan Chamberlain had a physical in November, just before his death, and was given a clean bill of health. His autopsy showed a slight constricting of the arteries near the heart from medium to high cholesterol levels, and damage to the right cerebral hemisphere of his brain. Maybe that was enough to kill him. But probably not. He flipped through the autopsy again, looking for the mass spectrometry screen. It was missing and he placed a call to Malcolm Cook.

"Malcolm, Bobby here," he said when he got the M.E. on the phone. "I just finished going through Chamberlain's autopsy. You forgot to include the mass spectrometry results."

There was a pause. "We didn't run mass spectrometry, Bobby."

"You didn't run a toxicology screen? Why not?"

"Bobby, the guy died in a room full of prominent doctors. Two of them declared him dead of a heart attack. What could I do?"

It took a minute for what Malcolm was saying to sink in. "You were told not to run the tox screen? In case the doctors were wrong?"

"Bobby…" The line was silent for a minute. "You helped me keep my job once. This could have the opposite effect."

"None of this gets out, Malcolm."

A long silence, then, "I was asked not to run toxicology on the victim. Just a slice and dice autopsy. Exactly what's in the report."

"I don't know, Malcolm, from what I'm looking at, there's no reason for Ryan Chamberlain to be in the ground. He had raised cholesterol levels in some arteries, but nothing that would have caused a massive coronary." More silence. After thirty seconds, Bobby continued. "Did you take tissue samples?"

"Yes."

"Do you still have them?"

"Christ, Bobby, do you know what you're asking?"

"Yeah, I do. I'm asking if you have liver or kidney samples that you can run through a mass spectrometer and generate a tox screen."

"I can't do that, Bobby. There's too much pressure on this one."

"From the docs?"

Bobby heard a heavy sigh over the line. Malcolm was struggling with how to respond.

"Listen carefully," Malcolm said. "Rose Ambers and Ben Olsen are both very prominent doctors. Top of the heap. They knew assessing a cause of death at the scene was a risk, but they both have big egos. They couldn't resist."

"I know what they're like," Bobby responded tartly. "I've had my share of dealing with people like that."

"Okay." Cook took a few more deep breaths. "Once I ran the initial autopsy, they were all over me. They saw exactly what you saw. That Chamberlain's death may have been more than just a heart attack. But their reputations mean more to them than the truth. They made it clear that if I ran the tox screen my career was dead in the water. If I let it go I was in for life."

"Fuck, Malcolm, you sold out. How could you?"

"I'm not as brave as you, Bobby. I can't just get turfed and keep moving along. I need my job."

Greco sat back in his chair and ran his free hand through his hair. *I'm not as brave as you, Bobby.* What the hell was *that* supposed to mean? How could Malcolm Cook think it didn't almost destroy him to be set up—to have his life yanked away from him and see his career with Orlando PD go up in smoke?

"Okay, I'll make you a deal," Bobby said. "Come in on the weekend, or work late at night, I don't care. Run the tox screen for my eyes only."

"And if I don't?"

"Don't even go there, Malcolm. We're too good of friends for that. I will never divulge how I got the information. You have my word on that."

Silence, then, "Okay, Bobby. I'll call you when I have the results." The line went dead.

chapter fifteen

Monique's retina scan cleared security and she entered the anteroom of The Fort. She swiped her pass card, typed in her code, then placed both hands independently on the glass. The system approved her fingerprints and she strode into the building as an airtight door closed quietly behind her.

June Childers' office was in section six and Monique moved through the complex with purpose. She needed the debugged software along with the files for the modified missile body, and she needed them now. Armand was getting impatient—his buyer was putting pressure on him to deliver, and that responsibility was hers alone. She spotted Childers speaking with one of her programmers and waved. The scientist waved back, wrapped up her conversation and headed over to meet the boss.

"Morning, Alexis," she said cheerfully. "How are things?"

"Very well," Monique said. "Everything ready to go?"

June's brow creased slightly. "You're early. I haven't encrypted the files yet. Give me an hour, maybe two, and they'll be ready."

"No need," Monique said. "I'm taking them straight to the safe in my office."

June was at a loss for words. The head of the company was asking her to circumvent the rules. She shook her head. "I can't release the data without encrypting it first."

"June," Monique said, drawing close to the woman. "Download the data. Today." She spun on her heels and left.

June Childers watched the new CEO leave. Something wasn't right, but she couldn't put her finger on it. Alexis Chamberlain had every right to ask for the technology and to put it in the vault in her office. The FBI had given her clearance to do exactly that. But they hadn't, at any time, said it was okay to move the data from one place to another without encrypting it. She stared through the glass into the adjoining laboratory where the JASSM prototype was suspended from the ceiling by tungsten wires. Her team had made six adjustments to the missile, and without all six of those changes the prototype was still visible from space. JASSM was incredibly complex, and from working on it she could see how the scientists at the Pentagon had missed the mark. Given the level of secrecy surrounding the project, and what was at stake, sending unencrypted technology outside Building Nine wasn't going to happen, even if the recipient was Alexis Chamberlain. She made a decision.

Her series of tests had stripped away the problem like layers of an onion, each crucial to the final outcome. If she were to download one of the interim solutions, she would be giving Alexis a missile that appeared completely invisible until actual production. She could deliver the correct files later, prior to the production run, encrypted and in accordance to the FBI's strict rules.

June set to work, downloading the incomplete version of the missile. Alexis need never know.

Bobby glanced up as Jill entered his office, clutching two thick packages and a single sheet of paper. She set them on the edge of his desk and smiled.

"Here's what you wanted to know about Synergy and Alexis Chamberlain," she said.

"Wow, that was quick. Good work."

She left his office still smiling, and he looked over the single sheet she had set on his desk. It was an email from the Orlando Police Department. A white van, registered to Alred's Cleaning, had been reported stolen on Saturday, January 10, and recovered late in the afternoon on Monday,

January 12. Nothing was missing and the van hadn't been damaged. Bobby noted at the bottom of the report that forensics had dusted for prints, but come up empty. That ruled out kids taking it for a joyride. And nothing was missing. Why would someone steal a vehicle that was so easily recognizable? Something wasn't adding up. He set the page on his desk and ripped into the package on Synergy Industries.

Twenty minutes later he had a headache. Annual corporate reports and financial statements were like reading Greek, and Synergy was great at record keeping. He could tell the company was in the black, and the government contracts had been delivered on time and on budget. That triggered bonus options, which boosted their profit margins. Since going public, they were a reliable performer on the NYSE, and their stock was rock-solid at sixty-one dollars. There were no outstanding liens or caveats against them, and no employees had filed grievances. Their legal department had two lawyers and four assistants—small for a firm of their size.

Synergy had top-level security clearance from both the National Security Agency and the Federal Bureau of Investigation. The latest weapon they were working on was the Joint Air-to-Surface Standoff Missile. Bobby read an overview on the missile, but it was far too complicated for his high school math and physics. He filed it away under *rocket science* and switched files. It was time to find out about Alexis Chamberlain.

She had been born Alexis Rothchild. Bobby set the file on the desk and rolled his eyes. Mr. Silver Spoon meets Ms. Silver Spoon. The Rothchild family had amassed some of Florida's most valuable coastal property, spanning all the way from Miami to West Palm Beach. The woman came from serious money.

Bobby sipped his coffee and continued reading. Alexis Rothchild had been an over-achiever since her grade school days. She was consistently top of her class throughout high school and had graduated from MIT as an electrical engineer with a physics minor. Even with such a crushing course load she had managed a 3.9 GPA, and then had followed up with her Masters, producing a thesis on random signal theory.

"Shit," Bobby whispered to himself. "She's a fucking rocket scientist."

Bobby drank the last of his coffee, wondering how anyone could compete with these kinds of people. He closed the file and scratched his chin. This was one impressive woman. Born into wealth, never needing to work, yet she spent six grueling years getting her Masters. She was raising two children, had helped Ryan build Synergy from scratch and was well liked wherever she went. Alexis was socially adept, and thinking back to their encounter at Heathrow, he realized that while he had been the one asking the questions, she had been in control. If he read her tone and body language correctly, she didn't really care about the six million dollars. It was nice that it would eventually show up, but it wasn't going to change anything for her.

He walked over to the whiteboard. Under *the cleaners*, he wrote, *rich man and woman* and *stolen van*. Why would wealthy people steal a van and pose as cleaners? They could simply drive up to the front door in their Mercedes and ring the bell. Perhaps they didn't want to be recognized. Maybe they were from her past? Was the whole thing some sort of kinky sex triangle? Were they famous?

The sex angle immediately faded as a possibility. The gardener had described the two visitors as middle age—not an age group usually associated with wild, kinky sex. If Alexis Chamberlain was looking for something on the side, the players would be young and attractive. He ruled it out. Then he started asking why someone with a recognizable face would steal a cleaning van in order to arrive incognito. It was a ridiculous idea. They would simply drive up in a car with tinted windows and walk into the house with hats on and their heads down. That one was out.

Could it be someone from her life before Ryan? Who then? Right now there were too many questions and not enough answers.

Bobby was on a caffeine high and gave the coffee pot a wide berth on his way down the hall, thanking Jill for the info as he passed. The high heat and humidity hit him as he pushed his way out the door, and he hurried to his car, calling Jill as he took off.

"One more thing." He floored the BMW and sped south on North Thompson Road. "Could you get me a number for the Rothchild residence."

chapter sixteen

A few minutes before quitting time June Childers headed for Alexis's office with an armed escort and a small package in her hand.

Rhonda ushered her in, and Monique looked up from her paperwork. "Is that it?"

"Yes. The modified files for the casing and the stealth software." She placed the hard drive on the edge of the desk and took a seat. The FBI had allowed individual pieces of Synergy's work to be kept in the CEO's safe, but never more than three at a time.

"Excellent. Any problems?"

"No, none at all. I downloaded the new body shape first. Those files are all prefixed with *ex*. The second set of numbers is for the stealth technology. They're prefixed with *st*. Pretty simple actually."

"Is it encrypted?"

Childers couldn't help looking perturbed. "Yes."

"I'll be careful with it. Thanks again." Her tone indicated the meeting was finished.

The scientist rose from the chair and left the room.

Monique Dupres ran a manicured fingernail gently over the drive and a shiver went down her spine. She had already downloaded and copied the files from the other ten departments, and with this, she had a working prototype of the missile. Cortez was going to be over the moon. She connected the drive to her computer and started the decryption program. It ran without a hitch and indicated the file was now ready to be viewed. She put another thumb drive in the computer and clicked *copy*.

The expected transfer commands did not appear on the screen. Instead, a few lines of code June Childers had inserted into the header sprang to life. The subroutine instructed the drive to erase all stored data. Monique could only watch helplessly as the top-secret updates for the missile disappeared off her screen, file by file. Finally the screen went dark red and a line of white text scrolled across.

Attempting to copy this disc was illegal.

Monique grabbed a handful of pens and hurled them across the room, peppering the far wall like shotgun pellets. "You bitch," she whispered viciously under her breath. "You goddamn bitch."

The door opened and Rhonda stuck her head in. "Is everything okay, Mrs. Chamberlain?" she asked.

"Yes, fine, Rhonda." She was so angry she could barely breathe. "Sometimes computers make me want to pull my hair out."

Rhonda grinned slightly. "That's funny coming from you," she said.

"Why?"

"You design them." She shut the door behind her.

Monique stared at the closed door, thinking how ridiculous she must have looked, getting mad at her computer. Becoming Alexis had been difficult, but in many ways continuing the charade was even harder. Her mannerisms, her voice, her words, everything had to be exactly as Alexis would react. Often times, Monique found herself thinking in French, and that was dangerous. She had to be careful.

She stood and paced about the room until she was thinking more clearly, then went back to her desk and disconnected June's hard drive. There might be a way to get the scientist to recreate the drive without her knowing it had been erased. The more Monique thought about it, the more convinced she was it could be pulled off. She opened the wall safe and tucked the useless drive inside. This was going to hold things up for a couple of days, but that wasn't important. What mattered was getting a functioning copy to Armand. Monique checked her watch and shut down her computer. June Childers had gotten the best of her this time, but the next round would be different.

It was a few minutes to six and dusk was settling over Orlando. Bobby checked to see who was calling his cell, but it came up *private*. He took the call anyway.

"Hello," he said. "Greco here."

The voice in his ear was excited, almost breathless. "Bobby, its Malcolm. Can you get over here?"

"Sure. Are you still at the office?"

"I am. I'll wait for you. How long until you get here?"

Bobby checked his watch. He was about half an hour drive from the ME's office. "I'll be there at six-thirty."

"That's good. I'll wait at the front doors for you. The place is locked up."

Bobby hung up and pulled a U-turn. Malcolm Cook didn't often get flustered about things, and something had him upset. It was a no-brainer that something had come up on the Chamberlain file. When Bobby pulled into the parking lot, his friend was waiting inside the building, next to the front doors.

"Hi," Bobby said. "I take it you got some results."

"Come in and I'll show you what I found." He led Bobby into the depths of the morgue and when they arrived at the lab Malcolm flipped on the lights. "I kept liver and kidney tissues, plus blood and marrow from the cadaver. First I ran microcrystalline tests, then a thin layer chromatograph. I prepared a slide with droplets of blood and silica gel, then watched the capillary action as the liquids separated. Under ultra-violet light there was nothing. Absolutely nothing traceable."

"Is that normal?"

"Sort of, providing the victim hadn't used a stimulant like cocaine or ingested some sort of poison. But we're looking for something that might have caused the heart to stop. Right?"

"Right," Bobby said.

"Well, look what I found when I ran the samples through the mass spectrometer." He held out a sheet of paper with spikes and troughs on it. There were numbers on both the vertical and the horizontal axis. "The machine breaks up molecules by bombarding them with high energy electrons, reducing each substance to its basic building blocks. Since no two substances have exactly the same chemical makeup, they don't break up the same. Each has its own individual chemical signature."

Bobby knew how a mass spectrometer worked, but stayed quiet. He glanced at the toxicology screen it had produced, checking out the areas where poisons most commonly occurred. He held it out for Malcolm. "There's nothing on it," he said.

"To the untrained eye." Cook didn't take the paper from Bobby. He pointed to a spike with a mass of 303. "Do you know what that is?" he asked. Bobby shook his head, and Malcolm continued. "It's verapamil."

"What the hell is verapamil?"

"It's a channel blocker," Malcolm said. "It's used for patients that don't respond well to lithium or carbamazepine. It regulates the heartbeat."

"You're saying it's a prescribed drug?"

"Yes, but drugs approved by the FDA have reasonable therapeutic indices. This one did not."

"Okay, Malcolm. Now you're talking Greek. What are you saying?"

Malcolm Cook looked Bobby in the eye. "My guess is that someone had access to a supply of verapamil before it was diluted into pills for distribution. Or they extracted the active ingredient from pharmaceutical pills. Whichever way they did it, they got an extremely high dosage into him without triggering any other spikes on the spectrometer." He paused for a moment. "Someone pumped enough verapamil into Ryan Chamberlain to cause his heart to stop."

Bobby was quiet for a moment. "So he was murdered."

"Yes."

Greco rubbed his unruly hair with both hands and sat down on one of the lab stools. He stared around the lab at the beakers and test tubes, the Bunsen burners and all the other stuff he had used when he was struggling with high school chemistry. Now these same pieces of equipment were telling him something no one else knew. That the very wealthy CEO of a company developing top-secret weapons for the US government had been skillfully executed. Bobby's head was spinning. It didn't get much worse than that.

Malcolm sat down next to him. "What are you going to do, Bobby?"

The ex-cop shrugged. "I promised how I got the results would stay between you and me, but it changes the way I'm looking at certain people. Alexis Chamberlain, for starters."

Malcolm nodded slowly. "The wife."

"Yes, the cool-as-a-cucumber wife." He turned to Malcolm. "Tell me, my friend, can this channel blocker be ingested orally? Like, shall we say, with food?"

"Yes."

"And he died having dinner, in a room full of doctors. Now isn't that something."

chapter seventeen

Clayton Riggs watched Bobby poke at his steak. He had been holding something back through lunch, something Clayton figured he wanted to get off his chest, but wasn't sure how. It was Friday and Bobby had called the meeting.

"What's bothering you?" Riggs asked.

Bobby didn't even look up from his plate. He continued to poke the piece of beef, then switched to the potato. Finally, he gave a Clayton a short glance.

"I haven't been working for you very long, Clayton, but I think you're a fair man." Riggs didn't respond, just took a sip of rye and coke and waited. "I've got something on the Chamberlain case that's good and not so good at the same time."

"What's that?" Riggs asked.

Bobby looked him in the eye. "This has the potential to get really ugly, and I need your word that you won't repeat what I'm going to tell you until I say it's okay."

"How can I do that? I don't know what you're going to tell me."

Bobby didn't respond.

"And it involves the Chamberlain case," Riggs said.

"Yes."

"First Eastern Life has the right to know what's going on. If what you tell me is relevant to the case, then I have to divulge it."

"Then I can't tell you what I know. Even if it costs me my job." Bobby Greco locked eyes with his boss. The mutual respect between the men was either going to be enough to get them through this, or Bobby would quit. He wasn't going to hand over Malcolm Cook.

As they sat in silence, Clayton Riggs saw the look in Bobby's eyes and knew he wasn't going to win this one. If he wanted Bobby Greco on his payroll he had to back down. Slowly, he nodded. "Okay, it stays between you and me, but this doesn't get swept under the carpet indefinitely."

Bobby knew all too well how investigations worked. Down the road, other evidence would come up that would lead to the conclusion that Chamberlain had been killed. The tox screen from Malcolm Cook would never see the light of day. "It can come out when the time is right."

"Fair enough. What have you got?"

"Chamberlain was murdered."

Riggs' blood pressure went through the roof. "Aww, fuck." It took a minute for him to gather his thoughts enough to ask, "How sure are you?"

"One hundred percent. I got my hands on a toxicology screen from Chamberlain's tissue samples. Someone drugged Ryan Chamberlain with a channel blocker called verapamil. It causes the heart to slow, or stop, depending on how much you give the person."

"Christ." Riggs slumped back in his chair.

Bobby nodded. "There's more. A man and a woman showed up at the Chamberlain house last Sunday. They were in a stolen van, dressed as cleaners. The landscaper who saw them said they looked rich."

"A landscaper?" Riggs sounded skeptical.

"He's a very believable witness." Bobby paused, then added, "And Alexis Chamberlain has changed how she hits her tennis backhand."

Clayton just stared blankly at him and Bobby continued.

"It's important. Let's say you play a sport, like tennis, just below the professional level. You consistently hit your backhand with two hands on the racquet. Then out of nowhere, you start using only one. For you or me that's not a big deal, but for someone playing at that level it's huge."

"Okay," Riggs finished his drink, pushed his glass out of the way and waved at the server for another. "Where does all this point?"

Bobby shrugged. "Right now, I don't know. But I *do* know one thing from working homicide. If something *is* wrong and you keep digging, you usually figure it out."

Clayton sat quietly for a couple of minutes, taking it all in. His new drink arrived and he toyed with the stir stick. "So why all the secrecy?"

Bobby lowered his voice. "The ME who gave me the tox scan is a friend, and it turns out the doctors who pronounced Chamberlain dead at the scene paid him a visit. They pressured him into finding the same cause of death they did. If it were leaked he didn't run a toxicology screen with the autopsy his career would be over, and that's the last thing I'd let happen. Without the tox screen we would have nothing. I owe him."

"Okay." Riggs pushed his index fingers into his temples. "If we let even the slightest hint of this out, the press will go nuts. We've got a dead guy who left a quarter-billion-dollar estate, a beautiful wife, and a company producing top-secret government weapons. Holy shit."

"Yeah." Bobby raised his glass in a mock toast. "Holy shit."

Clayton leaned in and asked, "How long do we have before we have to respond to First Eastern Life?"

"We're four days into our two week extension, so that leaves us ten."

"Okay," Clayton said. "That's the least of our worries right now. I'll handle that end of things."

"Thanks, Clayton."

"What's next?"

Bobby's appetite was back, now that Clayton was informed and on side. He cut into his steak and dipped it in the barbeque sauce. "I have a meeting lined up with Alexis's parents and a few of the key staff members at Synergy. No moss sticking to this stone, my friend."

It was Friday after work and June Childers pulled her Toyota into the Starbucks parking lot. She hustled into the coffee house and immediately spotted the man she figured was Robert Greco. He was sitting on a tall stool at the front window.

Bobby recognized June from her photo on the Synergy website and gave her a quick wave as she entered. The picture didn't do her justice. To him, she was a knock out. He felt his throat constrict as she walked toward him in snug-fitting jeans and a white T.

"I'm June Childers. You must be Robert Greco." She offered her hand.

"Everyone calls me Bobby." They shook and his eyes darted to her left hand to check the ring finger. It was empty.

"Give me a minute," she said. "I'm going to grab a mocha."

"Sure."

Bobby watched her as she walked to the counter, thinking that he already knew a couple of things about June Childers. She was not going to be in anyone's debt—her tone of voice had told him she was buying her own coffee. And the way she walked was self-assured and confident. June Childers was an athletic, powerful woman. She was also the last of the interviews with Synergy staff, and so far he had nothing.

She returned to the table with her drink and pulled up a stool. "So you're an insurance investigator." She stirred her steaming-hot coffee. "Do you have some ID?"

He produced his business card. "Riggs & Company."

"Sounds interesting." She smiled. "Is it dangerous?"

"No. It's quite boring actually."

"And you're investigating Ryan's death."

"We are. It's a formality, really. Talking to a few of the people who knew him is standard procedure before the insurance company pays out on a policy."

She sipped her mocha. "All right. Ask away."

"From what I've gathered so far, it appears Mr. Chamberlain was pretty happy with his life—with his company, his wife, his kids. Would you say that's correct?"

"Yes. Ryan was totally in control of his life. He knew exactly where he wanted Synergy to go and he was well on the way to taking it there. His family adored him. He and Alexis had a great marriage. His death, it was an absolute tragedy."

"So it appears." He toyed with his coffee cup for a second, then asked, "How are things at Synergy since his death?"

"I don't see how that is relevant to your investigation. I'm not comfortable answering questions about a company that deals with government military secrets."

Bobby hadn't expected Childers to be a pushover and it wasn't a surprise that she had shut him down. "It *is* relevant, Dr. Childers. I'll try to keep the questions from touching on anything that might be confidential."

"All right, ask your questions. I'll answer the ones I'm comfortable with."

"How is Alexis Chamberlain doing now that she's running the show?"

"Alexis is very competent."

"Do you think she's the same as before Mr. Chamberlain's death, or has she changed?"

She cocked her head slightly. "That's a strange question."

"Not really. When tragedy strikes, people often react in predictable ways. Some withdraw, others become extroverts. I was just wondering if she seemed any different."

Childers gave that question some serious thought. "Yes. I would say Alexis has changed. She's more focused, perhaps even a bit aggressive in following through on the work that Ryan started."

"Was she involved in the company before his death?"

"Well, she seemed to take more interest in Synergy just before he died. She started coming to the office more frequently, sometimes even on weekends."

"So that was new for her? Coming to the office?"

"It was."

"Did she seem on edge at all?"

"Not really," June said, then reconsidered. "Well, maybe a bit. She lost it with the security guard at the front gate when her retina scan failed."

Bobby leaned forward ever so slightly. "I'm not sure what that means."

She gave him a long, hard look, deciding whether to give him any more, then continued. "Synergy installed a new security system that uses high frequency light waves to map out a person's retina, then compares it to the one on file. If they match the green light goes on, if not the light flashes red. I guess her scan was red that morning."

"Do you remember which Sunday that was?"

"I'll try." She pulled out her phone and scrolled through her calendar. "Ryan and I were discussing a particular project back in October, so it would likely have been either the 12th or the 19th." Her eyes flicked back and forth between the two dates for a few seconds and Bobby remained quiet. Finally she said, "October 12th." June cocked her head slightly and looked directly at him. "Sunday, October 12th, I'm positive."

Bobby was completely caught off guard by the look. It was intense, and, if he was reading it correctly, suggestive. He wrote the date in his notebook and tried to figure out if he was simply imagining her intentions. He wasn't sure.

He glanced up and she met his gaze. "You said Mr. Chamberlain went to the security building and straightened things out."

"That's correct. From what I know, there haven't been any problems since."

Bobby didn't want the interview to end, but he was done and if he stretched things out and longer she would pick up on it. He held his hand out and they shook again. "Thanks very much," he said. "Could I call you if I need any further information?"

She reached over and slipped his notebook from his hand. She jotted down three phone numbers, closed the book and gave it back to him. "I'd like that." She left him sitting in the coffee shop, his mind whirring.

It took him a minute before he opened the notebook. He stared at what she had written. There were three numbers—her direct line at work, her cell number, and her home number. He closed the book slowly, and a grin crept across his face. June Childers was, he thought, a very outgoing woman.

He was having an extremely good day.

chapter eighteen

June stopped in the store next to the Starbucks and found a birthday card for a friend, then returned to her car. She glanced back at the Starbucks as she unlocked her door, and saw Bobby still sitting where she had left him, sipping the last of his coffee and thumbing through a magazine.

If she was any judge of character, there had been some chemistry between them at the meeting. The truth was, from the moment she first saw him, she was interested. He was intelligent, handsome, and had honest eyes. Bobby Greco might be a man worth getting to know.

She slid into her Toyota and closed the door. Meeting new people and letting them into her world was a problem. June had secrets. Secrets that normal people could never know. She worked for the National Security Agency and was, essentially, a spy, NSA's inside person at Synergy.

She hadn't started out with any aspirations of becoming an NSA operative. She was a typical college student—hard working, popular, and able to drink beer with the best of them. In her undergraduate years at Johns Hopkins University, June switched from pure mathematics to coding and cryptography because she enjoyed probability theory. Most of her friends couldn't even begin to comprehend the level of math she routinely worked with and they called her the Giant Brain.

When she graduated with a doctorate in cryptology, the NSA came calling. Her skills were perfect for a government agency set up to both create and break codes. After four months traveling through Europe and considering their offer, she returned and accepted the position of Cryptologic Scientist.

From her office window June had watched the traffic flowing past on the Baltimore-Washington Parkway, the people in the cars oblivious to the top-secret world inside the NSA complex. Crypto City, as it was known, housed thousands of employees whose spouses and families had no idea what they did when they went to work. The place was a dark hole, where highly skilled people like June Childers disappeared for eight to ten hours a day, then reappeared at dinner time. It was that part of the job, the one that kept her from building any meaningful relationships, that June found hard to bear.

After a few years, she wanted something else, but knew the NSA wasn't going to just let her walk out the front door. She went to her superiors with an idea they liked—let her work in the real world, in highly sensitive areas where NSA wanted eyes and ears. They agreed to her proposal, and with a fake resume in hand June left Crypto City for a new position with Synergy. She moved into a comfortable house in Orlando that backed onto Lake Wildmere and all was well.

Until Ryan Chamberlain's death.

Things were different after that. She had noticed changes in his wife that were troubling. Alexis was more aggressive, to the point of demanding June download the unencrypted stealth technology onto a hard drive. June had considered calling her contact at NSA to report Alexis's breach of protocol, but had simply encrypted a flawed version and added some code that would wipe the drive clean if someone tried to copy it. She'd handed over the hard drive and considered it done.

Then Bobby Greco showed up, asking questions. She was starting to think she should have made the call.

Bobby drove south on the Florida Turnpike toward Palm Beach a bit faster than usual. His appointment with the Rothchilds was at six-thirty and he didn't want to be late. He reached the exit onto the 704, paid the toll and cruised into West Palm Beach over the Royal Park Bridge.

The Rothchild mansion was on South Ocean Boulevard, occupying a massive lot dotted with Royal and Canary Island palms. He turned in and parked his car near the front door and left the keys in the ignition. He sprinted up the stairs, rang the bell and waited, the gurgling of water in the fountain the only sound.

A middle-aged man in a freshly pressed suit opened the door and welcomed him in. He led Bobby down a wide hall with frescoes of tiny cherubs dancing on popcorn clouds to a large drawing room with overstuffed chairs, then invited him to take a seat. A few minutes later the Rothchilds entered.

The first thing that struck Bobby about Percy Rothchild was his size. Six-four and thick through the chest, he wasn't what Bobby expected from Alexis Chamberlain's father. Neither was his face, with its wide, harsh features. He marched up to Bobby and extended a large hand.

"Robert Greco?" he asked.

Bobby nodded. "Yes, sir."

"I'm Percy Rothchild—my wife, Etonia." He motioned to the tall, large-boned woman who had accompanied him into the room. They were a classic example of a husband and wife who look well suited for each other. She gave Bobby a tight smile when she shook his hand and the three of them sat at a grouping of chairs.

"What can we do for you, Mr. Greco?" Etonia Rothchild asked. It was polite, but to the point.

What can you do for me? Tell me enough about your daughter so I can figure out if she murdered her husband.

"I'm with Riggs & Company, as you know. We were commissioned by First Eastern Life to take a look at the circumstances surrounding Mr. Chamberlain's death. I assure you, it's simply a formality."

"Of course," Percy Rothchild said. There was more than a tinge of sadness in his face "Ryan was a wonderful man. We all miss him."

Bobby treaded carefully with the next sentence. "Your daughter is the beneficiary of a six-million-dollar insurance policy. We need to do our due diligence."

"She doesn't need the money," he said, staring out over the expanse of ocean behind the house.

"I know that," Bobby said respectfully. "Still, it's a large sum to the insurer."

Percy nodded. "Well, let's get on with it, shall we."

Bobby opened his notebook. "How did Alexis seem to you, both before and after her husband's death?"

Etonia Rothchild answered. "Before his death, things were completely normal. They kept to a routine, you know, mostly for the children. Stability is so important for kids. When Ryan died, she took it extremely hard. She's coping by diving back into work, it's keeping her busy and her mind active."

"Do you mean by taking control of Synergy?"

She nodded. "Alexis knows the company better than anyone else, so she was the logical one to step into Ryan's shoes."

"Did Ryan's death come as a surprise to you?"

The old man thundered out a response. "Of course it did. The man was thirty-nine years old for God's sake."

Bobby got the feeling that Percy Rothchild was struggling to keep his emotions in check. He could have baited the man, but refrained. "Was everything okay with Ryan and Alexis? You know, their marriage, the kids, that kind of stuff."

"They had a wonderful marriage," Mrs. Rothchild answered quickly for her husband. "Zach and Patricia are a joy, and she and Ryan loved the kids to bits. Alexis was very happy, if that's what you're asking."

"I imagine she's under a lot of stress with running the business and taking care of the children."

"She's sent Zach and Patricia away to school." Percy Rothchild didn't sound happy about that.

That bit of information came as a shock. "The children aren't in Orlando with her?"

"No, they're in a private school in Virginia. It's supposed to be very good." Etonia said, straightening up.

"They should be at home," Percy snapped. "I don't care how stressed she is. Hire a bloody nanny."

Etonia Rothchild shot her husband a withering glance. "It's her choice, Percy."

Bobby turned to Etonia. "How long have the children been away?"

"Since early January. They started at the beginning of the second semester." She shifted slightly so she was looking at her husband. "We just wonder if Patricia isn't a bit young to be away at school."

Bobby jotted the information in his book and continued. "Your daughter was very accomplished academically. I imagine she attended private schools." If she had, it might explain why she enrolled her children in one.

"Certainly, but there are very good private schools right there in Orlando," Percy answered.

Bobby pointed to a family portrait hanging on the wall some twenty feet away. In it were Percy and Etonia Rothchild, flanked by their children. "Four children. All tennis players?"

"They all played," Etonia said. "Alexis was the only one to stay with it."

Bobby focused on the photo. Alexis appeared more mature than the others. "Is she the oldest?"

Etonia glanced at the photo. "She is. After Alexis we discovered that I could have children."

Bobby got up and walked over to the photo and took a closer look at each of the four children and the parents. Alexis was the only one with fine features, the rest had broader faces like Percy and Etonia. "I'm sorry. I don't understand."

"Alexis is adopted." Percy looked at his wife. "The doctors told us Etonia couldn't have children." He smiled. "Wrong, weren't they."

She took his hand. "They really were."

Bobby raised an eyebrow. That certainly explained the difference between Alexis and her siblings. "Does Alexis know she's adopted?" he asked.

Mrs. Rothchild answered. "Of course. We told her when she was thirteen. She was beginning to ask questions about why she was so…" She paused. "…different from her brothers and sister. We felt it was only fair that she knew."

"I see. Did Alexis ever ask about her birth mother? Search for her?"

Etonia walked over and stood next to Bobby. She adjusted the photo slightly, and Bobby knew she was reliving the experience.

"We told her the name of the adoption agency—Adoption Advocates—but she never followed up. She made it quite clear that we were all the family she needed."

"Do you know the identity of Alexis's birth mother?"

"Yes, but that is privileged information." Her response was curt and closed the door on the issue.

Bobby nodded at the picture next to the one of the family. In it, President William Neilson and his parents were posing with Percy and Etonia and their children on a beach. "You know the president," he said.

"We do," Percy answered. "They're our neighbors in the Hamptons."

Bobby stared at the photo for a minute, trying to get a sense of the level these people lived at. A twenty-million-dollar West Palm Beach mansion, a beach house in the Hamptons, and personal friends with the president and his family. He failed miserably.

"Well, thanks for your time," Bobby said. They saw him to the door and thanked him for coming.

He kept to the speed limit as he headed back up the Turnpike. The trip to Palm Beach had been fruitful. Alexis Chamberlain was adopted. That was more than a little interesting. And she had sent her kids off to private school a couple of months after her husband died. Percy Rothchild was right when he said she could have hired a nanny. It seemed strange that a woman wouldn't want her children close by after such a loss. He had two more points to add under Alexis Chamberlain on his whiteboard.

Kids sent off to school and *Alexis adopted.* Two more pieces of the puzzle.

He stared through the window into the darkness of the central Florida night.

What would be next?

chapter nineteen

Leu Gardens was quiet on Saturday morning. It was too early for tourists, and there weren't enough locals to create a crowd. It was exactly the kind of place Armand Cortez sought out. He spotted Monique on a bench overlooking Lake Rowena, unrecognizable to anyone but him, with a short black-hair wig and sunglasses. He sat down next to her and looked out over the still water.

"What the hell happened?" he said. "You were going to deliver the files yesterday."

She didn't like his words or his tone. "I had everything," Monique snapped back. "There was some sort of code on the drive that wiped it clean when I tried to copy it."

"You had the files and you erased them." It was an accusation, not a question.

"Yes." She watched a couple walk by, hand-in-hand. "I'll make her give me another copy on Monday."

"This is *not* good." He reached out and cupped her chin in his hand, forcibly turning her head to face him. "Downloading them again. She'll suspect something."

Monique stared straight into his eyes. "No, she won't. I'll deal with it on Monday." She tried to push his hand away, but couldn't. "You can have it on Tuesday. Surely to God your buyer can wait three days."

He leaned in toward her. "You know my buyers are not patient people, Monique."

"Tuesday," Monique repeated.

"Tuesday, then." Cortez finally let go of her, but she continued staring at him. "If you give me the only copy of Childers' data, what are you going to hand over to the Pentagon?"

She tossed her hair as she looked away. "That's not a problem. June can make another one in a week or two. I'll tell her the one she gave me was corrupted."

"Ahh, I see." He turned away, to the lake and the towering oaks bordering it. The scene was too good for a postcard. "The insurance adjuster. Bobby Greco."

Monique let out a sigh. "What about him?"

"He's poking around. He met with Childers."

She relaxed a bit. "That's probably okay. He interviewed a handful of Synergy employees."

Armand turned toward her. "He drove down to West Palm Beach last night and met with the Rothchilds."

"What?" Monique was almost speechless. "Why?"

Armand's gaze intensified. "I have no idea."

"Jesus." Monique was shaken, but quickly regained control. "Maybe he's just being thorough."

"Maybe," Armand said. "And maybe he's becoming a problem." She didn't respond, and he continued, "Why did you want to meet without your mother?"

Her eyes narrowed a touch. "We need to discuss Alexis."

Armand looked back at her, a slightly bemused look on his face.

"You know we can't put her back," Monique said. "She'll expose us."

Cortez smiled, but his eyes had a cruel edge to them. "Alexis has no idea what I look like. She's no threat to me."

Monique's jaw clenched so tight they could both hear her teeth grinding. "She's a threat to *me*, Armand. I'm her identical twin. Everyone knows what *I* look like."

Cortez turned back to the lake and the smile faded. Finally, he said, "You know what you're asking."

She slid along the bench so they were only inches apart, aware that this was the moment that would determine her future. "I *am* her."

Cortez remained silent.

Monique settled back on the bench and managed a smile at a man walking by with his dog. "Where she is right now, anything could happen."

"What about the children?"

"I can deal with them," she said without hesitation.

Armand kept an impassive face, not giving her any indication of what he was thinking. From the start there had been no way Alexis could ever go home. She would tell her story and the government would connect the dots back to Synergy and the stolen missile technology. The moment that happened, they would be like bloodhounds on the trail and eventually there would be a knock on his door. The man he had tasked with executing Alexis was already in place and waiting for instructions. Alexis had been collateral damage from the onset. Sylvia's attachment was a problem, but she would eventually get over the accidental death of a daughter she had never met. Things were fine, nothing had changed.

"The money is slow coming in. Are you having problems?" he asked. He had made Monique responsible for siphoning off a hundred and fifty million dollars from the Chamberlain estate to untraceable offshore accounts. That cash was a large piece of the total take and something he did not want to go sideways.

"Not really," she said. "I have to deal with money managers at every turn. They want to know why I'm freeing up so much cash from the investment funds. I can only move a few million at a time."

"I understand." He took her hand and squeezed it gently. "Get me what I want and I'll take care of Alexis."

She leaned in and kissed him on the cheek, then dug in her purse and pulled out a key chain. "I have a tennis match at Heathrow at one o'clock on Tuesday. The hard drives will be in my locker." She removed the smallest key on the ring and handed it to him. "Locker 427."

Cortez got up to leave. "Oh, and about Alexis. Don't tell your mother."

She smiled at the humor.

Monique watched him walk along the path by the lake until he was out of sight. He was in his sixties, a handsome and respectable looking man. People smiled when they passed him and he smiled back. *If they only knew*, she thought. How many men had he executed? How many soldiers and innocents had his weapons killed? The numbers were staggering.

She stood and headed back to her car, the morning sun glittering off the lake like diamonds. Orlando was hers now. Maybe it should always have been. When she and Alexis were born it could just as easily have been her who had remained, adopted into a life of privilege. She had drawn the short straw and spent her time in the shadows, out of sight and ready to move on a moment's notice. Armand had been the only father she'd known—a ruthless arms dealer capable of murder on a grand scale, and compared to her mother he was the warm one. She hadn't exactly had the easiest life.

She found her car and headed out, back to Twelve Oaks and the stratospheric life of Alexis Chamberlain. She glanced in her rearview mirror and smiled at her reflection. "Good morning, Alexis," she purred.

chapter twenty

Bobby rolled out of bed just after ten on Saturday morning. He wasn't a morning person, but as his mind started to clear, his first thoughts were of June Childers. She had made one hell of an impression on him.

He showered and shaved, all the while trying to decide whether to call her. By the time the last of the water was gurgling through his coffee machine, he had made his decision. Call her. He flipped open his notebook and tried her home number. She picked up on the third ring.

"Hi, Bobby." She was breathing a bit hard. "You caught me halfway out the front door. I was heading to the office."

"Oh, you're working today," he said, a touch of disappointment in his voice.

"I set my own hours on the weekends. Why?"

He sucked in a deep breath. *Go for it.* "I thought you might like to have dinner. Tonight, perhaps?" There was a pause for a few seconds and Bobby felt his stomach drop to the floor.

"Dinner tonight would be nice, Bobby. Do you want to pick me up?"

"Sure." He gave the air an arm pump. "What's your address?"

"47 Oxford Street. It's in Longwood."

Bobby knew the street. He'd worked a homicide in an upscale house a few blocks away. It was a great neighborhood. "Near Lake Wildmere?"

"Exactly. What time?"

"Seven o'clock okay?"

She wondered if he could feel the smile in her voice. "Perfect. I'll see you at seven."

Bobby let out a sigh of relief, hung the phone up and wandered out to his patio. That had been tough. It was a long time since he'd phoned a woman and asked her out, and as he stood on the deck he realized his hands were shaking. He could sit across a table from a murderer and stay focused and calm, but one call to an attractive woman and he was a bundle of nerves. Funny how that worked.

Bobby eased into one of the deck chairs and thought about Ryan Chamberlain and the six-million-dollar insurance policy. Alexis was the beneficiary and topped the list of suspects. On one hand she didn't need the money. On the other, now that her husband was dead the entire estate was hers. Maybe money *was* the motive. He was uncovering details that weren't obvious at first, but wasn't sure exactly where it was all leading. He closed his eyes and did a mental recap.

Alexis had been adopted by the Rothchilds. That one had been a shocker, and talking with the adoption agency was high on his to-do list. What else? She had failed a retina scan sometime in mid-October and security had rescanned her eyes. That may have been a malfunction in the new scanning equipment, but it was another possible piece of the puzzle. Then there was her tennis backhand—hitting the ball with two hands during the club championship and then with one hand a couple of months later. The devil was in the details, and he was not prepared to discount that one in particular.

Then Alexis sent her children to a private school in Virginia. He kicked around whether he would have done that if he were in her circumstances. Partner recently deceased, fabulously wealthy with a large, empty house, and able to hire whatever help was necessary. He decided the last thing he would do is send the kids away. He'd want them close by, yet she had exiled them. That one was quickly working its way to the top of his list of strange behavior.

What he *didn't* know, was what all this meant.

Bobby pulled out his phone. He needed to make a dinner reservation and he looked up the number for Charlie's Lobster House. He dialed and reserved for two at seven-fifteen, then killed the call and Googled *Orlando security firms*. There were plenty so he refined his search criteria by adding *retina scans*. Only two companies came up that offered that technology. The first, Able Security, was a family owned business, and the person who answered said they hadn't worked for Synergy. RTS Security was a different story. A pleasant-sounding employee named Calvin was working and picked up. Bobby identified himself and his company, and asked if they had worked for Synergy.

"Yes, we installed a retina scanning system there back in early October. Why?"

"Some of the companies we work for are trying to improve their security, and I'd like to know more about how your system works."

"Sure. A lot of our business comes from referrals. When would you like to come down?" Calvin asked.

"The sooner the better."

"I could meet with you today if you want."

"Today is fine," Bobby said.

"Our offices are on Dowden Road, in Taft. Number 749. Do you know the area?"

Just the mention of Taft dragged him down. Back to the warehouse, to the kid lying on the concrete floor with a chest full of shotgun pellets. To the disappearing gun and the end of his homicide career. "I know the area."

"Is one o'clock okay?"

Bobby snapped back to the present. "That's fine. I'll see you at one."

Bobby entered the time and address in his phone. He hadn't driven anywhere near there since the incident. Since his life came apart. He liked Clayton Riggs and his new job, but it was a far cry from homicide. He reclined in the warm sun and looked up Adoption Advocates on his phone. Their office was in Largo and when he called a lady with a soft voice named Evelyn answered. Bobby identified himself.

"I'm calling about a baby your agency placed about thirty-five years ago. Would you still have records on that adoption?"

She laughed. It was an easy-going, friendly laugh. "Yes, of course, Mr. Greco, but I'll tell you right now we can't divulge any privileged information, and that covers just about the entire file. What was the name of the family who adopted the child?"

"Rothchild. Percy and Etonia. They live in Palm Beach on South Ocean Boulevard. The child's name is Alexis, born July 14th, 1983." Bobby had found that the amount of information floating around on the Internet was directly proportional to how wealthy and famous people were. In the case of Alexis Chamberlain it had only taken about five minutes to find her birth date.

"The Rothchilds," Evelyn said, her fingers tapping on the keyboard. "Oh, yes, here it is."

"Is there anything at all you can tell me about the adoption?"

"Well, there was a midwife involved, and Alexis was adopted three days after she was born. That's about it."

"Is that normal? I mean for the adoption to be so quick?"

There was a long hesitation, then Evelyn said, "We're talking hypothetically here."

"I understand," Bobby replied.

"All right. It can happen if the birthmother relinquishes all parental rights to the child before leaving the hospital. Once that consent is signed, it is irrevocable."

"Hypothetically, could the birthmother receive financial support from the adoptive parents?"

"Most times, yes. They're given medical and living expenses while they're pregnant, and then usually for a few months after the child is born."

Bobby was beginning to get a picture of what had happened. "So, if the adoptive parents are paying for expenses during the pregnancy, then the adoption must have already been arranged. Is that correct?"

"In many cases, yes. The birthmother can pick the family she wants to adopt her baby. If the adoptive family agrees, we handle the paperwork."

"So a young woman, pregnant and financially stressed, could choose a wealthy family for her child."

"Yes, but keep in mind wealthy families are often choosy about the baby and who the young parents are."

"So the family would meet with the birthmother and then make their decision."

"Yes."

"Is it possible to get the name of the hospital where Alexis was born?" Bobby asked.

"I'm sorry, Florida law prevents that, even when a midwife is present."

"Okay, Evelyn. Thanks for your time."

"You're welcome." She hung up.

Bobby looked down at the notes he had jotted in his notebook. Alexis's mother, whoever she was, had decided to give her daughter up for adoption before the birth. Percy and Etonia Rothchild had likely taken a close look at both the young woman and the father before offering to adopt the baby. And Evelyn had said *Florida law prevents that, even when a midwife is present,* which meant Alexis had been born in Florida. It wasn't much to go on, but it was something. Still, he wasn't sure what to do with it.

Bobby felt his hackles come up as he drove into Taft. He passed the building where Chad Sommers had died and he felt a strong urge to go after the vice cops who had used him and the kid. No matter how badly he tried to put it behind him, he still wanted his pound of flesh. He'd managed to control his anger, mostly because homicide cops know better than anyone how badly things can go for someone bent on revenge.

He pulled into the parking lot in front of RTS Security. The building was on Dowden Road and fairly new, with a pale stucco exterior and large windows. Bobby approached the reception desk and an attractive twenty-something redhead smiled back at him.

"Bobby Greco," he said.

"I'll let Calvin know you're here." She wore a headset and hit a button on the switchboard, then spoke softly into the microphone. She looked up and said, "He'll be right out." Bobby took a seat and picked up a copy of Sports Illustrated, then dropped it as a young man, nicely dressed in black slacks and a collarless shirt appeared from the hallway. He held out his hand.

"Hi, I'm Calvin Graftaas."

"Good of you to meet with me on such short notice," Bobby said.

"Not a problem. Saturdays are usually slow. I've got a presentation set up for you in the boardroom."

"Thanks." Bobby started to feel guilty about burning the man's time. *Forget it*, he thought, *I need this information.*

In the boardroom, Calvin pointed to the table. There was a projector, three small metal boxes and an assortment of high-tech electronic gear, including a laptop computer. "This is the basic system we sold to Synergy." He picked up one of the boxes and pointed it at Bobby's face. "Don't blink," he said. A green light filled the room for a split second, then nothing.

"What was that?" Bobby asked.

"I just scanned your right eye," Calvin said. "We always use the right eye, never the left. Each retina is different, so if we scanned a person's right retina, then tried to cross correlate it with their left one, it wouldn't match." As he spoke, Calvin typed a few commands on the laptop. "I just wirelessly downloaded your retina onto the hard drive, so you're in the database now."

"This is really slick," Bobby said.

"Now I'll scan your retina again and ask it to find a match." He picked up a second device from the table, slightly larger than the first, aimed it at Bobby and pushed a button. Another green light flashed, then after a second or two there was a beep from the computer. Calvin turned the screen around so Bobby could see. The machine had identified him as Robert Greco of Riggs & Company.

"That was quick." Bobby said.

Calvin nodded. "The database it searched has over two hundred thousand retinas stored on it, and it found you in under three seconds."

"You're kidding."

"Nope. The only thing I did before you arrived was set up a file with your name and company."

"And the system is completely portable?"

"Yes. Synergy uses the scanners at their front gate, and at the entrances to each of their restricted buildings. It's wireless, so the guards can carry the scanners with them when they're on patrol. What do you think?"

Bobby was serious when he said, "I would recommend this system to our clients." Then he paused. "But it can make mistakes."

Graftaas's smile faded. "No, Bobby, it doesn't."

"Do you know Alexis Chamberlain?" Bobby asked and continued when Calvin nodded. "She told me her retina scan failed back in October. They called her husband and he came down to the front gate. They couldn't get a match so they scanned her retina a second time."

"That's impossible," Calvin said. He was obviously struggling with the confidentiality aspect of opening the file, then his curiosity got the better of him. He typed a few commands, then frowned. "There are two files for Alexis Chamberlain," he said. "There should never be two files. Let's see how that happened."

Bobby moved around the table and stood beside Calvin, watching over his shoulder as he isolated both files and downloaded them to the printer. He grabbed the first one as it appeared. "Oh, okay. This makes sense," he said.

"What happened?"

Calvin waited for the second sheet to print off, then set them on the table and pointed to the printouts. "This one was entered by Ryan Chamberlain, not by our staff. The date the picture was taken is Tuesday, September 30th. That picture was downloaded into the database the following day at 10:08 a.m."

"Isn't that before you set up Synergy's system?" Bobby pointed out.

"It is, but I know what happened. I gave Ryan and Shawn Falstaff a couple of mobile scanners to try out. That way they could see how easy the system is to operate. Ryan snapped a picture of his wife's retina at 8:32 p.m. on September 30. That photo stayed in the system until she failed her scan on October 12th."

"That doesn't seem right," Bobby said. "If the picture of her retina was faulty, it shouldn't have worked for almost two weeks before failing. How many times did she enter the complex in that two-week period?"

Calvin checked the screen. "Four." He was getting nervous about divulging so much information.

"All right," Bobby said, pacing about the room. "Mrs. Chamberlain is able to access the complex between September 30th and October 12th. Then her scan fails. Somebody rescans her right eye and she has access again. Is that right?"

"Yes," Calvin said, eyeing the printouts. "Wayne Elliot rescanned her retina and entered it a few minutes after she was refused entry."

"So Alexis and her husband must have gone directly from the guard gate to the security office."

"I guess so," Calvin said.

Bobby glanced at the screen. He could see the line entries for when Alexis Chamberlain entered the Synergy complex between October 12th and November 22nd. He did a quick count. Thirty-one. Bobby's head was spinning from all the new information.

"Can you put the two retina scans beside each other on the screen. Perhaps the one Mr. Chamberlain did was too fuzzy or something."

"I can, but please don't take a screen shot." Calvin returned again to the laptop. One scan popped up on the screen, a mass of tiny blood vessels covering the surface of the retina. A moment later, a second picture appeared on the other half of the screen.

"I'll be damned," Calvin Graftaas said. "They're not the same."

chapter twenty-one

Bobby slipped in the back door to Riggs & Company and it locked shut behind him. He brewed a fresh pot of coffee and poked around in the fridge for something to eat. There was a package of frozen lasagna, and he heated it in the microwave and headed for his office. He set the food on his desk, pulled out his whiteboard and added some new notes.

Alexis Chamberlain

-tennis
-the cleaners
-who is Alexis Chamberlain?
-kids sent to private school
-adopted
-Rothchilds
-did birthmother pick them?
-failed retina scan Oct 12
-new scan Oct 12
-Sept 30 through Oct 12 (4 visits)
-Oct 12 through Nov 22 (31 visits)

Synergy Industries

-government contracts
-JASSM

Ryan Chamberlain

-life insurance
-respiratory failure
-mass 303

Bobby finished writing and sat back in his chair, sipping the coffee and taking a mouthful of lasagna. He double-checked a date in his notebook. Alexis Chamberlain had won the tennis tournament on Wednesday, October 8th and the awards ceremony was three days later on Saturday. On October 8th Alexis Chamberlain's retina was still the same and she hit her tennis backhand with two hands. Skip ahead to October 12th and her retina scan looked completely different. Why? When he watched her play tennis on Monday, January 12th, she had used a single hand on her racquet. Again, why?

She had made a meager four visits to her husband's office prior to failing the retina scan, and a staggering thirty-one trips between then and when Ryan died. Why the sudden interest in what was happening at the office? After Ryan was murdered, she sent her children to private school in Virginia. Why would a grieving wife do that? Then two rich looking people showed up at her house, dressed as cleaners. Bobby kicked that around for a minute, then thumbed through his notebook until he found Jared's cell number and dialed it.

"Hello?" It was Jared's voice.

"Hi, Jared. This is Bobby Greco. We spoke briefly outside a house on Twelve Oaks a while back. I was asking questions, trying to figure out who stole a necklace. You remember?"

"Of course. What can I do for you?"

"Just one more question, Jared."

"Sure, man."

"The woman who arrived in the cleaning van, was she attractive?"

The phone was silent for a minute. "Yeah," the landscaper finally said. "She was a looker."

"Was she thin, overweight, somewhere in the middle?"

"Thin, man. Definitely thin," he said without any hesitation.

"Do you think she would have been good looking when she was younger?"

"Yeah, she was probably a knockout when she was young. Why?"

"Following up on a clue, that's all. Thanks, Jared."

"Sure, no problem."

Bobby hung up and drew a line from *the cleaners* to *did birthmother pick them*. It was a long shot, but maybe the woman who visited Alexis was her birthmother.

Bobby's eyes lingered on one of the items under Ryan Chamberlain. *Mass 303*. To anyone who happened to wander into his office, it meant nothing. But to him, it meant Chamberlain had been murdered. And the way things were stacking up, the prime suspect was Alexis Chamberlain. Or whoever she was.

Bobby pulled into Longwood at ten minutes to seven. He stopped on Oxford Street at the north end of the lake and waited. He wanted to be on time, but not early. At exactly two minutes to seven, he slipped the BMW into gear and pulled away from the curb. Number 47 was a stylish two story backing onto the lake, beautifully landscaped with soft lights illuminating the trunks of the palms in the front yard. He steered the car into the driveway and took a deep breath. It had been a while since he'd been on a date.

He knocked and June opened the door and waved him in. "I'm ready. Do you want to have a quick drink before we leave?" she asked.

Bobby checked his watch. "The reservations are for quarter after seven. We should probably get going."

"Sure. Hang on while I lock up."

He stood in the foyer and watched as she closed a pair of garden doors that led out to a lakeside patio. She grabbed her keys from the kitchen countertop and slipped into a pair of soft leather boots. Her cream-colored denim fit snug on her hips and thighs and matched her sweater. Her makeup was subtle, but did the job. June Childers, Bobby thought, was a very beautiful woman.

"Done," she smiled at him. "Let's go."

Soft music played as they entered Charlie's Lobster House. It was a safe choice for dinner—most everyone who lived in Orlando knew of it. The restaurant had a New England feel, with fresh lobster and oysters at the top of the menu and tables covered with crisp white linen.

Bobby ordered a beer and she followed suit. "I can't believe you've never eaten here before," Bobby said. "Charlie's is very popular."

"I haven't been in Orlando very long," she said. "It's the job. I have to move every now and then."

He couldn't help wondering how long she would be in Orlando. "Do you plan on staying with Synergy?"

"I'd like to, but that might change when my current project wraps up. I'm not sure what I'll be doing then."

"Can you talk about what you do for Synergy?"

"The basics." She took a small swig of beer. "A lot of my work revolves around a mixture of pure and applied math, so there are lots of applications. Satellite trajectories, missile guidance systems, communications in a vacuum, that sort of stuff."

"So you could rig my TV to get free Netflix."

She feigned shock. "That coming from an ex-cop. You surprise me."

He was no fool. Of course she knew about his past. Google *Robert Greco* and a whack of news articles about the incident in Taft popped up. "So you know about that," he said.

She nodded. "It was pretty easy to find."

"At least you said okay to dinner. That's got to count for something."

"It does." She was quiet for a bit, then said, "I'm a pretty good judge of character."

He smiled and looked at the dinner specials.

She set her menu on the table and said, "Do you want to tell me what happened?"

He could handle this in two very different ways. Clam up and let her wonder, or tell his side of the story. It was an easy decision. He liked her and didn't want a wall between them right from the start.

"I was set up," he said. "A couple of vice cops had an informant they needed to get rid of and they used me to do it."

After they ordered appetizers, Bobby gave her the entire story. When he finished the monologue he sat back and waited.

"Their story is full of holes, Bobby."

He knew exactly where the holes were, but he was curious to see if she did. "What do you mean?"

"The drug deal was obviously set to go in the rear of the building, not the front. By the time you made it to the back door and let yourself in, Sorrenson and Ross would already have noticed the light in the back of the warehouse. It only makes sense that they would have checked it out, but they didn't. They stayed up front, in the dark, and let everything play out. Red flags should have been going up right away."

"I made that point. No one wanted to listen."

"It's too bad the drug dealer isn't talking. He knows what happened. If there was some pressure on him he might give up the real story."

"I had my chance, presented my case to Internal Affairs and got kicked off the force. According to the DA, I was lucky I wasn't facing a murder charge."

"The truth has a way of coming out, Bobby," she said.

It wasn't just *what* she said, but the *way* she said it made him take a second look at her. He wasn't sure what that meant. "I'm not sure it matters now."

"Reputation always matters," she said.

The appetizers arrived and they talked about Bobby's kids, his excellent relationship with his ex-wife, and his new job while they ate. When they were finished and waiting for their main course, he shifted the conversation.

"Alexis Chamberlain," he said as a second beer arrived at the table. "She's an interesting woman."

"How so?" June asked.

"Well, I thought you could tell me. I've noticed a few things and it's got me wondering."

She leaned in a bit and whispered. "I feel like you're starting an interview." She leaned back and smiled. "Am I being interviewed, Detective Greco?"

Bobby felt the fool. This was a date. "Okay, busted. I shouldn't mix business with pleasure. Sorry about that."

She stared at him for a long while without breaking eye contact. "No, it's okay. Let's go there. It might get interesting."

"Okay." He arranged his knife and fork on his napkin. "Does Alexis seem different to you? I mean, since her husband's death."

"That's a good question." Her eyes narrowed slightly, and she looked at him closer. "A very good question. I'd like to ask where it's coming from before I answer."

"Her husband dies and she sends the kids to a school in Virginia. She suddenly starts showing up at the office all the time. Her tennis game has changed." He shrugged. "Maybe it's nothing, but I don't know her and even I'm sensing something is different."

"I can't say I noticed any of those things, but now that you mention it, she does seem…" She searched for a word, but couldn't find a better one. "…different. That's accurate, I think."

"In what way?"

June had no intention of telling Bobby about Alexis demanding the unencrypted stealth specs. Still, she could manipulate things a bit and give him something.

"Alexis has gone out of her way to cultivate a friendship with me. It could be because she's lonely since Ryan died. Maybe she just wants a new friend. I don't know."

"So she's more approachable? Nicer, for the lack of a better word?"

June shook her head. "With me, yes, but with the other staff she seems colder. Harsher, quicker to hit the boiling point. It's like when Ryan died, a switch flipped and she lost her warmth—her empathy."

Bobby sensed she had more, but wasn't giving it up. He wasn't going to push. "Good to know," he said.

The entrees arrived and they dug into their meals. After, as they were driving home, June said, "The door is open if you'd like to come in for a coffee."

"Love to." Bobby tried not to grin, but was entirely unsuccessful.

When the evening was finally over and he was at the front door, she leaned in and kissed him goodnight. Just a quick one, but they both knew what it meant.

She watched Bobby walk to his car, happy with her decision to go out with him. He was intelligent, a gentleman, fun, and attractive. Good things to build a relationship on. She knew he would call, and they would see each other again. This was going somewhere.

June waved as he backed out of the driveway and accelerated down her street. She closed the front door and cleaned up the coffee cups, convinced he was telling the truth about what had happened in the Taft warehouse. If anyone could put pressure on a dirt bag drug dealer to cough up the truth it was the National Security Agency. Down the road, if they were making a go of it, she might be in a position to help him.

chapter twenty-two

The wrap-up meeting for JASSM was first thing Monday morning in the Admin Building boardroom. All eleven departments had finished their work and the hard drives were safely stowed in the vault in Building Nine. Monique listened as each division head gave a final update on their status, and discussed some of the wrinkles they had ironed out over the past couple of months.

"Well, that is excellent news," Monique said when everyone had presented. She glanced around the table, occupied by some of the top scientists in the country, feeling more than a bit smug. They were all clueless. What a coup—walk in the front door posing as the CEO, ask for the JASSM files and then walk out with them in her briefcase.

Oh, Alexis, she thought, *being you is the gift that just keeps giving.*

She gave Shawn Falstaff a nod and he started handing out envelopes with names on them. "Bonuses for a job well done."

When everyone had their envelope, Monique said, "Well, open them."

There were a few sharp breaths as they saw the amounts, and a lot of smiles. The team tucked the checks in their pockets and waited.

"On time and under budget. The Pentagon is happy, and so is the Board of Directors. You guys deserve this." She gave everyone a wide smile, then said, "One more thing. I got word this morning from the Pentagon that they need a backup copy of our work. Please download all your files onto another hard drive and have it to me by mid-afternoon today. That's about it."

The staff filed out, each of them thanking her on their way to the door. She accepted their kudos, all the while watching June out of the corner of her eye. Childers was still at the table and not moving. When they were the only two left in the room, Monique said, "What's up?"

"I was wondering who requested the backup copy."

"As I said, someone at the Pentagon. It's classified." She picked up her phone and the notes she had brought with her into the meeting.

"I'm not comfortable with that," June said. She remembered her conversation with Ryan that Sunday in the lab, and he had been specific. *One hard drive, encrypted.*

"June, I need an additional copy of your work by this afternoon." Monique stared at her without blinking. "It's not a negotiation."

June stood and slowly started to move for the door.

"How long will it take you to generate a new one?" Monique asked.

"At least three hours," June said. "Probably closer to four."

Monique looked at her watch and smiled. "It's noon. I'll expect the hard drive by four at the latest."

June left the office and headed for Building Nine. She stopped in one of the grassy areas between buildings and fished a cell phone out of her bag. It wasn't the one Synergy had given her, it was a burner cell attached to an account at the NSA. She dialed a number and a man's voice answered.

"Brad, it's June Childers."

"June, it's great to hear your voice. We miss you over here. How are things at Synergy?"

"Not bad. I like it here."

"I doubt this is a call just to catch up," Brad said. "What can I do for you?"

"Someone at the Pentagon asked for a second copy of the completed JASSM files. Could you find out who it was?"

There was a brief silence, then, "I can try, but that place is like a labyrinth. It might take some time."

"Do the best you can."

"Sure," he said. "Hey, I wasn't kidding, we really miss you."

June felt a tinge of sadness at the words. Brad Lawrence was one of the rare people she had met through work who had become a good friend. Now she hardly ever saw him, or anyone else from NSA headquarters. It stung every now and then.

"Yeah, I miss you guys too. Call me on this number when you get something?"

"Will do. Talk soon."

"Right." She tucked the phone back in her bag.

She stood in the sun and felt the warmth on her skin. Something about it was erogenous, and she imagined the tiny rays tingling her skin were Bobby Greco's hands. That he was gently caressing her, kissing her on the lips and then sweeping her off her feet and heading for the bedroom. Thinking about it made her want to see him again, and soon.

June gave her head a shake and continued on to Building Nine, cleared security and settled in at her desk. Byron Broten, one of her senior staff members, poked his head into her office as she started downloading the files to a new hard drive. He looked stressed.

"June, we might have a problem with the particle size being deflected off the tip of the wings. We're two microns out and can't make it work. We've tried everything."

"Shit," she muttered under her breath. This was something she needed to handle herself.

She stood and pointed for him to sit at her desk. "This a list of files I need transferred onto the external hard drive. Exactly these files, Byron, no exceptions. When you're finished, take the drive to Alexis Chamberlain and deliver it personally. She's expecting it no later than four o'clock. No one else but you and she are to touch it. Do you understand?"

"I do, not a problem," he said.

"No one but Alexis." June looked him in the eye, then turned and left her office. The lab was a considerable distance and she walked fast, her heels clicking on the tile floor. The brisk walk settled her a bit and by the time she arrived she had smoothed over any misgivings about Alexis having another copy of the files. She had likely been overreacting. Ten minutes later, with her head bent over a stack of printouts, it had faded to the back of her mind.

Monique took Armand's call on her cell. He got straight to the point.

"Did Synergy have any dealings with RTS Security?"

It took a moment for Monique to connect the dots, then she said, "We did. They installed a new security system that scans the employees' retinas. Why?"

"Bobby Greco paid them a visit."

Monique sat down at her desk and took a moment to settle her nerves. "That's not good."

"No, it isn't." Silence, then, "When was the last time you spoke with June Childers?"

"Less than an hour ago."

"Did she have the files?" Armand asked.

"She's copying them right now. I'll have them later this afternoon."

"Greco and Childers went out for dinner last night. He ended up back at her house for a couple of hours."

"What?" Monique jerked upright in her chair. She was breathing hard now. "Do you think he's piecing things together?"

"No idea, but it's an issue. Check the files from Childers carefully when you get them."

"I understand." She expected a response, but Cortez had ended the call. Monique thought back to her exchange with June. She had been a bit different, colder, and Monique cursed Bobby Greco and that stupid insurance policy all to hell.

Mostly, Bobby liked Monday mornings. There was something fresh about them, starting a new week and all that. This Monday felt even better than usual, as it came on the heels of a successful date with June

Childers. He smiled at the other staff and listened to a couple of bad jokes while getting his morning coffee. Finally, he made his way to his office and shut the door, then pulled out the whiteboard and made two new entries.

Under *Alexis Chamberlain*, he added, *Childers new friend* and *Cold to staff*. He sat back and stared at the red, erasable ink on the white surface. It was beginning to tell a story. He stood up and made one more entry. Under her column he underlined, *Who is Alexis Chamberlain?* Somehow, now, it didn't look out of place. Where was this going?

"Are you Alexis Chamberlain?" he said quietly.

The moment he said it, he regretted it. There were a hundred reasons why the woman had to be herself. It was virtually impossible to create an exact duplicate of another person. According to the dates on the whiteboard, if that *had* happened, the switch would have been on or about October 12th. It was impossible. No imposter could fool a husband for almost six weeks. He shook his head. The idea was absurd. He looked back at the whiteboard, at his notes under Ryan's name.

Mass 303. The man had been murdered. Someone had administered a lethal dose of Verapamil, skillfully enough that it went undetected by two prominent doctors. The question was, how did the poison get into his system? During the autopsy, Malcolm Cook would have noticed a prick from a hypodermic, so Ryan must have ingested the poison. But Ryan's plate, remaining food, and his cutlery had been tested for anything abnormal. It was standard procedure and nothing was found.

Did Alexis Chamberlain eat the same dish as her husband that evening? He jotted down one more note under her name. *Dinner?* He pulled out his phone and made a note to visit Heathrow on Tuesday. It might pay to have a chat with the executive chef. He glanced up as Clayton Riggs opened the door.

"How's it going?" He pointed at the whiteboard. "That list keeps getting longer. Is that good or bad?"

"That depends on how you look at it."

"Okay, I had a call from Horace Vander Linden this morning. He's wondering if we're going to need the entire two-week extension. I told him we likely will." He sat on the edge of Bobby's desk, concern written all over his face. "Do we?"

Bobby gave Riggs a run down on the latest information, then sat back while his boss digested it.

"Christ." Riggs backed off and shook his head. "Okay, I can keep the wolves off your back for a few more days. Whatever you have, it needs to be solid. Get corroboration. Nail it down."

Bobby nodded. He already had enough to save First Eastern the six million. The question was, how much more of the puzzle could he solve.

"I worked homicide, Clayton," he said. "I know how to tie things down."

Clayton got up and walked to the door, then turned back. "I'm trusting you on this, Bobby."

chapter twenty-three

Byron Broten had downloaded most of the files to the hard drive. The revamped missile body structure was finished and Byron started on the stealth software. He checked the filenames, and stopped. They were wrong. Dr. Childers had given him a list that included the versions from two weeks ago. They had fine-tuned those ones, the revised files were more recent. She had instructed him to download the wrong files.

Byron knew his boss better than anyone. She hated being bothered with details that could be handled by one of her staff, yet she was intensely detail oriented. How could she have given him a list with the wrong files? He stopped and tapped his fingers on the desk. There was no way June would want anything except the correct data going to Alexis Chamberlain. He made a decision.

The files with the corrected data were heavily encrypted and only a handful of people could decrypt them. He accessed the decryption algorithms and started the program. In a little over two hours he had downloaded the final files to the portable hard drive and called Alexis's assistant to let her know he was on his way. It took the better part of ten minutes to clear security and get to the CEO's office. Alexis was waiting when he arrived.

"Byron," Monique said. "What happened to Dr. Childers?"

"She's busy on a small problem with particle deflection." He held out the drive and she took it and set it on her desk.

"This particle deflection problem, is it connected to the stealth technology?" she asked.

Byron shook his head. "No, nothing like that. It concerns the missile's trajectory. It's for future use. She's looking ahead, you could say."

"That sounds like June." Monique stood. "Thanks for dropping off the drive."

Monique closed the door once Byron had left and walked back to her desk. Hands shaking, she connected the drive and carefully checked its contents. June had come through for her and she let out a huge sigh. She had the stealth technology. Monique slipped the drives in her purse, then powered down her computer, flipped out the lights and told Rhonda she was off to a tennis match. Armand Cortez would have his treasured plans right on schedule.

She breezed out of her office feeling like an actor who just had their name called at the Oscars. She smiled when she passed the staff and even told a guard at the front gate to have a nice night. It was a high like never in her life, almost an out of body experience. They'd just pulled off one of the greatest heists in history, and the best part—the victims didn't even know they'd been robbed.

Bobby dialed June's work number. Her voicemail answered and he hung up. He wanted to ask her out again, but not by leaving a message. He got back to work and called a few local hospitals, asking if they still had birth records from July of 1983. They did, but the files weren't well organized. The person searching would have to start in January of 1983 and scroll through every birth, one by one. The only faster way was if there was something out of the ordinary to search for, like stillborn children, caesarian sections, multiple births, and births where the mother died during labor. The task of locating Alexis's birthmother was next to impossible. Bobby gave up on the hospitals and tried June's number again. This time she answered.

"Hi." Her voice brightened when she realized it was Bobby.

"Hey, how's your day going?"

"Much better now that you called," she said. "I had a problem that took the entire afternoon to fix."

Sometimes, he thought, *problems just don't get solved.* "At least you fixed it."

"So what's up?"

"I thought you might like to go out again. Maybe tomorrow night. Dinner, a movie, something like that."

She didn't answer for a few seconds, then, "I'd love to. Tomorrow is Tuesday, right?"

"Yup."

"Then let's skip the movie. Tuesday is cheap night and the theatres are always packed. How about dinner at my place?"

Inside his head Bobby was doing a happy dance. "That sounds great. What time?"

"Seven is good."

"Fantastic. I'll bring some wine."

"Red, if that's okay with you."

"Love it. See you at seven."

He hung up and smacked his fist on the desk. Christ, dating was like being in high school again. The exhilaration. The chase. The catch. His smile faded. What happened after the catch? This was all new to him. The rules had changed and now he wasn't sure.

Bobby mulled over a few things. Did convention say the man should bring the condom or was that up to the woman? Was bringing one making an assumption that could deflate things? Literally. He finally decided against the idea. It was a Tuesday night. Who in their right mind had sex for the first time on a Tuesday night?

He looked up the number for the Country Club at Heathrow on his phone, and when the line connected he said, "Could you put me through to the kitchen?" A moment later a voice answered and Bobby asked to speak with the head chef.

"Hang on a minute." Sounds of a busy kitchen floated through the receiver. Bobby checked his watch. Four-fifteen. It was a stupid time to call, he thought, just as a voice came through.

"This is Jurgen Strauss. How may I help you?"

"This is Bobby Greco at Riggs & Company. I'd like to ask you a few questions about the night Ryan Chamberlain died. Do you have time now?"

"Not right now." Strauss sounded agitated. "I could manage a few minutes tomorrow, after lunch. Two o'clock."

"That works. Thank you very much."

Bobby hung up and entered the appointment on his phone. Heathrow at two, June at seven. Tomorrow was shaping up to be a damn fine day.

June Childers held the phone for a second longer than necessary, still feeling Bobby's presence on the other end. They were having a second date and she was happy with that. It had been a wonderful kiss on the first date and she was wondering how far things should go tomorrow night. Bobby would be an excellent partner, but it might be too quick. She snapped out of it as Byron Broten stopped by to say goodnight.

"I'll see you tomorrow, Byron," she said, then added. "Did you get the files to Alexis?"

"Sure did. I left the summary of the download on your desk. It's in that pile of paper." He pointed to a stack of paper on one side of her desk.

"Thanks, Byron. I'll find it later."

She was in a fine mood, and didn't feel like wasting it on the office. A bit of shopping for a new top and a latte at Starbucks fit the bill. She shut down her computer and headed out, her mind still on Bobby Greco.

chapter twenty-four

The Country Club at Heathrow was bustling as usual, but the lunch crowd was thinning and Bobby pulled into a parking spot by the front door. He'd made a good choice when car shopping ten years ago. Biting off payments on a BMW had seemed extravagant at the time. *What cop drove a bimmer?* In retrospect it had been a good move, the car was immaculate and fit in everywhere. He used the fob to lock it and entered the club.

The front desk had his name on the day's guest list. That impressed him, especially since the chef had barely acknowledged their conversation except to concede a five-minute meeting the next day. Obviously the man was a good listener and well organized. Bobby asked for directions to the kitchen and headed off.

Jurgen Strauss was Austrian, with blond hair and deep blue eyes. He greeted Bobby with a thick accent and took a break from what he was doing, motioning for his guest to follow him through the busy kitchen. Bobby had seen enough restaurant kitchens to know that this one was especially clean and well run. He commented on that as Jurgen reached the back door and pulled out a package of cigarettes.

"We run a tight ship, Mr. Greco," Jurgen said, lighting his cigarette. "The members of the club expect it. So what can I help you with?"

The sun was bright and Bobby slipped on his sunglasses. "What do you remember about the evening Mr. Chamberlain died?"

"In what way?"

"Did Mrs. Chamberlain have the same dish as her husband?"

Jurgen took a long drag on his smoke. "That's an interesting question, Mr. Greco."

"Call me Bobby, please."

"Okay. As I said, it's an interesting question."

"Why?"

"Because Alexis doesn't like lamb. She and Ryan are here all the time with the kids and I remember once, about a year ago, trying to get her to give it a go. She'd tried it in New Zealand and had no taste for it. So it was very strange, that on the night Mr. Chamberlain died, she ordered lamb."

"And Ryan had lamb as well?"

"Sure did." Jurgen's blue eyes stared right into Bobby.

"You're positive?"

Jurgen looked irritated for a second, then backed off. "Yes, Bobby, I'm sure. Ryan's plate and cutlery were immediately wrapped in plastic for the police. They took it for analysis."

"Did they just take his place setting?"

"Yes. One plate, two forks, three spoons and one cup and saucer. We got them back about two weeks later."

"So the police never sampled any of the other food at the table?"

"No." He looked intrigued now. "Should they have?"

"Forensics knows what they're doing," Bobby said. "I'm sure they followed procedure."

Jurgen crushed out his cigarette, then leaned against the wall, apparently not in any rush to get back to the kitchen. "What's this all about?" he asked.

"Sorry, confidential."

"Of course."

"Thanks very much, Jurgen," Bobby said. "I appreciate you taking the time to speak with me."

The chef smiled. "Stop in and have lunch sometime."

Bobby shook his head. "When I win the lottery."

"My treat," Jurgen said.

"Then I'm in. Thanks."

Bobby walked through the kitchen and headed for the front entrance, stopping at the schedule board for the tennis courts on the way to glance over the entries. Alexis Chamberlain had booked a court from one to two-thirty. He spun on his heels and headed back into the club. He found her quickly enough, and stood in the doorway, watching.

According to the scoreboard, Alexis was losing. The first set had gone to her, and the second to Susan Blair. Blair led the third set four games to three and Bobby watched as she served a cannonball that threw Alexis off balance. She barely managed a soft return and Blair hammered it back, winning the point. Forty-fifteen. Blair moved to the adjacent court and served for the game. She blasted it down the centerline for an ace. Game to Blair. Five games to three.

Bobby watched Alexis Chamberlain on the changeover. She was furious. The Blair woman was taking it to her and she didn't like it, not one bit. *Why get so pissed off?* Bobby wondered. It wasn't like this was the club championship, and hardly anyone was watching. He glanced into the gallery. A paltry seven people were in the seats, and one of them caught his eye.

The man was in the farthest row, near the top of the stands. He was mid-fifties, with jet-black hair and a dark complexion, fitting the landscaper's description. There was a woman with him, but she was mostly blocked out from Bobby's vantage point. Bobby slipped out his phone and touched on the camera icon. There was more to this guy than a bored businessman taking in an afternoon tennis match. The way he moved ever so slightly when Alexis stretched to make a return gave him away. He was pulling for her. Bobby snapped off four shots without anyone noticing.

He turned back to the match. Alexis was serving, the match tied at four games. She raked an ace down the centerline, evening the score at deuce. Again, another excellent serve, but this time Blair returned it with a deep lob that caught Chamberlain too close to the net. She scurried back, struggling to return a weak crosscourt drop that Blair then smashed down her throat. Advantage, Blair.

Alexis Chamberlain was incensed. She faulted on her first serve, then put her second serve in play. Blair returned it hard, with a vicious topspin. Chamberlain lobbed it deep, backing her opponent behind the line. Blair let it bounce and volleyed hard down the right line. Alexis dove for the ball, missed it and slid along the clay surface on her elbows and knees. She came up grimacing, and bleeding.

Alexis limped to the net and grabbed a towel. She held it tight to her knee and kept it there for a minute, then dabbed her elbow. The bleeding had mostly stopped, and she dropped the towel courtside. She motioned to Blair she was ready to continue, but for all intents and purposes the match was over. Blair ran her around the court like a rank amateur and Alexis lost the game, giving up the third set 6-4. Game, set, and match, Blair.

Bobby kept to the shadows as the two women shook hands and walked off the court, Alexis still favoring her leg. The injury must be painful, he thought, yet she had refused to concede. The man in the stands was leaving and Bobby caught a fleeting glimpse of the woman with him. Bobby thought about heading to the front doors to get a better look at them, but dismissed that idea. He had something else on his mind.

Alexis Chamberlain had torn the skin on her knee badly enough to bleed. And blood on a towel was an excellent source of DNA. He wanted that towel. Bobby slipped out and stood by the gate of the chain link fence surrounding the courts. He looked about, then quickly lifted the latch and strode out onto the clay surface, in full view of the stands and the lounge that overlooked the play area. He kept walking and didn't stop until he reached the net, then bent over and picked up the entire pile of towels, slipping the bloodied one under his shirt. He turned and stopped in his tracks.

A muscular young court attendant was staring at him. "What are you doing?" he asked.

"Oh, just grabbing my wife's towels. She left them after the match."

"Those towels belong to the club, sir," the man said, closing in on him.

Bobby looked down. "Oh, you're right. They're not hers. She must have used the club's today. My mistake."

He dropped the armful of white towels in the man's hands and walked off the court, to the front door and out to the parking lot. He opened his trunk and slipped the towel from under his shirt, dropped it in a large plastic bag, then headed back into the club. After half an hour of watching for the man and woman he gave up and returned to his car. They must have left while he was stealing the towel.

Bobby drove back to the office, considering what to do with the evidence. He knew some guys at homicide who might run the DNA tests for him, but he wasn't sure if he had any influence left inside the department. He needed time to think. He updated the whiteboard by adding *lamb* next to *dinner*, and noted *DNA* in Alexis's column.

The man in the stands was obviously tied to Alexis, so he wrote that under *Alexis*. He drew another curved line upwards, this time connecting *dark skinned man* with *the cleaners*. The more he thought about it, the more convinced he was that the man the landscaper had described was the same one he had just seen at the tennis club. The woman with him could well be Alexis's mother, but what was their motive? What did they have to gain?

Actually, that was an easy question to answer. Ryan Chamberlain's estate, which had come in at a staggering two hundred and fifty million dollars, could be the motive. People had committed murder for far less. He picked up the plastic bag with the bloodied towel and stared at it. His cop senses were kicking in again, and they were telling him that grabbing the towel was the smartest thing he had done yet.

June had been in meetings all day, and it was mid-afternoon before she finally freed up enough time to go through the stack of paper on her desk. She shuffled through them until she located the list of files Byron had downloaded and delivered. She scanned the first few pages, nodding as she went. Everything was fine. She made it to the last page and froze. Line by line, she read the filenames as a sense of dread washed over her. This wasn't right. Byron had changed the last sixteen sub-files.

He hadn't given her the flawed files. She had the real thing. June threw open her laptop in a total panic and accessed her decryption software with shaky hands. She scanned the list of files decrypted earlier in the day, and every last one matched Byron's list.

"You fucking idiot." She slammed the paper down on her desk. "What have you done?"

Alexis Chamberlain had a fully functional stealth version of the Joint-Air-to-Surface-Standoff Missile in her possession. The weapon was in the hands of a person June Childers didn't trust. She leapt up and her chair went flying backward into the wall. Her palms were sweating and she was breathing so fast she had to force herself to settle down before she had a full-blown anxiety attack. She finally picked up her chair and sat down, light headed and spent. The damage was done.

She checked her watch and did some basic math. If she called her contact at the NSA and relayed the news, dinner with Bobby wouldn't happen. The question was, how crucial was the breach? If it even *was* a breach. Alexis was the CEO and had every right to the information, so giving her the hard drive was nothing more than following protocol. All she had was her suspicions, and if she called it in, an investigative team would be assigned and she'd be in the hot seat. There would be a lot of questions, most that she wouldn't have answers to, and they would inevitably ask if anyone else knew. If that happened, she had to either give up Bobby or lie.

June made a decision to sit on it for now.

chapter twenty-five

The prawns were sizzling, the was salad crisp and fresh, and the steaks cooked medium with a hint of pink. Bobby couldn't imagine even Jurgen Strauss putting together a better meal than June Childers had prepared.

"Dinner was fantastic." Bobby leaned back in the patio chair. "Better than fantastic. It was perfect."

Her cheeks took on a touch of color. "Well, thanks."

Across fifty feet of well-trimmed grass lay the calm waters of Lake Wildmere, with only an occasional ripple shimmering in the moonlight. Crickets chirping and a hint of soft music coming from the house were the only sounds.

They were sitting close to each other and she let her hand brush against his arm. "I feel comfortable with you."

He grinned like a kid with candy money in his pocket. "We do seem to get along."

They sat without talking for a minute, alone with their thoughts, then she asked, "How was your day? You know, chasing fraud and all that."

"Actually, I had a very interesting day. How about you?"

"Today was crap."

Bobby turned slightly so he could look at her profile. He'd noticed that she seemed a bit on edge, but had put it down to them getting to know each other. Maybe it was more than that. "What happened?"

June waved her hand through the warm night air. "I asked one of my staff to copy some files and he downloaded the wrong ones."

"Nothing irreversible, I'm sure," Bobby said lightly.

June glanced at him. "That's the problem. It's completely irreversible. I shouldn't have brought it up—I can't discuss it."

Bobby's interest was piqued, but now wasn't the time to push. He'd come back around to it later if the opportunity presented itself. "Well, I can discuss some of what I did today."

She swiveled a bit, resting on her elbow. "I'm listening."

"I visited Heathrow and talked with the chef. It turns out that Alexis Chamberlain hates lamb."

"So, I don't like lamb either. What makes that interesting?"

"Alexis ordered lamb the evening her husband died."

June sat up. "And Ryan ordered lamb as well?"

Bobby nodded. "I've dug up some pretty strange stuff in the past few days. It's confidential and I can't say much."

"Try me. I'm pretty damn good at keeping secrets."

"I want to, but..." He ran his finger around the rim of his coffee cup as he decided how much to tell her. Finally, Bobby said, "Okay, this is highly confidential and possibly dangerous."

She leaned toward him. "What is it?"

"I have evidence that points to Ryan Chamberlain being murdered."

June's face showed a moment of surprise, then it faded. She ran her hand through her short hair and looked out over the lake. Slowly, her head began to move up and down. "That doesn't surprise me as much as you might think."

"Really?" Bobby said. "It sure as hell surprised me."

"Oh, it's a bombshell all right, Ryan Chamberlain being murdered. And it leads into what's going on with Alexis." She stared in his eyes. "What do you know, Bobby?"

"This has something to do with the project you're working on, doesn't it?"

"Yes, I think it might. And it's important you tell me what you know about Alexis Chamberlain."

"This goes no further than right here and now."

June set her glass on the table, exactly in the center of the coaster. "No further, unless we both decide it has to."

"I'm not sure what you mean by that. Care to explain?"

"If you find out what that means, then we're all in a lot of trouble." Her voice had changed. It was all business now.

Bobby looked confused. "Who *are* you, June Childers?"

"You first," she parried. There was a hint of levity in the words, but the underlying message was clear. She wanted what he knew.

"I'll make you a deal." He stood and walked a few steps toward the lake on the soft grass, then turned to face her. "If what I tell you is consistent with what you're holding back, you give it up. Do we have a deal?"

"Deal." There was no hesitation in her voice.

"All right." He took a deep breath. "I don't think Alexis Chamberlain is actually Alexis Chamberlain." Bobby watched for a reaction, but there wasn't one.

"I agree," June said.

Bobby was gobsmacked by her reply. He returned to the chair and sat down. "You suspected?"

"I did, and that creates a hell of a problem for me." She leaned forward and set her cup on the table, then stared out across the lake. She was treading a very fine line. After a couple of minutes, she leaned back in her chair. "The other day, Alexis, or whoever she is, asked me to download some highly restricted information about a missile we're building."

"JASSM," Bobby said.

"Ah, right. We talked about it at Starbucks," she said and he nodded. "It stands for Joint Air-to-Surface Standoff Missile, and it's probably the most dangerous conventional weapon there is right now."

"What makes it so dangerous?"

"We developed a stealth version. It's completely invisible on ground-based radar and from space. A country with fighter jets could launch this thing at high altitude, have their jet fly home, and then watch as all hell breaks loose. There would be no way to prove who fired it."

"So someone could use it to start a conflict. North Korea, Libya, Syria—it's probably a long list."

"Exactly."

"Holy shit." Bobby jerked upright, his eyes wide and unblinking. "So what makes you think Alexis is someone else?"

"I don't think she is in the literal sense. She's the same person, but she has a completely different agenda than when Ryan was alive. She's up to something and it has to do with the missile."

"Well, that's not what I meant." Bobby said. "I think Alexis Chamberlain has been replaced."

"What?" June said, her mouth slightly open. "What are you saying?"

"I think Alexis Chamberlain is an imposter. The switch happened sometime back in early October."

"That's crazy, Bobby. Impossible." She saw the look on his face and realized he wasn't kidding. Losing the stealth technology was starting to look like an explosion with shrapnel flying in every direction. "What proof do you have?"

"A fair amount, actually. Most of it is small, almost inconsequential stuff, but when you put it together, it adds up."

Bobby pushed himself off the chair and walked to the edge of the lawn. He needed a minute to settle down and make sure he was thinking straight. Finally, he said, "In October, Alexis switched from using two hands on her tennis backhand to one. Someone who plays tennis at her level doesn't do that. When I noticed, I started looking for other inconsistencies."

A slight breeze had picked up and the palm fronds were beginning to sway ever so slightly. She pulled on a sweater and joined him on the lawn. "What else did you find?"

"I took a closer look at what happened at Heathrow the night Ryan died. The logical place to start was with the autopsy. I found out the ME's office was pressured not to run a toxicology scan by the doctors who diagnosed a heart attack as the cause of death. I know the coroner and got him to run one—Ryan had traces of a drug called Verapamil, which can cause the heart to stop."

"So you found a smoking gun."

"I did. I was sure Ryan was murdered, so I started asking who would benefit."

"Alexis."

Bobby nodded. "Her retina scan—I saw the before and after pictures and they're not even close. Her retina is completely different now than it was in October."

"Which is impossible."

"Unless it's a different person." He paused, then asked, "Did you know she's adopted?"

June shook her head. "I didn't."

"A man and woman disguised as cleaners visited her house, and I saw the same people at Heathrow, watching her play tennis. I think the woman might be her birthmother."

June could barely believe the scope of what Bobby had uncovered. "That's why she sent the kids away to school."

"I think so. Eventually they would have figured out she isn't their mother."

"Oh, my God." June's head was spinning. "If what you're saying is true, then who has the JASSM files?"

He grabbed her elbow to steady her as she reeled from the news. "That's what happened yesterday? One of your staff copied the wrong files and gave them to her?"

She looked like she was going to be sick. "I left a list of files to copy, but he changed some of them. He gave her the real thing. I was holding back the final version of the missile because I suspected something was wrong, but I couldn't have even imagined anything like this."

Bobby's hand was still on her arm. "There's something you're not telling me."

She looked away from him. From the moment she had signed on with the NSA she had suspected this moment might arrive. Her commitment to the agency was solid, and she had every ounce of respect for the non-disclosure agreement in her file, but these circumstances were compelling enough to consider breaking it. She turned to face him, but remained silent.

"You're not who you seem to be. I can sense it." He let go of her arm. "Who are you, June?"

She *wanted* to tell him, she *needed* to tell him. Still, the ramifications could be catastrophic. A long time passed before she said, "I could go to jail."

He thought about that and finally nodded. "Then you need to know without any doubt that you can trust me to keep your secret. If you can't, I understand."

June broke away and walked down to the shore. Being near the water always calmed her spirit. It gave her clarity of mind that usually led to good choices, and this was an important one. Her contract with NSA was very clear—she was not to divulge her status to anyone outside the agency. She respected that, but without Bobby Greco she wouldn't have pieced things together. That is, if he was right. There was always the chance that everything he had laid in front of her could be explained and that Alexis was the person she had always been.

She leaned against a palm and stared across the water, suspecting Bobby was right. How it could have happened, she had no idea. Who was involved was a total blank as well, but she knew it had to do with the missile they were developing. Someone was trying to steal the plans. Hell, someone *had* stolen the plans. Byron had messed things up more than he could ever know. Alexis had tried to copy the first drive and erased the data, and then lied about the Pentagon wanting a second copy. By now she could be passing the information to someone else.

The burning questions were what to tell Bobby Greco and how to deal with the loss of the stealth technology. She made a decision and felt a huge weight lift off her shoulders. Bobby had returned to the patio and she walked over to where he was sitting patiently waiting for her.

"I work for the National Security Agency." It was that simple. The truth was out. She sat down next to him.

His jaw literally dropped. "Seriously?"

"Seriously." She took a few minutes and filled him in on her role and the problem Byron had created when he gave Alexis the final specifications.

The color had completely drained from his face and his voice was hardly a whisper. "Jesus, this is really bad."

"More than you can even begin to imagine," she said.

He felt blindsided, dazed even. His entire focus had been on who Alexis really was, and the cause of Ryan's death. He'd figured money was the motive. Kill the rich guy and drain the bank. This was different. This was a crisis that could start a war.

Bobby ran a hand through his unruly hair. "Okay, now what?"

She put her head in her hands—doing nothing was not an option. "I should have gone to the NSA." She paused, then added, "But it all seemed so farfetched, like it couldn't be real."

"Well, you didn't." Bobby phrased it carefully so it was non-accusatory. "Where do we go from here?"

June was hunched over, looking deflated and beaten down. "I'm not sure. All I know is that if you're right, I have to get those plans back."

Bobby was up and pacing. "Let's take this one step at a time. First, we need to be sure whether this woman is or isn't Alexis, and I think I have a way to do that. When I was at Heathrow today she was playing tennis and she slipped and scraped her knee. She was bleeding and wiped it off with a towel. I managed to grab it. Is there someone at your agency who could run a DNA test on the blood?"

June brightened a touch. "I think so, and we have Alexis's DNA profile on file at Synergy. That would give us definitive proof."

"Right. I'll get you the towel." He took a long look at her. "You're not a trained field operative, are you?"

She shook her head. "No. I'm pretty much a math nerd who's in over her head."

Bobby felt a surge of confidence. The one that came when the case he was working started to open up and things began falling in place. He'd taken one small detail and built a plausible case through logic and solid footwork. Now he had a connection to the National Security Agency and all their resources at his fingertips. This was going places.

"There's one other thing," Bobby said. He continued when she nodded. "I managed to get a picture of the man who was at the tennis club. Could your contacts at NSA also have a look and see if they can identify him?"

"I'm sure they can."

"That's great," he said, taking a long, hard look at her. She was exhausted and overwhelmed, and it was time to wrap things up for the night. Clear heads made good decisions. "I should go. We'll pick this up tomorrow morning."

"Quite the date," she said, getting up and joining him.

"Well, there were no awkward silences."

Despite the circumstances, she couldn't stop the smile. "No, there weren't." She turned out the patio lights and closed the sliding doors behind her.

They walked to the front door and he took her hand. "Are you going to be okay?"

She looked at him and took a deep breath. She couldn't think of anything to say.

He took a half step toward her so they were only inches apart. "We've done pretty darn good on our own so far, and now there's two of us. And all your contacts over at NSA. We'll figure this out."

"Oh, Bobby," she said. "This was never what I envisioned when I joined the NSA. This is insane."

He gave her hand a squeeze and let go. The whole mess was as crazy as it sounded. "Talk to you tomorrow. Get some sleep."

"Sure." She let his hand slip from hers. They both knew it wasn't going any further for a while. If ever.

June watched his taillights fade into the darkness and closed the door. She leaned against the wall and knew her decision to tell him had been the right one. They were both caught up in the theft of top secret government documents and there was no going back now.

She had one more thought as she shut off the lights and got ready for bed. If the woman wasn't Alexis, then who the hell was she?

chapter twenty-six

Armand Cortez asked for a table on the courtyard, tucked away amongst the palms and hibiscus. The hostess at Le Boheme seated them next to a small gurgling fountain and smiled when he offered a generous tip. They had chosen the Grand Bohemian Hotel for its opulence and its discretion. The staff were extremely protective of their guests' privacy, and the front desk asked very few questions, perfect for someone traveling under a false name.

It was lunchtime and Armand kept a close eye on the people drifting into the restaurant. His laptop with the missile technology from ten of the eleven drives was secure in the hotel safe. The hard drive with the stealth specs was in his jacket pocket—he never let it out of his sight, and having it with him at all times kept him on edge. Waiting for the buyer to call and set the final meeting was excruciating. He had executed his part of the deal perfectly, but the rest was in the buyer's hands and out of his control. He hated that.

"It's almost over," Sylvia said, sensing his unrest. "And Monique was brilliant."

Armand smiled and relaxed a bit. "She really pulled it off."

He watched as two men in suits entered the restaurant, then turned back to face Sylvia when they met a friend and ordered drinks. "Monique's having a slow go of it transferring the money. It's going to take time, weeks perhaps."

Sylvia leaned forward and slipped her sunglasses down a touch. "Make sure she doesn't get carried away." She nestled back into the large wicker chair.

"There will be plenty left for Alexis," Armand said. "We're only taking the cash and liquid assets. Alexis will still have the house, her Synergy stocks, and more. She'll have over a hundred million."

The server arrived with menus and Armand watched Sylvia choose a bottle of wine, all smiles and nice to the young woman taking her order. Armand wondered how happy she'd be if she knew of the deal he had arranged with Monique. Alexis was never coming back. How could she? It was an impossible circumstance, and once he was positive they wouldn't need Alexis as a bargaining chip, he would call the man who was holding her.

Sylvia turned her face to the sun and closed her eyes. "What a way to go out."

Armand tried to keep from smiling, but couldn't. The whole thing was completely audacious. "We've had a good run of it."

A chilled bottle of wine arrived in a silver bucket, water beading on the sides in the midday heat. The server poured a taster in Sylvia's glass and waited while she took a small sip. Sylvia nodded and motioned for the woman to fill their glasses.

"Where do you think your buyer will want to meet?" she asked when they were alone.

"Somewhere in Europe. I won't know until they call," he said, surveying the room again.

"Do we stay in Orlando until then?"

"I think we should, in case Monique needs us," he said, knowing that would make her happy. "The Americans have no idea we're in the country, so we're as safe here as in Paris."

Sylvia nodded in agreement and sipped her wine. Lunch arrived and as they ate she steered the conversation around to buying a second home, somewhere away from Paris. They bantered about a few options, finally settling on the Croatian coast. They already had a small safe house there and had fallen in love with the area. The country was beautiful, steeped in history and the Mediterranean climate suited them. Armand finished his lunch and gave Sylvia a wink as he got up from the table.

"I'm going to the spa," he said.

Sylvia smiled like a schoolgirl. "I'll be in the room."

Armand was in the hall leading to the spa when his burner cell rang. It was Stephen Bishop. He moved off to the side and took the call.

"What do you have for me?" he asked.

"Bobby Greco was at Heathrow Country Club yesterday afternoon."

Armand stiffened. "What time?"

"He arrived just before two, and left at about three."

Armand thought back to when the tennis match had ended. Christ, Greco had been at the club at the same time as him. His hand was shaking slightly as he asked. "Do you know why he was there?"

"One of the attendants thought he had a meeting with the kitchen staff."

Armand tried to picture whether Greco had been nearby during the match. There was no recollection. "Anything else?"

"He spent about four hours at June Childers' house last night."

Armand felt his blood pressure rising. He could barely form the next words. "Is that it?"

"Yes."

"I need you to do one more thing," he said, keeping his voice as even as possible. "Get me a *complete* file on Greco—his friends, his family, every bit of information you can dig up."

"No problem."

"Thank you." He hit the end button and kept his back to the wall for support. Greco was becoming a major problem, one that might need to be removed.

Sylvia left the restaurant and wandered slowly through the lobby, then headed back to the suite. She drew a hot bath and slipped out of her clothes. The water was soothing and she settled in for a long soak, her mind a million miles away.

Sylvia Dupres had secrets. She had always had secrets, things that even Monique and Armand didn't know. She had grown up in extreme poverty behind the iron curtain, and was old enough to remember the day the state police barged into their cramped apartment and dragged her father off. Even now, the anger and resentment of authority still clung to her. Her mother was harassed by the police and became so beaten down that after six months she sent Sylvia to live with her grandmother. She hated everything about her exile. The small village was so backward, and the tiny house freezing and without indoor plumbing. A month after she moved in, word arrived that her mother had been murdered. Sylvia was seven.

The summer she turned seventeen she packed up her meager belongings and made a run for it, travelling through the countryside at night, stealing food from farms and sometimes going days without eating. After two weeks, within eyesight of the border, a guard caught her. A beautiful girl, she traded her virginity for her life.

She spent the next year in a displaced persons camp waiting for an approval for her visa application to America. She boarded the ship with only two priorities—safety and security—and to her that meant marrying a rich man. Becoming pregnant with Monique and Alexis was no accident, their father was exactly what she needed. When things didn't pan out exactly as she planned, she kept a level head and worked with what she had. She played it perfectly.

Sylvia laughed at the scope of her deception. "Oh, Armand," she whispered to herself. "If you only knew."

The bathwater cooled and she climbed out, her thoughts turning to Alexis. Dropping her daughter back into her life in Orlando wasn't going to be easy. Alexis would talk to the authorities and tell them everything she knew. Powerful agencies would be searching for them, and Monique would need plastic surgery to alter her face. All three of them would need to disappear. Sylvia wasn't sure if Monique could ever have a normal life again, but then again, had Monique *ever* had a normal life.

Sylvia wrapped a towel around herself and walked into the opulent suite. She had always known there would be a heavy price for her duplicity. Killing Alexis was the only other option, and that was unthinkable. She felt a tear pooling at the edge of her eye and wiped it away. Tears were a sign of weakness, and if she had learned one thing from Armand over the past twenty-seven years, it was to never show weakness, not even to those closest to her.

The admin building was officially shut down for the night, and the fourth floor was dimly lit by an emergency light near the exit door. June Childers moved quietly through the maze of desks and cubicles until she reached a door at the back of the room. She swiped her access card and entered a small office with a bank of computers against one wall.

June felt the cables on the back of each of the computers, searching for one that did not have an Ethernet connection. The PC she wanted was a silo, with no Internet or database connection, nothing except an electrical cord. The system contained the DNA profile of each person employed by the company, and security breaches were impossible unless the person hacking into the system was in the office and sitting at the keyboard. To do that, they would be required to enter Synergy's main gate, pass a second retina scan at the admin building, know the access codes to the main doors, and have a current pass card to the series of locked doors leading to the floor's computer room. Which was exactly what June Childers had done to get in.

While her security clearance allowed her access to the HR files, she wasn't really supposed to be snooping around in them. Especially in the middle of the night.

She found the computer, neatly tucked away on the west wall. Smart, she thought, to put the stand-alone system in with the others, to make it appear as simply one of the group. She powered it up and typed in her password. She was sweating now, and her hands shook as she retrieved the DNA profile for Alexis Chamberlain. She slipped a thumb drive into the USB port and copied the file. June cleared the screen and left the room, ensuring the lock clicked shut behind her. The security guard was at his post when she arrived back in the main foyer.

"Goodnight, Sammy." She swiped her card through the reader and the light went green.

"Goodnight, Dr. Childers."

June headed out the front doors and walked directly to her car. She wasn't cut out for this clandestine stuff. She felt a presence behind her and spun about as she reached her parking spot. Nothing. She jumped in, started the car and backed up, her heart rate easing as she drove out of the parking lot and onto the main road.

Bobby Greco was waiting at her house with the decaf brewing when she arrived. She bypassed it and poured a whiskey, downing it in one gulp, then poured another. This one she sipped.

"Nerves a little frayed?" Bobby asked, chuckling.

"A little? Holy shit, that is dangerous." Her adrenaline was still surging.

"Did you get Alexis's DNA profile?"

"I did."

"*Now* you're a spy," he said.

She sat on the couch next to him, staring at the ceiling. "I guess I am. On the NSA payroll and stealing classified information. I didn't imagine I'd ever be doing this sort of thing."

"You did well," Bobby said.

She smiled and a short silence settled over the room.

"Are things set for Saturday?" he asked.

She nodded. "I have our flights and hotel reservations booked. We're good to go." She paused, then said, "D.C. is going to be intense."

"Well, it *is* the National Security Agency," Bobby said.

June settled back into the couch, her mind shifting ahead to the secretive complex where she'd worked for all those years. With the stealth version of the missile missing the thought of going back inside sent a chill through her.

"My God, Bobby, how did all this happen?" she asked.

Bobby was on his feet and strolling about with his coffee. "That's what we need to find out."

chapter twenty-seven

Orlando to Washington D.C. is not a long flight, but on January 24th, the two cities might as well have been on different planets. A cold front had pushed down from Canada, blasting D.C. with frigid northerly winds and dumping three inches of snow on the ground.

Bobby tucked his jacket under his chin and tried not to breathe the icy air. June laughed at how ridiculous he looked, her breath escaping as quick puffs of steam. She slipped into the back of the first cab in the queue and shut the door. It was wonderfully warm, and they both turned their attention to the storm outside as they headed for the Annapolis Junction. When they were close, June pointed the driver toward an exit ramp and he followed it over a massive earthen berm, slowing at the crest.

"Welcome to Crypto City," she said, watching Bobby's reaction to the spectacle laid out in front of them.

Strategically placed boulders dotted the roadside and the cab reduced its speed to a crawl. Motion detectors and cameras on tall poles surveyed them as they approached the main gates, and a series of barbed-wire fences and thick cement barriers negated any chance of a vehicle approaching at any rate of speed.

"This is quite the place." Bobby stared out the window as members of the special forces patrolled the area with 9mm submachine guns clearly visible, their black uniforms contrasting sharply against the brilliant white snow.

She glanced over at him. "Oh, you haven't seen anything yet."

The cabbie dropped them off at the front gates and a young NSA employee who introduced himself as Graham picked them up. Bobby got the impression he was lying, even about his name. Graham drove them through the complex to a tall glass building and stopped directly in front of the main entrance. He accompanied them into National Business Park-1 where, not surprisingly, security was intense. June produced her identification and registered Bobby Greco as her guest, then entered her password, scanned a card key, entered another numerical sequence, and had her fingerprints scanned. They were admitted, but only after walking through a sensor that would pick up even the tiniest trace of metal.

When they entered the elevator, June hit twelve. The doors opened and she led the way down a long hall to a well-equipped lab where a man in a white coat was hunched over a series of printouts. He glanced up, smiling when he saw her.

"June." He came to the door and shook her hand. "Man, it's good to see you. Like I said on the phone, we really miss you."

"Thanks, Brad." There was a hint of emotion in her voice. "I miss you guys, too." She turned to Bobby. "This is Bobby Greco. Bobby, Brad Lawrence."

Brad nodded at Bobby and shook his hand, then looked back to June. "That request from the Pentagon for another copy of the JASSM files. As far as I can tell, it never happened."

"That's interesting," June said, concern written all over her face.

"Very." He sat on a desktop and tilted his head a touch. "So what's the big secret?"

"This." She pulled the thumb drive containing Alexis's DNA profile from her pocket. "And this as well." She held up the towel. "We need to know if the blood matches the DNA profile on this stick."

"Whether they're the same person? That's what you want to know?"

"Precisely."

"That should be easy enough. It'll take a few hours."

Bobby pulled his phone out and touched the camera icon. He found the picture of the man at the tennis club and turned the screen so Brad could see it.

"I took this two days ago in Orlando. Is it possible to run it through your system and see if you could put a name to the face?"

"Sure, I'll get one of my guys to have a look."

Bobby shook his head. "I'd appreciate if you did it. It's important this stays between us. Okay?"

Lawrence hesitated for a moment, then shot June a cautionary look. "Discretion has its limits."

"This can't go upstream," June said. "For now at least."

He thought about it. "For now," he conceded, "but that could change."

June knew it was the best she was going to get from him. "Okay."

"This will take a while. Are you staying in D.C. overnight?"

"Yes," June replied. "At the Park Hyatt Washington."

He looked at his watch. "It's almost noon. I'll try to get things wrapped up by dinner. I'll call you and then drop by the hotel."

June gave him a sincere smile. "Thanks, Brad."

Bobby snapped his fingers. "I just thought of one more thing."

Brad shrugged. "Shoot. It's your tax dollars at work."

"Could you access the national DNA record center and run a cross correlation with the DNA profiles from both the blood and the hard drive. It might be a way to identify the birthmother."

Lawrence shook his head. "That's highly unlikely. Our DNA database is limited in scope—nothing compared to what the British have." He saw the disappointed look on Bobby's face. "I'll try, but no guarantees."

"Good enough." Bobby shook Brad's hand as they walked to the door.

"Time will tell," Brad said, the bagged bloody towel in his hand.

A uniformed guard drove them to the outer gate of the complex where a cab was waiting to take them back to the city. Bobby wasn't used to snow and ice and felt his neck muscles tense up every time the car lost its grip on the road and started to slip. By the time they arrived at the hotel he was exhausted. June suggested a stop in the lobby lounge and he was all for it. They found a table near the fireplace and ordered a couple of beers.

"What do you think the test results will show?" she asked. "Same person?"

He shook his head. "I'm really not sure." He thought for a while longer, then added, "How can someone be an exact duplicate of another person? So exact, that she could fool her husband for six weeks. I don't see how that is possible. Still, a lot of things point to it. She's definitely acting differently. The tennis shot, sending the kids off to school, the failed retina scan, her sudden interest in Synergy, mysterious people at her house, and Ryan Chamberlain murdered. It's all a bit too much for coincidence."

"So, what's your final guess? Alexis or not Alexis?"

"You first," he said, setting his drink on the table

"Okay, fence sitter, I'll go on the record. I don't think that woman is Alexis Chamberlain."

He didn't look surprised. "That's it? That's your decision?"

"It is."

"Okay." Bobby finished his beer and motioned to the waiter for another round. "Since you're willing to go out on a limb, I'll join you. I agree."

They did a little fist bump and settled in with their fresh drinks. When they were finished they rode the elevator together and headed down the hall to their rooms. June's was first and Bobby stopped at the entrance as she slid her key card through the reader. He studied her profile as she pushed open the door, wishing he could follow her into the room. She turned and smiled, and they agreed to meet in three hours for dinner. The door closed.

June leaned against the frame and took three long, deep breaths, this was definitely not the time to dive into a relationship. Regardless of what Brad Lawrence discovered, she was in a precarious position. In her estimation, Alexis was not trustworthy, and she had the plans to the missile. Her supervisors at the NSA were going to find out at some point, and then all hell was going to break loose. This was the time to hunker down and keep a cool head.

Armand Cortez and Sylvia Dupres were back at Le Boheme for dinner when a text message buzzed his phone. Cortez's face darkened.

"What's that?" she asked, waving her wine glass at his cell.

"It's from Monique," he said quietly. "Something's not right at Synergy."

Sylvia reached for the phone, but he shook his head. "She didn't say what, just that we should contact her." He set his knife and fork aside and motioned to the waiter. "Bring the check now, please."

They hustled back upstairs and arrived in the room shortly after six. Armand poured a drink to steady his nerves, then picked up his cell and called Monique.

When she answered, her voice sounded tense. "June accessed one of our secure computers on Thursday and downloaded Alexis's DNA profile."

"Is there any work-related reason she would do that?" Cortez said, not really believing there was.

"No, and she came in late at night after everyone had left for the day. The building is smart-wired and it didn't register any lights going on. She did it in the dark."

Armand took a long slow drink and set his glass down. There was absolutely no doubt in his mind that Childers and Greco were collaborating, treating things like they were working a homicide file. "Send me Childers' personnel file immediately. Do you have her fingerprints and DNA on your computers?"

"Yes. Both. I'll send them over." There was a short break, then Monique said, "I'll bring them myself."

"No, use a courier." Armand said sharply. "All direct communication between us stops now. Once I have her information, I'll deal with her." He hung up and made a call to an international number.

"Dimitri, put a team together and have them in Orlando tomorrow morning." He set his phone on the table and turned to Sylvia, the veins in his neck bulging.

"We have a problem."

chapter twenty-eight

Brad Lawrence looked totally stressed as June ushered him into her suite. He had a file with him and was holding it so tightly that his knuckles were white. The NSA operative perched on the end of the sofa where Bobby was waiting, and June sat down between them. He looked like a different man than the one they had visited five hours earlier. If Bobby read the look correctly, Brad Lawrence was scared.

"You look like you could use a drink," Bobby said. Brad nodded and Bobby got up and headed for the bar fridge.

"Scotch, if they have it."

Bobby found a little bottle of scotch and added ice. When he delivered the drink, Brad opened the folder. The picture Bobby had taken of the man at Heathrow was on top.

"We might as well start with this guy," he said, turning to Bobby. "Where did you say you snapped this picture?"

"The Country Club at Heathrow. It's a tennis club in Orlando."

"At first when I ran this guy through our computer it came up empty. Then I refined the search to include matches with a lower allowable threshold."

"What do you mean by that?" Bobby asked.

"When the photos on file are grainy or out of focus the ID program can sometimes find a match when the parameters aren't quite as tight. I did that and it had no problem finding him." Lawrence held up a grainy photo that barely resembled the man from Heathrow. "The minute it found him a red light flashed on my screen and in less than five minutes a couple of serious looking guys were at my door. They weren't very nice."

"What happened?" June asked, looking concerned.

"They wanted to know why I was running his picture through the identification program and demanded to know where I got it. I told them I downloaded the picture from another file on the mainframe and ran it to see if the program was working properly."

"Quick thinking," Bobby said. The man was no dummy.

"They bought it, but were really pissed off. They told me to never pull such a dumb stunt again." He leaned over and tapped his index finger on the photo. "Do you know who this guy is?"

"No idea," June said.

"His name is Armand Cortez. He's an arms dealer. World-class. Our guys, and the CIA, would like nothing more than to capture or kill him. They don't care which. Anyway, from how quickly the field ops were on me, and their attitude, I'd have to say he's on their most wanted list."

June didn't move for a few moments, then swallowed hard. "An arms dealer," she said. Her throat was suddenly dry and her voice almost inaudible. "Jesus, Bobby, he's an arms dealer. It's pretty easy to connect the dots."

Bobby picked up the grainy photo and studied it. "It's probably safe to assume he already has his hands on the files."

"But why would Alexis give them to him?" June asked.

"That's a damn good question," Bobby said. He turned and asked Brad, "What did you get on the DNA comparison?"

"Some really weird shit." Brad gave June a sideways glance that spoke volumes. He was worried for her. Brad set the file down and gulped down the last of his drink. Bobby got up and poured him another.

"What did you find?" June asked.

"Stay with me on this. I want you to understand what I did, so you'll believe me when I say I'm sure about the results." He took a long sip of the scotch. "I ran the blood sample from the towel through a standard Polymerase Chain Reaction test. PCR test for short. I used the Takara Hot-Start PCR because it ensures the polymerase is bound until the temperature is raised."

"To eliminate primer dimers from forming during reaction assembly," Bobby said.

Brad was visibly impressed. "Yes. How do you know that?" he asked, then snapped his fingers. "Orlando homicide."

"Right. You pick up stuff when you're around it for a few years," Bobby said. "Sorry to interrupt."

"It's okay. I'll be a little more technical now that I know you've got some knowledge of DNA testing. The test targets ten standard markers to come up with a DNA profile. Once these fragments of DNA were isolated, I looked for differences in length on all ten, then compared the result to the DNA profile on the thumb drive you gave me." He laid the two profiles on the table in front of Bobby and June.

They were absolutely identical.

"Well I'll be damned," Bobby said. "The DNA and the blood on the towel are from the same person."

"So it would appear," Brad said.

"Where are you going with this?" June asked, sitting on the edge of her seat and

staring at the profiles.

"So far, there are no differences in the DNA makeup of the two samples, but I wanted to run a paternity test as well."

"Good idea," Bobby said, then explained to June. "It has a different set of benchmarks."

"I had to take a back to front approach on this one. Usually for a test like this I

would have a DNA profile on both parents, which would give me eight genetic markers to work with. Unfortunately, I didn't have the genetic makeup of the parents to use as a base. Instead I compared the eight markers, person X to person Y, and they were identical."

Bobby leaned back in his chair. "So we were wrong. Alexis is Alexis. There was no substitution." He shook his head in disbelief.

June simply let out a heavy sigh.

Brad Lawrence finished his scotch as they spoke and held up his glass. Bobby caught the cue and grabbed the last scotch from the bar.

"You two thought these samples would prove to be two different people?"

Lawrence asked. They both nodded. "Well, you were partially right and partially wrong."

"What does that mean?" June's brow was wrinkled in confusion.

"Just because those eight markers match perfectly doesn't mean the samples came from the same person. In fact, they came from two different people."

Both Bobby and June sat forward, staring at the DNA expert. "How is that possible?" June asked.

"Do you know what the word monozygotic means?" he asked.

June sat without moving for a second, then slumped back in her chair. She stared at Brad, eyes wide. "Sure," she said.

Bobby was in the dark. "I've heard the term, but I can't place it."

June explained. "Monozygotic is a term used to describe two living beings created from one fertilized egg. In layman's terms, it means identical twins."

Bobby looked at Brad and shook his head. "How does that help us? The DNA from identical twins is identical in every way. It's a scientific fact that there is no difference. I had a case where we suspected a twin had murdered her sister's boyfriend, but we couldn't prove which woman did it."

Brad perked up. "Well, you're talking to the one guy at the NSA who deals almost exclusively with this. I defended my PhD on this very issue. Bottom line is, I discovered a small difference."

"What sort of difference?"

"The DNA forms the body's genetic code, and it's that code that is utilized when the body manufactures proteins. But…" he said, pointing a finger at Bobby. "…the molecular structure of these proteins are different, even in identical twins."

"Why isn't this common knowledge?" Bobby asked. "It could help homicide departments in their forensic investigations."

"When I joined the NSA, they put a clause in my contract that prohibits me from publishing any of my research. It belongs to the agency."

Bobby gave Brad a sympathetic nod. "Are you convinced that Alexis Chamberlain has a twin sister?"

"Yes. The woman whose blood is on the towel is the identical twin of the one whose DNA profile you gave me. It is definitely not the same person."

Bobby stood up, drink in hand, and started walking about the room. This was taking on all the idiosyncrasies of a homicide file, and that was something he understood. Murders usually looked chaotic and messy, but from a cop's perspective everything is ordered and at some point the clues fit together to form the whole. He continued to pace as he started speaking.

"Sometime near the middle of October, Alexis Chamberlain was abducted and her twin sister planted in her place. Armand Cortez is likely behind the switch. He probably waited until the tournament at Heathrow was over—too many eyes on Alexis at that time to risk it. Someone might have noticed the difference in her backhand shot."

"One hand, not two," June said.

"That bugged me from minute one," Bobby said. "So did the cleaning van." He saw the blank look on Brad's face and explained. "A landscaper saw two cleaners entering the Chamberlain house, but he insisted they looked off to him. His description of the man fits Cortez to a tee, and I was starting to suspect the woman was Alexis's birthmother." Bobby stopped and raked his fingers through his hair. "So what we have now is the mother, the twin, and Armand Cortez controlling both the Chamberlain fortune and Synergy."

"If they switched Alexis for her twin right after the tournament, that would explain why she failed the retina scan the very next day," June interjected.

"Exactly, meaning since October 12th Alexis's twin has been in the house. Between October 12th and November 22nd Ryan began to suspect something was seriously wrong."

"Why November 22nd?" Brad Lawrence asked.

Bobby eyed the man closely. "This is confidential."

Brad gave him a sideways look. "No shit," he said. "This is definitely confidential. What you have to say *and* what I have to say."

Bobby wasn't sure what the comment meant, but was pretty sure he was going to find out. He took a deep breath and dropped his bombshell on Brad. "We have definitive proof that Ryan Chamberlain was murdered."

"What?" Brad shook his head. "It was all over the news. Everything said he died of a heart attack."

Bobby continued. "They managed to get a fatal dose of Verapamil into him in a very public place."

Brad glanced over at June, wide-eyed.

"Hard to detect," she said. "It didn't show up in the autopsy."

Bobby was nodding. "As things stand, everyone thinks he died a natural death and we need to keep it that way for now. We don't want to spook Cortez."

"What the fuck, June." Brad was up off the couch and storming about the room. "What the fuck have you dragged me into."

She leapt up and met him by the window, rubbing his arm as he stared out into the snow that had started falling. He didn't move, but was clearly not happy.

"Why didn't you go through the regular channels? Why come to me?" he asked.

June shifted a bit so they were facing each other. "The whole thing seemed so preposterous, and we didn't know what to do. We needed to find out if it was real before we went up the chain. Can you imagine the briefing note?"

He didn't answer for a moment, then said, "Yeah, that would be a doozie."

She managed a tight smile. "We were just trying to keep things quiet."

Brad took a long look at her, then said, "Please don't tell me there's more."

June walked away and leaned on the edge of the couch. "Cortez had Alexis's sister get the JASSM data from all eleven departments. They have a working copy of the missile."

Any hint of anger on Brad's face faded to fear. "What?"

"They have the stealth version of the JASSM missile."

"Ah, shit." He continued to stare at her, sucking in long breaths and slowly letting them out, his eyes glazing over. "Anything else?"

"That's it. That's what we know so far," Bobby said.

Brad walked to the bar on unsteady legs and poured another drink. He sipped it, staring at the carpet. "There's more."

June tensed at the sound of his voice. Whatever was coming was not good news.

"Sit down." Brad waited until both Bobby and June were sitting and focused on him. "I ran the DNA profiles from both Alexis and her twin through the databank, looking for a birthparent."

"And you found her?" June asked.

"I wish," he said, shaking his head. "I found the father."

They both stared at him. "What?" June asked. "Are you sure?"

"Positive. This man is the father." He took a single sheet of paper from the folder and laid it on the table.

June recoiled and shook her head. "Brad, that's not possible."

Bobby grabbed the page and looked closer. "Oh fuck."

All three of them stared at the paper. On it was a full color photo and a line-by-line bio of the man's accomplishments. Lawyer, senator, Democratic candidate for president, winner of the Electoral College vote, President of the United States.

"William Neilson?" Bobby asked. "The president? Are you sure?"

"One hundred per-fucking-cent."

The room went dead silent.

chapter twenty-nine

Cortez picked up on the first ring.

Dimitri Petrov had cleared customs at Orlando International Airport and was on his way to the car rental. Cortez gave Petrov an address and told him to be there in one hour.

The meeting place, a Perkins restaurant near the Florida Mall, was about half full, normal for a restaurant near Disney World on a Sunday morning. Petrov and his two accomplices were dressed casually in shorts and golf shirts, and they fit right in as they were shown to a table. They spoke fluent English and ordered breakfast, knowing Cortez would only stay long enough to give them their assignment, not to eat. Right on time, Cortez slipped quietly into the restaurant and joined them.

Cortez acknowledged the men with a nod of his head, impressed with how easily they blended in. He personally knew each of them and felt Petrov had picked his team well. Tony DaSilva, early thirties with dark hair and probing brown eyes, was a master at making a crime scene appear accidental. Roberto Juarez, a Spaniard, was simply a cold-blooded killer who looked and acted like a nice young man.

Cortez ordered a coffee when the waitress came by, then slipped an envelope across the table to Petrov. "His name is Robert Greco. Everyone calls him Bobby."

Petrov checked for Greco's address. "Should we pay him a visit?"

"No," Cortez said curtly as he sipped his coffee. "That would invite attention. We'll take care of Greco by removing the people listed on the next page."

Petrov flipped the page over and scanned the information and photos. "Should they die accidentally?"

Cortez looked at DaSilva. "Yes, an accident. It will stop Greco in his tracks."

"What's our time frame?" DaSilva asked.

Cortez drained the last of the coffee. It was excellent. "Today, tomorrow at the latest." He stood and left the restaurant without looking back.

Dimitri Petrov turned the pages around so Tony DaSilva and Roberto Juarez could see the victim's faces. Juarez couldn't resist a smile at the sight of Janis Greco and her two young children.

Bobby barely slept Saturday night. He slipped out of bed, showered and dressed, then knocked on June's door. She was awake as well and they headed down to the hotel lobby for an early breakfast.

Their conversation was all about what Brad Lawrence had dumped on them the previous evening. Lawrence had gone a step further than simply running a paternity test, he had also dug into one of the NSA databanks and pulled off a past history of the president's life to see if their theory made sense.

The timing worked perfectly. In the mid-80s, William Neilson was a young, married, upwardly mobile member of the senate. He was pressing the flesh a lot, developing the alliances and contacts inside the political machine that would later carry him to the presidency. Now it appeared he had pressed a bit too much flesh, in particular with a woman who wasn't his wife. The result was twin girls who were now thirty-five years old, one of which was Alexis Chamberlain.

"So who's the other girl?" Bobby said as they sipped their coffee and waited for breakfast.

"Who indeed," June said. She set her cup on her napkin. "Do you think Neilson knows about this?"

Bobby shook his head. "My guess is that he doesn't, but some things are beginning to make sense."

"Like?"

"When I was interviewing Percy and Etonia Rothchild, she mentioned that the Neilsons are their neighbors in the Hamptons. Even if William Neilson didn't know about Alexis and her sister, you can bet the parents did. It's too much coincidence for them to own beach houses a hundred yards from each other."

"So the birthmother brokered some sort of a deal with the Neilsons, and the Rothchilds took one of the girls. She probably got a whack of cash."

"No shit," Bobby said. "Neilson was a senator at the time. A scandal would have derailed him."

"His parents stepped in and took care of things. The Rothchilds didn't think they could have children so they were more than willing to take Alexis. All those summers, the Neilsons had their granddaughter right next door."

"Exactly." Breakfast had arrived, and Bobby pushed his eggs around on the plate. "But why only one daughter? How would you choose? Why not adopt both babies? Surely the Neilsons would have pushed for that as well."

June was already halfway through her stack of pancakes. She finished chewing and swallowed. "Unless they didn't know about the second girl."

Bobby's fork was an inch from his mouth and he stopped right there. "The woman at the adoption agency said a midwife was involved." He set the fork on his plate, his mind racing. "You might have just nailed it. It's possible that no one but the birthmother and the midwife knew there were twins."

"Oh my God, this just keeps getting better." June looked around the bustling restaurant. The other diners were enjoying their meals, oblivious to their conversation. "So the president has two daughters, and no one knows about the second one."

They sat in silence, staring at each other. Finally, Bobby said, "Well, this is a bit of a clusterfuck."

"A bit?" June said.

They slowly got back to eating breakfast. After a few mouthfuls, June pushed back her plate and sipped her coffee. "Do you think Cortez knows what he's sitting on? That she's Neilson's daughter."

Bobby gave that some serious thought. There was no reason why anyone except the girls' birthmother had to know. It was entirely possible she was holding a trump card, waiting for the right time to play it. In fact, the more Bobby thought about it, the more he was convinced Cortez didn't know who the father was. That would be worth millions, and Bobby couldn't imagine Cortez leaving it unexploited.

"I don't think he has a clue," Bobby said.

"Do you think their mother is the woman with Cortez?"

"Oh, yeah, I'm pretty sure it's her."

June nodded, both hands cupped around her coffee mug, drawing some comfort from the warmth. "We need help. I *have* to report up. Brad Lawrence isn't going to keep quiet for long. Anyway, there's no chance we can handle this ourselves."

Bobby took a bite of toast. They both knew that was the understatement of the year. "Yeah, we need help."

"So we're agreed."

"We are," Bobby said. "Then there's Alexis. We have no idea if she's still alive."

June thought about that. "She well could be. What mother would let someone kill their child? Even this one."

Bobby stared out the window. Big, fluffy flakes were fluttering down and blanketing the cars in the parking lot. He figured June was right, if Cortez was still with the girls' mother, she would never go along with having her daughter killed. In the worst case, Alexis could be used as a negotiating tool. He watched a driver skid into the parking lot and hit the curb and briefly wondered why people lived in cold climates.

"I think you're right," he said. "They're holding her somewhere."

"Devil's advocate," June said. "Right now it's the perfect crime. No one even knows it's been committed. They can't let Alexis walk back into her life, so how do they ever release her?"

"They can't," Bobby agreed. "The clock's ticking."

June let out a huge sigh and buried her face in her hands. "Ryan was a good man," she said, looking up at Bobby with anger in her eyes. "They're monsters. They murdered him and now they're going to kill Alexis."

Bobby eyed June closely. For him this was an investigation, albeit one that was getting out of control, but for June it was personal. He reached out and took her hand.

"And you're the only reason she has a hope in hell," he said.

chapter thirty

Tony DaSilva cut through the chain-link fence surrounding the utility compound and ducked inside, then disappeared between two vans bearing the local gas company logo. He hotwired one of them, slipped it into gear and pulled out of its parking spot. At the front gate an electric eye triggered the automatic hydraulic arm and the gate slowly opened, then closed immediately behind him.

DaSilva turned east on Sand Lake Road and slowed to a crawl. Roberto Juarez and Dimitri Petrov jumped in and the vehicle pulled into the Sunday afternoon traffic. They turned south on the 423, then took the 528 to Orangewood Boulevard. He kept to the posted rate of thirty miles per hour as Juarez and Petrov yanked on the overalls they had found in the van. When they pulled up in front of Janis Greco's house, all three men were dressed as gas company employees.

DaSilva went to the front door and knocked. It didn't matter if the woman and kids were at home. If they were, he would simply tell them a story to get into the house. If they weren't, he would pick the lock and let himself in. There was no answer and he jimmied the door. Once inside, DaSilva checked the kitchen. Perfect, there was a gas stove. That made his job so much easier.

Eight minutes later he left the house, closing and locking the door behind him. The next meal Janis Greco prepared would be her last. He jumped into the truck and they returned the van to its parking space in the compound, then closed the slash in the fence as best they could. It was unlikely anyone would notice and even if they did it would be a mystery. No vehicles had been stolen, no equipment was missing, no offices were broken into. Just kids playing a prank.

The three men checked into a hotel for the evening and after a quick meal they hung around the room waiting for the news. When the house exploded, it would quickly become the top story of the day. The only question now was whether Janis Greco would eat early enough to make the six o'clock news.

Bobby and June flew back into Orlando, arriving a few minutes after three on Sunday afternoon. June's car was at the airport and she offered to drop Bobby off at his ex-wife's house, but he declined and headed for the taxi queue. They had been together for a long stretch and he needed a few hours apart to reset and think. The only thing he knew for sure was that he wanted to see his kids.

The airport was crowded with tourists looking forward to a few days in the Disney parks and it took a while to get through the queue. The ride to his ex-wife's house was short, less than fifteen minutes, and he glanced at his watch as the cab pulled up. Four twenty-three. Bobby trudged up to the front door, bag in hand, and tried the door handle. It was locked. He rang the bell, no answer. He walked around back and gave the patio doors a quick tug. Nothing. He sat down on a deckchair to wait.

He missed being a regular dad to his kids. Living in a different house wasn't how he had envisioned things when he and Janis were together and their lives humming along. She had managed the stress of being a cop's wife for a few years, but eventually it had ground her down. Bobby didn't blame her, not many of the guys on the force stayed married for more than ten years. It was like water flowing over rock—it eventually wore away the foundation, then everything collapsed.

He heard the sounds of Sarah and Lizzie getting out of their mom's car and waited on the deck for them to come running through the house. There were giggles and squeals when they saw him, and Lizzie pressed her grinning face against the glass doors. Janis showed up a second later and opened the sliders.

"Daddy." Lizzie came running and gave him a bear hug. "Are you going to take us for pizza tonight?"

"You bet, sweetie," he said softly. He lifted her up above him, then dropped and caught her. She gasped, then let out a wild laugh. Her older sister, Sarah, peeked out from the kitchen.

"Hi, dad." She skipped over to him. At six, she was getting a little big to be thrown about. Bobby gave her a hug.

"Hi, darling. Did you guys have fun with Mom today?"

Both their eyes brightened. "Yes. Mom bought us some new toys. She said they're from you," Lizzie whispered to him. "She said we were supposed to thank you."

He looked up and saw Janis at the patio doors, watching him and the kids. She had that look in her eye, the one that said she still loved him.

"Hi, Jan," he said, rising from the chair. He gave her a quick peck on the cheek as he brushed by her into the house. "Would you mind if the kids and I take your car for pizza? I caught a cab from the airport."

"No, not at all. I'm just going to curl up in front of the television. A full day at the mall is almost enough to kill me."

"No kidding," he agreed. "Are the kids hungry?"

They answered that question by jumping all over him, screaming how much they needed pizza. He took the car keys from Janis and headed out.

"I'll be about an hour, maybe an hour and a half," he said as she followed them to the front door.

"Take your time," she said, and winked. He knew it meant *Please take them and give me some time to just put my feet up and rest*. She shut the door.

The kids jumped into Janis's car and he made sure they were strapped in properly, then slid into the front seat. A neighbor from the house next door gave Bobby a wave. The man was well into his sixties and walked with a slight limp as he started up Janis's sidewalk.

"Can I help you?" Bobby asked. Janis was trying to get some peace and quiet, and maybe he could handle this.

The neighbor turned to the car. "Oh, it's probably nothing, I just wanted to make sure Janis was okay, what with the gas company showing up today and all."

Bobby's cop-senses kicked into gear. "The gas company was here?"

"Yeah, they showed up about an hour ago, spent five or ten minutes in the house, then left."

Red flags were going up everywhere. Janis was at the mall an hour ago and the house was locked up tight. The only way someone could have entered was if they broke in, and if they did, then they weren't from the gas company.

"You said they were here for five or ten minutes?"

"About that."

"Shit." Bobby threw open the door and yelled at the girls. "Don't move."

He sprinted up the sidewalk for the house and hit the front door at full tilt, throwing it open. Janis was in the kitchen, standing by the stove.

"Don't touch it," Bobby yelled, flying across the room and jerking her back from the stove. He looked her square in the eyes. "Get the girls out of the car. Go somewhere at least three or four houses away. Do it now."

"Bobby, what's..." She stopped when he held up his hand. Janis moved slowly at first, then headed out at a dead run.

Bobby turned his attention to the stove. If someone had tampered with a gas appliance, chances are it would be the range, not the hot water tank. The stove would only ignite if someone was standing in front of it with their hand on the control. The hot water tank could kick in anytime to keep the water warm. He was sure—if something was rigged it would be the stove. Bobby knelt down and peered along the crack between the top of the oven door and the body of the stove. Nothing on his left. He moved to the other side. Again, nothing. He slowly opened the door a fraction of an inch and checked for a trigger wire. There wasn't one, and he opened the door all the way.

The interior light was working and he could see inside the oven. The burners looked normal. The corners were smooth and there was no place inside to attach a triggering device. He checked the hinges and the light bulb, then closed the door and stood up. The stovetop was typical, with two large burners and two small ones. One by one he lifted the grates and peered into the opening below. He could see the gas lines and the electronic ignition switches for each burner. What was he missing?

He glanced down at the tile floor, then kneeled down and ran his fingernail along the grout line out front of the stove. It came away covered with heavy, greasy dust. That didn't make sense. The dirt would accumulate under the stove, not in front of it. Someone had recently pulled the appliance out from the wall.

Bobby got off his knees and opened Janis's junk drawer. He found the flashlight and flipped the switch. The beam was weak, but better than nothing, and he climbed on the counter and aimed it behind the stove. The space was no more than an inch, and it was difficult to see all the way down to where the gas line came through the drywall. He held his breath and gave the stove a slight push. It moved slightly and he sniffed in deeply for a few seconds, anticipating the smell of natural gas. Nothing. He shone the light down the crack again, now able to see where the main line connected to the stove. He was no gasfitter, but he knew instinctively that the tiny plastic piece attached next to the stopcock did not belong.

Bobby leaned against the cabinets, thinking what to do. While he didn't want to blow the house, and himself, into the next county, the last thing he needed right now were a bunch of emergency trucks parked on the street. Whoever had planted this device had been here this afternoon and would be waiting for the results. A gathering of trucks and people would clue them in pretty quickly that someone had found their handiwork. That option was out.

Leaving the stove in its current state was out of the question. From what he could see there was no way of knowing exactly how the device worked, but he was pretty sure it was a trigger mechanism of some sort. He made a decision, and slid off the counter onto the floor. Grasping the edges of the stove, he pulled it slowly out from its alcove until there was enough room to get in behind it. He jumped back on the counter, then lowered himself carefully into the space between the stove and the wall. By squatting and hunching his back, he was able to bring his face to within six inches of the gas line. Now he could see how the device worked.

It was a tiny ignition switch that had been spliced into the gas line. The cut had been sealed with some sort of yellow putty that closely resembled the main line, and it was on the source side of the stopcock, so closing the valve was useless. Bobby stood up and leaned over, reaching into the junk drawer and feeling for some duct tape. He found a partial roll near the back. He gave it a quick kiss, and knelt back down to take a closer look before beginning.

The device was set to pop open the moment there was any sort of internal pressure, allowing the gas to leak into the room. Turning on any burner or the oven would create that pressure. The switch had a rudimentary timer on it. He couldn't tell how long it was, but he guessed it was very short. A few seconds after the stove was turned on, while the homeowner wondered why they smelled gas, the switch would spark. With all that leakage from the high-pressure line, the explosion would kill anyone close by. The device, being plastic, would be completely destroyed in the ensuing fire. Murder made to look accidental.

The device was held in place only by the putty, and Bobby carefully slipped it off, then wrapped the hissing line with duct tape, tight enough to cut the escaping gas flow. He wound a bunch more tape around the cut, then hoisted himself from behind the stove and pushed it back against the wall. He pocketed the trigger switch and, with hands and legs shaking, went in search of Janis and the kids.

Bobby found her six houses down, talking with a neighbor woman he'd met once or twice. He stayed on the sidewalk by the road and motioned for her to come over. When she and the girls reached him, he said, "Kids, head home and mom and I will be right behind you. We need to talk for a minute."

The kids scampered ahead while he and Janis walked toward the house.

"Someone rigged the stove to blow." He slid the device from his pocket and held it out.

The color drained from her face. "Someone tried to kill me, and the kids?" she asked. Her voice was a whisper.

Bobby nodded.

"Who? Why?"

"I don't know. It might be related to a case I'm working on. I can't think of any other reason someone would do this."

The initial shock was wearing off and her anger was setting in. "Who did this?"

He took her by the shoulders, tight enough to settle her down. "This case, these criminals, they're powerful. They have resources very few people have and it looks like they're willing to use them."

"But why me and the kids?"

"They likely want to distract me. Send me a message to get me off the case."

"Distract you?" she said, fury in her eyes. "Blowing up my house and killing us is a distraction? We're a fucking distraction?" She was starting to lose her composure. "Who the hell are these people, Bobby?"

Lizzie and Sarah were standing fifty feet up the sidewalk watching them now. Bobby turned Janis so they were face to face.

"You need to leave," he said, taking her hands. "I want you to take the girls and head for Jim and Louise's cabin. The one on the Alapaha River, just south of Ocilla. No one knows about it. You'll be safe there."

"Jesus, Bobby." Janis looked scared. She had spent years as a cop's wife, hearing the stories, knowing the risks, but there had never been anything like this.

"The one in Georgia," she said slowly. "Where we stayed after Sarah was born."

"Yes, that's the one. Do you remember how to get there?"

"Straight up the Turnpike to Tifton, then head east." She was mapping it out in her head as she spoke. "Yes," she said, more forcefully now. "I remember. I can find it."

"There's no way anyone will be there at this time of year. The key is always in the birdhouse on the big elm beside the cabin. Leave now, stop at the bank and get lots of cash. I'll pay you back later. Don't use your credit card, your cell phone or your debit card. Nothing that would give someone looking for you a clue to your location. Strictly cash, do you understand?"

Janis looked over at the girls, waiting patiently for them to finish talking. "I understand. How will I know when it's safe to come home?"

"I'll call you. Turn on your phone once a day and check for messages."

"What if…"

"What if something happens to me?" He took out a pen and scribbled down Jacky's personal number. "This is for Jacky Foster at the office. Don't call her unless it's absolutely necessary, and not from your cell."

"She's the backup," Janis acknowledged.

"She is," Bobby nodded. "Right now, I need to disappear. I'll get a burner cell and Jacky will have the number."

"Okay," she stuttered.

"Jan, we're going to get through this. In the meantime, you need stay out of sight and keep your head low. Okay?"

She saw the look in his eyes. She'd seen it before, when a killer was on the loose and he was on their tail. He had always got the guy. She nodded. "Okay, we'll stay at the cabin until we hear from you." She relaxed her grip on his hands. "Be careful, Bobby."

chapter thirty-one

Bobby called June and asked her to pick him up at the Florida Mall in half an hour. She agreed, and after she hung up Bobby found a mobile phone store and bought two untraceable burner cells. He left a message on Jacky Foster's home phone with his new number and asked her not to give it to anyone else. He kept rehashing what had happened at Janis's house, barely able to keep his anger in check. The bastards had actually tried to kill his family. Now he knew exactly how June felt—this had just got very personal for him as well. At six-thirty he made his way to the northwest doors, where June had already pulled up and was waiting for him.

"What's going on?" She looked worried as she drove for the exit.

"Pizza got canceled." Bobby was at his boiling point, and she listened without interrupting as he told her what had happened.

Traffic on Winegard Road was hectic and moving fast, so she pulled into a strip mall. "Unbelievable," she said, leaning her head against the steering wheel.

"Well, it happened."

She was shaking slightly and could barely find her voice. "My God, Bobby. Are you okay?"

"Not really."

From where June had parked they could see a neighborhood pub with an OPEN sign flickering in the window. Bobby pointed and said, "I need something to eat."

The pub was a dated hole in the wall, and a good place to get off the street and out of sight. A few men were playing darts and both the pool tables were in use. The waitress, dressed in a short skirt and a crisp white blouse, stopped by and took their drink orders.

"I think you'd better call in sick tomorrow," Bobby said. "If Cortez knows about me, he knows about you. It's time for us to get lost."

June didn't look very happy about that, but finally nodded her agreement. "You're right. When they find out their attempt on Janis and the girls didn't work, they'll probably come after both of us. It looks like my cover is blown."

Bobby shook his head. "They may not know about your connection to the NSA, but you can bet they're aware you and I have been talking."

"They could have traced my break-in at Synergy."

"Do you think so?" Bobby asked.

"Probably," June said. "I used my keycard to access the room where Alexis's DNA profile was stored. Honestly, I have no idea if the computer I broke into tracks who logs in and when. If it kept a record, they could easily figure out which file I opened. That means they'd know what I was after."

"So it's a maybe."

June shrugged. "Regardless, they'll see that I came in late at night and was poking around."

Bobby considered what that meant to them. "Let's assume the computer had a monitoring program of some sort. That means they're onto you and know what you're looking for. I'm definitely on their radar. I probably have been since the first time I spoke with Alexis's twin at Heathrow. Chances are, they've figured out we know about the substitution."

June looked disgusted. "Now they're hunting us. I need to get this information to the NSA. It's long overdue."

"Maybe," Bobby said slowly.

He thanked the waitress as she dropped two pints of draught beer on their table. "I think we need to do two things first. We should have a chat with Debbie Mayther. She was Alexis's tennis partner when they won the mixed doubles at Heathrow. She's also a doctor. Maybe she can help us figure out who the birthmother is."

June's eyes narrowed slightly. "Do you know her?"

"I met her outside the tennis club and asked her a few questions. Mayther and Ryan were good friends and she gave me her card. Told me to call if I needed anything else."

"Okay, if that works we'll know who the birthmother is. What then?" She picked up her glass and took a drink.

"We meet with the president."

June's head snapped up. "What?"

He ignored the question. "We meet with William Neilson," he repeated.

She actually managed to laugh. "Right, you and me. We're going to call up the White House and just ask for the president. Then we're going to tell him to open a spot on his calendar ASAP. Dream on, Bobby."

Bobby took a drink of beer and wiped the foam from his upper lip. "You know how if you look hard and long enough, we're sort of all connected in one way or another? The whole six degrees of separation?" She nodded and he said, "Well, I know someone."

"Who? Who do you know that can get us into the Oval Office?"

"I know a guy from my early days on the force. He ended up working for some lobby group in D.C. and made friends with Derek Adler. Now they play squash all the time."

"Derek Adler," June said quietly, "is White House Chief of Staff."

"He is, and he has daily access to the president. However, before we call him, we need to find out the identity of Alexis's birthmother."

"Because?"

"When we meet with Neilson, we have no credibility unless we can identify the woman he had an affair with. If we go into the meeting with her name, he'll hear what we have to say, otherwise, forget it."

"That makes sense," she said slowly. "And if he doesn't listen?"

"We go to your contacts at the NSA and the president goes up in flames."

June was nodding now that she understood Bobby's reluctance to go straight to the NSA. "Good thinking."

"I'll contact Debbie Mayther tomorrow and see if I can track down the birthmother. We need to get to Washington, but they're going to be watching for us."

"I can book a car," June said. "NSA gave me a false driver's license and a credit card. I've never used it."

"Where is it?" Bobby asked.

She pointed at her purse. "I was told to always carry it."

He shook his head. "Holy shit, the things the average person doesn't know about our government." He thought for a minute, then said, "We're going to be driving all night."

She toyed with the last few chips on her plate. "Jesus, Bobby, I can't even go home."

"No, you can't. We need to get a hotel room for a couple of days." He reached over, took her hand and squeezed it lightly. "I dragged you into this. I'm sorry for that."

She put her free hand on top of his. "I was part of this the moment Ryan was murdered. I just didn't know it at the time." June let her hand linger on his, it felt warm and reassuring.

The three men sat in their hotel room, eating Chinese take-out and monitoring the newsfeeds on their phones. So far there hadn't been any mention of an explosion in Orlando, but the online media might not be at the scene. The local news was starting on the television and they turned up the volume. An attractive brunette with a flashy smile appeared and started into the night's top stories. There was nothing, the trigger mechanism hadn't been activated. The question was, why not?

Tony DaSilva frowned. Janis Greco should have used her stove by now. Regardless of which burner she turned on, the gas line would have ripped open and the twelve second fuse ignited. The house should be a pile of toothpicks. DaSilva stood and slipped on a light windbreaker.

"I'm going to drive down and check things out," he said to Petrov. "Do you want to come?"

"No, I'll stay in case Cortez wants us. Take Roberto with you."

The two men left the hotel and headed for the South Florida Parkway. When they passed Sea World, DaSilva turned east into Janis Greco's subdivision and parked two blocks from her house.

"Stay here," he said to Juarez.

It was a few minutes before midnight as DaSilva walked slowly along the sidewalk. Most of the houses were dark, the owners already in bed. He turned onto Gardenbrook Lane and strolled past the target house. It was dark. He walked down three houses, then quietly cut between two homes and doubled back, approaching Janis Greco's house in the darkness, his black windbreaker and pants blending into the shadows. The patio doors were tightly secured, but he picked the lock with no problem and slid the door open. It rolled back noiselessly in its track and he moved through the kitchen to the hallway, sensing something was wrong. All three bedroom doors were open, moonlight spilling into the hall. He quickly checked the kid's rooms, then the master. They were all empty.

He returned to the kitchen and slipped a flashlight from his jacket pocket, then leaned over the counter and aimed the beam between the stove and the wall. There was duct tape where he had installed the ignition switch. He cursed under his breath, tucked his flashlight back in his pocket and left the house, jogging down the block to where Roberto Juarez was waiting.

He snatched the cell phone from the seat as he got in and dialed a number. "Cortez is going to go fucking nuts."

Janis Greco saw the signage for Tifton and swerved over to the off-ramp. She glanced in her rear view mirror—both Sarah and Lizzie were asleep, safely strapped in with their seatbelts. If what Bobby said was true, and she was sure it was, they had missed being blown to pieces because a nosy neighbor had happened by. Her hands started shaking at the thought of what would have happened. She tried to put it out of her mind and forced herself to concentrate on the road.

The moon was little more than a sliver hanging low in the sky. It was mostly obscured by thick groves of trees bordering the road, and ahead of her the black asphalt disappeared into the night as a bank of fog rolled in. Janis followed the faint white center line snaking through the Georgia countryside, peering out the windshield and watching closely for her turnoff. She had only visited the cabin twice, and both times it had been during the day. Even then the dirt road was difficult to find, its edges crowded out by trees and shrubs. She saw it at the last possible second and slammed on the brakes, steering hard right. The car made the turn, bouncing over the washboards at the intersection with the highway. The road smoothed out after a hundred feet or so, and Janis stole another quick look at the kids. They were still sleeping.

She drove carefully—sliding into the ditch on such a scarcely travelled road was a recipe for disaster. The curves came without warning, and she crawled along, teetering dangerously close to the ditch. She tried her high beams, but in the fog that only made things worse. The short drive from the highway to the cabin took almost an hour, and her shoulder muscles were knotted like misshapen tree roots by the time she reached the overgrown access leading to the cabin. She let out sigh of relief when she saw the house.

It was exactly as she had remembered—a small two-story with a shed on the east side. There was running water and electricity, but only if she could get the generator working. Janis found the key, let herself in and made up two cots for the girls, then she woke them and shoed them upstairs to bed. They went without prodding, and when she was sure they were both sleeping she headed for the shed to check the generator. A full can of gas sat next to the door and she filled the tank, checking the fuel filter before attempting to start it. Everything seemed fine and she pushed the ignition switch. It coughed a few times then kicked on, sending a low droning sound through the threes. The house lit up and she felt the knots in her shoulders fade a touch. She wandered over to the dock at the edge of the Alapaha River, slipped off her shoes and dangled her toes in the murky water. She had been here before, perched on this exact spot, but never under circumstances like this.

Someone had tried to kill them, and she was having a hell of a time wrapping her head around that. Bobby had dealt with some pretty rotten scum during his years in homicide, but the threats had never been aimed at his family. Now things had escalated beyond comprehension and here she was in the backwoods with the children. A shudder ripped up her back at the thought. She slipped her feet from the cool water and headed for the house.

The generator was still whirring in the shed, and she plugged in the fridge and removed the wood block holding the door open. It would be cool by morning. When the kids woke, they would drive into Ocilla for groceries. She made her way up to the empty bedroom and slipped under the covers, exhausted. How long, she wondered. How long would she and the children have to stay here, cut off from their home and their friends? She tried to drift off, but her mind wouldn't stop racing, always bringing her back to the same place.

Whoever they were, could Bobby stop them?

chapter thirty-two

Debbie Mayther, the new head of neurology at South Seminole Medical Center, was returning to her office after a meeting when her assistant held up a message.

"Bobby Greco would like to set up an appointment with you concerning Ryan Chamberlain."

Debbie recognized the insurance adjuster's name from when they had talked at the tennis club. "Thanks, Arlene. I have a few minutes right after lunch today. Have him come in then."

When Bobby arrived, he had to wait almost an hour before being ushered into Mayther's office. She was on the phone and waved him toward a chair. The call took a couple of minutes, then she hung up and apologized.

"A small crisis," she said, shaking his hand and taking a seat behind her desk. "I take it this is about Ryan."

"It is," he said. "Thanks for fitting me in, and for the offer to help."

"Do you?" Mayther asked. "Need help, that is."

"I do. I need to find the name of a woman who gave birth in Florida through a midwife on July 14, 1983."

Mayther's eyebrows went up at that. "And how is this relevant to Ryan?" Before he could answer, she added, "That's Alexis Chamberlain's birthday. Any chance it could be a coincidence?"

Bobby smiled. This woman was nobody's fool. "No, it's not a coincidence."

Mayther studied him for a few seconds. "Midwife, you say. That sounds specific."

She was fishing, but he wasn't biting. "It should help narrow down the search."

Debbie Mayther nodded slowly. "Alexis was delivered by a midwife?"

"I suspect she was." Bobby waited a moment, then leaned forward, "*Trust me*, this is important."

"You're asking me to access confidential Florida State hospital records." She settled back in her chair, watching him.

"That's partially correct. The records aren't confidential, just very hard to access without a direct link into the health care system. The problem is, I need the information now. I don't have time to go through the regular channels."

"So I'm saving you some time."

Bobby nodded. "Basically, yes."

"And this benefits Ryan Chamberlain somehow."

"Believe it or not, yes. More than you can imagine."

Mayther was intrigued by what was unfolding, but reluctant to simply cave and give Greco what he wanted. She knew he was correct about the records being in the public domain, and after weighing both sides of the situation, made a decision. She pulled her keyboard toward her. "July 14, 1983. Right?"

"Yes."

She keyed in a few strokes, accessing the data banks for all births in Florida. A lengthy list appeared under July 14, but she cut it down to a single entry when she limited the search to females delivered by a midwife. She hit print and pulled the sheet off the LaserJet next to her monitor.

"Please don't tell anyone where you got that," she said politely.

"Not a chance."

Bobby took the sheet of paper and quickly scanned it. Emily Larouche was the midwife, Sylvia Dupres was the mother. He glanced up at the neurologist and nodded, then got up and offered his hand. "Thanks. This really helps."

Outside the front door, Bobby used his burner cell to call Jill on her personal phone, purposely bypassing the Riggs and Company switchboard in case Cortez was monitoring it. He gave her Emily Larouche's name and asked if she could try to locate her. He was less than six blocks from the medical center when his phone rang. It was Jill.

"You finally gave me an easy one," she said.

"Emily Larouche?"

"Yup. She's eighty-six and living in a senior's residence here in Orlando."

Bobby smiled. Luck was finally with him. "Send me the address," he said, then added, "Do me a favor?"

"Sure."

"Tell Clayton I won't be in for a couple of days, and give him this number. I'm not taking any calls on my usual phone right now."

"Is everything okay, Bobby?" Jill sounded worried.

"Everything's fine. I'll explain later."

The line died and a moment later Bobby's phone pinged. He pulled over, entered the address into his GPS and set out to see the woman who had delivered the president's daughters. The drive took twenty-five minutes, and he pulled into a visitor's spot in front of Bonavista Village. It was a single story, brightly-painted building surrounded by mature trees and a large duck pond thick with bulrushes. He entered the main doors and asked for Emily Larouche. The receptionist glanced out the front door and pointed to a woman sitting by herself on a bench near the water.

"That's Emily," she said.

Bobby walked back outside and circled the pond until he arrived at the bench. "Emily Larouche?" he asked.

She was tiny, almost skeletal, with thin grey hair and deep blue veins showing through paper-thin skin. She gave Bobby the once over, then motioned to the empty half of the bench.

"Have a seat," she said, her voice quiet and melodic.

Bobby sat and turned slightly so he was facing her. He introduced himself as an investigator for Riggs and Company, then said, "Did you ever work as a midwife?"

She looked at Bobby with interest. "I did."

"I need to find out about a birth that happened a little over thirty-five years ago. July 14th, 1983 to be precise."

She drew in a sharp breath, then exhaled slowly and pushed back her shoulders and folded her hands on her lap. "I was beginning to think no one would ever ask."

Bobby took a long time to respond. There was no sense rushing things. Emily Larouche had lived with her secret for thirty-five years. "Do you know who the father is?" His tone of voice left no doubt that *he* knew.

She nodded, and a wisp of hair fell across her face. She brushed it away. "I do."

Bobby had every confidence that none of this could have happened without the involvement of William Neilson's parents. They were the puppet masters, the ones who had kept his daughter a secret all these years. "Sylvia Dupres had an arrangement with Laura and Garth Neilson," Bobby said.

The old woman didn't break eye contact with him. "Sylvia went directly to Laura, and she told me that Laura handled everything. Her husband had no idea what was going on." A faint smile passed over her face. "Laura was a tough one."

"Tell me about it," Bobby said.

Emily pulled her shawl around her shoulders. "Laura Neilson got my name from a mutual friend and asked if I would oversee a pregnancy and birth. She offered a good deal of money. Enough that I didn't have to think about it very long. I said yes, and it was then that I met Sylvia Dupres."

"When did you know she was expecting twins?"

That caught her off guard. "So you know about that as well." When Bobby nodded, she said, "Early on."

"And you never said a word to anyone? Not even Laura Neilson."

"I was with Sylvia for seven months. She was young and vulnerable." There was a softness in her eyes. "That woman used her wealth and power to take the child and then she discarded Sylvia like a piece of garbage. It was hard to watch how she was treated." The softness disappeared as she talked about the president's mother. "Sylvia was a good girl, and after all these years she hasn't taken advantage of William's position."

That much was true, although Bobby wasn't so sure Sylvia Dupres was all that honorable. "So William Neilson had no idea Sylvia was pregnant with his child, and no one but you knew she gave birth to twins."

"That's correct."

"Why are you letting this out now?" he asked.

"I'm not telling you anything you don't already know. If you'd come fishing, you would have got nothing." She straightened up a touch and lifted her chin. "It has been Sylvia's choice to stay silent, and I have kept her secret."

Bobby was more than a little impressed with the elderly woman. She was sitting on what could be the biggest story to come out of Washington in years, yet she had never said a word.

"What are you going to do now that you know?" she asked.

"If at all possible, keep it quiet."

"That would be best." She glanced at her watch and stood up. "If there's nothing else..."

Bobby thanked her and watched as she grasped her walker and made her way into the building. All those years, he thought, carrying that knowledge. He wasn't sure he could have done it. The winter sky was clear and cool as he walked back to his car, and he shivered, chilled to the bone at the thought of the complicity that had kept William Neilson and his daughters apart.

Traffic was heavy and it was a slow drive back to the hotel. Once he was parked, he went to the room and collected June, then headed back to the lobby where the staff had lit a fire. They ordered drinks from the bar and June settled in, waiting for Bobby to fill her in on what he had found.

"The mother's name is Sylvia Dupres, and I even managed to find the midwife who delivered the girls."

"You're kidding."

"I am *not* kidding." Bobby spent the next few minutes recapping his conversations, then sat back and sipped his drink.

June couldn't conceal her shock. "So Laura Neilson kept all this from her son, and he has no idea Alexis Chamberlain is his daughter. Man, that woman is some piece of work."

"She's pretty ruthless all right."

"And Laura Neilson had no idea Sylvia Dupres had twins."

Bobby shook his head. "Only Dupres and the midwife."

June contemplated what Bobby had told her, then threw her hands up in exasperation. "Well, that's just great. If we can get to the president, then we're the ones who have to blindside him with this."

Bobby hadn't really thought of it from that angle. This was personal and would cut right to the bone. Despite all his accomplishments and the position he held, it was likely going to be the biggest bombshell of his life.

The lobby waiter came by with a carafe of coffee and Bobby had him fill his cup. "Has his Chief of Staff called yet?"

June motioned for a refill. "Nothing from Adler this morning. What did you tell your friend, the one who plays squash with him?"

"Rex Blythe. That we needed to speak with Adler today. He was going to try and contact him sometime this morning."

"How do you know Rex Blythe?"

Bobby gave her a wily grin. "I kept Rex's brother, Brian, out of jail a few years back. He was a suspect for a murder, but I dug up some evidence that pointed in a different direction. Rex told me to call if I ever needed anything."

"Do you think he can arrange a call with Derek Adler?"

"I hope so."

"So now we wait?" she asked.

"Now we wait."

Cortez listened intently when the overseas call came through, then said okay and hung up.

"Our buyer wants to meet in Cannes," he said to Sylvia. "We'll fly to Paris tonight or tomorrow morning. Set up the flights." He paused, then added, "Please."

Sylvia nodded, flipped open her laptop and started typing. Armand was on edge, and when he asked her to book the flights, he meant now, not in five minutes. Delta had a trans-Atlantic flight into Charles de Gaulle departing in three hours. She booked two business class tickets and pulled their suitcases out of the closet. They were already packed. She returned to the couch and sat next to him.

"Excellent." He leaned over and kissed her on her cheek. "Dimitri is on his way up. I need to see him before we leave."

Sylvia was already at the front desk checking out when she spotted Dimitri hustling through the lobby on his way to the suite. When he arrived, Cortez motioned for him to sit.

"Why is Janis Greco still alive?"

Petrov looked up at Cortez. "Tony rigged the gas line to explode when she turned on the stove. We went back later that night and the trigger mechanism was gone. Someone removed it and put duct tape over the splice in the gas line."

"So someone found the trigger on the gas line."

"Yes."

"Did the police or the gas company come to the house?"

Petrov hesitated. "Not that I know of. They could have been gone by the time we arrived."

Cortez gave him a look. "Do you think the police are going to find a gas range rigged to explode and then just leave?" He crossed his arms. "*She* didn't find it. That leaves her husband, Bobby Greco."

"Okay." Petrov shifted uncomfortably on the sofa.

"I'm leaving for France," Cortez said. "You need to hang back and take care of Greco. If he's with a woman named June Childers, remove her as well."

"I understand. What about Janis Greco, another accident?"

Cortez squeezed his fists so hard his knuckles went white. "I don't care, just fucking kill them."

Petrov felt his pulse begin to race. Cortez was dangerous when he was calm, angry was an entirely different thing. He wanted to ask about payment, but didn't dare.

Cortez eyed him like a cat would a mouse. "Two hundred each. When all five are dead I will wire you an even million."

"That's generous," Petrov said as he stood and backed toward the door.

Cortez gave Petrov a sharp glance. "Don't miss this time."

Derek Adler ushered the president's three o'clock into the Oval Office and retreated. He was up on the day's events, with one exception. Rex Blythe had insisted he call a man named Bobby Greco in Orlando. No other information, just that. It wasn't normal procedure by any means, but Rex had been adamant. He picked up the phone and dialed. A man's voice answered.

"Bobby Greco, please," he said.

"This is Bobby."

"Mr. Greco, this is Derek Adler. Rex Blythe asked me to call."

"Mr. Adler, thanks for calling."

"Of course." Adler voice was clipped and he tapped his foot on the carpet. Shorter was better.

"I have information concerning a personal issue in the president's life that has become a matter of national security. If the circumstances were to go public, the president would be completely blindsided. It could do irreparable harm."

Adler was momentarily set back by Greco's abruptness. "What sort of issue, Mr. Greco?"

"Not until I'm sitting opposite President Neilson."

Adler was almost at a loss for words. "You want me to set up a one-on-one meeting with the president based on *your* word that this information is damaging?"

"Mr. Adler, it goes far beyond reputational damage. This needs to be dealt with and my next call will be to the NSA. Where I go with this depends on you."

Adler's mind was churning. He had already run a quick Google search on Bobby Greco and numerous articles had popped up. The gist was simple—Greco had killed a man in Orlando and been booted off the police force. Still, the request to take this call had come from Rex Blythe, and the man was solid. "What do you propose, Mr. Greco?"

"To meet privately with him," Bobby said. "Within the next twenty-four hours."

Adler was teetering. "I can't just break the president's appointments, some of them set months ago, so he can take a private meeting with you."

Bobby needed to close the deal. "Okay, it's your call. Just be aware that I've recorded this conversation."

"Give me something, Mr. Greco."

"It concerns an affair and a rogue arms dealer, both with direct ties to President Neilson."

Adler felt the color drain from his face. "I tell you what," he said slowly, thinking on his feet. "Get to D.C. and I'll see you tomorrow. If I'm convinced the president should talk with you, I'll arrange five minutes. That's the best I can do."

"That will be fine. What time tomorrow?"

Adler checked his schedule. "Eleven o'clock."

"I'll be there. And I'll have an associate with me."

"What's his name?"

"*Her* name is June Childers. She's NSA."

There was a brief pause and Bobby could hear Adler's fingers on his keyboard. "Fine. I'll see you tomorrow morning. I'll advise security you have a meeting with me."

Bobby touched the end button on his phone and grinned at June. "We're in."

chapter thirty-three

Tony DaSilva took the contract on Janis Greco and her family, and Roberto Juarez was tasked with killing Bobby and June.

Armand and Sylvia had already departed for Paris, leaving Dimitri and his crew to clean up the loose ends in Orlando. To remain inconspicuous they checked out of their current hotel, then registered at the Embassy Suites south of the Altamonte Mall. Tony and Roberto shared a business suite in the wing overlooking the atrium, and once they were settled in they got to work.

Within a couple of hours Tony DaSilva had set up a tracking system that would send him an alert when anyone with the last name of Greco moved through an airport or bus depot in Florida. Car rental agencies and cruise ships were easy, and while few people traveled by train, he was watching there as well. He also ran a surveillance bot on Janis Greco, although he held little hope of getting a hit. He tied a simple cross-correlation program into the credit card networks that would tell him if she used her charge cards. Once he had everything running smoothly, he went to Roberto's room and put the same programs on his partner's computers, this time using Robert Greco and June Childers as the keywords. He switched on the printers and poured a drink.

"Cortez will go ballistic if we miss again," he said to Roberto.

Juarez nodded. "No shit. We have to find them." He glanced at the screen. "Will this work?"

"Oh, yeah," Tony said. "People on the run are careful, but they make mistakes. Only professionals don't screw up. She's an amateur."

There was a knock on the door and their hands instinctively went for their guns. DaSilva moved quietly to the washroom while Roberto answered the door. It was Dimitri Petrov. The men relaxed and let him in.

Cortez had called Dimitri from the business class section of the aircraft, his mood considerably improved. When he first arrived in Orlando, Ryan Chamberlain was alive and Synergy was an impenetrable fortress with the JASSM technology securely locked inside. Cortez was feeling that he had pulled off the impossible. Monique now controlled the Chamberlain fortune and the missile technology was safely tucked in the laptop bag under the seat ahead of him.

For good measure, Cortez had decided to up the ante for Greco and his ex-wife. The kitty stood at half a million dollars each and Dimitri was at the hotel to deliver the good news.

"Armand called from the plane," Dimitri said, accepting a cold beer and a cigarette. Both men watched him closely as he lit up. "He's now paying half a million each for Greco and his ex-wife."

"Excellent," Roberto grinned, pounding his fist on the credenza. A beer tipped over and poured onto the carpet. He ignored it.

Tony pulled another cigarette out of the pack. "Such a tragedy, a woman and her two young children. And her being such a looker. Bet she's an excellent fuck."

Dimitri's eyes narrowed. "Just get it done. I'd hate to think of the consequences." He stubbed out his cigarette. "If you screw up, Cortez will send a team for you."

A heavy silence fell over the room, the soft buzz from the overhead lights the only sound. Roberto kept his eyes focused on his glass, slowly rotating his finger around the rim. Tony DaSilva locked eyes with Dimitri for a moment, then broke it off and stared at the carpet. Dimitri was only the messenger.

Dimitri swallowed the last of his beer. "I'm leaving early tomorrow morning. You know how to contact me. Call the moment the job is finished."

Petrov walked across the soft carpet to the door. He glanced back, but both men had their heads down, staring at the ground, deep in thought. He closed the door behind him and walked the length of the hallway, already considering who he would send if DaSilva and Juarez were to fail. He stopped at the elevator and stared at his reflection in the steel doors, wondering if he had always been so crass. In the time it took the elevator to reach the ground floor, Petrov had wiped any traces of doubt from his mind. He was a professional and his allegiance was to Armand Cortez. If that included the cold-blooded murder of a woman and two children, then so be it.

The generator was humming along and Janis Greco checked the fuel level. It was a touch over three-quarters full, and she switched it off, topped up the gas and checked the oil, then restarted it. She closed the shed door behind her, shutting out the noise, and walked down to the dock and leaned against one of the posts.

The early morning Georgia sun was just peeking through the leafy canopy across the river. Dew pooled on the wide leaves of the wild grass, then trickled down to the forest floor, and warblers chirped and swooped low over the water. Above the river the sky was turning deep blue as Janis turned and headed back to the cabin where Lizzie and Sarah were still fast asleep.

She started breakfast, using the provisions someone had left behind last summer. A few packets of porridge, some hardened brown sugar and rolled oats were all there was to work with. She boiled water and mixed them together, forming a sludgy looking concoction that she spooned out into three bowls. The girls were up, and by the time they had taken a trip to the bathroom the gruel had cooled enough to eat.

"This is more fun than school, mom," Sarah said, chipping away at the sugar.

"For sure." Lizzie spooned in a mouthful of porridge.

"You don't even go to school yet," Sarah admonished her younger sister. "*Mommy*."

Janis sat at the table, ready to address the injustice. "Sarah, it's not Lizzie's fault she doesn't go to school yet, she's just not old enough. She'll be in grade one in two years."

"And I'll be in grade three by then," the older girl crowed. There was no denying her the advantage of age.

Janis sipped on a hot cup of tea and pondered her next move, reluctant to drive into Ocilla, but knowing the trip was inevitable. The other thing she *had* to do was call Sarah's school and let them know the girl would be missing classes for a while. Sarah and Lizzie finished their breakfast, dressed and ran out to play. She cleaned the kitchen and watched her children run about the grassy field between the house and the river, having fun, completely unaware of how close they had come to dying or to what had brought them here.

"C'mon girls." She banged open the back door and stood on the porch. "We're going to town."

Tony DaSilva was monitoring the land line in the Greco house when Sarah's school called. They left a brief voice mail for Janis to get in touch and advise them if Sarah was authorized to be missing classes. They also left the school's phone number. Tony hacked into the trunk line that serviced the school and initiated a program to track all incoming calls. It didn't work on local calls, but he could identify any that were long distance and trace them back to their origin. Once he had the program up and running, he drove to the Greco house and continued his surveillance.

Nothing had happened since the previous evening, other than regular mail delivery and a man in his late sixties delivering flyers. Patience was the key. In time, the woman would make a mistake and then he would pounce.

He thought of the half million dollars and smiled.

chapter thirty-four

The drive from Orlando to Washington D.C. had taken almost thirteen hours, and both Bobby and June were exhausted. The streets were slick with ice and it was snowing lightly as they pulled into the city. Neither of them were good at driving in winter conditions and they decided to leave the car in a mall parking lot at the edge of the city and catch a ride.

They gave the driver 1600 Pennsylvania Avenue as the address and got a bit of a look for that. They crawled through the city, across the Potomac on the Memorial Bridge and into the heart of the nation's capital. When they arrived, June paid the driver and they trudged up to the security gate where an armed soldier was on duty and watching them approach.

"Bobby Greco and June Childers. We have an eleven o'clock meeting with Derek Adler."

The man scanned the sheet of paper on his clipboard, then drew a line across the page. "I'll have a car drop you at the west wing. Put your bags in the scanner and walk through the metal detector." They came out clear and he handed them two numbered claim checks. "You can pick up your things on your way out." His voice was polite but firm.

June slid into the rear seat of the car and Bobby followed. The driver left them at an entrance close to Derek Adler's office, and a guard accompanied them through a maze of offices until they reached a small waiting room. Adler's door was closed and his assistant poked her head in and let Adler know his eleven o'clock was here. It was four minutes to the hour.

Adler came to the door and waved them in. He was in his mid-forties and dressed in a tailored blue suit and Italian leather shoes. His oval face seemed cast in a perpetual frown, and he removed his wire-rimmed glasses after he shook their hands. He motioned to the chairs that faced his desk as he walked back to the other side and sat down.

"Mr. Greco, Dr. Childers." He nodded for them to begin.

Bobby started. "Is what we say in this office recorded?" he asked. Adler shook his head and Bobby continued. "The president has an illegitimate child."

Derek Adler's face remained a mask. "That's quite a statement. Could you elaborate."

"I'm working on an insurance investigation that led us to run a DNA profile on the claimant. William Neilson came up as a perfect match for the father. We are absolutely sure, with no margin for error that President Neilson has a daughter."

A touch of worry crept onto Adler's face. "All right, let's assume you're correct. It's damaging, but containable. What else do you have?"

"That's just the beginning," June interjected. "She's linked to a foreign arms dealer, murder, kidnapping and treason." She watched Adler intently, waiting for a response.

Adler stared across his desk at his visitors. He could read people and knew they were serious. He glanced at the open NSA file on his computer screen. June Childers, Cryptologic Scientist, sought after for her knowledge of codes and a capable undercover operative. NSA had inserted her at Synergy Industries to work on the Joint Air-to-Surface Standoff Missile. She was the lead scientist on the stealth software, and now she was in his office talking about an arms dealer. The two were most almost certainly related.

Adler glanced at Greco's dossier on his second screen. He was a different matter altogether. The incident of him killing a drug dealer during a botched deal was front and center. Adler set his jaw and looked up at his visitors who were waiting patiently for his decision.

He addressed June. "You said there are foreign arms dealers involved. Does this have ties to the missile you're working on at Synergy?"

"It does," she said.

Adler leaned back in his chair and weighed the pros and cons of what was in front of him. He decided the key criteria for giving Greco and Childers an audience with the president was Childers' position inside NSA. She was credible and had too much to lose unless they were serious.

"The president has a gap after this evening's function." Adler leaned forward. "I'll arrange for a short meeting then."

They both nodded they understood.

Adler said, "There was no record of you arriving at Regan National from Orlando."

"We drove," Bobby replied.

"I see. Check into the Hyatt Regency. It's in the four-hundred block of New Jersey Avenue. I'll call you between nine and ten this evening and give you an address. Also, I'm assigning a security detail and they'll be tailing you."

"Good to know," Bobby said.

Adler stood, but didn't offer his hand.

Bobby and June were greeted outside Adler's office by an aide who walked them back through the labyrinth of halls to the entrance. They were driven back to the front gate and they started on foot down Pennsylvania Avenue. They turned right on 15th Street and walked past the Ellipse to the Washington Monument. June twisted a bit and looked at his profile. She'd met a lot of strong, dedicated men in her life, but never anyone quite like Bobby Greco.

He felt her eyes on him and looked over at her.

"Let's just get through this," he said quietly. His hand touched hers and she held onto it.

Ocilla, Georgia is a clean, quiet community of 3,200 souls. No fake news, no mass shootings, no terrorists—just Main Street America—a place where people know their neighbors and outsiders feel welcome. That was the Ocilla Janis Greco drove into on Tuesday morning. She pulled into the Jiffy-Mart on the southern edge of town, unlatched the kids from their car seats and followed behind as they skipped into the store.

"Morning, y'all." The cashier, a woman in her late fifties, smiled as they entered. "Can the young-uns have a candy?"

Janis returned the smile. "Sure," she said. "And thanks."

She left Sarah and Lizzie with the cashier, pulled out a cart and started shopping. She moved up and down the aisles, waving to the girls each time she rounded a corner. The woman had found some puzzles for them to work on while mom shopped and they were having a great time.

When Janis finally pushed the cart up to the till it was overflowing with paper towels, spices, flour, pancake mix, sugar, syrup, toilet paper and fifty other basics that weren't at the cabin. As she unloaded, the cashier rambled on about how nice it was to see a new family in town.

"We're not staying long," she told the woman. The name on her tag was Barbara. "We're just visiting for a while."

"A long while by the looks of it, honey," Barbara said. "Where y'all staying?"

"In a cabin, by the river," Sarah said, looking up from her puzzle. "It's really neat. We've got a little dock for a boat, and..."

"Barbara doesn't need all the details, Sarah." Janis smiled as she cut off her daughter in mid-sentence. *No one needs the details*, she thought. The quieter they were about their stay, the better. "Do you have a phone I could use to make a long distance call?" she asked.

"There's a pay phone outside with one of those card reader things on it for a callin' card," Barbara said cheerfully, packing the groceries into paper bags. "I never could figger out how them things worked."

"Me neither," Janis lied. "I don't have a calling card. Do you have a phone in the store? I can pay you cash to use it. More than what the call would be."

Barbara gave Janis a second look. "Sure, honey. Why not? There's a phone out back in the office. Let's put these groceries in your car and then get you on the phone."

"Thanks." Janis handed Barbara cash for the groceries. "Thanks a lot, I'll be quick."

chapter thirty-five

Derek Adler called Bobby's hotel room with specific instructions. Be at Gourmet Coffee Company on Columbia Street at ten past eleven. Come by cab and stop across the street, the driver is not to wait. Keep both hands in plain sight while crossing the road. And finally, do not enter the coffee shop if another vehicle is driving by. Wait until the street is empty. Bobby jotted the instructions down as Adler gave them. He acknowledged that he understood and hung up.

"There it is," he said. "A private audience with the president." The reality of it was sinking in. They were about to have a clandestine meeting with the most powerful man on the planet. He held his hands out in front of him. He was shaking.

"Intimidating, isn't it," June said, perching on the edge of the sofa. She was sipping hot chocolate and absentmindedly flipping through a visitor's book the hotel provided for its guests.

"Yes," Bobby admitted. "I've never met anyone this important."

"I met him once," June said, looking up at him. "Not like this, of course, but I had the opportunity to shake his hand."

"Where was that?" Bobby asked, dropping onto the couch next to her.

"An NSA function. He was in Baltimore for a meet-and-greet with some department heads. He actually stopped and spoke with me for a minute."

"That doesn't surprise me. I'm sure you were the best-looking rocket scientist at the ball."

She grinned, and even blushed a touch.

At a quarter to eleven, Bobby and June slid into the backseat of a cab and gave the driver the address on Columbia. She asked him to pace the trip to arrive as close to eleven-ten as possible. Right to the minute meant a larger tip. The man smiled and told them he could get it to the second if that was better.

Columbia Street was dark when the car pulled up across from the Gourmet Coffee Company. The businesses were shut for the night and a *Closed* sign hung in the coffee shop window. Inside, there was a single light on near the front of the shop. June paid the driver, and when the road was deserted they crossed. They entered a small foyer and the door swung shut behind them. Inside, they were met by a man and woman, both with earpieces. Secret service.

"Bobby Greco?" the woman asked. It wasn't really a question. She already knew.

"Yes."

"Could you and Dr. Childers take off your coats, please." Her voice was civil, but there was no mistaking that when she asked them to do something, they were going to do it.

They slipped out of their coats and handed them to the agent. The woman patted Bobby and June down thoroughly, then directed them toward the rear of the café. It took their eyes a moment to adjust as they walked across the old softwood floor, the boards creaking as they made their way. There were two men sitting at a table against the back wall, one of them was Derek Adler, the other was William Neilson.

"Good evening, Mr. Greco, Dr. Childers," the president said. His voice was subdued, quiet even. Neilson looked every part the president, attired in his usual dark blue suit. His eyes were intelligent, but tired.

"Good evening, sir," Bobby answered as he took a seat. June's voice mirrored his a second later.

"You have some very interesting news." The president took a sip of coffee and said, "Go ahead."

Bobby had replayed his opening line a hundred times in his mind. It needed to grab the president's attention without being crass or theatric. He cleared his throat and said, "This all starts with Sylvia Dupres."

Neilson's face barely changed. "Continue."

"We know that you had a relationship with her thirty-six years ago. Sometime in October of 1982, when you were in the Senate."

The president's face took on a distinct red hue, but he remained silent.

"Sir, your time together..." Bobby fidgeted in his seat. "She had a baby girl."

"Derek mentioned that." Neilson took a deep breath, then asked quietly, "Who is she?"

"Alexis Chamberlain."

The president shot Adler a look, who gave a slight shrug of his shoulders. Neilson turned back to Bobby and shook his head. "I've known Alexis Chamberlain and her parents all my life. She's a Rothchild."

"She's adopted," Bobby said.

Half a minute passed, then Neilson said mostly to himself, "*Alexis*."

He got up from the table and walked to the front of the café, his back to everyone. Clearly, he was letting the shock dissipate. When he returned, he said, "This doesn't add up. Sylvia would have had her hand out. And Alexis, she'd never be involved in something like this."

Neilson looked at June for an explanation, but everything stopped while an agent escorted the café owner into the room. He poured fresh coffee and was promptly led out.

"There's more," June said.

The president pulled up a chair between Bobby and June. "I'm listening."

"Sylvia Dupres had twins. Alexis has an identical twin." June stopped for a moment to give him a chance to take it all in, then continued. "There's no birth record for the twin. No one but Sylvia and the midwife know she exists."

The president stared at her, his mouth open ever so slightly as the scope of the problem hit him. Finally he wet his lips with his tongue, took a drink of coffee and said, "And you figured this all out...how?"

June gestured to Bobby, who shifted in his seat to face Neilson. "I was working a routine insurance investigation and it became apparent there were changes in Alexis's behavior after her husband died.

Idiosyncrasies that seemed off to me. Eventually June and I figured out that Ryan Chamberlain had been murdered, and we started taking a closer look at Alexis."

The president held up his hand. "Ryan Chamberlain died of a heart attack."

"No, sir, he was fed a lethal dose of Verapamil."

"Verapamil?" the president asked.

"It's a drug used to treat angina and irregular heartbeat," June replied. "In a concentrated form it can bring on a heart attack."

"Why didn't this show up on the autopsy report?"

"He died in a room full of prominent doctors, and two of them pronounced him dead of a heart attack on the spot. The doctors put pressure on the ME's office to not run a toxicology scan."

Neilson glanced at June, then looked back to Bobby. "What else?"

"We're quite sure that this man," Bobby slipped his hand inside his jacket and pulled out the photo of Armand Cortez, "is working with Sylvia Dupres and they are behind everything. We have DNA evidence that proves the woman running Synergy isn't Alexis. The only possible explanation is that her twin has taken her place."

June held up the reports from Brad Lawrence. "It's all in here," she said.

Adler stepped forward, took the file and quickly flipped through it.

"How sure are you of all this?" the president asked.

"Positive," Bobby answered. "There is zero room for error."

Neilson looked at Adler, who had a very worried expression on his face. Neilson sucked in a deep breath and rubbed his fingers on his temples. He closed his eyes and took a minute to piece it together. If what Bobby Greco was saying was right, then Alexis had lost control of the Chamberlain fortune and Synergy Industries. The woman now in charge was his daughter, and a killer. Alexis Chamberlain, his other child, was missing. It seemed impossible, a bad dream. He opened his eyes, but the room hadn't changed. Bobby and June were still there, silent and waiting for his response.

"Synergy," the president said quietly. "Our contractor for the stealth version of the JASSM missile."

June answered. "It's why we're here, Mr. President."

The room was so quiet Bobby could hear everyone breathing.

"Who is *this* man?" Neilson pointed to the picture of Cortez that Bobby had set on the rough wooden table.

"Armand Cortez, a known arms dealer," June said.

Neilson looked again at Adler, who said, "Cortez is high on our list, but until Mr. Greco snapped this, we didn't have a decent picture of him."

"Then how did you identify him?" Neilson asked.

"The NSA computers matched this photo to a grainy, twenty-year-old one on file," June said.

Neilson drew a hand across his brow and set his elbow on the table, his face etched with concern. No one spoke for a minute. Finally Neilson said, "Who else knows what you've told me tonight?"

"Malcolm Cook over at the Medical Examiner's Office," Bobby replied. "He ran the toxicology screen on Ryan Chamberlain. Brad Lawrence, a scientist at NSA who took care of the DNA profiles and identified Armand Cortez. Cortez and Dupres, of course, and they're not working alone. Someone tried to blow up my house and kill my wife and kids yesterday."

"What?" the president asked, yet more concern washing across his face. "Are they all right?"

"They are, for now at least," Bobby said.

"Well thank God for that." Neilson leaned forward in his chair. "This is…" he let the sentence trail off, then added, "…ugly."

A lengthy silence followed, then June said, "We have to stop Cortez from selling the JASSM technology. He has the stealth version of the missile."

"Leave that with us," Adler cut in. He had regained his composure, and his eyes were sharp and focused. "Do you have any idea where Cortez is right now?"

Bobby shook his head. "No, we don't. That's not the only reason we have to move quickly."

The president nodded. "Alexis."

"Do you have any idea where she is, or if she's even alive?" Adler asked.

"No."

Neilson looked at Bobby and June. "Is there anything else?"

"That's the gist of it, sir."

Adler stepped in, signaling the end of the meeting, and Neilson rose. He shook both their hands. "We'll be in touch."

Adler ushered the president through the rear door, the secret service detail in tow after taking the cup and spoon the president had used. Bobby and June were left in the dimly-lit café while the owner came out to clear the table.

When they were alone again, Bobby said, "That was exhausting."

June leaned back in her chair and let out a long sigh. "I feel like a massive weight just came off my shoulders."

"Right," Bobby said, not entirely agreeing, but reluctant to say anything. The stress was pushing up his neck into his brain and his head felt like it was going to explode. Janis and the kids were top of mind right now, and until Cortez was reined in they were in danger.

They left the café and a cold wind hit them. They walked to the end of the darkened street, shivering, then a few more blocks before a cab cruised by. Bobby waved it down and they gave the driver the address to the Hyatt Regency.

"What do you think will happen now?" June asked.

Bobby shrugged. "It's up to Neilson. He's used to making decisions. They'll likely have something mapped out by tomorrow."

"You know, I feel sorry for him. Two hours ago he was just the president. Now he's a man under attack from every direction. This will destroy him if it ever comes out."

Bobby nodded. "He has one thing to be thankful for."

"What's that?"

"He just found out he has twins, and one is Alexis Chamberlain."

"Yeah," June said slowly. "And one is evil."

Bobby looked at her out of the corner of his eye. "Well, put that way…"

chapter thirty-six

Neilson stared out the window as the presidential limo drove toward the White House. Many unexpected things came at him—it was all part of the job. But what had happened in the last hour was unprecedented. There were two distinct crises, and losing the weapon technology was the more pressing. If Cortez managed to get it to market, the buyer could use JASSM to start a war. But as much as he tried to keep it top of mind, the thought of Alexis Chamberlain continued to push to the surface. Right now, he needed Derek Adler's clear head to steer things as they moved ahead.

"We have two problems," Adler said, mirroring the president's thoughts. "The missing missile technology and Alexis. We need to handle them separately."

"What are you thinking?" Neilson asked, his face ashen.

"We bring in General MacIntyre and Glenn Taft to deal with the missile. Taft has the intelligence to track Cortez and MacIntyre can deploy a SEAL team to take him out."

"Taft is CIA," Neilson said. "You're thinking Cortez has left the country."

"Most likely. He's not going to hang around once he has what he came for."

Neilson considered Adler's suggestion. "Have them meet us in your office in an hour."

Adler nodded. He knew the lack of recording devices was the reason for the location.

The president continued. "After we've dealt with Cortez we'll have Taft hang back and tell him about Alexis. It's a job for the CIA."

Adler was already dialing.

The limo pulled into the White House and Neilson headed up to his private quarters to change his clothes and splash some water on his face. His wife was already asleep and he didn't wake her. He wondered how having a daughter from a previous relationship was going to sit with her, but shook it off. He didn't need any more problems right now.

When he arrived at Adler's office, all three men were waiting. Glenn Taft, Deputy Director of the CIA, was a trusted friend, while Mark MacIntyre was a career soldier out of the Pentagon with strong ties to covert military personnel.

Neilson sat in one of the chairs facing Adler's desk and got straight to business. "Glenn, Mark, thanks for coming. Derek, can you bring us up to speed?"

Adler kicked into gear and laid out the bones of the problem regarding the missing missile technology, providing both men with a comprehensive file on the issue to look through as he talked. When he was finished he waited for questions.

"Do we have any idea where Cortez is right now?" MacIntyre asked, holding the picture Bobby had taken in his hand.

"No."

Taft snapped a picture of the photo with his cell phone and forwarded it, then dialed a number and spoke quietly for a minute. "We have the computers running it through a facial recognition program. If Cortez got on a plane in the last few days we'll find him."

Adler made a quick note on his pad, then asked, "Can you circulate his name and picture to your field agents?"

"Already done," Taft said.

Adler simply nodded—Taft never missed a step.

"Well, we've lost a dangerous weapon," Neilson said. "What can we do to get it back?"

MacIntyre stood and walked about the room. "We're dead in the water until we know where he is. Once we have a target location, I can get a team in place in a few hours." He glanced through the file Adler had given him. "It would help to know who the buyer is."

"That's a limited list," Adler said. "Probably the Syrians, Libyans or the North Koreans."

Taft nodded. "He's not selling this to some splinter group. They couldn't afford it. I agree with Derek."

Taft's cell phone rang and he answered it. He jotted a few lines on a piece of paper and hung up. "Got him. He and a woman boarded a flight out of Orlando for Paris on Monday."

"Paris," Neilson said. "Can we expect the French to cooperate?"

Taft considered what the request would look like to the French government. "I think so. Keep in mind that we're on their turf and asking for a favor. They'll likely want something in return. I'll get someone on it."

"Mark, any problem getting a team to Paris?" Neilson asked.

"No. Trent Jamison and Kyle Andrews are available. I believe you're acquainted."

Neilson actually managed a smile. "Good men." The two SEALs had led a successful covert op into Somalia to rescue an American journalist. He had met with them personally afterward.

Taft's phone pinged and he spent a minute checking the message. "We've got something on Cortez. An operative in Magadan reported a possible sighting about three months ago, in mid-October."

"Magadan?" Neilson asked.

"Russia."

The room went entirely silent for a minute. Finally, the president said, "Add the Russians to the list."

"Christ, Bill." MacIntyre's voice conveyed what they were all thinking.

Neilson stood and the rest of the men were on their feet immediately. The meeting was over. MacIntyre grabbed his file and headed for the door, Taft behind him.

"Glenn, hold on for a minute," Neilson said.

Taft waited until the door had closed behind the general, then said, "Is there something else?"

Neilson pointed to a chair and Taft sat. "There is."

Adler spent the next few minutes on the subject of Alexis. When he was finished, the head of the CIA said, "You didn't know?"

Neilson shook his head. "Not a clue, Glenn. I got blindsided about two hours ago."

Taft stared at the floor, his mind racing. He looked up and said, "We need to find her."

Neilson's stomach was churning. "Alexis's safe return is crucial, but we need to keep a lid on this."

Taft knew he and the president were thinking the same thing—that the damage to the administration would be catastrophic. "Do you have any idea when she went missing? If she's still in the country?" He paused, then added, "Or if she's still alive?"

Neilson shook his head. "Honestly, we have nothing other than what Greco and Childers gave us. He thinks they substituted the twin sometime in October."

"All this because he noticed the difference in her tennis backhand," Taft said, shaking his head.

"That was the first clue he picked up on," Adler said.

"How many people would notice that?" Taft pursed his lips and asked, "What do you want to do about the twin? I realize she's your daughter, but she has control of Synergy. She could do a lot of damage."

"The damage is already done," Neilson said sharply. He took a sip of coffee, then added, "I need your opinion on that, Glenn. Do we pick her up, or leave her in place and hope she leads us to Cortez?"

Taft had already considered both options. "Leave her. We'll keep tabs on what she is doing at Synergy, watch her email, tap her phone, tail her—she may give us Cortez. If we scoop her up, Cortez will know we're onto him and burrow in even deeper. Plus, if she stays where she is, we don't need to explain anything."

Neilson nodded. "Derek, what do you think?"

"I agree with Glenn."

"All right," Neilson said. "We leave her where she is. How soon can you get some warm bodies searching for Alexis?"

Taft was careful with his reply. "Obviously, you want this to be a covert operation," he said, then continued when the president nodded. "That ties my hands a bit, as I need to be very selective of who I put on it. Still, we can be up and running by noon today. No stone unturned, Bill."

"Thanks, Glenn." Neilson stood, then asked, "What about your man in Magadan? The one who put in the report about spotting Cortez."

Taft shrugged. "He's in Siberia for a reason."

Taft slipped a paper out of a thin pile and double-checked an entry. "Our intel has Cortez in Orlando during that time, so I wouldn't put much stock in it. But…" Taft tapped the file on Bobby Greco, which was sitting on Adler's desk. "He's sharp, it couldn't hurt."

After Taft left, Neilson dropped into one of Adler's chairs. "Jesus, what a night."

"It's a mess," Adler agreed.

Neilson reached out and picked up Bobby's file and flipped through it. "What do you think?"

"His solve rate with Orlando Homicide was at the top of the bunch. He's tenacious and observant. If Glenn isn't willing to put manpower on it, like he said, what would it hurt?"

"And Childers?"

"They seem to make a good team," Adler said. "Having an inside track at NSA without us having to initiate it would be helpful. I'm good with her."

Neilson set the file on Adler's desk. "See if Greco and Childers are willing to take a trip to Magadan."

"Yes, sir."

"And find out what actually happened when Greco shot that drug dealer."

Adler typed a quick note on his phone. "Will do."

Neilson started for the door, then stopped and looked back. "Derek, thank you for everything tonight."

"Of course, sir."

chapter thirty-seven

Bobby was in the shower when Derek Adler called, and June, already finished getting ready and waiting in his room, answered. When the water stopped she tapped on the door and he poked his head out of the bathroom.

"Adler wants to see us in an hour," she said. "You should hurry."

"Right."

Bobby shut the door and dropped the strategically placed towel. He rubbed his hand over his chin, feeling the morning stubble. He dried off, brushed his teeth and tried to get his unruly hair under control. He pleaded with it, told it he had to meet with important people, but it didn't care. He gave up and slipped into yesterday's clothes, then joined June where she was sitting watching a morning news program. She burst out laughing when she saw him.

"You could use a hair brush," she said, giggling. He looked hurt and she walked over to him, reached up and ran her fingers through his thick hair. She smiled. "Much better." She handed him a piece of paper with the address.

Bobby took it and entered 1811 13th Street on his phone. A pin appeared on the map just north of Logan Circle, about twenty blocks from the Hyatt.

"Did Adler make the call himself?" he asked.

"He did."

Bobby raised an eyebrow and checked his watch. "Still dealing with the A-team. We have twenty minutes."

"I'm ready, are you?"

"As ready as I'll ever be," he said as they hustled out the door and took the elevator to the main floor.

A cab was parked out front and they jumped in and asked the driver to let them out at Logan Circle. The morning rush hour was light, and after the cab dropped them off they set out down 13th Street at a brisk pace. A *For Sale* sign hung in the window of number 1811, an upscale attached home with gray siding and a bright red door. Bobby opened the wrought iron gate and they walked up the sidewalk to the front door. He knocked and the same security detail from the night before answered. After a quick frisk they were ushered into the living room, where Derek Adler was waiting.

"Please have a seat," Adler said, motioning to the sofa.

"President Neilson is very appreciative of your efforts." There was a slight pause, then, "And your discretion."

"Of course," June said.

"We identified Armand Cortez and Sylvia Dupres on CCTV leaving Orlando for Paris on Monday. Do you have any idea where they might be staying or who they are meeting?"

"None whatsoever," Bobby said.

Adler leaned forward and picked up a folder from the coffee table, then opened it and slid out a page. He glanced at it and held it out. June took it. "It's possible Cortez was in Russia sometime around the middle of October. It's a long shot, but since this involves Alexis the president wants it looked into."

"Understandable," Bobby said.

"President Neilson is looking to send you two."

June could barely conceal her shock. "What would that entail?"

"Traveling to Siberia for starters. We would arrange your transportation and connect you with the CIA operative working the Magadan station. You'd be mostly on your own from that point."

The room was silent for a moment, then June asked, "What about access to NSA personnel and computers?"

Derek Adler nodded at June. "You'll have top priority clearance to the NSA databank. You will report directly to me."

"I can't just go MIA," June said.

"I'll take care of that." Adler jotted a number on the back of his business card and handed it to her. "My personal cell number."

June glanced at Bobby. His face was awash with worry.

"Janis and the kids," he said.

"Is there anything we can do to help?" Adler asked.

Bobby had a pretty good idea how that would work, and considered the offer. Adler would set a series of events in motion that would eventually filter down to the local police force putting a man or two on Janis. That could cause more damage than good.

He shook his head. "I think it's best to leave things as they are. She and the kids are off the grid right now—no email, no cell phone and she's not using her bank or credit cards. Probably best not to draw any attention, but thanks for the offer."

"We don't need to do this," June said to Bobby.

He got up and paced about the room. *What am I doing now to help Janis?* he thought. Not much, if anything. It wouldn't really make a difference if he was in Orlando or Magadan. Janis was safe, hunkered down in the cabin until this nightmare was over. The faster they could find Cortez, the quicker she and the kids could return home. He made his decision, standing on the sidelines was out.

"I'm in," he said. "But I need to return to Orlando for a day or two before we go."

"That's fine," Adler said. He looked at June, who nodded her consent.

Adler managed a small smile and stood up. "That's great. Get ready, things are going to move fast from this point. Turn on your cell phones and keep them charged. You'll get a call with instructions." He handed June a thin file folder. "The information you need is in here."

She took the folder and the secret service ushered Bobby and June out of the house. Adler was right behind them and slipped into a waiting car and was gone. A black SUV pulled up and the secret service agents got in and it sped off. Bobby and June were left standing by themselves in the quiet street.

"What's in Orlando that you need to wrap up?" June asked.

"Cortez and his guys are going to be looking for Janis and the kids. I have a couple of ideas that might flush them out."

She looked worried, but tried to make light of it. "Well, don't get yourself shot."

"I'll try not to." He glanced up and down the street. "What now?"

She held up the file. "Let's find a place to sit and look this over."

"Right."

It took ten minutes to walk to the nearest coffee shop, and once they were settled in they scanned the half page report. The operative, codename Breaker, claimed to have witnessed Armand Cortez enter the airport bar at the Magadan executive terminal on October 14th. The agent said Cortez sat down with some men, ordered vodka, drank it and then left. Breaker was insistent in his report that the man was Cortez.

"Breaker," Bobby said. "They really give these guys code names."

"They do," June said. "The National Security Agency does, and I'm sure the CIA is no different."

Bobby shook his head. "Crazy shit, all this."

They poked through the rest of the file, but it was mostly on Magadan and what to expect when they arrived. The main thing they both took from the briefing—it was going to be cold.

"I hate cold places," Bobby stood and buttoned his coat. "Let's pick up the car. We've got quite the drive back to Orlando and the roads are crap."

June laughed. "I don't think you're going to like Siberia."

chapter thirty-eight

Deep in a restricted area of CIA headquarters in Langley, six men and two women were hunched over computers and splayed out maps of Paris. A tall stack of empty pizza boxes was testament to how long the team had been working on finding Armand Cortez.

Trent Jamison was leaning against a table in one corner, watching, his thick forearms wrapped across his chest. As a Navy SEAL, patience was one of his greatest assets, but even for him it was wearing thin. Almost twenty-four hours had slipped past with nothing more than the French authorities confirming Cortez's arrival in Paris late Monday night. Almost unrecognizable from the photo Bobby Greco had taken, the man now had a goatee and heavy, black-framed glasses. His companion was a striking blonde, but the CIA experts had dissected the airport photos and determined she was wearing a wig. Once they arrived in Paris it was expected they would again change their appearance. Tracking them with a facial recognition program was going to be difficult.

Kyle Andrews looked up from a computer screen, then walked over to Trent. "We need to get moving."

Trent, who was five-eleven and tipped the scales at two hundred, was a sliver shorter and lighter than Kyle Andrews. Both men carried little body fat and looked every bit the lethal weapons they were.

"Agreed," Kyle said. "These guys can pass along anything they find."

One of the CIA operatives, a tall woman with short black hair, pulled a sheet off the printer and headed their way. "This guy just popped up on our radar," she said, handing over the page.

"Thanks, Abby," Kyle said.

Trent and Kyle took a long, hard look at the photo and accompanying data sheet. The man had pale skin, black hair cut short to his scalp, and a mustache that curved down past the corners of his mouth.

"Lorenzo Missoni," Abby said. "He just flew into France—came in through Cannes on the south coast. He could be the broker Cortez is dealing with. This guy, he'll charm you into letting your guard down, then slit your throat before you can move. The man is a total psychopath."

"Probably a prerequisite for the job," Trent said. "Do the French have anything for us yet?"

"No, but they've entered the CCTV photos of Cortez and Dupres into their facial recognition program. Their intelligence agencies are aware Cortez has sensitive military information and what his intentions are. They want him as badly as we do."

"Can we stop the deal from happening by watching Missoni?" Trent asked. "At least we know where he is."

Abby shook her head. "That was our first thought, but we're not positive Missoni is the contact for the deal. If we key in on him and he's not the guy, we could end up with nothing."

"Where is Missoni now?" he asked.

"To the best of our knowledge he's still in Cannes."

"Okay, the focus is on Cortez," Trent said. "We should be in Paris."

"Already thought of that." Abby glanced at the wall clock. "Your flight is in three hours."

Trent felt a surge of adrenaline. "That's good news."

"There's speculation that the North Koreans could be the buyers," Abby continued. "They have fighter planes capable of launching the missile from high altitude."

Kyle nodded grimly. "Nothing good about that."

Trent checked his briefing file. "The data that was stolen from Synergy is on eleven portable hard drives."

"Maybe," Abby said. "I've spoken with our contact at Synergy and she said it would be possible for Cortez to condense ten of the original drives onto one, or even copy them to his computer. The most important data is the stealth component and it's on a separate hard drive that is impossible to copy or download. If they try, it will release a virus that will destroy the data. There's no way to circumvent it."

"Okay, that's what we concentrate on," Trent said. "Is there any way to recognize that drive from the others?"

"Yes," Abby said, pulling another sheet from the file. "It's labeled 03-417-J/S with a black felt pen."

Trent jotted down the file name. "If we get this one, we've stopped anyone from getting the stealth version of the missile?"

"Yes."

Trent looked at Kyle. "At least we know what we're looking for."

"Anything else?" Kyle asked.

The CIA operative shook her head. "Just to wish you good luck."

Trent smiled. "Luck doesn't have a lot to do with it."

Tony DaSilva's nexus picked up the long-distance call to Lizzie's school. He opened a reverse directory program and entered the number, complete with area code, and five seconds later the call's origin popped up. A Jiffy-Mart store on Raymond Street in Ocilla, Georgia. Tony pulled the address up on Google Maps, then zoomed out, reducing Ocilla to a tiny spot on his screen. He jotted down the roads that would take him there, then left the room in search of Roberto Juarez.

"I've got a hit in southern Georgia," he told Roberto. "I'm going to follow up on it. You need to watch the surveillance systems in case something else comes through."

"Yeah, no problem. I'll need a key to your room."

Tony flipped him the plastic card and left the hotel. There was no reason for an elementary school in Orlando to receive a call from a small town in Georgia. No reason except a mother calling in her daughter's absence. Janis Greco was in Georgia. She may be on the move, but he would find someone who had seen her and make them talk. It was something he was quite good at.

President William Neilson thanked his aide for the notes from the morning meeting of the appropriations committee. He slipped on his reading glasses and began looking over the document. He reached the fifth paragraph, then set the sheaf of papers on his desk and removed his glasses. He sat in his chair, his head churning. The past twenty-four hours had been a nightmare. His life had come apart.

Sylvia Dupres. 1982. The woman was beautiful, intelligent, and witty. He, an eager young senator, ready to change the world. She had enthralled him with her sense of humor, her easy-going nature, and her body. She flaunted it, wearing thin blouses and short skirts that drove him from temptation to action. When he finally succumbed he was discrete to a fault. Even his most trusted aides were excluded from the secret, and Sylvia had kept her end of the bargain, never revealing their affair. It must have been tempting over the years as she watched his rise through the American political machine, yet she had never mentioned it. For that, at least, he respected her.

Neilson felt his blood pressure rising. There was only one person who could have orchestrated something this complex and underhanded. His mother. He knew that over the course of his career Laura Neilson had pulled strings, protected him, caused embarrassing moments to go unnoticed, but he had no idea her complicity could be this crass. A daughter, and she had hidden her from him. His hands balled into fists, and he had to keep telling himself she was still his mother until the anger subsided.

Everything was falling into place now. His parents' friendship with Percy and Etonia Rothchild, the neighboring beach houses in the Hamptons, his mother always doting on Alexis. Of course she wanted Alexis nearby—she was her granddaughter for God's sake. He had always shared a great relationship with Alexis, and his mother had encouraged it. All those times, face to face with his daughter and never a word. He could barely control his fury. He picked up the phone and dialed a number from memory.

"Mother," he said when Laura Neilson answered. "I'd like to see you. I'll send a plane to Houston later today."

"I have an invitation to the Gallagher's tonight," she said.

"Phone and tell them you won't be attending. I need you in Washington." He was struggling to keep his voice civil. "Someone will call and tell you what time they'll be by to get you. I have to go now. Goodbye."

He was shaking with rage and could barely think straight. He had to keep it together. Dealing with the fact that Alexis was his daughter was one thing, but the other girl, an imposter complicit in murder and kidnapping, that was an entirely different can of worms. Christ, what a mess.

If the public ever got wind of what he had learned in that coffee shop two days ago, all hell would break loose. In reality, his transgression was limited to an affair more than thirty-five years ago, but if the press found out they would hunt this down relentlessly. His administration had handed the JASSM contract to a company controlled by his daughter—then had the technology stolen. No one would believe he didn't know he and Alexis were related. On top of it all was Ryan Chamberlain's murder, and his other daughter's involvement. That would sink him on the spot.

Bobby Greco and June Childers. Until two days ago, he didn't know they existed. One thing was certain—they could have sold the story to the highest bidder and retired, rich. Yet they had come to him and quietly explained that he had a problem. That, beyond anything, proved they were completely trustworthy, and now in addition everything else they were chasing a long shot in Siberia.

The teams were in place to handle both crises. All he could do was hope and pray they came through for him.

chapter thirty-nine

"I don't think they're keeping Alexis in Orlando," Bobby said as he drove past a highway mileage sign. They were two hours out and he couldn't wait to hit the edge of the city. The drive from D.C. had been long and his neck muscles ached. "She's too wealthy and recognizable."

"Still," June countered, "We know Cortez spent a lot of time here hunkered down in a hotel."

"They probably wanted to stay close to the twin." He shifted around in the seat, trying to get comfortable. "At least until she delivered the missile technology."

June stared out the window. "Maybe, but if they rented or bought a place, and kept her drugged in the basement, no one would see her."

"That's possible, but I think Cortez had this planned a long time ago and was waiting for the right moment to set things in motion. He would have made arrangements in advance to move her."

"Okay, let's say you're right. So what are the different methods of getting her out? Commercial air doesn't work. She would have to be conscious at the airport and that would give her an opportunity to alert someone. The same thing with a bus or a train. That leaves a private vehicle or even a boat."

"Probably," Bobby said. "They wouldn't want to cross an international border with her, like Canada or Mexico. That would be far too risky."

"Or Russia," June said. She unclasped her seatbelt for a second, retrieved a sheet of paper from her pocket and buckled up again. She smoothed the paper on her lap. "This report of Cortez in Russia could have some legs."

"It's interesting all right," Bobby agreed.

She took her time reading it out loud. When she was finished, she said, "This guy is adamant the person he saw was Armand Cortez, but that puts him in Russia. He can't be there and in Orlando at the same time."

"So how does Cortez get there and back so fast?"

June thought about it, then lit up. "Bobby, the twin is in charge of Synergy right now."

"She is. What are you thinking?"

"Synergy has a private jet. A Gulfstream V-SP."

Bobby snapped his fingers. "Ahh-ha."

She nodded. "I flew on it a few times with Ryan. It has a range of something like sixty-five hundred nautical miles, and it cruises at Mach point eight. With that plane, they could fly almost anywhere without dragging Alexis through an airport."

"Cortez showing up in Russia two days after Alexis was abducted is a bit of a coincidence."

"It certainly is, and they had access to the Gulfstream," June said.

"They would still need to clear Russian customs."

June shrugged. "Russian customs? No problem, Cortez has lots of money."

Bobby took her hand and gently squeezed it. "We'll get the flight records for the Gulfstream. That's good thinking. Stuff like this, it breaks cases open."

She stayed silent, enjoying his hand on hers.

A few miles outside the city, Bobby called Jacky Foster's personal cell. "I'll be there in about an hour. Anyone watching the office?"

Jacky was confident in her reply. "Nothing so far. I've kept an eye out since you called from Washington. It should be okay for you to come in."

"See you in a bit."

They pulled into Orlando under a deep gray sky that was threatening rain. Still, it was far friendlier than Washington and its snow-covered streets. They drove through the city to Bobby's office and parked a block to the south. He trusted Jacky, but Cortez's men could have showed up in the last hour. He scanned the parked cars carefully, and after a few minutes he was convinced no one was watching. They pulled into the lot and went in through the back door. Bobby took June straight to his office.

"I've been thinking," Bobby said when they were behind closed doors. "Cortez would never have tried to kill Janis and the kids unless he knew I was involved, but Jacky says no one is watching the office. That doesn't add up, unless they're monitoring it electronically, waiting for us to call and give away our location."

"That makes sense."

"So let's do something about that," he said, buzzing Jacky. When she arrived, he said, "Are you up for a little adventure?" He opened his desk drawer and withdrew his Glock.

Jacky's face took on a glow. "Hell, yes, Bobby."

"You got a vest?"

She nodded. "What self-respecting ex-cop doesn't?"

"Good, you're going to need it."

Monitoring every call in and out of Riggs & Company was boring, and Roberto Juarez was quickly tiring of it. He considered running out to grab a sandwich, but five minutes later he was glad he had stayed. A call from a blocked number came through the switchboard at twelve-eighteen. It was Bobby Greco and he asked to speak with Jacky Foster. Juarez listened to the conversation in real time, recording it in case he needed to replay it later. The message was simple.

"I need the plane tickets now, Jacky," Greco said.

"I'm leaving early today. I'd rather not wait around the office for you." Whoever Jacky was, she sounded irritated.

"That's fine. I don't want to come into the office. Where are you headed after work?"

"I'm meeting my sister and her kids in Wekiwa. You could pick them up there."

"Whereabouts? It's huge."

"We usually go to Kelly Park. The kids like tubing down the springs. You know, where the springs widen out into the lagoons," Jacky said.

"Yeah, I think I can find it," Bobby responded

"Just follow the river south from the springs."

"Okay. When?"

"I need to finish a couple of things. Give me about two hours. Let's say two-thirty. Okay?"

"Sounds good."

"I'll be at one of the picnic tables."

"See you at two-thirty."

The conversation ended and Juarez replayed it, this time jotting down the details. He glanced at the clock, it was time to get moving so he could survey the area and pick the best spot to wait for Greco. He opened a map of Orlando on his phone and located Wekiwa Springs State Park, a massive tract of land covering the better part of 8,000 acres. The north entrance was the best access to Kelly Park, and he entered the address on his phone. Juarez closed his computer and left the hotel room.

June caught a cab from Riggs & Company to the Orlando Executive Airport. She bypassed the main terminal and took the secondary road, locating the Synergy hangar without any difficulty. As the cab pulled up she caught a quick glimpse of the Gulfstream through the partially open outer doors.

"Could you park and wait for me?" she asked the driver, then headed in.

Synergy's waiting room was opulent, with a fully stocked bar against one wall and leather couches and chairs for sixteen people. A young woman in a business suit poked her head out from the back room. She smiled.

June recognized her from previous visits to the terminal and pulled out her Synergy ID, clipping it to her belt. "It's Leah, right?"

"Oh, Dr. Childers. I didn't recognize you." She came around the counter. "Can I help you?" she asked.

"I'm sure you can," June said, rolling her eyes. "I need to review the flight logs for the fourth quarter of 2018. Expense accounts not adding up."

The woman glanced at June's ID and nodded. "Of course," she said. "I'll bring them out." She disappeared into the hangar, then reappeared a minute later with a large black book and handed it to June. "We keep our records by the quarter, so this is what you asked for."

"Thank you."

June opened the book. At first glance it was Greek to her, but the closer she looked the more it made sense. There had been thirty-seven flights over the quarter, each registered in Zulu time and showing a departure airport and an arrival airport. The route the pilot flew accompanied each flight plan and was designated by V followed by a number. Flight levels gave the required altitude, and the pilot set the airspeed. She noticed that the flight plans were all filed through a flight service station, then the plan forwarded to Air Traffic Control once the routing was in the system. Now that she had the basics, she concentrated on the date. Her finger slid down to October 13th. Three flight plans were filed for that day. One was from Orlando to Seattle, the second from Seattle to Anchorage, Alaska.

She studied the Seattle to Anchorage plan carefully. Eleven minute after takeoff the Gulfstream had switched from Seattle Air Traffic Control to Vancouver ATC. From there it flew on airway V-440 over sectors in Comox, Port Hardy, and Sand Pit. Eighty-seven miles north of Sand Pit, Vancouver ATC had relinquished control to Anchorage. The Gulfstream landed at the Alaskan airport less than three hours after it lifted off from Seattle. One more flight plan was filed for October 13th. The Gulfstream was to depart Anchorage for Shemya, an old air force/army base in the Aleutian Islands. A separate flight plan was filed October 14th for the return flight.

June took a photo of the page with her phone and handed the book back to the woman, indicating the records looked fine. June paused near the door, then turned and asked a final question.

"Why would Synergy's jet fly to the Aleutian Islands?"

"I believe they were picking up assay reports and samples from a gold mine."

"They brought back gold with them?" June asked and Stephanie nodded. "How much?"

"A few ounces perhaps. They showed it to me. It didn't look like gold. More like dull yellow rocks."

June thanked her, and once she was back in the cab she unlocked her phone and opened a map of the Aleutian Islands.

Bobby circled the lagoons in Kelly Park, watching for activity near the ponds and in the surrounding bushes. The day was dull and hazy with a wind that stirred the leaves on the trees. The poor weather had kept most people from the park, but he could hear kids laughing as they floated down the nearby stream. Across the freshly-cut grass was a cluster of picnic tables where Jacky Foster was sitting, the airline tickets visible on the table beside her. She was reading a book and eating a bag of potato chips. Her upper body looked a touch thicker than usual and Bobby felt a wave of relief that she'd worn her vest.

Bobby stared hard at the periphery of the clearing. The trees were dense, but not quite as thick as a natural forest. He could see the outlines of kids through the pines as they walked their tubes back up the boardwalk to the natural springs at the head of the river. His sixth sense kicked in, and he had the distinct feeling that whoever was searching for them was here. He slipped the Glock from his shoulder holster, released all three safeties and checked the clip—twelve .38 caliber bullets were tucked neatly into the tight space. He snapped the clip back in and continued looking for someone out of place in the park. A person without kids, moving slow, watching rather than enjoying. Then Bobby spotted him.

Across the lagoon was a grove of aspen that almost hid the man's shape, but not quite. He was in a perfect position to take out anyone crossing the open grass to where Jacky sat at the picnic table. Bobby tucked in behind a squat evergreen and considered his next move. Darting out from the trees and rushing the man was foolhardy. If he moved to the right, his route would cross the river and then two lagoons. It was too long and complicated and he decided to head to his left. The distance was shorter, but the tree cover wasn't as thick. To take the man alive, Bobby needed to get within fifty feet, then get a bead on him and yell for him to get his hands up. It sounded good, in theory at least. Then again, everything always sounded good in theory.

Bobby crept back from the clearing, crouched and ran fast. His legs started to burn, but speed was crucial as the killer would soon realize Jacky was a plant. He was about three-quarters the way around when the man spotted him midway between two groups of trees. Bobby jerked his gun up into the firing position and squeezed off a round as he spun and rolled for the nearest cover. Three slugs cut through the underbrush, narrowly missing him. There was no sound from the other gun, it was silenced. Bobby knew Jacky would be on the move, running for the trees, and he raised his head slightly, then ducked as another bullet whistled past his ear. The guy had him pinned.

A small tributary snaked off the main riverbed and flowed just behind him. Bobby tucked the Glock into his waistband, rolled over a couple of times and splashed quietly into the water. It was just deep enough to cover his body if he lay horizontal and hugged the bottom. Tufts of grass and small bushes bordered the waterway, and he floated slowly downstream. When he reached the entrance to the deeper water, he clung to the side and carefully raised his head above the riverbank.

The shooter was looking north and moving stealthily through the thick grass toward his last position. Floating toward Bobby on the river was a group of six youngsters in tubes, no older than ten or eleven. They'd heard the shots and were looking around for the source. At any second they would spot him lurking in the water with a gun and give away his position. He had to decide whether to take aim on the shooter and yell for him to surrender, or to shoot. In a split second, he had his answer.

From his vantage point he could see the picnic table where Jacky had been sitting. The table was empty, and on the ground next to it was a body. It was Jacky. The bastard had quit firing at him only to turn the gun on a woman.

Bobby readied himself, then hoisted his body from the water, aimed and pulled the trigger. The Glock spit bullet after bullet, most shots hitting the target, sending the man into convulsions as the slugs drilled through flesh and bone. He tried to swing his gun about, but Bobby's aim was getting better with each shot, the last drilling into the man's neck. He spun around from the impact and went down. Bobby stood there, dripping, as the kids floated past on their tubes.

They stared at him, speechless. Bobby had his back to them and kept it that way as he holstered his gun and pulled himself out of the water. He wanted to check on Jacky, but he needed to get the gun away from the perp first, just in case. He ran over to the inert body and kicked the gun off to the side. Once he was up close, there was no question whether the guy was dead. Half his neck was gone and at least six bullets had torn through his chest cavity. Bobby turned and jogged to where Jacky lay unmoving next to the table. He felt behind her ear and let out a huge sigh of relief. She had a steady and strong pulse. He carefully rolled her over, looking for entry or exit wounds and found blood on her shoulder. When he peeled away her shirt he saw that the bullet had missed the vest by an inch and gone right through her shoulder. He set her gently on the ground and ran to the river. He cupped his hands and filled them with water, then hurried back and dumped the water on her face. She woke, clutching at her shoulder and gasping in pain.

"Thank God," Bobby said.

"What happened?" Jacky asked, her fingers instinctively going to where the bullet had ripped through her shoulder.

"Looks like you took a bullet in your shoulder and smacked your head on the table on the way down. It must have knocked you out." He helped prop her up. "There are going to be cops everywhere in the next five minutes. If you can move, we need to get out of here."

"I think I can."

Bobby helped Jacky to her feet and they made for a thick grove of trees. In the distance, sirens cut through the humid air, and by the time they reached Bobby's BMW, the police were arriving and racing into the park from the north. Bobby had Jacky lie flat in the rear seat and they slipped out of Kelly Park the back way without being stopped. Once on the freeway, Bobby placed a call to Derek Adler in Washington.

"You may want to get some friendly faces down to Kelly Park in Orlando," he said as he drove. "I just killed one of Cortez's men."

"Oh, Christ." Adler was silent for a minute, then he said, "I have someone I can call. I'll take care of it."

"I need some medical attention," Bobby said.

"You're shot?" Adler sounded worried.

"Not me. One of my associates. Can you help?"

Again, silence. Then, "There's a Dr. Roger Amhurst in Lake Mary. It's close to Kelly Park. Can you get over there in time?"

Bobby glanced back at Jacky. She was breathing steady and had decent color in her cheeks. "I can. What's the address?" Bobby keyed it into his phone as he drove, then cut onto the 436, and headed for the I-4. Even with Orlando nearing rush hour he was making good time. "That must be quite the Rolodex you have, Derek."

"Call me when you get there, Bobby. I need to know what's going on."

Bobby sped through the city, his mind racing. He'd just killed a man, Jacky was shot, Janis and the kids were in hiding, and he and June were pitted against an international arms dealer. The whole thing was spinning out of control.

chapter forty

Paris was basking under an unseasonably warm spell, melting every trace of snow and sending Parisians into the streets with spring on their minds. People were cheerful and drinks were flowing freely in the bars. Mopeds zipped through the traffic as on a summer day and lovers strolled through the Cité, Armand and Sylvia among them, holding hands and blending in with the masses.

They meandered to the tip of the Cité, then angled north across Pont Neuf and along the southern edge of the Louvre, past the burned out nave of Notre Dame. There was a touch of sadness to their step, and not just because of the loss of the cathedral in the fire. In a few days Cortez would close his final deal and they would leave their home behind. Caution dictated it.

Cortez knew there were three distinct ways the end of the deal could play out. By some miracle, Monique could remain in Orlando and live her life out as Alexis. Cortez gave that about a one percent chance of happening. Greco and Childers were already poking around and the house of cards was sure to come crashing down at some point. Another possibility was that Monique overstayed her welcome and ended up in an American prison. She was thriving on the prestige and status of being Alexis, and he gave that about a twenty percent chance. The third and most likely scenario was that Monique continued to drain the Chamberlain fortune until the last possible moment, then made a run for it. That would leave Alexis dead and Monique taking over his business. His money was on that.

"I'm ready for all of this to be over," he said. "Monique will do well once I'm out."

Sylvia pulled him close as they walked. "It's not the career I would have picked for her."

Armand smiled. "She's damn good at it. No one is going to push her around."

"You're going to have a lot of time on your hands," Sylvia said.

"Maybe I'll learn to golf." He winked at her.

Sylvia laughed. "Right, you on a golf course."

Cortez looked at his phone as it vibrated, it was Dimitri and he touched the button. "What is it?"

"Roberto caught up with Bobby Greco in Orlando this afternoon." Dimitri hesitated, then said, "He didn't come back and he's not answering his phone."

Cortez stopped in the middle of the sidewalk, listening and running his hand over his tightly combed hair.

Dimitri continued. "So far, there's been no news coverage."

The implications of that weren't lost on Armand. "Someone is keeping it quiet," he said. They needed to focus on a softer target. "Leave Greco for now. Tony stays on the ex-wife and kids. When he takes them out, it will bring things to a complete halt."

"Agreed," Dimitri said. "I'll call when it's done."

Armand wanted to smash the phone on the pavement, but simply slipped it into his pocket, reminding himself the end game was still the same.

"Trouble?" Sylvia finally asked.

"Just some details that need taking care of." He glanced over at her and smiled.

Greco and Childers hadn't pulled Alexis's DNA profile for no reason, but it was impossible to know whether they had figured out the switch. One thing was certain, Monique needed to step things up, her time in Orlando was running short. He realized Sylvia was speaking to him.

"What about Alexis?" she was saying. "When can she return?"

Never, my dear, he thought. *Alexis is nothing more than a bargaining chip if things go wrong.*

Cortez took her hand and started walking again. "Monique is still siphoning off the money. Once she's finished and safely back in Europe, we'll release Alexis."

He felt the pressure of Sylvia's arm against his side as she tucked in closer.

"Wonderful," she said as they continued to walk slowly down the sidewalk.

Armand loved Paris and was thirsty for a last visit to his favorite haunts. He called the hotel and requested a limo pick them up—Versailles was at the top of the list.

chapter forty-one

It was late when Bobby arrived back at the hotel, having spent a few hours at Jacky's bedside. She had taken three bullets, two of them in her vest, and would have been dead without it. Bobby was still shocked at how things had played out, and when his alarm finally went off at six o'clock the next morning he was still awake, unable to sleep after the day's events. He knocked on June's door at half-past six and they headed down to the hotel lobby for breakfast.

"The doctor says Jacky should be fine," Bobby said after they ordered. "The bullet went right through her shoulder. It broke a bone, but nothing that won't heal."

June looked horrified. "That's good news—I guess." She flipped through the *Orlando Times*. "Not a word about a shooting in Kelly Park. Not even a tiny blurb tucked away in the back pages."

"I pump twelve bullets into some slime ball at mid-day in one of Orlando's favorite parks, and it doesn't make the newspaper or the television. How is that even possible?"

"Friends in high places," June said. "Amazing what that can do."

He straightened the cutlery on the napkin. "Tell me about your trip to the Synergy hangar."

She opened the photo of the flight log on her phone. "The flight to Seattle makes sense," she said as the coffee arrived. "Synergy has business connections there, but look here, there's a flight from Seattle to Anchorage. It doesn't make sense that anyone from Synergy would be traveling to Anchorage."

"Right," Bobby said, reading the next line. "And then fly on to the Aleutian Islands. That's even stranger." They were quiet for a minute. "What's the flight range of the Gulfstream?"

"Over six thousand miles if they keep the speed to Mach point eight or lower. The distance decreases quickly after that."

"They probably wouldn't need to fly faster than Mach point eight. What is that in miles-per-hour?"

"Six-hundred, give or take."

"What a machine," Bobby said.

June nodded. "I read the specs, it has a longer range than a Boeing 767, and flies faster and higher. It's quite the toy."

Their breakfast arrived and Bobby dug into his eggs and toast. He opened a distance calculator on his phone and used the app to measure the distance from Anchorage to Shemya Island, at the far western tip of the chain. It was around 1,350 miles as the crow flies. He set the phone on the table.

June finished the last of her orange juice and pointed at the image on Bobby's phone. "Are you getting anything there?"

"This may have some juice."

"How so?" she asked.

"The flight times from Orlando to Seattle, and then to Anchorage all look reasonable. But the one to the Aleutians doesn't look right."

"Why not?"

"The flights are registered in Zulu Time. That's airline speak for Greenwich Mean Time. They arrived in Anchorage at 21:00 Zulu, then departed at 23:00 for Shemya. The Aleutians are on this side of the dateline, so they would have arrived at 01:30 Zulu Shemya time. But they didn't. Their logged arrival time is 03:00 Zulu, and that's not right. It's out by an hour and a half."

June turned the screen slightly so they could both see it. "If the time increased by two hours Zulu, then chances are they made another stop."

Bobby nodded. "Let's see, Anchorage is about 61 degrees latitude. If we move another hour and a half to the west on about the same latitude and at the same airspeed, we get…" Bobby ran his hand along the map, across the northern Pacific, the Kamchatka Peninsula, and finally the Sea of Okhotskoye. He traced the line to the nearest point of land and placed his finger on the closest Russian city. "Magadan."

"Well, isn't that one hell of a coincidence."

Bobby's mind was racing as he spoke. "Okay, let's hypothesize. Is it possible to drug Alexis Chamberlain and get her onto the Gulfstream without someone at the Synergy hangar seeing them carry her aboard?"

"Yes, it's possible," June said. "There are no windows on the back of the terminal and the ground crew leave once they've fueled and loaded the plane."

"The flight crew," Bobby said. "They would definitely have noticed."

"Not necessarily. The pilots aren't employed by Synergy. They're drawn from a pool of pilots accredited to fly the Gulfstream."

Bobby was completely taken aback. "Synergy owns a plane without a pilot?"

"It's common practice," June said. "The plane is ready to go at a moment's notice, but there's no guarantee the pilots will be. They may have just flown the maximum number of hours and have to rest. FAA rules are really strict on that."

"But there was no flight plan to Magadan."

June shrugged. "Salaries and benefits for airline pilots haven't kept up with the times. I'm sure the pilots are well paid, but a wad of cash can be pretty persuasive."

"Okay, I guess. What about the cabin crew?"

"One person, and they could have requested that she not work the flight."

Bobby slowly nodded. "Then it's possible."

"Once Alexis is on the plane, they fly to Seattle and refuel, then enter Canadian airspace and land in Anchorage. No customs, no immigration, because they're still in America. They file a bogus flight plan, and instead of the Aleutians, they fly to Magadan. They must have had someone on that end in their pocket, or Russian immigration would have caught them."

"Could they have changed the flight plan while they were in the air?" Bobby asked.

June was on her phone and Googling ATC and North Pacific. "Aha. The entire north Pacific between Alaska and Russia is a blank zone in ATC coverage. It's monitored by AWACs, so yes, they could have received the new flight plan once they were en route. The Gulfstream could have flown into Magadan, dropped off its cargo and headed back to Anchorage. As far as anyone would know, the plane never left American soil."

"They brought back some gold," Bobby said. "Claiming that was the reason for the trip."

June was on her phone again, this time searching *Magadan*. The city's homepage appeared and she opened it getting a whole lot more than expected. Magadan was striving to become a tourist destination, but it was the city's history that caught her attention. It had been constructed back in Stalin's day to service the Gulag camps that housed Russia's political prisoners. An administrative home to mass murder, the port city of 200,000 on the Sea of Okhotskoye had been closed to all outsiders, including Russians, until the mid-1980s. Very little was known about the settlement before that, except that it housed a top-secret Russian naval installation during the cold-war era. June pointed to an article from 2001.

She read the entry. "*In November of 2001, Vladimir Putin officially opened Julietta, a gold and silver mine in the Kilganskiy Massiv Mountains northwest of Magadan. The mill is in full production and provides a major source of jobs to the local economy.*" She slowly turned her head and caught Bobby's eye. "Gold."

Bobby nodded. "And they returned home with unprocessed chunks of gold."

"What now?" she asked.

"Time for our lift to Magadan. Let's call our friends at the White House and see what strings they've been pulling."

chapter forty-two

Alexis Chamberlain stared through the tiny window out across the frozen valley. The wind was howling today, the worst it had been since she had arrived some three months ago. It whipped the snow into waves of white ice that froze exposed skin in seconds. Between gusts she could see a distant hillside and lone tree that were her only connections to the outside world. A noise at the door distracted her for a moment and she watched with detachment as one of her captors entered with dinner. It was the one called Ivan, the Russian. He smiled at her, his bad teeth showing behind thin lips. She ignored his attempt at civility and looked back out the window. She heard the door close and walked slowly across the room to the food. If she was to survive, she had to eat.

Her prison was a one room shack, about thirty feet square. It was built of decades-old wood, caked over with plaster and painted at one time in two colors. The bottom three feet of the room was dark red, the upper portion a distasteful shade of yellow. Heavily gouged wood pillars stood every ten feet, holding up the overburdened roof. Alexis lived in constant fear that the weight of the snow would cause it to collapse.

She sipped on the soup. It was better today, with tiny pieces of meat. Usually, it was little more than a clear broth. She dipped her bread in and chewed it slowly, willing it to fill her stomach. It never did. She finished the food and placed her cup near the door, hoping the men would only come in far enough to retrieve it and no further.

With the daily meal finished, she made a mark on the second post from the door. She counted the marks, one for each day, even though she already knew the outcome. One hundred and six. She pulled her sweater around her shoulders in a vain attempt to keep the cold away, and moved silently back to the window, looking for her tree. The white gusts dissipated for a few seconds and she saw it, one piece of green against a backdrop of swirling white. It was about halfway up the barren hill to the south of her prison, rooted in almost solid rock. It swayed back and forth, but never broke, bending with the forces of nature and surviving. Just as she was.

The rich bitch from Florida they called her. It didn't bother her in the least. She ignored them, knowing from day one that none of the three men watching her held any sort of authority. They were not the people that could release her from this living hell. That belonged to someone they called Armand or Senór Cortez. She assumed they were the same person.

It was colder by the window, and she moved back to the center of the room where her wood stove radiated some heat. She picked through her wood pile carefully, putting one small piece on and closing the door. The embers caught the new kindling and a small fire burst to life. The temporary warmth felt so good. She knew how to conserve her wood, a lesson she had learned the hard way. Her captors gave her a load of wood once a week, and she if she used it too quickly she almost froze for the last day or two. If she had any left over, they reduced the next week's supply. Today was the fifth day of the week and her meager pile was perfect, just enough left for two full days and no more. She curled up on the tiny mattress next to the stove and attempted to sleep. It wouldn't come. Finally she got up and walked about the room a few times, using the exertion to warm herself.

Of all the pain and humiliation she felt, nothing compared to the natural act of using the toilet. Alexis knew they watched, there were cracks in the walls and no curtains on the window. She always tried to wait until after dark to use her bucket. She lay down again next to her life sustaining stove, grateful that they hadn't tried to rape her yet. She knew that Ivan wanted to, but he wasn't the top man. Another Russian named Adnan was in charge. He kept Ivan in his place, and to some degree, her safe. His word was final, thank God. The third man, a European they called Lars, was seldom there, but when he showed up even Adnan cowed to him. He spoke rudimentary Russian with a Swedish accent, and when he visited they spoke English or French. She understood both. Lars was back now, and she wondered why.

They regularly complained about how long they had been stuck in this uninhabited wilderness, and how they wanted to leave and get back to civilization. On his rare visits, Lars reminded them of the financial rewards for watching her, and that seemed to placate them. He would stay for a couple of days, then leave, going back to the real world, of showers and central heating. That angered Adnan and Ivan, and they both drank heavily in the days after he left. Those were the times she feared most for her life.

She thought of Florida. Ryan, the children, their beautiful house, the life she had known. She replayed her last day in Orlando again and again in her mind—everything they had done, how she had held the kids close and wished them a good night. Her evening with Ryan at the club. The awards ceremony. The drive home and getting ready for bed. Then a noise, and slipping out of bed. What had happened after that was a blur. A figure, a blow to the head, waking up on an aircraft, a needle, and then the cold. Always the cold.

Alexis curled into the fetal position and tried again to sleep. This time, mercifully, it came. Her dreams were pleasant, chasing her children through the backyard to the lake. She finally caught them and they rolled together on the thick grass. A man appeared above her as she lay facing the deep blue sky. It was Ryan. Life was good again.

chapter forty-three

Friday dawned clear and warm in Ocilla. By ten o'clock, the air conditioner at the Jiffy-Mart had clicked on and was pouring cool air into the old single story building. Barbara Ziegler felt the chill from the overhead units and slipped on a sweater despite the sun shining through the storefront windows. It was a slow morning and she chatted with her customers, most of whom she knew, as she checked their groceries through the till, hoping the day would pass a bit quicker.

An attractive man in his thirties entered the store and walked up to the customer service counter. Barbara finished bagging an order and headed over to where he was waiting. He smiled as she approached, revealing even white teeth. God, she thought, this is one good looking man. He was a few years her junior, but what the hell. She still had a good figure.

"Hi," she said, smoothing her uniform. "Can I help you?"

"I hope so," Tony DaSilva replied politely. "I have a friend staying near Ocilla. She used your phone on Tuesday. She's a lovely woman, has two children. I just wondered if you knew where she's staying?"

Barbara thought for a moment, then snapped her fingers. "Yes, I remember. She was up from Florida, I think."

"That's her. She used your phone to call her daughter's school."

Barbara was instantly suspicious. "How did you know that?" she asked. Her tone had changed, now more guarded.

Tony laughed. It was an easy-going chuckle. "Call-display," he replied. "I was there, with the principal, when Janis called in. Your number and the name of your store showed up on the school's phone." He rolled his eyes back in his head. "Technology."

"Yeah, I guess," Barbara said. She felt foolish now that she had doubted him. "Why are you looking for her?"

"Janis is a good friend and she's going through some really tough times right now. I wanted to find her and talk. Give her some support, you know."

"Of course," Barbara said. "I'm not sure exactly where she's staying though."

"Probably in one of the local motels," Tony said, smiling. "I'll find her. Thanks for your time."

"She's not staying at a motel," Barbara said. "One of the girls said they were staying at a cabin by the river. One with a boat dock."

Tony tried to look mildly interested. "Any idea what river that would be?"

"If it has a boat dock, it would likely be the Alapaha. It could be the Satilla, but most of the people coming up from Florida stick to the Alapaha." She leaned forward. "It's not far off the Interstate. You turn off at Tifton and then take one of the little side roads. There are tons of them."

Tony felt a tinge of desperation creep into his voice and he struggled to control it. He knew if he pushed much further, she would begin to suspect and he would have to kill her. The last thing he needed right now were state troopers wandering about questioning outsiders. He backed off. "Thanks so much," he said. "I'll have a bit of a look about. If I don't' see her I'll just head back to Orlando. She'll be back soon." He watched the woman physically relax.

"Oh, I think she'll be a while. Her and the little 'uns bought a mess of groceries and supplies. She's at the cabin for a spell."

Tony grinned at her. "As long as she's safe, that's all that matters."

His grin was infectious. Barbara smiled back. "Right. Well, good luck, mister."

"Thanks."

Tony traded the air-conditioned building for the warm Georgia sunshine. He glanced to his left. Somewhere down that road was a turnoff that led to the Alapaha River, to the cabin where Janis Greco had holed up. Problem was, the countryside was chock-full of twisty back roads that led to hundreds of other cabins or just to dead ends. Trying each one was out of the question, he didn't have the time. He needed information.

Tony drove into Ocilla and located the Office of the Municipal District. He asked for a 1:50,000 map of the area, plus any building permits issued for cabins. Then he added boat docks to the list. The clerk was busy for almost an hour printing off the township plats and digging up building permits. Finally she stacked the results on the desk.

"That'll be three hundred and twenty-six dollars," she said.

Tony paid the fees in cash and left with the maps in hand. He checked into a nearby motel and got to work. He laid the topographical maps on the floor and started locating the cabins constructed with a permit. Then he added in the ones with boat docks. The exercise took him almost six hours. When he was finished, he sat sipping a beer and staring at the map. It was a daunting task, but the answer was in front of him. Which one? Which cabin was Janis Greco hiding in?

He decided to start with the ones closest to Ocilla and work his way out toward Tifton. Keying in on the lots with boat docks was tempting, but he knew most people built that sort of thing without the proper permits. The sun was dipping low and he turned on the television. Nothing was to be gained by starting out in the darkness. Tomorrow would be soon enough.

Trent Jamison and Kyle Andrews sat in the middle of a paper storm scattered about their Paris hotel room. They had checked the local hotels for all of Cortez's known alibis, including the name he had just used while in Orlando. Not one hit. Reports were filtering in from CIA, Interpol and NSA operatives all around Paris, still nothing concrete had come to light. The most promising item was from a French cop they had spoken to in the Versailles district. He insisted that Cortez, who had been wearing glasses and had a goatee, was with a woman whose description matched Sylvia Dupres. They had been resting on a bench near the Latona Parterre before walking down Royal Avenue to the Fountain of Apollo.

Kyle Andrews placed some stock in the sighting. Cortez's CIA file mentioned several times that he was a connoisseur of the arts, and *Castor and Pollux* was the kind of masterpiece that might attract him. Andrews went to work on it. He called the upscale taxi companies and limo services, checking their daily logs for Thursday. He got some hits. Six fares from different hotels had either stopped by Versailles or spent the day at the palace. Andrews left the hotel to track down the drivers, but after showing five of them the sketch of Cortez, he was at a dead end. He had one driver left, and headed out to meet with him.

Kyle called Trent as he pulled away from the curb and into the thick Paris traffic. "Anything on your end?" he asked.

While Kyle was chasing down the Versailles angle, Trent was out canvassing the concierge desks of Paris's five-star hotels with a photo of Cortez and Dupres. It was a long shot—the city had too many upscale hotels to cover in such a short time. Cortez could be anywhere, even at a converted country estate outside the city for all they knew. One thing was certain, they were running out of time and the link to Paris was getting stale.

"Nothing," Trent said. "He could be anywhere."

"Yeah, I'm 0 for 5 so far. Got one guy left."

"Good luck."

Kyle killed the call and concentrated on driving. He met with the final limo driver at a taxi queue on a busy street, but the man shook his head after looking at the picture. Kyle stood on the corner, listening to a couple of limo drivers complain about waiting around for hotel guests while they visited the sights. Some places they could get a coffee, others they were forced to sit and wait, sometimes for hours, without any food or drink. Kyle walked slowly down the sidewalk, thinking.

The street adjacent to Versailles was lined with coffee shops. The chauffeurs would have ample time on their trips to Versailles to hang out at their favorite café and get to know the staff. If Cortez *had* been at the palace on Thursday, maybe one of the café workers would remember a driver who had spent time waiting for a client. The more he thought about it, the better it seemed. Rather than try to find the specific hotel, he would find out which hotel limos had been at Versailles yesterday afternoon, then target those hotels. It was still a needle in a haystack, but the haystack was a lot smaller.

His cell phone buzzed with a text message from their handlers. *When you locate Cortez, imperative to find out where he is hiding Alexis Chamberlain.* Kyle texted back *Received and understood.* All they needed to do now was find him.

chapter forty-four

"Your ride to Magadan is ready to go," Derek Adler said. He gave June the details, confirmed that she had written them down correctly, then hung up.

"Adler has our schedule," June said. "We leave Orlando for Oakland at noon today." She held up the paper with the notes. "This is who we're supposed to meet at the airport. He said we'll find out the rest of the itinerary when we're airborne, and the CIA operative who spotted Cortez will meet us when we get to Magadan."

"Great," Bobby said, rubbing his hands together. "Which airline are we flying?"

"That's the interesting part," June replied. "It's FedEx."

"What?" Bobby stared at her. "FedEx?"

"FedEx." She was already throwing clothes in their suitcases. "Let's hope we have better luck than Tom Hanks."

"No idea what that means," Bobby said.

She rolled her eyes. "*Cast Away*. He ended up on a deserted island."

"Ah, right, but it was tropical, with palm trees. And you'd be there. I think I'd like that."

"You're impossible," she said.

Two hours later Bobby and June were hustling across the tarmac at Orlando International, surrounded by a fleet of FedEx giants, all in various stages of loading or unloading. The terminal manager, Alan Mackie, kept them close to his side as he wove carefully through the pallets being readied for shipping. They approached a DC-10, fully loaded and fueled, and Mackie waved at the ground crew.

"Is this the one to Oakland?" he asked the foreman, who nodded. "I've got two passengers for you," he yelled over the din of the jet engines. He held up a sheet of paper and the man yelled back that they had to hurry. Mackie pointed to the stairs attached to the side of the plane. "Quick," he said. "They're getting set to pull them back. Run."

Bobby and June ran to the plane, the stiff wind from the turbines pummeling them as they got closer. The stairway was already detached, and two ground crew members held it tight to the fuselage as they boarded. The co-pilot came back from the cockpit and met them.

"Hi, I'm Ron," he said, extending his hand. He pointed to a couple of seats amid the mass of cargo. "Buckle up, we're cleared for takeoff and there's only one bird in front of us. We'll be off the ground in about ten minutes."

Bobby and June thanked the man, stowed their bags under the seats and snapped the seatbelts in place. The giant cargo plane was already moving and lifted off into the bright Florida sky dead on its departure time. After a few minutes, Ron came back to check on them. He brought a few magazines with him.

"We don't get many passengers," he said cheerfully. "They're usually company bigwigs, so we have to be extra careful with our procedures. In fact, FedEx has a rule that no one rides with us unless they're employees. That makes you two quite the exception. You must have some well-connected friends."

"Yeah, something like that," Bobby said, grinning.

"Either of you want a coffee?"

"Sure," June said quickly, then added. "If it's not too much trouble."

Ron disappeared into the cockpit and returned a few minutes later with two cups of steaming coffee and a paper plate full of muffins and butter. Bobby and June dug in, it was after lunchtime in Orlando and they hadn't eaten since early morning. Their conversation quickly turned to Alexis Chamberlain. *If* she was in Magadan, and there was no certainty of that, how would they find her? She would be under guard—one man, two, three, more. How well armed were they? The only weapon Bobby and June had was his Glock 28, which Bobby was surprised they had allowed on the plane. Somehow, Derek Adler, or perhaps William Neilson himself, had pulled some huge strings.

They were part of a team now. CIA, Interpol, and probably a handful of other agencies all working toward two distinct endgames. The first was to take down Armand Cortez and retrieve the missile technology. The consequences of failure on that front, Bobby thought, were staggering. And while finding Alexis Chamberlain and bringing her home fell a distant second, Bobby was keenly aware of its importance to the man waiting in the Oval Office.

Cortez took the call from Cannes on Friday evening, tempering his eagerness as he listened to the instructions from Lorenzo Missoni, the buyer's agent. The exchange would be Monday, in three days. Once Cortez had checked into a hotel, he was to call Missoni and they would arrange a meeting place. Armand held the phone for a moment after it clicked and went dead, staring out the window at the magnificence of the Opéra. What was it like, to have lived your life creating such beauty? Such a legacy.

What was *his* legacy, Armand pondered. Wealth and power, a man to be feared? Bullets, tank shells, missiles, and land mines—he had brokered death on a massive scale. Now he had to kill yet again, this time closer to home.

Alexis. He felt no joy at the thought, but any other way was impossible. Lars was in Magadan and soon, when Alexis was no longer of any use, he would give the order.

chapter forty-five

Janis Greco perched on the edge of the dock, watching Lizzie and Sarah splash in the shallows close to the shore. Four days had slipped by since she had pulled into the clearing in front of the cabin with her sleeping children. Now it was Friday, and she was contemplating a trip back to town.

She wiggled her toes and the water rippled out from her feet, the tiny waves dissipating into the breadth of the river. These were days that she would never have back, and she wondered how many more would pass before this ordeal was over. Right now, everything depended on Bobby taking care of things, and that thought reassured her. He was so capable.

Lizzie came scampering over, insistent it was suppertime. Janis gave her a hug, perhaps a little too tight and a little too long, then retreated into the house and began preparing the meal. She looked through the fridge, taking stock. She had enough broccoli, tomatoes and cucumbers for two more meals. Everything else was gone. She would have to visit Ocilla by Sunday at the latest.

"It'll be fine," she chided herself. "We'll be in and out in a few minutes."

The meal came and went, and she washed and stacked the dishes, ready for tomorrow's breakfast. The children finally tired of playing outside and Janis read them a book until they drifted off. This part of the day was the worst. She was filled with worry and missed Orlando and her quiet life there. Hell, she missed Bobby. They were divorced, but that didn't mean she couldn't still love him. There had been plenty of men calling on her after she was single, but no one measured up to Bobby, with his quick wit and good looks. She sighed and pulled on a sweater.

The evening was clear and the sky filled with tiny pinpricks of light, each one a star. She was so small, so insignificant to the universe. Yet to Lizzie and Sarah, she was their entire world. The girls loved her and needed her. She had to get through this, if not for herself, then for the girls. Janis knew that Bobby would never have put her and the children in harm's way intentionally. Still, he wasn't here now and the burden of keeping the girls safe fell on her shoulders.

Janis returned to the cabin and headed for the kitchen. She knelt down by the table, over top of a trap door in the floor, and pulled on the handle. It creaked open, releasing a musty smell and revealing a dark hole with moist earth walls. She grabbed a flashlight off the counter, switched it on and took the narrow stairway down to the dirt floor. She knew what she was looking for and where it was. The beam of light cut through the blackness until it illuminated a shotgun. Janis tilted the light so she could see where to place her feet as she walked, couching to avoid the low ceiling. The gun was hanging on its rack and a stack of ammunition sat on a narrow shelf above it. Both were wrapped in thick poly to keep out the moisture. She took the shotgun and the shells off the rack, then climbed back to the kitchen and closed the trap door. She ripped the poly off the gun and pumped the forend along the magazine tube. The metal was dry and it slid effortlessly. She opened one of the boxes of ammunition and carefully checked the shells. The poly had done its work, and she fed six shells into the loading port and snapped on the safety.

Janis threw the poly in the garbage bin and stashed the gun and the shells in an overhead cabinet in the living room. She didn't like having a loaded gun in the house with the girls, but the fear of needing it had finally won the tug of war. Somehow just knowing it was there made her feel safer, and she turned off the lights and headed for bed.

If someone was coming for her children, they had to get through her first.

Friday night and the White House was quiet. It was William Neilson's favorite time of the week. His job was twenty-four/seven, but most of the west wing emptied out for the weekend. He took a deep breath and leaned back in his chair, alone in the Oval Office.

The president looked about the room—he loved this office. He hadn't even dared dream of it back in '82 when he had the affair with Sylvia Dupres. For all the hundreds of senators and congressmen across the country, there was only one president. Somehow, as the others had fallen off the path, he had held firm to his convictions and persevered, first winning the Democratic nomination and then the election. He had earned the right to live in this house, to sit at the desk and to govern the country.

Yet now, it all hung by a thread. He was guilty of having the affair, something he regretted to this day, but that was all. The rest of this nightmare had grown of its own accord.

Armand Cortez was in France, intent on selling top-secret American arms technology that could easily trigger a war. A killer, posing as Alexis Chamberlain was his daughter, and worse, she was complicit in the arms theft and the murder of Ryan Chamberlain. And what sent his mind racing every time he thought about it, was that the real Alexis was missing.

There was a soft knock on the door and Derek Adler entered. "Your mother is waiting upstairs in the lounge."

Neilson nodded. "Thanks, Derek." The root of his problems had arrived from Houston and he wasn't feeling very charitable. In fact, he was having trouble containing his outright anger.

Neilson shut down his computer and headed for the upper lounge. When he arrived, his mother was settled on a couch with a cup of tea and a small plate of biscuits. She smiled when she saw him.

"William, what is this all about?"

He sat in a chair facing her, unable to hide his fury.

The look on her son's face wasn't lost on her, and she crossed her hands in her lap and sat up a bit straighter.

"Alexis Chamberlain."

Laura Neilson, the untouchable matriarch of America's first family, had been caught. She didn't move, not a muscle, her eyes stayed on his, not giving an inch.

Neilson wanted to leap from his chair and scream at her that this was betrayal at the highest level. That no mother would ever do something like this to her son. Instead, he said, "Why?"

There was fight in her eyes. "It would have destroyed you." She reached out to touch his arm, but he recoiled and she slowly set her hand back in her lap.

Her coldness actually surprised him, and he stood and walked to the window in a last-ditch attempt to settle himself. "My career. You mean my career. You hid my daughter from me for my career?"

His rage was building and his hands formed tightly clenched fists. His breath was so short he could barely form words. "Were you ever going to tell me?" She didn't answer, and he said, "Were going to let it die with you?"

"William, look where you are." Her voice was firm, the same one she had used on him when he was a misbehaving child. "If your affair with that woman had gone public you would have been ruined. I did what I had to." She crossed her arms over her chest.

Neilson stared out the window at Washington's monuments, his fists still balled up. "The beach house in the Hamptons. The Rothchilds showing up at Christmas and our trips to West Palm Beach. All of it so you could see your granddaughter. And me, the patsy." He was close to exploding now. "All those times, but you couldn't be truthful. You couldn't come clean."

He walked back across the room and stood directly in front of her. "Sylvia Dupres, she played you."

A moment of shock registered in the woman's eyes, then the calculated restraint returned. "How is that?"

"She had twins."

Her eyes widened and a flash of panic crossed her face. "That's not possible," she finally managed.

He sat down on the edge of the sofa and leaned forward so he was only two feet from her. "That's why she insisted on a midwife. If she had been in a hospital there would have been birth records for both the girls. Then she took your money and disappeared with my other daughter."

The color drained from Laura Neilson's face.

"Identical twins, mom. Another granddaughter, and you didn't have a clue."

Laura Neilson slumped back in the chair.

"Oh, and it gets better," he said, his voice louder and crackling with anger. "Sylvia Dupres ended up with an arms dealer, and they've taken Alexis. They murdered Ryan Chamberlain and stole top secret technology that could start a war. Right now—right this minute—I have men in the field trying to find her, if she's still alive. And right now, I'm not all that fucking hopeful."

She was breathing hard, her chest heaving in and out. She looked small and broken, the fight gone, nothing left but a shell.

"Thanks for helping me with my career." He headed for the door. "Your flight back to Houston is waiting."

Near the Fountain of Neptune, a thick boundary of trees separates the palace of Versailles from a strip of four-story row houses. With their French Provincial façades, the coffee shops at street level are popular with both tourists and locals, including the limo drivers from Paris's five-star hotels. Trent Jamison was interested in speaking with those drivers.

Late Friday evening, he went from shop to shop asking the staff which drivers had come by on Thursday afternoon. When he had finished he had a list of sixteen, all from different hotels, who had stopped in for coffee while their fares toured Versailles. He pocketed the paper and checked his watch. Twelve minutes past eleven—too late to speak with the concierges working the afternoon shifts. He'd have to wait until the morning.

Trent called Kyle Andrews to check if his partner had anything to report. Nothing. They were spinning their wheels. Cortez could be anywhere. They decided to call it a night and met at a café just north of the Eiffel Tower to eat and regroup.

"Anything at all from Interpol or the French intelligence?" Trent asked when they were at the café.

"Interpol found a house he'd been staying at a few months ago. The lease is paid in full for the rest of the year, but he hasn't been there for quite a while. The French police have set up surveillance, but it doesn't look like they're coming back."

"And from the CCTV coverage?"

Kyle took a long drink of water and shook his head.

"They may have left Paris," Trent said.

Kyle shrugged. "Maybe, but the CCTV coverage here isn't pervasive like in London, and the facial recognition software isn't as robust. They could easily be disguised or simply avoiding the cameras."

"They're probably doing both," Trent said.

He pulled out the list of hotels and split it down the middle, then gave half to Kyle. Eight each. If that failed, they would have wasted two full days on another dead end.

They were losing Cortez, and they both knew it.

chapter forty-six

The FedEx DC-10 connected through Oakland and continued north toward Anchorage. The first leg of their flight had taken six hours, but they had gained three on the time change. Anchorage appeared below them, a speck of light against the pitch black of the northern night. They circled once, waiting for another cargo plane to land, then made their approach and touched down. The pilot taxied to the terminal and the co-pilot came back to speak with his passengers.

"They held the Magadan flight for you," he said, a touch of curiosity in his voice. "That's the first time I have ever heard of FedEx delaying a bird other than for weather or mechanicals. Your plane is two gates over. I'll walk with you."

June and Bobby followed the man through the fuselage and out the cargo door at the rear. A blast of cold air hit them as they stepped onto the landing at the top of the metal stairs.

"Oh, my God," June said, wrapping her thin jacket tight to her neck. It did nothing to stop the Arctic wind from attacking her body. She could feel her core temperature dropping as they hurried across the snowy tarmac to a giant MD-11, its engines purring in anticipation of takeoff. They were ushered on, welcomed, and strapped in as the aircraft was pushed back. Once the plane had reached cruising altitude, the pilot stepped out of the cockpit to meet them.

"Is that all you have to wear?" he asked after they had been introduced and all three had hot coffees in their hands.

"We flew out of Orlando about noon Eastern time today. It wasn't quite this cold," Bobby said.

"Well, if you thought Anchorage was cold, you're in for a shocker. Magadan is unbelievable."

"Colder than Anchorage?" June asked in disbelief. "How is that even possible?"

The pilot laughed. "It's possible." He opened a locker against the bulkhead and pulled out two snowsuits and sleeveless fleeces, all with the FedEx logo on them. "These are rated to minus sixty, providing you have the proper layers on underneath. You need a T-shirt, flannel shirt, and fleece." He turned back to the locker and dug out some mitts, hats and boots as well.

Bobby scowled at the gear. "I don't think I can move in that many layers."

The pilot looked serious. "This weather is a killer. One mistake can leave you exposed. If that happens, you won't survive more than an hour or two."

The pilot retreated back to the cockpit, leaving Bobby and June sitting in nervous silence wondering what the hell they were doing on a cargo plane bound for Siberia. June dozed for a while and when she woke she could feel pressure on her eardrums. The plane was losing altitude. She looked at Bobby and he smiled.

"You slept for a few hours," he said. "We're on final approach into Magadan. We've been dropping for about twenty minutes. Can you see anything out your window?"

June rubbed her eyes and looked out the small, round portal next to her. Utter blackness. She shook her head. "Can't see a thing."

The plane banked left and then shuddered as the landing gear dropped. June kept watching out the window at the endless void beneath her, then she pointed. "Lights. There, Bobby, I can see lights."

He leaned over her and looked out the window. Ahead and slightly to the right was a clump of lights in the rough shape of a lobster claw. They grew in size and intensity as the plane latched onto the landing beam and entered Magadan ATC. They were losing altitude quickly now as they cleared the Sea of Okhotskoye and headed overland, the runway lights rushing up to meet them. The tires crunched heavily onto the ever-present snow and then gripped the frozen ground as the flight crew applied the brakes and reversed the engines until the plane came slowly to a halt. June unbuckled and pressed her hand against the window. It was cold, very cold. She watched as a lone cargo mover pulled alongside with three men, all heavily bundled in thick coats and fur hats. They sat, waiting for the cargo doors to open, puffs of steam exploding from their mouths with each breath. One of them pulled a bottle from a hidden pocket and took a hit, then passed it to the other two. The cargo doors opened and the bottle disappeared.

There was a noise up front and they glanced away from the window to see the pilot, dressed in about forty pounds of Arctic clothing. He grinned at them from above the fur lining on the coat.

"Stylish aren't they," he said. "You two need to get into your gear." He looked at June. "Have you tried on the boots yet?"

"They're a bit big," she replied, "but I can wear them."

"Excellent. There's a man waiting for you in the terminal. We're going to drop you at the main entrance to Russian customs. Afterwards, walk all the way to the far end of the building. He'll be waiting for you there."

"Thanks," Bobby said, extending his hand. "You guys did a great job getting us here."

"Well, good luck. And remember, dress for the weather, not for style. Got it?"

"Got it."

The pilot escorted them to the door and cranked it open. An icy blast funneled in, immediately dropping the temperature by fifty degrees. Bobby and June made their way down the slippery stairs to a waiting minibus and jumped aboard, their luggage in tow. The driver slammed the doors shut, said something to them in Russian, and drove toward the terminal, where columns of steam and smoke were pouring out of the building's many chimneys. As they pulled up to the entrance Bobby touched June lightly on the arm and mouthed, *Here we go.*

They piled out of the bus and made a run for the warmth of the terminal, the cold air burning their windpipes and stinging as it hit their lungs. Inside, they were struck by the size and condition of the building. The tile floor looked new and shiny, the paint was fresh, and it was difficult to see the other end of the large structure. They stood at the entrance, looking for directions to the customs and immigration desks. The signs hanging from the ceiling were printed in Russian and indecipherable, and other than a handful of people, all staring at them, the place was empty.

"I don't see where we clear customs. Do you?" Bobby asked. He shouldered their luggage and started walking, and June fell in beside him.

"No."

"They probably didn't expect any passengers from the FedEx flight."

"Right," June said, her voice unsure. "I think we bypassed customs somehow. We're not in the restricted area. We could just walk out those doors into the city."

Bobby looked at the doors. He and June were already about eighty feet down the hallway, with nothing between them and the exit to the parking lot.

"Let's keep moving and meet our man."

It was warm inside the terminal and Bobby unzipped his snowsuit and tied it around his waist. The coolness felt better and they stopped for a second while June did the same, then trudged to the far end without anyone giving them much notice. A young woman, about twenty-five with shoulder length brown hair and prominent cheeks smiled at them as they approached.

"Hello," she said in English, her eyes sparkling. "Are you Mr. Greco and Dr. Childers?"

"Yes," June said, shaking the offered hand. "And who are you?"

"My name is Yulia. John asked me to bring you to the VIP lounge. It's this way." She pointed to a door that led outside. Her face widened into a huge grin. "You'll get used to the weather."

"I doubt that," Bobby muttered as he zipped up his snowsuit and followed Yulia to a nearby building.

She opened the door and ushered them into a warm and inviting space with what appeared to be original artwork hanging on the walls and a full-service bar on the far side. A man was sitting in one of the soft leather chairs and he stood as they entered.

"Hello. You must be Bobby Greco and June Childers." He was just shy of six feet, with a thick red beard and mustache. "Welcome to Russia. You can call me John."

"Thanks," Bobby said, accepting his invitation to sit. "We haven't cleared customs and immigration yet."

He threw them a quick wink. "They know you're here." He motioned to the chairs. "Would you like a drink?"

"Actually, yes," June said. "What do you have?"

"Anything you want, but I'd suggest vodka. It's something the Russians do well."

"Okay," she said, sliding into a chair.

John motioned to Yulia and she ducked in behind the bar to pour the drinks. Bobby took a sip, surprised at how smooth it was, and the three of them settled in as Yulia hovered close by.

"I take it you're Breaker," June said.

"In the flesh."

"Nice," she said, taking a sip of her vodka.

"My favorite brand." He swallowed the vodka in one quick gulp.

They spent the next few minutes on small talk, and Bobby was getting the sense the CIA man wasn't a *by the book* kind of guy, and steered the conversation accordingly. After a while, he knew he'd played it right when John started to open up.

"So here's the deal. I've been in Magadan for three years now and I actually like it. The Russians know who I am and what I do, but they don't care. In fact, I think it makes them feel important to have a live CIA agent hanging around."

"So they leave you alone?"

"Not really," John said. "They give me all kinds of useful information. Nothing damaging to their side, you understand, but still, things that are beneficial to Washington. We have a great working relationship."

"Is that how you noticed Cortez?"

John leaned back in his chair and took a long, hard look at both of them. "This is off the record."

Bobby glanced at June and when she nodded, he said, "Agreed."

"I never actually saw Cortez."

Bobby sat forward. "What?"

John waved at Bobby to relax. "Don't worry, he was here."

"How are you so sure?" June asked.

"Nikolay is a reliable contact who knows what's going on. He and I were at a café in town a couple of days ago when I got a text from Langley with a name and a picture. I showed it to Nikolay and he lit up like a Christmas tree. Told me the guy in the picture was the one who flew in on a private jet last October."

"How could he be so sure?" June asked.

"Nikolay was adamant it was him," John said. He lit a cigarette and offered one to Bobby and June. Bobby accepted. "Cortez had two other guys with him, probably bodyguards, and they stood out like a sore thumb. Private jets and rich guys aren't something we get a lot of around here."

"You knew about the plane arriving in October?" June asked.

John nodded. "Of course. I got to the airport in under an hour, but it was already gone. I pulled the CCTV footage, but it was parked too far from the terminal and the wind was whipping up the snow off the ground. Visibility was crap and I couldn't get the tail number."

Bobby was puzzled. "They didn't refuel?"

"No," John said. "A car drove out on the tarmac to meet them, and Cortez came in here with them for about twenty minutes, met some guys, then went back to the plane. Nikolay is pretty sure some money changed hands."

"I'm sure it did," Bobby said. He looked over at Yulia, smiled, and held up his empty glass. She headed for the bar. "What about the daily flight logs for planes arriving at the executive terminal?"

"Erased," John said. "I checked that too."

Yulia intervened as she returned with more vodka. Bobby thanked her and said, "Is that possible? To make a plane disappear?"

"Sure, if there was some money on the table," John said.

"So all that happened three months ago. Skip ahead to when you're sitting with Nikolay and get the text. What then?" Bobby asked.

"It was obvious Cortez was on the plane, so I responded immediately that we had a sighting. I went back over everything—time of day, the CCTV footage, the disappearing flight log—then I got everything I could out of Nikolay and sent a report to Langley."

June had excitement written all over her face. "Jesus, Bobby, if Cortez *was* here then it's possible this might have some legs. What now?"

Bobby shrugged. "I have no idea how the hell we're supposed to find her."

"Ahh, the missing woman," John said, then continued when Bobby and June looked confused. "I received a coded message yesterday. A wealthy American woman was kidnapped and her disappearance could be tied in with Cortez. Then a couple of hours later I was informed you two were on your way. Since things were moving ahead, I started poking around."

"Find anything?" Bobby asked, leaning forward.

"In fact, yes." He motioned for Yulia to sit in a chair near June. "Yulia dug up something interesting."

All eyes turned to the Russian woman. She cleared her throat and said "I have a friend in Magadan. He works at Julietta, a gold mine in the mountains to the northeast of the city. He told me he saw something strange up there a while ago."

Bobby leaned forward. "What? What did he see, Yulia?"

"One of the old camps, an abandoned gulag, had smoke coming from the chimneys of two buildings. That's very strange, because Russians don't like those places. We don't visit them or stay there. There's too much history."

"So there's no reason for anyone to be at the camp," June said.

Yulia shook her head. "None."

Bobby's mind was racing now. If John was right, they needed to act. He looked at Yulia. "This friend of yours. Could we talk with him?"

"Yes, of course," she said.

Bobby waited a moment for her to continue, but when she didn't he prompted her. "When and where?"

She glanced at the wall clock. It was a few minutes after three. "Perfect timing," she said. "We can meet him now."

"At three in the morning?"

"No better time." She rose and slipped on her coat and gloves. "Better put on your snowsuits. The last I checked it was minus fifty-two."

chapter forty-seven

Trent Jamison was on his fifth hotel when he hit pay dirt. The concierge at Le Grand Hotel Inter-Continental remembered Cortez after staring at the photo for a minute.

"I remember him because he tipped very well," the concierge said. He stared at the photo again for another minute, then nodded. "That's him, I'm sure."

"What name was he registered under?" Trent asked in fluent French. That question drew an intrigued look from the hotel front man.

"Henri Bouchard, of course. Who else would he be?"

"You'd be surprised." Trent leaned in a bit and read the man's name tag. "Did he leave a forwarding address, Francois?"

"Yes, sir. But that would be confidential."

Trent moved closer to Francois and took out his government identification. He gave the concierge plenty of time to study the ID, then said in little more than a whisper, "This man is Armand Cortez. He is a ruthless arms dealer who is wanted by the English, the Americans, Interpol, and your own police. If you don't give me exactly what I want in the next ten seconds, I will have every one of these police agencies crawling all over this hotel inside twenty minutes."

Francois looked unsure—and scared. "I don't know, Monsieur. We must protect the privacy of our guests."

Trent pulled out his cell phone, dialed and spoke in English. "I've got him, he's at the…" He stopped as Francois held up a hand.

"He's staying at the Carlton Inter-Continental in Cannes," the concierge said.

"I'll talk to you later," Trent said into the phone and hung up. "Anything else?"

"He rented a car here at the hotel. We have some high-end cars for our wealthier clients, and he took a Maserati 3200 GT."

"License plate number?"

Francois walked to the concierge desk and opened a binder. He ran his finger down a short list of cars, then stopped. "LC 235 50."

"When are his reservations for?"

"He is to check in on Sunday evening. Tomorrow."

Trent leaned close to the man again. "This goes no further than you and I. Understood?"

"Definitely." There was a touch of fear in his eyes, but mostly relief.

Trent left the hotel and called Kyle from the Place de l'Opéra. The phone rang twice and his partner answered. "I've got him," Trent said. "He was registered as Henri Bouchard at the Grand Hotel. He's rented a car and is driving down to Cannes. He'll be staying at the Carlton."

"Excellent, I know the place." Kyle's tone couldn't mask his excitement. "It's on La Croisette and fronts onto the beach. We should be able to set up surveillance without being seen."

"We need to get a flight out of here."

"I'm on it," Kyle said, opening his laptop.

"I'll be back at the hotel in twenty minutes."

Trent assessed the situation as he drove back to the hotel. Cortez had rented a vehicle in lieu of flying or taking the bullet train, which meant he wasn't in a rush to get there. Even with winter conditions in the Alps, Cannes was no more than a two-day drive from Paris, suggesting the exchange wouldn't be happening until at least Monday. They had until then if they wanted to intercept him in Cannes, but that was leaving things to the last moment. It would be better if they could take Cortez out on the drive down.

The route between Paris and Cannes started off with only one viable option. The A-6 through Auxerre and south to Lyon. Cortez would be on that stretch on the first day, but it would mean setting up a trap on a busy highway on a Saturday afternoon and the French authorities would never go for it. The better option was on the second day, when he would be traveling through the Alps. The roads were winding and dangerous, and fatal accidents more commonplace. The problem was, which road would they take? From Lyon, heading south, Cortez had numerous options. The motorway ran due south from Lyon to Marseille, but Trent discarded that idea. Cortez had rented a high-performance car to enjoy the drive, not to stay on a major highway. He would tackle one of the mountain passes.

If Cortez chose to drive through the mountains around Grenoble, he could take the N85 through Gap, a truly treacherous stretch of road, or the tamer N75. But even the N75 would provide an opportunity to run him off the road if they intersected him at the Col de la Croix Heights. The question still remained, which route would he take?

If they missed him, they would be in the mountains, cut off from Cannes by at least six to eight hours of driving time. No, the risks were too great. They had to leave Paris for Cannes immediately and set up operations close to or in the Carlton. That way Cortez could not slip past them.

He parked in the loading zone of the hotel and gave the doorman the keys. They were checking out.

chapter forty-eight

Yulia was a cheerful and energetic host. She kept them entertained, pointing out the landmarks as they drove through the deserted streets of Magadan in the small hours of the morning. She skirted the question when June asked her about Magadan's history with the gulags, and turned the conversation back to the city.

"This is Port Trail," she said, gesturing to a road sign that read ШоссеПорТовое. To the right lay the Sea of Okhotskoye, frozen solid with giant chunks of ice jutting up like ragged icebergs above the smooth expanse of virgin snow. The bay lay dormant, and the taxi veered onto another street, trading the industrial sector for an area filled with four-story grey concrete apartment buildings.

"What road is this?" June asked as a rare street sign flashed by.

"ПоЛярная," Yulia said in Russian. "It means Polar in English. Fitting, don't you think?"

"No shit," Bobby said from the front seat where he sat next to the cab driver.

They drove in silence for a few moments, everyone looking out the windows at the bleakness that was winter in Siberia. The taxi turned and headed away from the water, and when they intersected another major street Yulia pointed out the prominent sign.

"Remember this one," she said grinning. "Every Russian city and town have a street by this name.

"Гагарина?" June tried to pronounce the word using English to sound out the letters as best she could.

Yulia burst out laughing. "Gagarin," she said. "You know this person?"

"Of course," June responded. "Yuri Gagarin, the first man in space. Sometime in April 1961, in Vostok I. He's very famous in America too."

Yulia brightened. "Really? That's nice that you know of Yuri Gagarin. He is a Russian hero." A minute later she said, "We are almost there."

They passed another major artery, this one named, проспект Карпа Маркса, and June let out a laugh. "I think I actually know this one," she said excitedly. "Boulevard of Karl Marx?"

"Almost perfect," Yulia said. "Prospect Karl Marx. You are practically Russian now."

"That was an easy one," June said. In reality, the Cyrillic alphabet was coming back to her. During her tenure at NSA, she had used other alphabets for both creating and breaking codes, and the Cyrillic was ideal. She glanced back out the window as the cab pulled off the main drag into a narrow alleyway.

The car's side mirrors had been removed, but even with them gone the houses and shops were almost touching each side of the taxi. Ahead, where the road widened and under a neon light, a group of people huddled together outside a large, wooden door. The driver pulled into a small alcove opposite the entrance and said something in Russian to Yulia. She took some rubles out to pay the man.

"We'll pay," Bobby said, digging in his snowsuit pocket. "How much in American dollars?"

Yulia thought for a minute, doing the conversion in her head. "Three dollars and sixty cents."

Bobby handed the man a ten. "Tell him to keep it."

Yulia spoke again in Russian, "Американец сказал оставить это. Он хочет чтобы вы ждали тут." The man responded by nodding and giving Yulia his cell number, then tucked the bill in his breast pocket. Yulia pointed to the door and said, "Let's go and see if Pat is here."

They followed her into Club Astra and through a large reception area, manned by two bouncers and a skinny woman checking coats. Yulia jabbered something in Russian at the nearest bouncer and he burst into laughter. He waved all three ahead and patted Bobby on the back as he went by.

"What the hell is so funny?" Bobby asked.

"I told him you're here to try out some Russian vodka. You think it's for pussies and won't make you drunk. He'll be by in an hour or so to see how you're doing."

"They're checking everyone for weapons at the door," he said. "I'm armed."

"The club doesn't care if visitors carry weapons, just Russians." She turned to him as they entered the club. "Foreigners usually talk first and shoot later. Russians, not so much."

Yulia led the way into the nightclub. Straight ahead was the dance floor, filled with people dancing to techno-pop music blasting from a wall of speakers. Off to one side were dozens of tightly packed tables, crowded with chairs and bodies. Opposite, a row of chairs was filled with young, attractive women. Between them was a gaping hole in the wall that led to the bar, away from the noise and confusion of the dance hall. The place was rocking and Bobby checked his watch. Three-thirty in the morning. Unbelievable.

Yulia headed for the tables, elbowing her way through the crowd and greeting many of the dancers with a smile and a handshake. Most people lit up when they saw her, and it was obvious that she was well liked. Once they had crossed the dance floor, Yulia stopped and hovered near one of the tables. It was round and fit eight chairs, all of them taken. Seven by women, the eighth by a man in his mid-thirties, wearing a ball cap and a very big grin. His smile got even bigger when he spied Yulia.

"Dobray noch, Yulia," the man yelled over the pounding music.

"Добрыи нотч, Patrick," she replied, leaning over the table and giving him a quick kiss. "I have some friends I would like you to meet," she continued in English.

He jumped up and pulled over a couple of chairs. "Sit down," he said.

He wasn't tall, perhaps five-eight, but looked wiry and strong with thick forearms and wrists. He had a nice face, sharply chiseled and weather beaten, with a prominent chin and happy blue eyes. He grinned at June when they were introduced, and she couldn't help grinning back.

"Hi, I'm Pat Murdoch."

"June Childers, and this is Bobby Greco."

"Sit down, sit down," he said after they had shaken hands. "I'll introduce you to my tablemates. Now pay special attention, there's a test after." He grinned again. "This is Natasha," he said, starting at the right and working around. "And this is Natasha. And next to her is Natasha." He stopped for a second and glanced at June. "It's a popular name." He cracked up at that and poured a vodka. He downed it in one shot and continued around the table. The names sounded strange—Onya, Svetlana, Katerina, Lena. All seven wore short skirts and were dressed for a party.

Jesus, Bobby thought, *it's a table full of Robert Palmer girls.*

Pat insisted Bobby and June knock back a couple of vodkas before he would even consider talking with them. They learned he was an ex-pat Canadian who had come to Magadan five years ago to install a mill at the gold mine, then stayed on as a foreman afterward. He liked the fringe benefits, which obviously extended to the attention of the girls at the table. Bobby and June downed two vodka shooters to Pat's satisfaction, and he pointed to a quieter part of the bar.

"There's a private room over there." Once the four of them had made their way through the crowd and were settled in, he asked them what they wanted.

"Yulia told us you saw some smoke coming out of a chimney at one of the old gulag camps," June said.

"Damn right I did," Pat said, downing another vodka. "Strangest thing. Nobody ever goes in those places. They're creepy."

"But you did?"

"I like to hike and ski in the mountains on my time off. Julietta, the gold mine where I work, is near Gora Shun."

"Gora Shun?" June asked.

"It's a mountain in the Kilganskiy Massiv." Pat sipped on a new vodka and motioned for Yulia to sit next to him. She gave him a sideways look, but sat anyway. "There are lots of mountains around here, but Gora Shun is the tallest. Big mother fucker. Anyway, the Kilgana River runs down the east side, and I was enjoying a little cross-country skiing about three weeks ago and I spotted some smoke. It was coming from two cabins tucked up against the western side of the valley."

June was leaning forward, intent on his every word. "What did you do?"

Pat's face took on a serious look. "What every good Russian would do. I had a drink of vodka." He burst out laughing. "Actually, I think I had two or three drinks. Then I did the second thing a Russian would do. I got the hell out of there."

"Why?" June asked.

The music died down a bit as a slow song came on and Pat sat back in his chair. "This is Russia, not the friendly cabins of northern Montana. If someone is living in an abandoned gulag, five hundred kilometers from the nearest city, they don't want to be found. Skiing down to the huts and knocking on the door would have been the last thing I would have done."

"Okay," Bobby said. "But you have no idea who was there."

Pat smiled. "I didn't say that." He turned to Yulia. "Did I say that, Yulia?"

She shook her head. "No, Pat, you never said that."

He turned back to Bobby. "Just checking." The table of girls from the main room had arrived and they were making themselves at home. Pat obviously didn't mind.

"This vodka is starting to affect my judgment. I think I need to dance," Pat said in English. Then he announced something in Russian and the girls jumped to their feet and followed him onto the dance floor. The DJ had stepped up the tempo and they watched him dance, surrounded by the women, the huge grin still plastered on his face. Yulia had remained at the table, and Bobby asked her a question.

"Is this guy for real? He's like a Canadian Crocodile Dundee."

Yulia smiled. "That's funny. I've seen the movie. Good description." She gave it some thought, then said, "Pat isn't scared of anything, but he's not stupid either. He knows when to stand his ground and when to back off. The Russian men have tried to intimidate him a few times because he is so popular with the girls. They haven't done so well."

"He's not very big," June commented.

"Neither are wolverines," Yulia said.

June watched them dance for a minute, then asked. "What's with the women? They're beautiful, and all doting on him."

Yulia let out a long breath. "Pat is very skilled, he earns twenty times what the average mine worker does, and he has a nice home in Canada."

"Still..." June said.

Yulia laughed. "This is a university city. Every one of those women has a degree. Five of them are engineers and one is a geologist. The Russian men are like puppies if any of those girls show them attention."

"No wonder the men don't like Pat," June said.

The song ended but Pat didn't. He kept up the beat, the girls moving to the non-existent music as the DJ rallied the crowd in fast Russian. Another song came on and the group jumped to life. Yulia continued, "He has another side to him. He has helped so many Russian people in Magadan, I can't even tell you how many."

"Like how?" June asked.

"With money. Nobody plays him for the fool, but when someone is in trouble he's there for them."

"An interesting fellow," Bobby said.

"Very," Yulia said. The way she said it made both Bobby and June look at her. She was watching Pat on the dance floor. The look in her eyes said it all. She was smitten.

After three songs Pat returned to the table and downed a shooter of vodka. "There," he said. "Sober as a judge." He grinned. "Now where were we?"

"You implied you might know who was at the gulag," June said.

"Ah, yes. The gulag. I saw a man moving between the two cabins. There were two things that struck me odd about that."

"What were they?" Bobby asked.

"He wasn't Russian, and he had a rifle."

"What?" Bobby asked. "How could you tell that?"

"Russians wear shapkas on their heads. This guy had on a toque." He lit a cigarette and offered the package to Bobby. "So I knew he wasn't Russian, which is really strange, because this place is so totally isolated that only a completely crazy Russian would camp there, never mind a foreigner. But the rifle was even stranger."

"Why's that?" June asked.

"It was American. And new. And it had a scope."

June nodded. They were getting somewhere.

"I mean, think about it," Pat said. "Whoever this guy is, he's in the middle of Siberia, in the dead of winter, at an abandoned gulag camp. He carries a rifle from one building to the other, maybe a hundred feet apart. He sets it against the outside of the building, opens the door, puts something in, then closes the door and locks it. Then he takes a good look at the hills before heading back to the other shack. And, why did the rifle have a scope? If he *did* have someone in the other building, the gun wasn't to protect himself from them, it was to shoot anyone who shows up unexpectedly. Like me."

"He didn't see you?"

"Christ, no. I kept low on the ridge, the sun behind me."

"Whatever it was he put in the shack, could it have been food? A meal of sorts?"

Murdoch thought about that for a minute. He scratched his head behind his ear, where his hair showed a touch of grey. "Yeah, I would say it might have been." Then he nodded. "Yeah, in fact it probably was. The way he carried it was like he didn't want to spill it."

"So it's possible someone is being held captive in that cabin?"

"Maybe. It's possible."

Bobby leaned over to June. "Around here it wouldn't be that difficult to smuggle Alexis out of an airplane and onto a truck, then up to the gulag. Even if she managed to get out of the shack, she's in the middle of nowhere with temperatures that would kill her in under an hour. I hate to say it, but hiding her here, if she *is* here, was a pretty smart move." Bobby saw Pat was staring at him and stopped.

"Are you guys going to tell me what this is all about?" Pat asked, lighting another cigarette. "If not…" he shrugged his shoulders, eyeing the women who had followed him into the private room.

"Well, there is one thing," June said, avoiding the question. "Can you show us where these cabins are?"

"Do you have a map?" Pat asked.

"I didn't mean on a map," June said slowly.

The Canadian stared at her for a while. "You want me to take you there," he said and she gave a slight nod. "It would be very dangerous. I'm not sure about that."

"Lives hang in the balance," Bobby said.

Pat shook his head. "Not mine."

"We think they may be holding a woman in the cabin." June leaned closer to the Canadian. "No one else is coming for her, Pat. Without your help…" She let the sentence die off.

The perpetual smile faded from Murdoch's face. "Why is she there?"

June studied the man, then gave him an abbreviated version of the story, without mentioning Alexis's connection to the president. When she was finished, she sat back and waited.

The devil-may-care attitude was gone. He scratched the stubble on his chin and stared at the table. June knew he was evaluating the risks, and wondering if there was anything in it for him.

"She's rich," June added.

It took a minute, then Patrick asked, "How rich?"

"About a quarter of a billion dollars."

That set him back. He downed another vodka. "How much?"

"Two hundred and fifty million dollars," Bobby said.

Both Yulia and Pat were wide-eyed and focused. Yulia grabbed Pat by the forearm and leaned against him.

"Holy shit," Patrick said. "That's a lot of money."

"It is."

He lit a cigarette. "And you need to find out if she's at the cabin."

"Exactly."

Pat sat quietly for a few minutes, thoughtful and calculating, "Okay, we need a helicopter." He looked June and Bobby in the eyes. "And we have to go in when it's dark, which means tomorrow night." He stood up, dumped a handful of rubles on the table and waved at two of the women sitting at the nearby table. They hustled over and he placed one on each arm.

He smiled, like a Cheshire cat. "I'd better make it an early night then."

Bobby and June left with Yulia. It was four in the morning and the short walk from the club to her apartment was brutal, with the temperature already hovering at minus fifty.

Yulia talked as they trudged along the frozen road. "With the wind chill, it can reach minus seventy. Exposed flesh freezes in a few seconds."

"I can't feel my feet." June sounded worried. "It's like I'm walking on stumps."

"My teeth are frozen," Bobby said. "I can't believe we were in Orlando this morning."

"Almost there." Yulia pointed to the next building. They entered through a side door that banged shut after them, then climbed up four stories to an ice-cold hallway.

"It's freezing in here," Bobby said as Yulia fit her key into the lock.

She glanced at him over her shoulder. "No one lives in the hallways."

The apartment was much warmer, but pitch black as she herded them in and lit a candle. The long day had taken its toll, and Bobby and June politely declined tea when it was offered, just hoping to crash for a few hours. Yulia gave them the bedroom and threw a few blankets on the couch for herself.

Bobby fell into bed and pulled the thick blanket up close to his neck, tucking his toes in to keep them warm. June was settled into the other side, with a bit of space between them. The loud music and crush of bodies at the club had worn him down and he was exhausted. It was quiet and he stared at the flickering candle, wondering how on earth he had ended up here. For the thousandth time he thought of Janis and the girls, and prayed they were safe. There would be no forgiving himself...

The bed moved slightly as June slid over next to him. She pressed her body against his and he slipped his hands around her and pulled her close. In minutes they were both asleep.

chapter forty-nine

Cannes.

To the French, it's a tiny jewel, home to the European version of the Oscars. To the uninitiated, the city is a nightmare of one-way streets, crowded sidewalks, overpopulated beaches, and non-existent parking.

Trent Jamison and Kyle Andrews arrived early evening, Saturday, January 31st. They disembarked from the Learjet Interpol had provided and bypassed airport security, which was good as their bags were filled with weapons. Private jets were common in Cannes, and they moved quickly through the airport, drawing little attention.

Trent raised an eyebrow when he saw their ride, a silver Porsche 911 Turbo parked exactly where their contact had said it would be. Interpol knew from their report that Cortez was driving a Maserati, and didn't want the SEALs losing him on the treacherous roads surrounding Cannes. Trent slid his hand across the top of the driver's side front tire, found the keys and unlocked the doors. They stowed their bags in the trunk and took Avenue Francis Tonner into the city center, where they checked in at the Carlton Inter-Continental.

They hustled up to their room on the third floor and set to work, laying their arsenal out on the beds and hacking into the hotel's phone and reservation system. Henri Bouchard was due to arrive tomorrow and had requested a penthouse. They went into wait-mode, cleaning their guns, loading the ammunition into clips, and charging their two-way radios.

Trent stood at the window studying the sparkling expanse of the Mediterranean. "How and when do we want to take him?" he asked Kyle, who was resting next to the guns on one of the beds.

"They don't check in until tomorrow, so nothing is going down until at least Monday," Kyle said. "If we can get to him quickly, then we eliminate the chance of him meeting with Missoni and passing the information along. If we wait until Monday, we may have to kill Missoni too."

Trent snorted. "Like we really give a fuck," he said. "I'd like nothing more than to take out Missoni. The guy is a royal prick. His Interpol file is about an inch thick."

"I know." Kyle gave his partner a look. He knew exactly where Trent's head was right now. In a foreign country, armed to the teeth, and ready to do whatever was necessary. It wasn't going to be the first time they'd left a mess behind. Every mission had its risks, and this one was near the top of the pile.

Trent opened a Perrier and took a long swallow. "You're right, tomorrow is probably the safest."

"He'll be armed."

"Yeah, I know."

"Do you think he'll have any muscle with him?" Kyle asked.

"Good question. It looked like he was alone with the woman in Paris, but the deal wasn't going down there. He's had plenty of time to arrange for his men to be here. My guess is that he'll have some guys with him."

Kyle chambered a round in his pistol, then ejected it. The gun was ready to go. "Think they'll be here, in the hotel?"

Trent shrugged. "Probably, but picking his guys out could be tough. They may already be here and we have no idea who they are, or how many." He finished off the Perrier and set the empty aside. "How do we keep the visibility down? Cannes is a crowded place."

"Good question," Kyle said. For the first time in their discussion he looked a little concerned. "We're in a five-star hotel. A shootout in the lobby doesn't work."

Trent walked over to the window and looked down at the throngs of tourists on the sidewalks and the beach. Taking him out on the street was the worst scenario for collateral damage. He turned back to face his partner.

"Can we get to him in his room?"

Kyle grimaced. "Tough to do. We're on his territory and he has an entire suite. With that many rooms, the chances of hitting him and his bodyguards when they're all together are zero. I don't think that will work."

"Yeah, you're probably right," Trent agreed. "If they're spread out in the suite, we're screwed." He was silent for a minute. "Perhaps when he's having dinner?"

"Who knows where he's going to eat?" Kyle said, his voice showing a touch of frustration. "He could settle into the hotel and not want to go out again. That means their suite or one of the restaurants in the lobby, which gets us back to where we started."

"Yeah, it does."

Kyle brightened for a moment. "What if we gassed the fucker?"

Trent gave the idea some consideration. "What have we got?"

"Nothing, but that doesn't mean we can't find something this afternoon," Kyle said.

"I'm not sure," Trent said. "It's either totally lethal or we use something more generic that we can release in the suite. Either way, some is going to get circulated back through the hotel. We don't have any schematics of the heating and air conditioning system, so we could end up killing God knows how many people if the gas got pumped back through the building. No, we need more time to isolate the incoming and outgoing air to the suite before we could try that."

"Okay," Kyle said. "It was just an idea."

Trent pursed his lips. "The roads are pretty treacherous around here. What if he were to go for a drive?"

"Run him off a cliff into the Mediterranean?"

"Accidents happen," Trent said.

"What about the hired help?"

"We deal with them as it happens. We've got the upper hand on whatever they're driving. The Maserati is quite the machine, but it can't keep up to the 911 once the turbo kicks in."

"With you driving, of course."

Trent grinned. "Of course."

"How do we get him in the car? Like I said, he may get here and just hole up in the hotel."

"Possibly. We've got eighteen hours, give or take, to come up with a reason for him to leave the hotel."

"Okay," Kyle said. "We try to isolate him in the car. That's the primary plan. The backup is to mow him down like a mad dog on main street. How does that sound."

Trent gave his partner two thumbs up. "Perfect."

chapter fifty

Yulia woke Bobby and June at six in the morning. The two-hour catnap wasn't much sleep, but some was better than none.

"Pat's ready for you," she said softly, as if not wanting to wake them completely. "I'll take you there in a few minutes."

Bobby ran his hands through his matted hair and let out a low groan, the vodka haze still with him. Christ, that little Canadian could pound them back. They had been with him at Club Astra for less than two hours and Bobby had a hangover lurking. He could only imagine how wrecked Pat would be. He pulled himself up on one elbow and looked about.

Yulia's apartment was Spartan, the entire place not more than four hundred square feet, but the paint was fresh and it smelled nice, with a hint of jasmine. A few photos hung on the walls and a small table with two chairs sat next to an apartment-size stove. Bobby climbed out of bed and walked unsteadily to the window and peered out. A lone streetlight threw a hazy glow over the deserted road below, where a few older model Ladas were parked at the curb. Across the street was a big concrete apartment building with its rows of tiny windows looking out over the frozen landscape. He turned as he felt a slight pressure on his shoulder. Yulia was behind him with a cup of tea.

"This will warm you," she said. She noticed him glance about the room as he sipped on the tea. "Do you like my apartment?" she asked.

"Cozy," he said.

She grinned. "I have the largest apartment in the building. And the nicest. This is the only apartment with a bedroom." She smiled and pointed to one of the pictures on the wall. It was a photo of Pat holding a hammer and some wood, taken in the very room where they were standing. "Pat built me the bedroom."

Bobby nodded. "This *is* a nice home you have."

June poked her head out of the washroom looking suitably awake. "Try brushing your teeth, Bobby," she said. "It's heaven."

He joined her in the washroom, and said, "I'm starting to get this thing with Pat now."

"What do you mean?"

"Look around. Yulia's an incredible young woman and there's no getting ahead for her."

June nodded. "That's where Pat comes in." She finished brushing her teeth and tucked away her toothbrush.

Yulia waited until Bobby and June were finished their breakfast, then said, "We should get going."

"Ready. Let's go find that crazy Canadian."

"Good," Yulia said, laughing. She followed them out of the apartment and locked the door behind her. Their footsteps echoed in the stairwell as they descended to the ground floor, and when they slipped outside they were hit with a blast of bitterly cold air.

"Shit," Bobby muttered. The air seared his lungs when he breathed in, then formed a torrent of steam as it left his mouth. He squinted at June, blinking to keep his eyelashes from freezing together. She stared back at him in disbelief. Yulia, however, was already trudging down the block.

"I guess we walk again," June said, falling in behind her.

"Walk or die," Bobby said. He started to pace his breathing, careful of how quickly he drew air into his lungs and after a couple of minutes it didn't hurt as much. He pulled his toque over his eyebrows and tucked his nose into his parka, leaving only a slit, and his body heat warmed the inside of the snowsuit. He didn't feel quite as cold now, just about right, actually. The pilot's warning about dressing for the weather was damn good advice, he thought.

There were no birds or animals and the only noise was the oddly appealing crunch of their boots on the crystallized snow. It had a clean, crisp sound that he found refreshing. Yulia stopped in front of another apartment building exactly like hers and they followed her in.

June crept carefully up the stairs. Her oversize boots were slippery and there were numerous places where the handrail hung limply from the wall. When they reached the fourth floor, Yulia knocked on a door close to the stairwell and after a moment Pat poked his head into the hallway.

"Good morning," he said cheerfully, waving them into the apartment. "C'mon in, it's cold out there."

"No shit," Bobby said, closing the door behind him as he entered.

"Don't be so negative," Pat said. "There's no wind. Wait until it's minus fifty *with* a wind. That's brutal."

"Yeah, Yulia mentioned that last night." Bobby was quickly getting the drift that at these temperatures wind chill was a big deal.

"Be right with you, I'm on the phone."

Bobby unzipped his snowsuit and began peeling off the layers. Murdoch's apartment was opulent by Russian standards, and filled with leather furniture, wrought iron coffee tables, and a fifty-inch flat screen television. Numerous photos hung on the walls, most of Pat with smiling Russians in fur coats and shapkas. Bobby took a closer look. The scenery in some of the pictures looked different, and several had a much younger Pat posing in a group with a helicopter in the background. Bobby pointed at them when Pat hung up.

"Where were these taken," he asked.

Pat glanced over. "Canada, in the Yukon, close to where I grew up. I worked as a millwright in one of the mines there."

Bobby tapped one with his finger. Pat had a rifle slung over his shoulder and was standing next to a massive grizzly carcass. "You shot it?"

Pat's smile disappeared, and he said, "It charged me. Didn't want to, but she would have killed me."

Bobby could barely imagine having a bear that size running at him. He sat down on the couch. "There are helicopters in a lot of the pictures. Do you have your license?"

Pat shook his head. "No, but I flew in and out of the mine site lots of times. Most of the pilots back in those days had flown in Viet Nam and they were loosey-goosey about the rules. Got pretty good at all of it," he said enthusiastically. "Logged a few hundred hours."

A fresh pot of coffee sat steaming on the counter and Pat motioned for them to help themselves while he took another call. He spoke in fluent Russian for a minute or two, then ended the conversation with a few *da*'s. He hung up and smiled.

"Speaking of helicopters, I found us one," he said. "*But*, we need to pay for it up front."

June figured she could get some cash out of John if she asked. Surely the CIA operative had some sort of operating budget for this sort of thing. "I'll take care of it," she said. In the worst case Adler would pay.

"Now let's see." Pat sat at the kitchen table where a topographical map covered most of the surface. "I've already lined up the chopper and the snowmobiles, and I think I've laid out the best route from Magadan to the gulag."

Bobby eyed Pat. Apparently he didn't suffer from hangovers. Lucky him. "You look chipper," he said, then added, "Don't you sleep?"

"Forgot to last night," Pat winked. "Anyway, things to do, we've got a rich person to rescue. There's only one small problem."

"What's that?" June asked.

"Chopper needs a fix, it's missing a piece."

Bobby sipped his coffee with unsteady hands. "What kind of piece?"

"One of the rotors," Pat said. "Better get going so we can get on it."

"We?" Bobby asked.

Pat shrugged into his snowsuit and slipped on a shapka. "I've done plenty of work on motors and landing gear, stuff like that. How hard can it be?" He stood at the door, waiting for them while they struggled into their gear.

June was still sitting at the kitchen table, putting a call through to John. "We need a bit of help," she said to their CIA contact, then explained where their investigation had led overnight. "The chopper is going to cost a bit. Can you to cover it?"

John's response was quick. "I'll meet you at the helipad. I've rented from Sergei before so it shouldn't be a problem."

"Excellent." June hung up, wondering if everyone knew everyone else in Magadan.

Nine hours later, while John discussed the terms with the owner, they watched Pat reattach the rotor to its housing atop the aircraft. The hydraulic lines snapped easily into place and he tested the strength of the bolts with a torque wrench. Pat sat next to the rotor for a few minutes reading the technical brochure, then made a couple of additional adjustments to both the main and the tail rotors. He scrambled halfway down a makeshift ladder propped against the machine and opened the casing that contained the engines. Bobby walked over and stood at the bottom of the ladder.

"Do you have any idea what you're doing?"

Pat leaned against the machine and set his wrench on the cowling. "Tell you what, I answer a couple of your questions, then you leave me alone to fix this thing," he said and Bobby nodded. "Okay, ask away."

"You said the problem was with the rotor. Why are you working on the engine?"

Pat pointed to the rotor. "This is an older model Sikorsky. It was probably built in Stratford, Connecticut to some pretty exacting American standards. The Russians pick up these choppers when the Americans figure they're going to start costing too much for regular maintenance and repairs. They use them for transporting people and equipment in and out of mines in Siberia. So even though it has a lot of flying hours on it, we have a good bird on our hands. But here's the problem. If you look about halfway along the rotor, you'll see a hairline crack. If we take off with full power, we'll snap it. These are Pratt & Whitney PT6B-36A engines, and I'm adjusting them to perform at about sixty percent efficiency. That's enough to lift off with four people and two snowmobiles, but not enough to shear off the rotor. Any other questions?"

Bobby looked as stupid as he felt. "No. Not really."

Pat picked up his wrench and stuck his head back inside the engine compartment. It took another three hours before he reattached the cowling and pulled the ladder away. He opened the cargo door and started one of the snowmobiles, then drove it up the steep ramp into the bay. He strapped it in place and did the same with the second snowmobile, then closed the hatch.

"Ready to go," he said, yanking open the hangar doors.

A fierce blast of snow pelted them as they rolled the chopper out onto the concrete pad. The pilot checked Pat's job of tying down the snowmobiles and nodded his approval, then sat up front and started going through the preflight procedure. Bobby and June retreated to the hangar and shut the doors, trying to keep some warmth inside. John was standing next to Pat, and his cell phone rang as they watched the pilot ready for takeoff. He answered, then turned away and retreated to a corner where no one could hear. Bobby glanced at June, but she just shrugged.

Bobby and June were still standing inside the hangar when John walked up to them. The look on his face was telling.

"Anything wrong?" June asked.

"Yeah," he said. "Plenty."

"What?" June asked

"Langley intercepted one of Cortez's calls. He's meeting with the buyer on Monday and he's already given the order to execute Alexis the moment the deal is done."

June's face went white. "Monday. That's tomorrow."

"Fuck." Bobby squeezed his hands into fists.

June turned away from the men and pressed her head against a shelf. She closed her eyes, thinking of the woman she had gotten to know so well, and who she respected. If Alexis *was* in the shack, she had been through hell on earth for the past three months. Now that she was on the verge of being rescued, the word to kill her had come down. June set her jaw, pushing away any feelings of disparagement. They were ready to go, and there was time. They could still do this. She turned back to face John and Bobby, who were both staring at her.

"We have time," she said. "Let's go."

Pat had returned to the hangar and was standing off to the side, listening. There was a spark in his eyes. "Chopper's waiting," he said.

The pilot was already strapped in and checking his instruments as they boarded. Pat sat in the co-pilot seat and they spoke in Russian as the engines powered up. What started as a friendly conversation quickly deteriorated into a shouting match. Yulia unsnapped her safety belt and went up front, and within seconds she was yelling at both of them. Finally the pilot unbuckled his belt and got out of the aircraft.

"What now?" Bobby asked as Yulia rejoined them and John poked his head inside.

Yulia waited until John was in the chopper and the door shut. "The pilot doesn't want to fly with sixty percent power. He said it was too dangerous."

"Aw, shit," John said.

He jumped out of the machine and ran over to where the owner was talking with the pilot. They all watched as the pilot stormed off and the owner shook his head numerous times. John held up his phone, but the man shook his head again. Finally, John returned and climbed back in.

"The pilot is adamant, he's not going to fly. It'll take at least a day to get another pilot here, and even then there's a good chance he would refuse to fly."

A long silence settled over the cabin, then Pat got up and pushed his way out of the craft. He headed straight for the owner and spoke to him for a few minutes. Pat nodded a new times and shook the man's hand, then ran back to the chopper and slid into the pilot's seat.

"Negotiated us a helicopter." He glanced back at John as he strapped in and put on the headset. "Better hope I bring this thing back in one piece or the CIA is going to be coughing up some serious cash."

John looked horrified. "Can you fly this thing?"

Pat grinned and tilted his head in the direction of the owner. "*He* trusts me."

John looked into the rear of the cabin. "Do you have the satellite phone?"

"I have it," June said. "We'll call if we need anything."

"Call no matter what," he said. "If you get her, if she isn't there, if you need help. Whatever is going on, call me."

"Got it," June said.

"You guys are on your own," John yelled as he jumped out the door. "Don't fucking crash."

The motors picked up as Pat readied for takeoff and Yulia returned to her seat. Bobby unbuckled, moved to the front of the cabin and strapped into the co-pilot's seat. He put on his headset and waited quietly for Pat to finish the pre-flight check, then spoke into the mic.

"You okay with all this?" Bobby asked.

"Getting us there or going after the bad guys?" Pat asked.

"Both."

"I can fly this thing." Pat's eyes narrowed and for once he looked deadly serious. "Come on, Bobby, this was never about just having a look around. Time to go hunting."

Pat had known from minute one that they were going up against whoever was at the cabins. Bobby swallowed hard, looking at the most capable partner he'd ever had.

"So you flew a Sikorsky back in Canada."

Pat looked at him like he had two heads. "Not so much."

"Shit," Bobby said.

Pat glanced back at the instrument panel, opened the throttles and lifted the chopper off the ground. It groaned under the reduced thrust from the modified engines, but continued upward. Snow kicked up off the pad and visibility was reduced to zero until they rose above forty feet, and Pat pushed forward on the stick. The chopper began moving ahead and they continued to climb, passing three thousand feet and leveling off at about thirty-three hundred. Pat explained why he had chosen that altitude.

"The mountains between us and where we're headed run as high as 6,200 feet above sea level, but we can follow a series of valleys that top out at about 2,500 ASL. The lower we stay, the better our fuel consumption and the less stress on the rotor."

"You're sure you can navigate the valleys?" Bobby asked.

Pat grinned at him. "I know this area really well. There's only one ridge of mountains between the gulag and the mine where I work. It'll be easier when the moon comes out and I can see where I'm going."

Bobby looked northward to the horizon where the last hint of sunlight was disappearing behind the jagged mountain peaks. "How long until we get to the mountains?" he asked.

"About an hour," Pat said.

"How long until we get some moonlight?"

Pat checked his watch. "About an hour and ten minutes." He kept a straight face for a few seconds, then started to laugh. "Just kidding. We'll make it."

Bobby sort of believed him. He stayed up front in the co-pilot's seat, watching out the windows for high hills or low mountains. "What exactly is your job at the mine?" Bobby asked after a while.

"Like I said, I'm a millwright. I work on large industrial machines. Conveyors, boilers, ball-crushers, all kinds of stuff. Basically, anything and everything."

"And that's why you're so good with machines?" Bobby asked.

"Yeah, probably. Up north, you do what needs to be done. You need to be a jack of all trades." He grinned and leaned over so he was closer to Bobby. "Yulia's hot don't you think?"

"Sure," Bobby said, rolling his eyes.

Pat pointed ahead to the horizon, the mountain peaks clearly visible in the moonlight. To their right, about five degrees off their flight path was a valley that snaked between two mountain ridges. The helicopter was still cruising at thirty-three hundred feet, well above the level of the valley floor when Pat changed course and steered toward the rift.

"From here on it's going to get a bit crazy, but if the visibility is okay I should be able to get us there. We're about three hours flying time from where I want to land. From there we take the snowmobiles, then walk the last mile or so. It's going to get rough. Think you can handle it?"

Bobby was torn between offering the guy a Bud Light and punching him. He settled for nodding. "Hey, anything a Canadian can do, an American can do," he said. He was surprised how funny Pat found that remark.

chapter fifty-one

When Alexis woke the fingers on her right hand felt like they were frozen. She rolled from her side onto her back and willed them to move. No response, just a numbness that extended up her wrist into the tendons and muscles of her arm. She massaged the area with her left hand and some feeling began to return. She breathed a sigh of relief, figuring she must have pinched a nerve sleeping on her side. Her hand tingled with pins and needles for a couple of minutes, then she sat up and looked about.

The wind was savage, howling through the valley and driving snow through the cracks in the wooden walls. She moved about the room packing the snow into the gaps to keep the wind out, then added a few sticks of kindling to her fire and rubbed her hands together over the tiny flames. The warmth felt good. After a few minutes she walked to the grimy window and peered out into the driving snow.

Her tree was still there, bending in the gale but holding firm. It was incredible that those scrawny roots could cling to the rocks. It steeled her resolve. Whatever her captors could throw at her, she would take it. The scraping sound of a key in the lock surprised her, and she moved back against the far wall.

Ivan was peering through a gap between the boards. He saw her huddled in the corner and threw open the door, the European they called Lars beside him. She cowered, shivering against the rough wood, glaring hatefully at the men. They stared back at her with disgust. Lars walked slowly across the room until he stood a few feet from her. He was Scandinavian, she decided, with his blond hair and icy blue eyes.

"Still alive." His accent sounded Swedish. "You should be dead by now." Finally he broke eye contact and walked about the room, kicking her blanket as he passed it. She shuddered at that, knowing she would be dead if he took it.

"If not for you, I wouldn't have to come to this God-awful place." He was quiet again for a minute, then moved close enough that she could smell the liquor on his breath. "But this will be my last trip."

Alexis was shaking uncontrollably now. He was leaving little doubt as to why he was there, and she wondered why he didn't just kill her now.

"I should let Ivan have you. That would break your spirits." His face was only inches from her now. "I'll think about that."

Eventually he turned and stomped out into the cold, and she grabbed her blanket and curled up on her bed. A few minutes later Ivan appeared with her breakfast. She waited until he had closed and latched the door, then skittered across the barren floor to the food. It was still warm and she devoured it with a vengeance. When she was finished she returned to the stove and stoked her fire. The embers caught and flames danced up from the ashes. The warmth gave her strength, and she had a fleeting feeling that something good was in the wind. She had no idea where the it had come from, but she clung to it.

She thought of the European. "You're not going to see me die," she whispered. Just saying it made her feel much better.

Derek Adler closed the door to the Oval Office behind him and strode over to where President Neilson was sitting behind his desk. He handed Neilson the latest update, at the same time telling him what was in the report.

"The FBI intercepted a call between Cortez and the twin."

"My other daughter," Neilson said quietly.

"Yes, sir. Cortez has given his men the order to kill Alexis once they've handed the missile over to the buyer." Adler stood in front of the president, waiting.

"Well, at least we know she's alive."

"Yes, sir." Adler wondered if that was true. She could already be dead for a multitude of reasons.

Neilson rose and stood at the window, staring out over the garden. "Anything new from the teams looking for her?"

"Childers is still our best bet. She and Greco are checking out a possible sighting at an abandoned gulag. No word since they left Magadan in a chopper about three hours ago."

Neilson nodded slowly, his optimism ebbing. At best, the Russian angle was a long shot, and it was all they had. "What's happening with locating Cortez?"

"The SEAL team arrived in Cannes about four hours ago. Cortez is traveling under the name Henri Bouchard and he's due to check in at the Carlton some time on Sunday. Our men are already set up in the hotel and waiting for him."

"Excellent." Neilson took his time before continuing. "My other daughter. It's time. Bring her in. Quietly."

Adler couldn't imagine what was going through the president's head at that moment. "I'll make the call."

Neilson stood in his office, lost in thought. He had read Solzhenitsyn and had been horrified with the accounts of life in the gulags, and now it was possible Alexis was trapped there in the dead of a Russian winter. In his heart, he hoped she was. If not, they would never find her in time.

It was incredible to think his mother was the genesis of all this. Her arrogance and meddling had caused Ryan's death, and now Alexis was under threat. His anger began to rise and he tried to calm himself by sitting at his desk and wading into the stack of papers waiting for his signature. It was hard, almost impossible, to focus. He sat back, staring at the ceiling in the waning hours of January, alone in his crazy world.

Daylight was fading and Tony DaSilva flipped on the dome light so he could read the map spread out on his lap. Another road off his list and he traced along the wiggly dotted line with his red pen. The map was littered with red lines, all of them branching off the highway toward the Alapaha River. He rubbed his eyes, tired from hours of staring at the tiny print and driving on endless muddy backroads that led nowhere. He ran his finger along the next turnoff. This one snaked back into the woods farther than most and he glanced up at the evening sky. It would be pitch black before he got to the end. He turned the car around and headed back to Ocilla.

He was frustrated and angry. The countryside was a maze of unpaved tracks twisting back into the bush and exploring each of them was wearing him down. The thought of how he would spend the money always reinvigorated him and he focused on it as he drove. Maybe a small villa in the Caribbean. No one down there asked where the cash came from. And he would certainly need a sports car and a Harley Davidson. All his, simply for putting bullets in three heads. Christ, it couldn't get any easier. But first he had to find Janis Greco and the girls.

Ocilla appeared as he rounded the sweeping curve at the edge of town, its street lights flickering on in the hazy dusk. Saturday night. He drove past the Jiffy-Mart and stopped in for a few groceries. The woman he had spoken with earlier was making change at her register and smiled when she saw him. He returned the gesture, picked out a few items and went through her till.

"Y'all find your friend?" she asked.

"No luck so far," he said. "I've just been hanging around in case she shows up, but I have to leave soon. Have you heard from her?"

"Not a word. Hasn't been in since she used the phone."

"Not to worry," he said. "She'll show up soon." DaSilva thanked her for bagging the items and strode out into the warm Georgia evening.

"Oh, yes," he said quietly under his breath. "You'll eventually show up, and when you do...."

chapter fifty-two

Gora Shun rose above the surrounding peaks, hardly a monster, but intimidating enough for Pat to stay well west of it. The wind was picking up as they flew farther into the mountains and the downdrafts buffeted the Sikorksy, making it hard for Pat to keep the craft level. He was constantly looking up at the rotors for signs of trouble, but the cracked blade was holding. He pointed to Gora Shun, speaking into the headset mic so Bobby could hear.

"We'll go past Gora Shun by about six miles. There's a canyon that runs east off the valley we're following now." He motioned to the flat expanse that lay ahead between two sets of hills. "Once we turn the corner it's going to get a little tighter."

"Tighter?" Bobby asked.

"The canyon isn't as wide. The sides are steeper. In fact, there's one place where..." he stopped and gave Bobby a quick look. "You'll see soon enough."

"How close to the gulag are you going to put us down?" he asked.

Pat shrugged. "If the wind keeps up, we can get fairly close, maybe within a mile or two. If it quiets down we'll have to land farther out." Pat glanced up at the rotors, checked his instruments, then said, "This thing is loud. Even with the hills and a raging wind, they'll still hear us if we're less than a mile out. Anyway, the snowmobiles will get us from the chopper to the cabins."

"Snowmobiles are loud too." Bobby stared out the window. It felt like he was on a different planet. Below him for as far as he could see was nothing but ice and snow, and it was unnerving to think they would be landing there.

"Not even close to this," Pat responded and offered Bobby a cigarette. "One thing about flying with me," he said. "Smoking is permitted."

"Do you take anything seriously?" Bobby asked.

"Absolutely. I take this very seriously. We could all die in a number of horrific ways, but what's the use walking around with a stick up your ass? Relax, have a little fun."

"Okay, I'm relaxing. Nice airline you're running here. Where's my fucking coffee?"

Pat grinned. "That's better."

They flew on past Gora Shun until they spotted the smaller valley to the east, and Pat banked the helicopter toward it. The full moon hung low in the southern sky, illuminating the twists and turns of the creek they were following as it wound its way deeper into the hills. The rock formations on either side of the chopper were closing in on them, and ahead the valley narrowed to a thin vertical chasm. They were cruising about seven hundred feet above the valley floor and within minutes the rock faces on either side rose over a thousand feet above them.

Bobby pointed to the narrow gap directly ahead. "Is that the place you were talking about?"

"Yeah, that's it," Pat said, completely focused on the upcoming gorge. "It's tight."

"Let's take it up and fly over the crest," Bobby said, pointing up to the open sky now far above them.

Pat shook his head. "No way. They'll hear us for sure. We have to go through. See if you can find a place where the rocks widen out a bit."

Bobby scoured the gorge. He saw a slightly wider spot near the valley floor and pointed at it. "Way down," he said. "Almost to the ground. Maybe eighty feet up."

Pat nodded, the walls too close now for him to look away. "Okay, I'll take it down." He slowed their airspeed and angled the chopper toward the valley floor. The gorge loomed ahead, no break in sight, and it was obvious the blades would never fit through. Even where they were, the walls were only thirty or forty feet from the tips of the blades. The thumping of the rotors was deafening, and the snow blew off the walls, swirling around the chopper and reducing visibility even further.

"How close are we to the ground?" Pat asked, his knuckles white on the stick.

Bobby craned his neck to look out the side window, but couldn't see anything but white. "No idea," he yelled back. "But we're damn close to the rocks on either side."

"That's an understatement," Pat said. "Do you see it yet?"

"No, nothing. Wait, just a second," Bobby's voice was excited. "Down about twenty feet and then straight ahead."

"Keep watching for the gap," Pat yelled. The muscles in his thick forearms were hard as rock from holding onto the stick so tight and his entire body was shaking from the vibrations.

"I see it," Bobby pointed. "Dead ahead now."

Pat pushed the stick forward, keeping their altitude steady as they broke through the chasm and hit the open skies on the north side of the gorge. There was a moment of silence, then Yulia's voice cut through the cockpit.

"Do you guys know what you're doing up there? We came really close to hitting those rocks."

Pat and Bobby gave each other a high five. "Piece of cake," Pat said. "Plenty of room to spare."

"Could have driven a semi through that," Bobby said.

Pat gave him a withering look, then grinned. "That's stupid. This thing's way wider than a semi."

They were moving ahead at a good speed, thirty feet above the valley floor. Pat pointed to his left and said, "We can get inside two miles now. We'll drop the chopper into one of these little rifts, have something to eat and get moving on the snowmobiles. If the wind keeps up we can get within about a thousand feet of the cabins."

Bobby gave the Canadian a long look. "Nice flying back there."

"Thanks," Pat said, and glanced over at Bobby. "Did I mention I've never landed one of these things?"

chapter fifty-three

Trent and Kyle had their surveillance up and running by ten o'clock Sunday morning. Their best guess was that Cortez and Dupres had stayed in Grenoble overnight, and that put them at least six hours from Cannes. If they were on the road by ten, that would have them checking in around four in the afternoon. Once an hour the SEALs brought their system online and checked if Cortez had registered. At three o'clock they got a hit. Henri Bouchard was now a registered guest, in suite 713. They put their plan in action.

A tiny bit of C-4 explosive with a remote trigger blew out the electrical sub-panel for the kitchen. In milliseconds the lights and the freezers were out and the kitchen staff in a frenzy. The gas lines to the stoves and ovens were working, but otherwise all they had was emergency lighting. An electrician arrived and delivered the bad news. The panel would require a minimum of eight hours to rebuild. The hotel manager recommended they offer a limited menu for dinner, but the head chef felt the risk to his staff was too great. The decision was made. They closed the kitchen.

A large sign was posted outside the entrance to the main restaurant and automated calls were placed to all rooms. One of Cortez's entourage took the message and passed it along to his boss. It hardly raised an eyebrow. Sylvia suggested they drive up to the casino in Monte Carlo for dinner, and Cortez, preoccupied with the exchange set for Monday, nodded his approval. Sylvia had one of the bodyguards call in a reservation for eight o'clock and headed for the spa.

The Maserati was parked in a preferred spot in the underground lot, clear of pillars and close to the elevators. A lone man, dressed in dark pants and a thin windbreaker, leaned against the wall, watching the car. Trent noticed the slight bulge under the man's right arm. He was armed.

The SEAL had entered the lot from the street entrance, running down the ramp beside a Mercedes and quickly disappearing behind a group of parked cars. He crouched behind a Renault, only a few yards from the Maserati, and slipped a pair of night goggles from his pack. When the fans from the ventilation system cut in, he slipped them on and texted Kyle.

In place and ready.

Kyle severed the power to both the primary and backup lighting systems. The lights flickered, then went out completely. Trent crept toward the Maserati, watching the guard. The man was confused for a minute, unsure what to do. He stood motionless, listening, then felt his way blindly toward the car, his hands outstretched in front of him in the pitch black.

Trent reached the Maserati and slid effortlessly underneath, the night goggles amplifying the tiny remnants of light from the distant ramp and giving him a clear view of the underside. He located the brake line and put a tiny slit in it, then attached a dark piece of rubber underneath to catch the brake fluid so it wouldn't leave a puddle. Trent slid out from under the vehicle on the far side, away from the guard, and moved quickly through the jumble of cars toward the street exit.

Turn them back on, he texted as he slid off the night goggles and stuffed them in his pack. The lights flashed back on as he opened the man-door leading to the street and joined the afternoon crowd on the Boulevard de la Croisette, just another barefoot tourist walking along the beach.

When he returned to the room, Kyle was signing onto a surveillance program and checking to make sure their hack into the hotel's computer was still in place.

"Room 713 called the casino in Monte Carlo," Kyle said. "They made a reservation for two people at eight o'clock."

"We're on." Trent slipped a clip in his AK-47 and looked down at the map spread across the table. "Damn, these roads look treacherous."

Derek Adler hustled down the hall to the Oval Office.

He knocked and entered, then walked quickly to the desk. "The men watching the Chamberlain house called in," he said. "She's gone."

Neilson couldn't believe what he was hearing. "How?"

Adler shook his head. "She was home and they had the house covered. When they went in this morning she wasn't there. All her ID is gone, the safe is open and cleaned out."

Neilson collapsed back in his chair. "Cortez got to her."

"It appears so."

Neilson was torn between being horrified and relieved. Bringing in the twin would have opened Pandora's Box, but losing her severed their connection to Cortez and a pivotal thread in finding Alexis. He closed his eyes and wished the whole thing would simply disappear. When he opened them, his Chief of Staff was still there, waiting.

"She can't have gone far. Find her."

chapter fifty-four

Janis Greco buckled Lizzie and Sarah into the car and pulled away from the cabin. The tires crunched on the gravel driveway and a few errant pebbles flew into the weeds as she hit the gas a bit too hard, anxious about the trip.

The sky was threatening, but the rain was still holding off as she turned onto the main highway leading to Ocilla. The road was clear, with Sunday traffic almost non-existent, and she set her cruise control to three miles per hour over the legal limit.

Half an hour later the clock on her dash read 9:58 as they entered Ocilla. The parking lot at the Jiffy-Mart was empty and a crooked *Closed* sign was visible in the front window as she cruised by and headed for the nearby McDonald's. The kids were bouncing in their seats as she pulled around the back of the restaurant, excited for breakfast. Janis tucked the girls in a booth away from the front windows and picked up their order. They gobbled down their food, then headed back for the edge of town and the Jiffy-Mart. There were a handful of cars parked out front and the sign in the door had been flipped over to read *Open*. It was straight now.

She recognized the cashier when she entered, and waved, trying to remember her name. The woman gave a cheerful wave back as she checked an order through for another customer. Janis shopped with the kids in the cart until it was too full for them to fit, and they were hanging off the sides as she pushed it up to the cashier. When she reached the checkout the woman's name came to her. Barbara.

"Hi, Barbara," Janis said, giving the woman a warm, Sunday smile.

"Good morning, honey." Barbara reached under the counter and pulled out a couple of suckers. "Look what I've got for you two." The girls giggled and thanked her for the treats while Janis unloaded the groceries.

"Did your friend catch up with you?" she asked as she rang through the groceries.

"What friend?" Janis asked, puzzled.

"The looker with the nice brown eyes." She winked. "He's been in twice. Asked about you both times."

Janis felt her knees go weak. Bobby knew where the cabin was, so it was definitely not him. "Did he say his name?" she asked, her throat dry.

"No, just said he was a friend of the family." She looked over at the girls, then said, "From the school. He was with the principal when you phoned, and he saw the call-display." She continued to ring the groceries through, oblivious to the look of horror on Janis's face. "I hope you don't mind that I know..." She glanced at Janis and stopped in mid-sentence. "What's wrong, girl? You've gone all white."

"What did you tell him?" she gasped.

"Oh no, sweetie. I shouldn't have told him anything," she said "Thank God I didn't know where you were staying. I told him in a cabin on the river, but he'll never find it. Not in a million years. Too many back roads around these parts." She had stopped working and gently set her hand on Janis' arm. "I'm sorry, honey. I really am."

"Okay." Janis was regaining her composure. "Let's just bag these so I can get out of here. We'll be safe at the cabin."

"Right, we have to hurry." Barbara worked the till quickly with shaking hands. She totaled the bill and made change. "Arnold," she yelled at a stock boy halfway down the aisle. "Give this woman a hand out with her groceries." She turned back to Janis, her face etched with regret. "I am so sorry."

"It's done," Janis said, and hustled from the store with the girls in tow.

The stock clerk tried to help, but Janis grabbed the bags from him and threw them in the trunk, slamming it shut as she yelled for the girls to put on their seatbelts. The rain started in earnest as she lurched onto the highway and almost put the car in the opposite ditch. She turned on her wipers and stared out through the rhythmic swishing until she reached their turnoff. The small dirt road was slick with mud and she drove slowly, terrified of sliding off the narrow tracks. The trip in took almost an hour and it was half past noon when the cabin came into sight, exactly as they had left it.

Janis bundled the kids into the house, got them interested in a game and then went back for the groceries. She tucked them away and stood in the living room, staring at the road that led back to the highway. It had brought them here, to this safe place, but it could also bring the killer to their doorstep. Outside, the rain pounded on the roof with an irregular beat and she felt a wave of anxiety and hopelessness flow over her. She looked over at Lizzie and Sarah playing at the kitchen table, helpless without their mother. They needed her.

Janis took a few deep breaths as the reality of their situation hit her. She was being hunted and the man was closing in. The first thing she needed to do was decide whether to stay or make a run for it. How long would it take him to find her, or would he? The cabin was tucked back in the woods and there were so many side roads. It could take him weeks to search all of them, and even then he might miss the cabin. Staying was dangerous, but so was running. There may be more than one of them, and they could be watching the roads. Just driving by them could mean the end. And if she *did* leave, where would she go? She made her decision—she was staying.

The girls were still in the kitchen, and after checking on them she returned to the living room and unlatched the clasp on the overhead bin. She removed the shotgun and ammunition. She made sure the safety was on, then looked around for a more accessible hiding place. The couch caught her eye and she slid the gun under the cushions then stood back and checked her handiwork. It was impossible to tell it was there, and it was tucked back far enough that the girls wouldn't know it was there even if they sat on the cushions.

She took a deep breath. It was the best she could do.

chapter fifty-five

Pat kept the helicopter less than a hundred feet off the valley floor as he searched for a protected place to set it down. He spied a small rift in one of the rock walls and angled toward it. The secluded niche was just large enough, and he was able to maneuver the helicopter into the opening without any danger of the rotors hitting the walls.

"Make sure your seatbelts are tight," Pat yelled as he prepared to land.

All four of them were thrown about in their seats when he touched down, but no one was injured. Pat powered the machine down, and when the rotors stopped turning there was nothing but the eerie sound of wind whistling up the valley.

"Bobby, siphon off a bit of fuel and start a fire," Pat said. "I'm going to tie down the rotors and show Yulia how to keep the engine from freezing."

"Got it," Bobby said.

By the time Pat and Yulia were finished going over how to start the engine, Bobby had a fire burning in a small, rocky alcove where they could all huddle close together for warmth. A tripod hung over the fire and Yulia was melting ice for drinking water and tea. She spotted June eating some snow and cautioned her.

"Don't eat that." She poured a cup of herbal tea and held it out. "It takes too much energy for your body to melt it. You can actually die of dehydration from eating snow."

"Didn't know that," June said. She sipped the tea and nodded her approval. "Oh, this is good."

Pat set a pot on the fire and tended it, stirring occasionally and adding a bit of snow every now and then. After the better part of an hour, he spooned it out into four cups, and they sat about eating the brown sludgy meal. When they had finished Pat checked his watch and did a quick mental calculation. He looked pleased with the final result.

"It's four-thirty," he said to the group. "Time for Bobby and me to go. Yulia, you know how to work the radio on the chopper and the satellite phone. Call John and let him know we're here. If Bobby and I are not back by six tomorrow night, then things have gone wrong. Put the call through then, no later. Do you understand?"

"Yes. I call John in Magadan at six tomorrow night. Give him our location. Have someone come out to pick us up."

"Do you know where you are on the map?" he asked.

"Within a mile or so," she said. "Close enough for a rescue."

"And you know how to start the chopper to keep it from freezing. How often and for how long."

"Once an hour for five minutes." She thought of something, and asked, "Where is the best source of heat in the helicopter?"

"The vent by the pilot's feet. Why?"

"I need to put the trauma kit there so it doesn't freeze."

"Right." Pat looked at the women and broke into a huge grin. "Couldn't do this without you."

Yulia beamed and Pat leaned over and kissed her on the cheek. He took one last look at the campsite, taking in all the details. The fire was far enough from the overhanging ice shelf that it wouldn't break off and come crashing down on the women. The helicopter was tucked away from the wind, but its rotors still able to spin without hitting anything. The trauma kit was in the chopper and Yulia was sharp enough to know she needed to keep the saline solutions and drugs from freezing. It was best to leave it in the helicopter, she was the only one with enough medical training to use the equipment.

Pat jumped to his feet, zipped up his parka and walked quickly to the helicopter. He opened the cargo door, and with Bobby's help unloaded the snowmobiles. The fuel lines were partially frozen, but eventually he got them both going. They let the machines idle for about ten minutes before Pat slid his leg over the seat and grasped both handles. He revved the engine for a second, gave Bobby the thumbs up and shot off across the smooth expanse of snow that covered the frozen river. Bobby opened the throttle on his machine and pulled in behind.

It was like nothing Bobby had ever experienced. The machine was fast and responsive, and glided over the snow as effortlessly as a hot knife through butter. He leaned one way, then the other, feeling it corner as he shifted his weight. It was like floating on air, and he hardly noticed the icy blast as they flew down the valley.

They headed north for about a mile and a half, covering the distance in good time. The valley floor was mostly flat, interspersed with small hills and rock outcrops that they took care to steer clear of. Overhead the sky was a mosaic of stars, clearly visible through the cold air. It was just after five in the morning when Pat angled toward a ridge on the east side of the valley. He pulled up in a spot that was mostly sheltered from the wind howling down the valley and killed the engine.

"Got a quarter for the meter?" he yelled over the wind when Bobby had powered off his machine.

Bobby shook his head. "You really are nuts, you know."

"I'm nuts to be out here helping you. It's fucking freezing."

Bobby looked around and all he could see was snow and rocks. "Which way to the gulag?"

Pat pointed to the ridge that towered over them on one side. "It's just over that outcrop. Once we're on top we'll take a few minutes to see if they have a guard posted before going in." Pat unzipped his parka and slid a gun out from somewhere inside the fur suit. It was a Smith & Wesson .44 Magnum.

Bobby tucked up against the rocks, pulled out his Glock and checked to make sure it wasn't frozen. Everything appeared to be working and he stuffed it back inside his snow suit.

Pat stashed his gun away as well and motioned for Bobby to follow. "Let's go."

It took longer than both Bobby and Pat expected to climb the rock face and it was well after five-thirty when they finally crested the ridge. A gale force wind hit them, whipping up tiny crystals of snow that cut into exposed flesh and stung their eyes as they peered over the edge. Below them was a group of six buildings, most in terrible condition and some with collapsed roofs. At least two of the shacks appeared to be in use, with smoke pouring from the chimney of one and dribbling slowly from the other. Bobby figured the two occupied buildings to be about a hundred feet apart, with no cover of any sort between them. Worse, the terrain between them and the cabins was an open, snow covered expanse of about four hundred feet. Once they moved from their protected position behind the ridge, there would be no turning back.

"What do you think?" Pat asked Bobby as they surveyed the scene.

"She's in that one." Bobby pointed to the cabin with the least smoke coming from the chimney.

"Agreed." Pat kept his eyes on the cabins. "You're the cop. How should we do this? Go after the woman first or second?"

"Leave her where she is," Bobby said firmly. "We go after the guys watching her, then we don't have to worry about her getting caught in the crossfire."

"Good idea. We take out the bad guys first." Pat leaned back against the rocks, blinking as the Arctic wind stung his face. "Any idea how many there are?"

"Not a fucking clue," Bobby responded.

There was a break in their conversation for a few minutes as they watched the buildings nestled into the valley below them. They were in Bobby's world now—the one where he had been so many times before. When and how to go after the bad guys. Bobby turned to Pat. "There's no sentry. Let's go, my friend. Time's a wasting."

chapter fifty-six

The rain was heavy, hindering Tony's view through the windshield and turning the back roads into grease as he searched for the cabin. By one o'clock he had had enough. He turned around and headed back down the narrow track to the highway. When he hit the edge of town he pulled into the Jiffy-Mart, locked the car and sauntered into the store.

The woman he had spoken with was busy bagging groceries and he picked out a few items and chose her till. She started to smile when she saw him, then her eyes went wide and her body stiffened. He knew immediately that she had seen Janis Greco. He kept the basket in his left hand and slipped his pistol from under his jacket with the other. It was below the basket and pointed at Barbara Zeigler's heart.

"Move," he said. "Out to the car or I'll kill you right here."

She swallowed hard and started to say something, but he made a shushing sound and she followed his instructions. He told her which car was his, and kept the gun trained on her as she walked through the parking lot and slid into the passenger's seat. He started the car, backed up and headed out of Ocilla. They drove for a couple of minutes until he was sure no one was following them, then started in with the questions.

"When did she come in?" he asked.

"Listen, mister, I got nothin' to do with your problems."

"Answer my question." DaSilva raised the gun slightly off his lap.

"She came in maybe an hour ago."

"And you said I was looking for her." He kept his voice calm, almost gentle.

"Yes," she said, relaxing a bit now. "I told her and she got all upset. I didn't know you were her husband, mister."

Tony had no idea what Janis Greco had told the cashier. *If* the woman thought he was the husband, then it was best to play along.

"I have to find her. She has the kids." Tony lowered the gun and set it in his lap. He put both hands on the steering wheel. It made no difference to him, he could still kill her before she could reach across the car. Letting go of the gun would calm her and get her to open up.

"Like I told you, she's staying at a cabin," Barbara said.

"She never told you where?"

"No."

"Okay, I tell you what." Tony kept his voice even and low, reassuring her that he was a rational man. "We'll look for her together. When we find her, you can go and let her know I'm in the car and ask for her to come out. She'll calm down, she always does. Then I'll drive you back to town." He looked over at her and smiled. "How does that sound?"

Barbara sat quietly in the seat, her mind racing. Who should she believe? The woman seemed reasonable, and the girls were relaxed at her side, so they obviously didn't feel threatened. Still, he had been at the school when the call came in, and there was no way the principal would have helped if there was any history of abuse. She thought about how she would react if her husband took the kids, and figured she'd be doing exactly what he was—desperately looking for them. What parent wouldn't?

"What can I do to help?" she asked.

"You say she left the Jiffy-Mart an hour ago," he said, and she nodded. "Then whatever road she took will have fresh tire tracks in the mud. I'll pull up and drive slow as we pass the roads. You look for tracks. Deal?"

"All right. You promise you won't hurt her when we find them?"

Tony glanced down in his lap at the gun. He shook his head. "Yeah, sorry about the gun. That was stupid." He slid it back into its holster. Out of sight, out of mind. "She's been gone for over a week now, and I'm worried she's getting a bit unbalanced. She has a history of not being so stable, if you know what I mean."

Barbara knew a woman in town who had problems dealing with everyday life. "I do."

Tony drove to the last access road he had checked, then slowed, stopping at each turnoff so Barbara could run across the road and check if a vehicle had driven through the mud recently. Nine roads nothing, then at the tenth she waved and pointed at the mud. Tony swung across the deserted highway and pulled in beside her. He eased himself from the car and looked down. There was no mistaking it. A vehicle had driven through the mud very recently. The tire tracks weren't even full of water yet. He smiled and they both got back in the car.

He drove on the road for about ten minutes before stopping. He glanced over, saw the look of horror on her face and smiled at her.

"Out of the car, please." He pointed at the door handle.

"Please don't hurt me, mister." Her eyes were welling up with tears. "I won't say anything."

He motioned again for her to open the door, and she did. He stayed behind the wheel and lowered the passenger window. She stood framed in the opening, soaking wet, her makeup streaking down her cheeks as her tears mixed with the rain. He slipped the gun from its holster and fired. The bullet hit her mid-chest, exploding as it drove through her heart, killing her before she hit the ground. Her body slid down a steep incline into the overgrown ditch, and Tony closed the window and drove ahead without looking back.

Half an hour later the cabin came into view. He could have missed it except for the light shining through the trees. *Amateurs*, he thought. A professional would never have left a light on, no matter how dreary the day. He parked a hundred feet farther up the road and doubled back, moving quietly through the underbrush. The cabin was surrounded by shrubs and trees and he got within twenty feet before coming to open ground. He stayed motionless in the trees, the rain dripping off the branches and slowly soaking through his jacket. Finally, a figure appeared in the house, a woman moving about in the kitchen. Janis Greco. She spent a bit of time at the stove, then set something on the table. A moment later two girls appeared, sat at the table and began eating. It was lunchtime.

Tony waited until Janis was seated, then crept through the bushes until he was facing the front of the house. The living room was dark and he raced across the lawn to the front door, hugging the rough wooden exterior of the cabin. Through the door he could hear children laughing, and his best guess was that they were still in the kitchen. He took a piece of thin wire from his pocket and slid it inside the lock, feeling for the tumblers. They clicked open and he slowly swung the door inward and slipped inside the house.

Tony closed the door behind him, took off his shoes and tiptoed across the living room to the kitchen door. He slid his weapon from its holster and took a couple of deep breaths. It was just a woman and two kids, he reminded himself before stepping around the corner and leveling the gun at Janis Greco.

"Don't move," he said, ignoring the children's piercing screams at the sight of the gun. "Put your hands on the table."

Janis's lips trembled as she did what he had asked. "Don't hurt my children. Do whatever you want, but for God's sake leave my children alone."

Tony stared down the barrel at her. Just like her picture, she was attractive and fit. He had hoped to have sex before capping her, and now that looked possible. He took a quick glance at the children, wide-eyed and terrified. They were cute, almost angelic. Too bad. He motioned to the stairs.

"Send the kids to their rooms," he said. "They'll be safe there."

Janis was trembling but managed to keep her voice steady. "Lizzie, Sarah, I want you to go upstairs and stay in your room. I have to talk with this man for a few minutes. When we're finished talking, I'll come up and get you. Don't come out of your room. Do you understand?"

Sarah and Lizzie nodded as they ran from the room and up the stairs.

Tony kept the gun trained on Janis. He made a slight gesture with his head toward the living room and she rose and walked past him, then stood next to the couch. "I'm glad you didn't go up in smoke in Orlando." He eyed her body, up and down.

"Why kill me?" she asked. "I'm nobody special."

"Someone thinks you are." He rounded the edge of the couch and pointed to her shirt. She started to unbutton it. "Your ex-husband pissed him off, and when he gets angry, people pay."

She let her shirt slip off her shoulders onto the floor. She reached behind her back and unclasped her bra. "If it's about Bobby, I'm not even married to him anymore." The bra slid down her arms, over her hands and landed on top of the shirt.

He was hungry for her, wanting her now that he saw her partially naked. "Your jeans," he whispered, his voice anxious, his breathing coming quicker. "Take them off."

She complied, sliding them over her hips then down her thighs. She leaned over and tugged the bottom of the legs one at a time until they lay in a heap on the floor. She wore bikini panties, and stood in front of him wearing that one scant piece of lingerie.

"Everything." He kept one hand on the gun as he unbuckled his belt and let his pants fall. Janis slid her panties down and stood facing him, naked. He was down to his underwear and from the bulge in his shorts, she could tell he was exited. She lay down on the couch, keeping her legs together. Her right hand slid down behind the cushion and she fished around until she felt the handle of the shotgun. She coughed slightly as she released the safety. Tony pulled off his underwear.

"You're going to enjoy this, sweetheart," he said, his one hand still on the gun, the other forcing her legs apart. She lifted her left leg up and out of the way of the barrel of the shotgun and leaned back hard, tilting the gun upward under the cushions. Then she pulled the trigger.

The blast sent the couch in one direction and Tony DaSilva in the opposite. The tight pattern of pellets caught him in the groin area and up, shredding his penis and peppering his stomach and chest with hot metal. He screamed and grabbed for his manhood. It was gone. Blood spilled from his wounds, then began to flow from his mouth. He grasped for his gun, which had skittered across the floor, but it was too far and he lay in a growing pool of blood, unable to move.

Janis Greco struggled to keep it together. She looked away from the bloody mess on the floor, picked up the pistol and placed it on the coffee table. Once she was dressed, she forced herself to look at the body again. He was still, his chest no longer heaving. She approached him carefully, touching her index finger behind his ear, feeling for a pulse. Nothing. She could hear the kids screaming at her from their room, and she yelled up to them that she was okay and to stay where they were.

Janis took a deep breath before pulling the body onto the area rug in the middle of the room and rolling it up inside. She dragged it outside onto the front porch, then returned to the living room to clean up the worst of the blood. Exhausted and shaking, she went upstairs to her children and led them out the back door to the car. As they drove off, Sarah asked what had happened to the bad man.

"Exactly what *should* happen to bad people," Janis replied.

She'd have to improvise, find a new place to stay. One mistake had almost got her and the children killed. No more calls from a traceable phone, cash only for every purchase, and she would trust no one. No more mistakes, not until Bobby had sorted this out.

chapter fifty-seven

Trent watched the Maserati leave the underground parking lot at twenty past six. Cortez's muscle wouldn't be far behind, and moments later two black, four door sedans tailed him into the Cannes traffic. The SEALs were waiting across the street, and Trent gave the three vehicles a long head start before pulling in behind. He knew where they were going, and now, how many vehicles there were.

"Did you get a look at the number of guys in each car?" He asked Kyle as they blended in with the evening traffic.

"Cortez and the woman in the Maserati, two guys in the second car, three in the third."

"That's what I got. Pretty much what we expected," Trent confirmed. "Which one do we take out first?"

Kyle stared out the window into the darkness. The sun had already set and it was a cloudy moonless night. Perfect conditions for what was ahead. "I say the one with three shooters. Just a numbers thing."

"Agreed." Trent upshifted to make a traffic light. "Let me know when. You know the road best."

"Will do," Kyle said.

Their plan was to come up fast behind the two escort cars and take them out with automatic fire and grenades, then go after the Maserati. The coastal highway was an insane series of switchbacks and tunnels, with steep drops down to the Mediterranean on one side and a sheer rock wall on the other. It was on that stretch of road where they intended to eliminate the arms dealer.

"What could possibly go wrong?" Trent asked, his fingers loose on the wheel.

"Yeah, no shit."

Trent kept well behind the procession as they passed through Nice, losing them a couple of times, then picking them up again a little farther down the road. Outside the city they continued northward along the coast to Villefranche-sur-mer. The highway climbed steeply once they cleared the tranquil village, its lights dotting the rugged mountains towering above the sea. The road hugged the cliff edge, snaking back on itself and weaving its way up the sheer rock walls.

Kyle put his weapon on his lap, the safety off. "Time."

"Ready," Trent said. "I'm moving up."

Trent passed the tailing car, settling in between the second and third vehicles. They kept the distance for a mile or so, then slowed slightly, creating a larger gap between the two cars with the bodyguards. Trent held the wheel steady as Kyle rolled the window down, pulled the pins on four grenades and held the clips down so the five second fuses didn't activate. They hit a switchback and Trent slowed, gearing down into first. He gave Kyle the nod.

"Do it," he said as he peered around the corner.

Kyle released the clip on the first grenade and tossed it out the window. A second later he repeated the action—then again and again until all four grenades were bouncing about on the road behind them. Trent floored the Porsche and wound out the gears. Seconds later the road behind them was obliterated. The vehicle took two direct hits and its gas tank exploded, the flaming wreck careening wildly over the embankment and plunging toward the water five hundred feet below.

Trent was gaining quickly on the second vehicle when Kyle leaned out the window and let loose with a quick burst of automatic fire. One tire on the car blew and the driver lost control. It veered sharply and smashed into the rock wall, then spun out and slid across into the guard rail where it teetered on the edge of the cliff. The men threw the doors open and piled out onto the road as Trent came up on them. He slowed and Kyle raked the scene with gunfire from one end to the other, the men jerking about as the bullets hit their mark. The carnage behind them, Trent floored the Porsche and took off after the Maserati.

Cortez was a skilled driver and already a good distance ahead of them. Trent hit the corners fast, the rear end of the Porsche sliding dangerously close to the cliff. He misjudged one slightly and the car bounced off the rock wall and headed straight for the guard rail. Trent fought the wheel and the front tires caught on the pavement at the last second.

"Holy shit," Kyle yelled as the car bounced off the wall. "Thought we were done."

Trent's knuckles were bone white on the wheel. "Too close."

He hit a rare straight stretch and floored it, the engine screaming as he pushed each gear to its limit and the speedometer edged over one-sixty. They came up fast on the next corner and Trent slammed on the brakes, wrestling to keep the car straight, then hit the gas the moment he started into the bend. The car rocketed through the turn and shot out the other end at eighty miles an hour. They were closing in. Three more switchbacks and Kyle pointed.

"We've got him," he yelled. "He's about a hundred yards ahead."

"We don't have him yet," Trent said, going pedal to the metal on the 911. The turbo kicked in and they continued to gain on Cortez through another tight corner. When they came out of the switchback, they were right behind the Maserati and Kyle leaned out the window with the submachine gun.

Cortez was not going to be taken down as easily as his bodyguards, and he steered hard left onto a tiny road cutting through a narrow gap in the rocks. It led inland, away from the sea and into the hills, and he hit the gas and opened the distance between the two cars. The Maserati was larger and heavier than the Porsche and couldn't hold the corners as well, but the Porsche couldn't match the Maserati's incredible acceleration on the straight sections of road. They jockeyed back and forth, with Cortez pulling ahead then Trent closing the gap when they hit a series of bends until they reached a village with houses bordering the road. Cortez didn't slow at all, screaming through the cluster of houses at an insane speed. Trent couldn't risk killing an innocent person and took his foot off the gas. Cortez raced far enough ahead that they lost visual contact.

"Ahh, shit," Trent cursed as they reached the edge of town and he hit the gas again.

Outside the village was a small traffic circle that led off in four directions, and Trent slammed on the brakes. Kyle jumped from the car and ran around the circle, his eyes glued to the road.

"Here." He pointed to the third exit. "Fresh rubber."

Trent jammed the Porsche into first and floored it, reaching one-forty before he had to slow for a group of stone buildings fronting onto the road. He geared down, the engine roaring as they rounded a sharp corner and passed the last of the houses. The moment they were in the clear the car was hammered with bullets. The Maserati's brake line had finally drained out and the car had careened into a stone wall. It was a mangled wreck, but Cortez was out of the car and firing with an automatic weapon.

Bullets strafed down the length of the Porsche, cutting through the metal side panels and ripping into the cockpit. Trent screamed and grabbed his left arm as the car swerved wildly and flipped, rolling once before landing back on its wheels in a field next to the road. Kyle threw himself into the door and it sprung open. He leaped from the car, rolling on his shoulder and firing as he regained his feet. He missed, but Cortez didn't. Four slugs slammed into his chest, sending the SEAL backward into the car. He slid down the door panel, the gun falling from his hand.

Trent ignored the searing pain in his shoulder and jumped out, racing for the stone buildings. Bullets churned up the dirt as he wove his way across the field and dove behind a house. A minute passed in silence, and Trent peered carefully from behind the shutters, drawing fire for his efforts. The bullets gouged out the rocks and sent tiny splinters flying in all directions. A couple cut into his face and neck and he grimaced as blood streamed down his cheek. From the edge of the building he could see Kyle, lying motionless.

"Shit," he whispered.

His mind was racing as he thought through his options. First off, he needed to figure out where Cortez was and the trajectory of the bullets could tell him that. He closed his eyes and envisioned the houses, the road, the field and the location of the Porsche when Cortez had opened up on them. The only way he could have shot Kyle and now be in a position to cover him was if he was at the corner of the house directly across the street. It might be possible to circle around and take him from behind. Trent moved quickly along the back of the house and glanced up the road. There were short rock walls on both sides, and he crouched down and ran behind one until the road had curved enough that Cortez couldn't see him cross. He hopped over the rocks, then sprinted across the street and slid in behind the wall on the opposite side, hugging it and moving fast for where Cortez was dug in. Speed was everything. In a few seconds Cortez would realize he was on the move.

Trent reached the target building and crept along the back side to the far corner, then risked a quick look. Nothing. He quietly made his way down the length of the building and inched up to the corner. He took a steadying breath and jerked out into the open, his gun leveled at chest height.

Cortez was still looking across the road. He heard Trent behind him and spun, his finger tightening on the trigger. Trent had seen this reaction before, the arms dealer wasn't going to drop the gun and surrender, the weapon was coming to bear. Trent fired and bullets raked Cortez from his chest up to his neck. He staggered back from the impact, collapsing in a heap at the edge of the building.

Trent kept his gun trained on him as he approached, then stood over the dying man. He bent over, his face close to Cortez. "Where is Alexis?"

Cortez stared back at the SEAL. "Fuck you."

Trent ran his fingers across Cortez's chest, feeling for an object inside in his dinner jacket. He found it and flipped the lapel back, then slipped the hard drive from the inside pocket. He glanced at the label. 03-417-J/S was written in black felt pen on the top side. This was what he had come for. He had the JASSM technology. He put the drive in his pocket and asked Cortez again, "Where is Alexis Chamberlain?"

"Piss off," Cortez wheezed. They were his last words.

Trent didn't bother moving the body. He left it on the edge of the road and hurried back to the Porsche. Kyle was still propped against the car, blood seeping through his shirt. Trent ripped it open, revealing a Kevlar vest with three bullets sticking out and one hole. A bullet had penetrated the high tensile steel and the wound was serious. He winced and hoisted the injured man onto his good shoulder and slid him into the front seat of the car.

Kyle opened an eye and whispered, "The fucker shot me."

"Yeah, but then I shot him."

"Good." Kyle closed his eye and passed out.

Trent took a quick look at the scene—the ruined Maserati and the bloody corpse. The French police would be there in minutes and dealing with them was something he didn't need. He stood at the driver's door for a few seconds, searching for the woman in the darkness. Nothing. He jumped into the car and gunned it, heading for the back roads and Nice, where he could get Kyle to a doctor. The Porsche churned through the dirt in the field and bumped back onto the road as the first sounds of police sirens floated on the night air.

Sylvia Dupres huddled inside the stone building, not making a sound until the roar of the Porsche's engine was gone. In its place the wail of approaching sirens grew louder. She took a furtive glance out the door to see if anyone was watching, gave Armand's limp body a quick look and started running. She stayed off the main road and cut across an open field for a grove of trees. The ground was soft and she kicked off her heels and carried them, her breath coming hard and fast by the time she reached the trees. A narrow road led back toward the coast and she settled into a steady jog, putting as much distance as she could between her and her dead lover.

The image of Armand was horrific and it wasn't going away. The dark red bloodstains, the blank eyes and contorted body—shot by some

American cowboy with a gun. She felt a rage rising up, clouding her vision, and almost stumbled and fell. Dupres steadied herself and concentrated on each footstep. Getting injured was not going to accomplish anything, what she needed now was to link up with Monique, and she stayed focused on that.

Thank God she had called her daughter and told her to get out of the Chamberlain house. A text had come back less than an hour later—*FBI all over, just made it*. Monique was adept at disappearing, she'd been at it all her life. She was somewhere in the US, changing her look and figuring out a way to get to Croatia, where a small house on the coast was waiting for them.

Sylvia's legs moved in a steady rhythm, her bare feet making tiny slapping sounds on the asphalt. She was growing stronger with each step and thinking clearly about what was ahead, not what lay behind. Monique had already drained tens of millions of dollars from the Chamberlain estate, and that coupled with Armand's millions made them very wealthy women. Vast wealth made it easy to take on new identities and disappear into new lives. No one was going to find them.

Armand's bloody corpse pushed its way into her mind again and she heard his killer asking, *Where is Alexis?*

A disconcerting thought occurred to her as she ran. Where *was* Alexis?

chapter fifty-eight

The six derelict cabins were an ugly scar on the virgin landscape.

Two dark figures popped up over the hard-packed snow on the ridge and skittered down the incline toward the cabins. The moon was low in the sky, but the light reflecting off the white surface left them fully exposed.

Pat whispered to Bobby as they moved, his breath coming in short burst of steam. "The snow we're walking on is just a thin crust, maybe three or four inches," he said quietly. "If anyone comes out of the cabin, kick hard and you'll break through. It's all powder underneath and they won't be able to see us. Just remember to turn sideways to breathe so the steam doesn't come out the hole. Got it?"

"Jump hard on the crust, then lay in the powder and breathe to the side," Bobby repeated.

"Right," the Canadian said as they continued down the slope.

As they closed in on the cabins, they could smell the smoke drifting across the open ground. They were less than a hundred feet away when a door on the far side opened, sending a sliver of light across the snow. Pat motioned down with his hand, and both men pushed hard on the surface. The crust gave way and they tumbled into a pile of loose powder.

The snow was blinding and they could barely breathe as they slid uncontrollably down the hill and away from their air holes. When they came to a stop, Bobby felt pressure on his arm and looked over. A touch of moonlight filtered through the icy crust above them, and he could make out Patrick's face, covered with snow. Pat put his finger up to his mouth and Bobby's panic ebbed as he watched Pat breathe, slow and steady. A minute later Pat wriggled around and pulled out his gun. He placed the barrel against the crust and twisted, first left, then right until the barrel broke through and a tiny bit of night sky appeared. He hoisted himself up so his eye was to the hole and watched for a minute, then slumped back into the powder.

"He's gone back inside," Pat said. Despite the darkness, Bobby could see a grin on the Canadian's face. "That was quite the ride down the hill, eh?"

The adrenaline was still surging and Bobby couldn't help grinning as well. "Fucking great."

"Should have thought of that," Pat said. "Being on a hill and all."

Pat widened the hole and poked his head out. It was clear and he pushed upward, thrusting his shoulders through the snow. Bobby did the same, and a few seconds later they were on top again and moving toward the cabins. There was no turning back now, they were less than fifty feet out. Pat picked up the pace, almost running across the snow and risking another collapse. The crust held and they reached the side of the cabin.

Bobby took the lead and pointed with his gun. "You go that way and wait at the window. When you hear me come through the door, smash the glass and shoot anything that moves." He turned and started down the side of the building, then stopped and turned back. "Except me," he added.

Bobby disappeared around the corner and Pat crept down the wall until he reached the window. He pulled out his gun, chambered a round and took the safety off. The hood on his parka limited his line of sight and he pushed it back, the bitter cold biting at his ears and exposed head. He ignored it and tensed up, waiting for the sound of Bobby kicking in the door. A moment later he heard his cue.

A crashing sound burst through the quiet, followed by three shots in quick succession. Pat hammered the glass with the butt of his gun and grabbed the grimy curtain covering the window, ripping it out of the way. Bobby was framed in the doorway, gun up and firing. Pat spotted a man moving fast toward the back door and squeezed the trigger. The pistol recoiled as it pumped out cartridge after cartridge and the man spun sideways as the bullets found their mark. Pat fired one last shot as the guy tried to get a bead with his gun, taking out his trachea and severing his spinal cord. Pat ducked as bullets chewed into the wooden window frame inches from his face, followed by a smashing sound from the far side of the cabin. It sounded like a body going through the other window and Pat figured one of the guys in the house had bailed. There was movement on his right side and he whipped his gun up to firing position. It was Bobby rounding the corner.

"I got one," Pat gasped. There was no humor in his eyes now, just determination.

"So did I," Bobby panted. "One went through the window on the south side."

"Yeah, I figured."

Bobby looked about. "We need to keep ourselves between him and Alexis's cabin. I don't want her being used as a shield." He shifted his focus back to Pat. "He's not dressed to be out in this weather. He'll get desperate and come looking for us."

"Okay. What do you want me to do?"

"Get into Alexis's cabin, and once you're inside protect her. Shoot anything that tries to come through the door."

"Unless it's you."

Bobby gave him an irritated look. "He's probably in one of the other shacks. I'm going to try and flush him out."

"I thought you were going to wait for him to make a move."

Bobby shook his head. "Reconsidered it. This guy wants us dead and has a loaded gun. We don't want him running around any longer than necessary. I'm going after him."

Pat grabbed Bobby's arm. "You're too much out of your element with all that gear on. Bad reaction time could get you killed. I'll go after the guy with the gun, you get to Alexis."

Bobby considered pulling the *I used to be a cop* card, but Pat was right, he was having a tough time functioning in the snow and frigid air. "All right, but for Christ's sake, be careful."

"Of fucking course I'm going to be careful."

Bobby hugged the cabin wall as he hustled toward the shack where Alexis was being held. He glanced behind him when he reached the corner, but Pat had already disappeared into the night. Bobby took a deep breath and made a run for it, legs pumping as he pushed through the snow. He reached the cabin and stopped at the door, listening. It was quiet. The latch was simple to operate from the outside, and he slid the bolt back and slipped inside, his gun in front of him with his finger on the trigger.

The interior was dark except for a dim light coming from a stove in the center of the room. He closed the door behind him, squinting as his eyes adjusted to the darkness. A figure was huddled against the far wall, and he moved closer.

"Alexis?"

Wild eyes stared back at him through a tangled mat of filthy hair. They softened at the sound of his voice.

"Yes." Her voice was barely audible. "I'm Alexis. Who are you?"

"I'm the cavalry," Bobby said. "We're going to get you out of here."

There was almost no reaction. She still looked terrified.

Bobby hustled over to her side and set his hand gingerly on her arm. He recoiled slightly at the feel of it, so thin and frail, like a skinny chicken wing. "One of the bad guys is still out there," he said. "We're not out of the woods yet."

She clutched at his arm. "Thank God you're here." Her voice was soaked with desperation.

"Where do you usually sit?" he asked. She looked confused and he asked again. "When they bring your meals, where do you normally wait?"

"Right here," she said. "It's the furthest from the door."

"Let's move. If the wrong guy comes through the door, I don't want to be sitting where he expects us."

"Okay," she said.

Alexis got up on unsteady feet. She followed Bobby across the room and they crouched against the wall. Bobby knelt in front of her with one knee on the floor and the other at ninety degrees to support his shooting arm. He held the position, focused on nothing but the door. Alexis began to say something, but he gave her a quick shush and she lapsed into silence. Minutes ticked by, then two shots in quick succession cut through the air. The reports from the guns were markedly different.

"They both got off a shot," Bobby said. "We'll know soon now." He felt her trembling as she crouched behind him, terrified.

They heard boots crunching on snow as someone approached the cabin. Bobby felt his muscles relax a bit. The person wasn't trying to be quiet—it must be Pat. He held his breath as the steps reached the door. It burst open and the room lit up with muzzle flashes. Two bullets smashed into the far wall before the shooter realized Bobby and Alexis weren't there and jerked his gun around, searching for them. He was fast and almost had them in his sights before Bobby got off a shot, hitting him in the head. His body jerked, then collapsed. Bobby stood and cautiously approached the body, kicking the gun from the limp hand and checking for a pulse. Nothing. He returned to Alexis.

"Let's go. The other cabin is warmer than this one. I want you to stay there while I look for Pat." He grabbed her emaciated waist and held her close to him, but she was stumbling as they walked. He lifted her up and carried her, protecting her as best he could from the bitter cold as they struggled through the snow. She weighed almost nothing, and he wondered how she had ever survived. When they got to the cabin Alexis knelt by the fire, shaking and wide-eyed at the carnage. Bobby dragged the bodies outside and threw them in the snow, then hustled off to search for Pat.

His best guess to where Pat might be was from the gunshots. That put the location somewhere to the southwest and he jogged through the snow, looking for a dark object against the endless white. He rounded the corner of one of the huts and stopped in his tracks. Pat's limp body hung from a protruding log. Bobby ran over and lowered him gently onto the bloodstained snow, placing his finger on Pats carotid artery, not sure he wanted to know the answer. *Come on, man, don't be dead.* Pat's pulse was strong and his heart was beating normally.

"Oh, you tough mother fucker," he said.

Bobby lifted his friend into a fireman's carry and slogged his way back to the cabin, kicking the door open and laying Pat down beside the fire. Alexis had thrown a few more pieces of wood on the flames and the room had heated up considerably. Bobby started to unzip Pat's snowsuit when a hand shot out and grabbed his wrist.

"What the fuck?" Pat asked.

"Relax. I'm looking for a bullet hole." Bobby leaned back and watched as Pat struggled to sit up.

"Holy shit, I feel like someone hit me with a shovel." He shook his head back and forth a few times, then he noticed Alexis sitting next to the fire. He stopped and stared at her. "My God, woman. You need to do something with your hair."

She smiled and burst into tears at the same time.

chapter fifty-nine

Pat was hurt bad.

How bad, Bobby wasn't sure, but he knew Pat needed medical attention. There were three satellite phones in the cabin, but all had passwords and were useless. There was no way to call for help.

Bobby kept a close eye on Alexis. Some of her strength was returning as she ate, but she was a skeleton. Her muscles were showing signs of atrophy and she would be a long time recovering. Three of them on one snowmobile would be too heavy, the machine would sink when they hit soft snow, and if that happened they would die of exposure. *If* he decided they needed to head back to the helicopter, Alexis would have to drive the second machine.

"Are you feeling better?" Bobby knelt beside Alexis and handed her a cup of hot broth.

"Yes." She was sitting with Pat, who was drifting in and out of consciousness. "Is he going to be okay?"

"I hope so. He took a bullet under his right lung. I think it missed his organs and there's an exit wound on his back, so it definitely went through. I'm pretty sure he smashed his head when he went down, so he has a concussion and has lost a lot of blood."

"Where am I?" Alexis asked.

"Russia."

"*Russia*." She leaned back on the bed of animal furs next to the fire. "How?"

Bobby refilled Alexis's tea and encouraged her to drink while he told her the story. He didn't hold anything back, except the identity of her father. When he was finished she sat without moving, a hint of tears mixed with determination in her eyes.

Finally, she said, "My children are safe."

"They are."

"And Ryan…" She couldn't keep the tears back. "He's dead."

"Yes."

Bobby had always hated that part of working homicide, telling people that someone they loved was dead.

She poked at the fire, thoughtfully adjusting the pile of wood, then asked, "What now?"

Bobby had been kicking that around in his head for a while. Yulia was the only one with the medical training to stop Pat's bleeding and get an IV going, and Bobby was pretty sure without it Pat was going to die. Yulia and June were calling for help at six o'clock, almost ten hours from now, and it would be a good long time after that before anyone showed up at the cabins. Pat would bleed out long before then, so waiting for help was not going to work.

"We need to get back to the helicopter," Bobby said, "and that's not going to be easy. Someone needs to drive the second snowmobile." He looked at Pat, semi-conscious and mumbling under his breath. "I don't think Pat is able."

Alexis sipped her tea and puffed out a tiny bit. "I've driven one, when we visited Denver in the winter."

"This is different," Bobby said. "We're not going to be on a groomed trail, it's minus fifty, and if anything goes wrong we will freeze to death. Plus, Pat and I on one sled will be too heavy. You'll have to take him on yours and he'll mostly be dead weight. He could tip your machine."

Alexis chewed on her nail. "We can't stay here."

"No, we have to get moving," Bobby agreed. "I've seen enough gunshot wounds to know Pat needs a doctor and an IV or he won't make it. And the snowmobiles are going to freeze solid if I don't go and get them soon."

Alexis nodded. "I understand. I'll watch Pat."

Bobby covered every inch of skin and doubled down on the gloves, wearing some with wolf fur that he had found in the cabin. When he was dressed, he grasped Alexis's hand and gave her a nod.

"I'll be about an hour."

He closed the door firmly behind him and started trudging up the hill he and Pat had slid down an hour ago. The incline was steep and halfway up he was exhausted and almost unable to put one foot in front of the other.

"Jesus, Bobby," he whispered to himself. "It's do this or die."

He thought of Sarah and Lizzie and managed another step, then another. One step at a time, careful not to break through the icy crust and go sliding back down the hill. A mistake now would be fatal.

Bobby refused to quit, and when he crested the hill he could see the snowmobiles sitting at the bottom of the rock outcrop. He started down the incline, careful not to slip on the icy stones. Ten feet from the bottom his boot went out from under him and he hit hard, bouncing and tumbling down to the valley floor. He lay in a heap, scared to move in case he'd broken a bone. Finally, he wiggled his toes and his fingers. Everything was working. He sat up and got to work.

Back at the helicopter, he had watched Pat warm the gas line with his body heat, and Bobby did the same before turning over the motor. The battery would only have so much power and he needed it to start the first time. The engine groaned, then caught. Bobby slowly gave it some revs and then let it settle into an idle. He repeated the procedure with the second machine and it started as well. He waited about ten minutes, then shut down the first sled and drove the other one down the valley until he found a place where he could get over the ridge. He circled back and reached the cabin a few minutes later, then shut the engine off and went in to check on Alexis.

"Got them both going," Bobby said when he'd stripped off enough clothing to talk.

"Good," Alexis said. She was sitting next to Pat looking worried. "He's worse, Bobby."

Bobby knelt down and listened closely to Pat's breathing. It was labored and there was a slight gurgling sound. The bullet must have nicked the lung. He was bleeding internally and his lung was likely beginning to fill.

"I'm going to get the other machine. You get him dressed for the trip, then find the warmest gear you can for yourself." Bobby took her gently by the shoulders. "You have to drive, Alexis. He'll die if you don't."

She nodded calmly, her scraggly hair moving with the motion. "I can do it."

He stared into her eyes for a moment, then said, "Yeah, you can."

Bobby started for the door, and Alexis said, "When you come back, can you stop at that little tree out there and break off a piece?"

It was an odd request, but he simply said, "Sure."

The second time up the ridge was harder. He had hoped to rest for a while at the cabin between trips, but Pat was going downhill too fast. Exhaustion set in and at one point he had to crawl on his hands and knees. When he finally reached the top he needed to rest for a minute and lay down on his back. The stars were gone and the sky was now vivid blue, and it felt so peaceful. As his eyes started to close, he remembered a story he'd read by Jack London where a man had stopped to rest and froze to death. He forced himself to get up and started down the rocky outcrop.

"Don't fuck up now. Your girls need you," he whispered to himself as he measured every foothold before putting weight on it.

He reached the bottom without falling. The snowmobile started easily and he followed the same route back, driving in the tracks to save fuel. When he reached the cabins he stopped at the tree and broke off a sprig, then headed inside. Alexis had Pat dressed and was ready to go. Bobby hoisted Pat up, got him outside and set him on one of the machines. He looped some rope around Pat's body and then knotted it to hold him on the bench seat.

"This is the gas." He twisted the handle slightly and the engine revved. "Don't let the front end of the skis dip under the snow or they'll dig in and throw you off. Keep the tips up."

"Like water skiing," Alexis said.

"Exactly." He helped her straddle the machine, then said, "We're only a couple of miles from the helicopter. Stay behind me, in my tracks."

"I will."

He pulled on his goggles and they left the cabins behind. Bobby kept glancing back to see how Alexis was faring. She was struggling to keep the skis in the tracks, mostly because Pat was shifting side to side. There was no other way, Pat's weight and his would be too much for the sled to plow through the loose snow. He'd learned on the way out to keep his speed constant—not so fast that the wind chill would be too much, and not so slow that the machine would sink in the snow. He took another look and she was still fifty feet back, on his tail. This was working.

Alexis could barely hold the handlebars. Her hands were cramping and she had no strength in her arms. The spray from Bobby's machine was a fine mist of ice crystals and stung like thousands of razor blades cutting into the tiny bits of exposed skin on her face. She wasn't sure she could make it another hundred feet when one of the skis hit a rock and threw the machine sideways. She channeled every bit of strength she had into keeping it from tipping, but Pat's body shifted and she felt the machine going over.

Alexis opened the throttle and threw herself to the opposite side, the engine screaming as the track spun wildly in the snow. She was sinking and the back end of the machine was settling into the loose snow, the tips threatening to drop under the crust. If she went under, Bobby would have to stop and they wouldn't get going again. She was going to kill all of them if she couldn't keep the machine afloat.

"You're not going to fucking win," she yelled and gave the handlebars one last wrench. The track caught and righted the machine for a moment. Alexis reached behind her and grabbed Pat and yanked his body back onto the middle of the seat. The sled settled into the snow, tips up and the track spinning, but she was out of Bobby's track now and breaking her own trail. Her adrenaline was surging and she felt a wave of confidence as she kept the throttle open and pulled up beside Bobby.

He glanced over, nodded and gave his machine a bit more gas to stay alongside her.

Yulia and June heard the high pitch whine of snowmobile engines at the same time. They ran out from the rift and stared into the blowing snow. At first all they could see were snowflakes whipped up by the wind, then two dark objects came floating out of the solid white, bearing down on them. The women stared at the machines, oblivious to the ice crystals biting at their eyes. When the sleds were finally close enough, Yulia turned to June and gave her a hug.

"Three people," she yelled. "They must have her."

"Oh, thank God."

The snowmobiles pulled up and both drivers killed their engines. Bobby jumped onto the snow and helped Alexis off her machine, then started untying Pat.

Pat came to for a few seconds and looked around. His face showed every bit of the agony he was fighting. He stared wide-eyed at Alexis and forced out a few words. "Bobby let you drive?"

"Yulia," he yelled as Pat passed out again. "Pat's shot and needs help. He's lost a lot of blood."

"Bring him to the chopper," Yulia said. "I'll rig up an IV."

"June." Bobby hoisted Pat and carried him toward the chopper. "Get our CIA friend on the phone and tell him we need a medivac right now."

June had the phone out and was dialing John's number by the time Bobby had Pat inside the helicopter. The CIA operative answered and listened to what she needed.

"There's a chopper at Julietta," he said. "I checked in with them a few hours ago and they're ready for our call."

"Julietta," June said. "That's the mine where Pat works."

"It is, and it's not far from you," John said. "I have your location from the GPS on your phone. They'll be there soon."

The line went dead and June headed over to join Alexis. She had stripped off her goggles and moved near the fire, where she stood staring at June in disbelief.

"Jesus, June," Alexis said, wrapping her arms around her and pulling her tight. Her frail body was shaking now, the adrenaline rush over and exhaustion setting in. She held her friend for a long time, then slowly relaxed her grip and looked her in the eyes. "I can't believe you're here."

"I am," June said, taking her hand. "*We* are."

They made their way to the helicopter to check on Pat, and when they got there it was obvious he was in trouble. Yulia had cut away his snowsuit and exposed his chest where he'd taken the bullet. She had an IV in his arm and Bobby was holding the saline solution so it was elevated and on a fast drip into the tube. Yulia was trying hard to stop the bleeding, but the defibrillator was out and ready, just in case.

She looked over at Alexis and June and yelled. "Close the door. It's getting too cold in here."

They backed off and Bobby slid it shut. The two women went back to the fire and sat huddling close to each other to stay warm.

"Who is he?" Alexis asked.

"One very enthusiastic Canadian." June glanced back at the chopper. "And someone very special."

They fed the fire and waited quietly. After about fifteen minutes they heard the distant thumping of a helicopter rotor. The volume increased and then it swept in over a nearby hill, headed directly for them. Help had arrived.

chapter sixty

The hospital corridor was dark and quiet, and for the first time in two days Alexis walked the entire length without holding the rail. She stopped at the door to Pat's room and listened. The nurse was in tending to him and they were speaking quietly in Russian. When she came out, Alexis went in and sat at his bedside taking his hand.

"Hi," she said.

Pat rolled his head slightly on the pillow so he was facing her. "You're my most regular visitor."

She smiled. "It's a short commute."

He managed a small smile, then grimaced in pain. His grip tightened on her hand. "Bit sore still," he said.

"The doctor told us you should have been dead." She cupped both her hands around his. "But Bobby said you're…" she paused, "*…too fucking stubborn to die*. Yeah, that was it."

Pat closed his eyes. "I'm glad we found you."

Alexis teared up, but didn't let go of his hand. "You're the bravest person I've ever met."

He took a couple of minutes to respond. "Oh, I don't know, Bobby's right up there."

She began to cry and buried her face into the pillow next to Pat. He tilted his head slightly so they were touching and neither of them moved for a long time. Finally, Alexis sat up and asked, "Do you want anything? Some water? A bite to eat?"

He shook his head. A few minutes later he opened his eyes and said, "I'm sorry about your husband."

A noise at the door caused Alexis to glance around. Yulia, June, and Bobby were looking in. She smiled and motioned for them to join her. "He's doing a lot better," she said.

Pat opened one eye and surveyed the newcomers. "No, I'm not," he said slowly, forming every word. "I'm still in mortal danger and require a lot of attention."

Bobby grinned. "I'm sure you do."

Pat closed his eyes, a big smile on his face. "All my favorite people."

An hour later, with Pat sleeping under Yulia's watchful eye, Bobby and June followed Alexis to a small lounge at the end of the hall. The furniture was worn, but to Alexis it was heaven. She sipped on her coffee and pulled a blanket over her legs.

"Tell me again how you pieced things together," she said to June. "I'm still a bit sketchy on the details."

"Of course."

June gave Alexis the story again, from the start. That Bobby had been fired by the Orlando police and had taken a job with Riggs & Company. How he had noticed her tennis backhand was different, and had begun an investigation that uncovered Ryan's murder, her kidnapping and the theft of the JASSM technology.

"And you're with the National Security Agency," Alexis said to June.

"I am."

Alexis shook her head. "It's unbelievable."

June waited a minute before continuing with how the rest of the events had unfolded, including Bobby tracking down the midwife and uncovering her mother's identity. "Only a handful of people know your sister exists," June said.

Alexis's face was a blistering shade of red and she couldn't hide the rage that was simmering inside. "Sylvia Dupres. My mother." The words were tinged with acid. Alexis was silent for a moment, but June and Bobby knew she wasn't finished.

"There were times when I wondered who my real parents were," Alexis finally said. "The Rothchilds were wonderful, but it's natural to have those thoughts." She slumped back in her chair, looking spent. "Now it turns out she's a monster."

"It's a lot to take in," June said.

"That's an understatement." Alexis took a few deep breaths and stared out the window at the snow-covered streets of Magadan. Her mind drifted back to the remote cabin that had once been a gulag. She couldn't begin to imagine the horrors the camp once held, the ghosts of all those tortured and killed in that desolate place. She would have been one more if it wasn't for Bobby and June. A hint of a smile came when she thought of Pat, recovering just down the hall. If she had ever owed a debt, this was it.

"You and Bobby found my mother, and you know who my father is, but you won't tell me."

"There are privacy issues and we're not at liberty to say anything," June said. "You'll find out soon enough."

"Is he involved in this?" Alexis asked.

"In a good way," June responded quickly. She glanced at Bobby, then said, "We've both met him and he's a good man."

Alexis pulled the blanket up over her chest and closed her eyes. Who was he? Despite June's assurance, if her father was anything at all like her mother he was sure to be a crushing disappointment. She took a deep breath and resigned herself to the fact that she had to wait.

Yulia came bustling down the hall with firm instructions about visiting hours being over and her patients needing their rest. She draped the blanket across Alexis's shoulders and gently helped her out of her chair.

"The doctor is ready to discharge you tomorrow," Yulia said.

Alexis beamed. "I spoke with her this morning. She said you're quite the nurse." Yulia blushed at the praise.

Bobby pulled out his cell phone and checked his texts. "Good news. Your plane is in the hangar at the airport. It arrived a few hours ago."

Alexis brightened at that. "We're going home."

She put her arms around June and Bobby, leaning on her friends as they shuffled back to her room.

The Gulfstream, with Synergy Industries emblazoned on its side, was a thing of beauty. It sat under a bank of lights on the tarmac, fueled and ready for its passengers. An SUV pulled up alongside and Alexis got out, then led the way up the stairs. Bobby and June tailed close behind.

A woman in a uniform greeted Alexis at the top of the stairs. Her face registered outright shock when she saw the gaunt face and body. "Mrs. Chamberlain," she stammered.

"Good morning, Glennis." Alexis expected a reaction and had decided that not acknowledging it would be best. "You know June Childers, and this is my friend, Bobby Greco."

"Welcome aboard," the flight attendant said.

They entered the plane and Bobby let out a low whistle at the plush interior. The women settled in as the pilots took the plane through a pre-flight check and got clearance from Air Traffic Control, while Bobby placed another call to Janis's cell phone. She was safe in a hotel in Georgia, and now had a two-person security detail in tow.

"Just tell me it's over, Bobby," she said when they connected.

"It's over," he said. "I'm sorry. None of this has been fair to you or the kids."

"These agents…" she paused, unsure of who had ordered them to protect her, "…they're waiting to hear that it's okay to go home. One of them said they'll know in a few hours."

"It should be. Cortez is dead," he confided. "A SEAL team took him out in southern France."

"Oh, thank God," the relief evident in her voice. "Sarah needs to get back to school, and I'd really like to go home."

"Call me when you get to the house and I'll stop by."

"Thanks, Bobby."

He sat with the phone in his lap, wondering how he had ever let her get away. Cortez had tried to kill her and the girls, but had come up short. Janis was the whole package—beautiful, intelligent and resourceful. He turned off his phone and closed his eyes, missing what they had when they were husband and wife. At least they had remained best of friends, and that meant the world to him.

The plane started moving and twenty minutes later was climbing fast, leaving the frozen Russian landscape behind. Bobby stared out the window at the vast expanse of ice and snow. He'd been there, on the ground, racing over the snow with Pat at his elbow in what was likely the craziest thing he'd ever done. They'd found Alexis and brought her back. What had seemed impossible was reality. He pulled down the window shade, reclined the seat and closed his eyes.

They refueled in Anchorage, then touched down again in Oakland to top up the tanks for the final leg across the continent. At eleven thirty-three the Gulfstream lifted off, its flight plan set for Orlando. Glennis brought hot coffee in china cups and set them on the table, and Bobby studied Alexis. He thought she was going to break down as she rubbed her fingers on the delicate cup and took a sip with quivering lips. He'd seen this emotional wreckage so many times and knew exactly what she was thinking.

After a while, she looked at June and whispered, "He's really gone, isn't he?"

June knew it was rhetorical and didn't answer. The woman was still coming to grips with what had happened.

Alexis was fighting the tears, staring down at the table, her shoulders slumped over. "I didn't get a chance to say goodbye. He was my husband. It's not fair."

"No, it's not." June glanced out the window, allowing Alexis some privacy with her grief.

"Well, at least I finally get to meet my father," Alexis said after a few minutes of silence.

"You do," June said.

Alexis had recovered a bit and there was a spark in her eyes. "Yes, as soon as possible."

June caught the yearning in her eyes and wanted to tell her more, to just blurt it out. Instead, she excused herself and walked to the rear of the plane and used the phone to call Derek Adler. She had been in constant contact with him, and Adler had cleared the president's schedule for the day. He was waiting for her call.

"What's your ETA?" he asked.

"We're about four hours out of Orlando, then another hour to get her home and settled in."

"Call me when you touch down," Adler said.

"Sure."

"Thanks, June."

She returned to the seat facing Alexis and said, "Your father is flying down to Orlando today. The plan is for him to drop by your house later this afternoon." June looked her in the eye and said, "Sound okay?"

Alexis looked a bit apprehensive, and finally stammered. "Okay, that would be fine. Thanks for setting it up."

"No problem."

Alexis stared out the window for a while, then said, "I'd like both of you to be there when I meet him."

The request took June by surprise, but after glancing at Bobby and getting a nod, she said, "Of course."

The Gulfstream was over the American heartland, moving at subsonic speeds. Getting from Magadan to Oakland, then going through customs was all Alexis could take, and she slept for most of the flight to Orlando. Glennis served them a meal after she woke, and then they all took turns freshening up in the washroom. As they were on their final approach to Orlando, Bobby phoned the Magadan hospital.

"He's still doing fine," Bobby reported to Alexis and June. "The risk of infection is getting less all the time."

"Thank God," Alexis said. "I owe him, and both of you, my life."

Bobby blushed slightly, which didn't go unnoticed by either of the women.

Alexis reached out and grasped Bobby's hand. "You're a hell of a detective."

Bobby ran his free hand through his thick mane. "Well, if it's any consolation, I think this is the most bizarre case I've ever worked."

The plane was banking now, coming around and lining up for the approach to Orlando Executive. She let go of his hand, but the look in her eyes left little doubt of her gratitude.

The Gulfstream landed, and the moment the door opened Alexis knew she was home. The warm, moist Florida air welcomed her, and she took a deep breath, relishing the earthy odor she had always taken for granted. *Never again*, she thought. She started down the stairs and saw her parents standing off to the side of the terminal. She gave them a quick wave, then turned to June and Bobby, who were following her.

"We'll wait in the lounge," June said.

Bobby and June headed for the terminal while Alexis walked over to where Percy and Etonia Rothchild were waiting. They threw their arms around her and were still holding each other when Bobby and June entered the building. It was the better part of an hour before Alexis found them and dropped into the chair beside June.

"I wanted my parents to come with us to the house, but they said they'd drop by later," she said, giving June a sideways glance. "They know what's going on."

"They're pretty connected." June took a quick look at her watch. "You guys ready?"

Bobby was stretched out on a recliner enjoying a glass of scotch. "Sort of."

A car was waiting, and as they piled into the back seat for the familiar drive to Twelve Oaks. Alexis felt the tears welling up as they pulled off the street and crawled slowly up the drive in front of the house. They stopped behind a black Lincoln Navigator and she stepped out into the warm Orlando sunshine. Home. She wiped her eyes and entered the foyer, staring at what had been stolen from her not so long ago. Her children would be home soon, but her husband was never coming back.

She felt overwhelmed. It all seemed like a bad dream, except there was no waking up.

A secret service woman was standing off to the side of the room and a man in a black suit appeared from the back of the house and joined them.

"Just making sure everything is secure, Mrs. Chamberlain," the woman said. She had an earpiece with a tiny coiled wire.

Alexis stared at the unexpected guests. "Thanks," she said slowly, then led Bobby and June into the living room.

"I'd like you to make a list of everyone who helped," Alexis said as they walked. "I'm indebted."

Bobby thought of Jacky, who took a bullet while sitting as bait in the park. Then there was Jared, the landscaper who had been so observant, and nodded. He suspected they would both get a leg up on life from all of this. "Will do," Bobby said. He studied the bank of windows facing the water. "Mind if I look around?"

"Sure," Alexis said. "I'm going to call the children's school and make arrangements to get them back home."

Bobby was all for having a poke around. After a tour of the main floor he headed out the patio doors and gave the back yard a long, hard look. The lake was wide and would be almost impossible to swim. The neighboring yards were secure and as he stood on the dock and looked back at the house, he couldn't help but wonder how the twin had escaped. She was, he decided, a very resourceful woman.

"Quite the place," Bobby said when he returned.

Alexis rejoined them and sat on the couch next to June. "That went well. I'm flying down tomorrow afternoon to pick up Zach and Patricia."

"Wonderful," June said. She couldn't help noticing that in one hand Alexis was clutching the sprig from the tree outside her cabin at the gulag.

Alexis stood and started pacing the spacious room. "I'm having trouble getting my mind around everything. Another woman, in my house, pretending to be me. Sleeping with my husband, mothering my children. I'm not sure I can live here."

The room was quiet, and June tried to imagine what was going through Alexis's head at that moment. After all she had been through, now sitting and waiting for her father to walk into the room. She had no idea what it would be like.

"My sister and my mother, they're still out there somewhere," Alexis started, then stopped.

There were voices coming from the foyer and the secret service woman came into the room and stood off to the side. June was up off the couch and Alexis moved close enough to her that their hands were touching.

William Neilson walked into the room and Alexis froze. A mask swept over her face, hiding her emotions as she stepped forward and shifted into business mode. "Mr. President."

Neilson walked across the room and stood a few feet from her, looking completely awkward. "Alexis."

There was a moment of complete confusion, followed by shock, then disbelief.

"*You*?" she whispered, her voice barely audible.

He nodded.

"How is this possible?" she asked.

Neilson kept the distance between them. It was up to her to make the first move. He took a deep breath. "An affair—thirty-six years ago."

She stared at him, the disbelief growing. "All that time our families spent together and you never said a word."

"I only found out a few days ago. I had no idea."

Alexis turned and walked to the window and stared across the lake, stone faced. "That's quite a coincidence, our families next door to each other every summer." She looked back at him. "Don't you think?"

Neilson had dreaded this moment, but the truth was the only option. "My mother—she arranged it."

"What?" Alexis was in shock. She walked to the couch and sat down. "Auntie Laura. My grandmother."

"Yes."

"Oh, my God."

Alexis stared at the floor and tried to comprehend what she was hearing. The scope of the deceit was almost beyond comprehension. After a minute, she looked up at her father and said, "Your mother arranged for the Rothchilds to adopt me."

"She did."

"And she never told you."

"No. Not a word"

Questions flooded her mind. What would it mean to be the president's daughter—how would it affect her life? Her children's lives for that matter, and what would she tell them? Could she stay on as CEO at Synergy? Would the secret service always be there? Would her sister come after her again, considering who their father was? The list was endless.

She looked up at him standing patiently, waiting for her response. She tried to imagine the shock and betrayal he must have felt when this was dropped on him. His own mother—her grandmother—the woman had broken every possible trust. Now, with all of this crashing in on him, he was standing in front of her with his emotions on his sleeve. William Neilson was every bit the man she had always thought him to be. And, he was her father.

Alexis felt the tears rolling down her cheeks and clumsily wiped at them. She walked directly to him, ignoring the mascara smudged under her eyes, and said, "I'm..." she searched for the right words, "... in shock." She dabbed away the last of the tears. "What now? How do we handle this?"

He managed a smile. "Well, that's a hell of a good question." He motioned to the back yard. "Want to sit by the lake and have a talk?"

"I'd like that," she said.

Neilson grinned as he thought of the times they had spent together, sitting by the water at the summer house. It was familiar territory. "Come on," he said, opening the doors to the back yard.

Alexis started walking, then stopped and looked back at June and Bobby. "Oh, you two," she said, a huge grin on her face.

Bobby stood at the window, watching them cross the grass to the dock. Neilson took off his shoes and rolled up his pants, and sat on the edge of the deck with his feet in the water. Alexis was sitting close enough that their shoulders were touching. Shades of days past.

"Question for you," Bobby said.

June was still staring through the patio doors. "What's that?"

"What do you think Pat would have said when Neilson walked in?"

She burst out laughing.

three months later

Clayton Riggs poked his head into Bobby's office. "There are a couple of plainclothes cops here to see you."

"What do they want?" Bobby leaned back in his chair.

Clayton shrugged. "No idea."

"Send them in," Bobby said. "The weekend can wait."

Clayton disappeared and came back a minute later with Stacey Daniels and a mid-fifties man dressed in a pinstriped suit. Bobby jumped up from his chair and broke into a wide grin when he saw his old boss from Orlando Homicide.

"Stacey." Bobby couldn't hide his emotions. "C'mon in."

"Hi, Bobby." She gave him a wide smile. "This is Bennett Archer, our new chief of police."

"Right, I saw something about that on the news." Bobby shook Archer's hand and pointed to the chairs facing his desk. Clayton was hovering at the door and Bobby motioned for him to stay. "How are things, LT?" Bobby asked.

"Excellent," she said as she got settled.

"So, what can I do for you two?" he asked, sitting.

Stacey's voice got serious, like it used to when they were looking at a case and things were at a critical point. "Some new evidence has come to light on the Taft warehouse incident."

Bobby felt his hackles rise and gave it a few seconds before responding. "What would that be?"

She pulled a file from her briefcase and set it on his desk. "Andy Rogers, the cocaine dealer, came clean. He's admitted to lying about you shooting Sommers in cold blood. Told us everything." She tapped the file with her fingernail. "It's all here."

Bobby didn't make a move to take the file, or to respond. He could feel Archer's eyes on him, probing for a reaction.

Finally, the chief cleared his throat and said, "It all went down exactly as you said. Sorrenson and Ross are up on charges."

Bobby didn't say a word. The setup had cost him dearly, and the fallout almost got his wife and children killed. He wasn't feeling overly forgiving.

Archer leaned forward, his hands resting on Bobby's desk. "We owe you one hell of an apology."

Bobby leaned back in his chair, asking himself what an apology from Orlando PD would mean in practical terms. He gave Clayton Riggs a quick glance, but the man's face was a mask. This was his call. He thought for a minute, figuring this whole thing was going to be a process, with lawyers and offers of compensation. It would take time, and he wasn't about to be in a rush.

"How about putting that apology in writing," Bobby said.

Archer stood and offered his hand. "We'll be in touch next week."

"That would be fine." Bobby shook

As they were heading for the front doors, Stacey hung back a bit and turned to Bobby. "*What* the hell is going on?"

He was confused. "I'm not sure what you mean."

"Rogers was dropped in our lap," she said, eyebrows raised. "The whole file was, with everything but a bow on top. There was evidence and corroboration to back up every detail. Nothing to chance." She gave him a hard look. "You've made some new friends?"

He smiled. "If you only knew."

Bobby retreated through the office and let himself out the back way to where his car sat waiting. He slipped it into gear and started out for June's house.

The phone rang and Lizzie's excited voice came through the speakers. "Daddy, when are you coming?"

"Yeah, dad." It was Sarah and every word was carefully measured. "When are you coming?"

"Soon, you little monsters. I have one more place to go, then I'm all yours."

"Disney," Lizzie yelled. "I want to see Mickey."

"Oh, sweetie, it's Mickey's day off," Bobby said in the most serious voice he could muster.

"Bobby, stop misbehaving," Janis chimed in. "You *do* realize they actually believe you."

"Okay, we'll see Mickey." He paused for a second. "And Minnie."

"Yay."

He was three blocks from June's house by the time he'd managed to get them off the line, after conceding to ice cream. Bobby parked and sprinted up the driveway. When she didn't answer the door he went around the side of the house and found her sitting on a bench by the lake. He dropped down beside her.

"That's it?" she asked. "It's officially the weekend?"

"It is."

"What time are the kids expecting you?"

Bobby checked his watch. "In about an hour." He rolled his eyes. "Disney World. Tough negotiators, those two."

Overhead, the sky was deep blue with a few popcorn clouds. The lake was calm and the palms barely moved in the still air. It was Florida at its best.

They sat quietly, enjoying the silence, then Bobby asked, "Any word on Sylvia Dupres or her daughter?"

June shook her head. "Nothing. I checked with Brad Lawrence over at NSA, and they found out the daughter's name is Monique, but they have no idea where they are."

"Incredible that two people can just disappear like that."

"It sounds like they've had lots of practice," June said, shaking her head. "The FBI almost had Monique. Nobody can figure out how she slipped away. And her mother, not a trace of her either."

Bobby thought about that for a minute. Sylvia Dupres was more than just a chameleon. She had played Laura Neilson, a powerful and resourceful woman, and it was entirely possible she had led Armand Cortez in the direction that best suited her. Maybe she and her rotten-to-the-core daughter were the ones pulling the strings right from the start. Worse, she still held a trump card—that the president had fathered illegitimate twins—and Bobby didn't doubt for a minute that she would use it when the time was right.

He turned to June. "It must be a worry for the president—having both Sylvia Dupres and her rogue daughter out there."

"No kidding," June agreed. "There may be some interesting times ahead for our president."

"Indeed," Bobby said. He shifted slightly so he was facing her. "You and I. Where were we when all this started?"

She smiled. "I cooked you dinner, we had a nice chat, then the wheels came off."

"I remember," Bobby said. "The food and the company were perfect. Want to try again?"

"I'd like that," she smiled. "Tomorrow night maybe?"

"Done." Bobby grinned and glanced at his watch. "I need to go. The kids will be waiting."

She gave him a sideways look. "Bobby Greco, that's why you came to visit me."

"What?"

"You wanted a dinner date."

He was totally busted. "Yeah, I did."

She leaned over and gave him a quick kiss. "Have fun with the girls."

His phone rang as he headed up the lawn and he checked the caller ID. "Hey, it's a FaceTime from Pat." He touched the green button and Pat and Yulia's faces popped up on the screen. Bobby jogged back, sliding in beside June so Pat and Yulia could see them.

Pat was beaming. "Hey, Bobby, what's up?"

"Relaxing by the lake at June's place," Bobby said, tipping the phone a bit toward her.

Yulia saw June and a huge grin splashed across her face. There were a few minutes of catching up, then Pat flipped the image on the camera around. A small, moored yacht appeared.

"Forty-three-foot Carver," Pat said. "Almost new, sleeps six and has an awesome motor. It's a beauty, and check this out." He flipped the image back so he and Yulia were on the screen, then held up what looked like a credit card. "It's a gas card. I never have to pay to fuel this baby."

"Courtesy of Alexis?"

"Yeah, and she paid off the mortgage on my house." He was all smiles. "Life is good, my friend."

Bobby thought about the call he'd received from the bank a couple of weeks back. Both his and Janis's mortgages had been paid in full as well. "I know what you mean."

"Where *are* you two?" June asked.

"Halifax, Nova Scotia. We're heading south today, for Belize. Thought we'd check in with you guys and see if we could stop somewhere along the coast and link up for a drink."

"Yeah, of course," Bobby said. June was nodding. "Cocoa Beach would work."

"Sure, Cocoa Beach. We'll call the day before we get there."

"Have you ever driven one of those things?" Bobby asked.

Pat pulled out a captain's hat and tucked it on his head. He grinned and leaned in so his face filled the screen. "Hell, no, but how hard can it be."

The screen went black.

If you enjoyed

One is Evil

Then be sure to sign up for Jeff Buick's newsletter and receive the prequel to this Bobby Greco novel (hey, it's never too late to get a good read for free) "No End of Bad Guys"

Visit www.JeffBuick.com to find out more

Buy Link: https://www.jeffbuick.com/books/no-end-of-bad-guys/

Get ready for Jeff Buick's next scheduled release!

A Killing Game

Buy Link: https://www.jeffbuick.com/books/a-killing-game/

Newsletter Link: https://www.jeffbuick.com/newsletter/

other titles by
JEFF BUICK

Bobby Greco series

No End of Bad Guys—September 2019
https://www.jeffbuick.com/books/no-end-of-bad-guys/

Curtis Westcott series

A Killing Game—December 2019
https://www.jeffbuick.com/books/a-killing-game/

AJ Costa series

Size Four—TBD
https://www.jeffbuick.com/books/size-four/

Stand-alone titles

The Krubera Conspiracy—March 2020
https://www.jeffbuick.com/books/the-krubera-conspiracy/

Bloodline—TBD
https://www.jeffbuick.com/books/bloodline/

The Art of Deceit—TBD
https://www.jeffbuick.com/books/the-art-of-deceit/

The Reluctant Truth—TBD
https://www.jeffbuick.com/books/the-reluctant-truth/

acknowledgments & kudos

While I'm the one who sits in my favorite Starbucks and types for endless hours to create this stuff, my books are a collaborative effort. These are my fellow co-conspirators.

Nothing would get done if it weren't for my incredible wife, Celia. She anchors me (in a good way) and keeps me focused. She is my encouragement, my reality check and my shoulder to rest on. She's also the best editor I've ever had. Lucky me.

Christina Curkovic is my awesome behind the scenes person. She takes care of everything, like those cool links so you can get to Amazon and find my books, and a hundred other things. If Christina suddenly disappeared and I had to do all that stuff, my creative side would shrivel up and die. She lets me write, so I adore her.

Michael Hartley-Robinson is a friend, mentor, and sounding board. He is my Saturday morning coffee guy, a source of intriguing plot lines, and a brilliant proof reader.

Laura Rushford is the BEST proof reader EVER. She is a like a heat-seeking missile for bad grammar (guilty) and misplaced/misused words (guilty again). Thank you, Laura.

Check out The Team page on my website for the rest of the crew. I could never do this alone: https://www.jeffbuick.com/the-team/

about the author

JEFF BUICK has been writing thrillers since 1998 and he has no plans to stop anytime soon. His first book was a Young Adult story called Download to Disaster that he wrote for one of his sons. It was about a bad guy taking down the Internet (which pretty much no one knew of back then), and it's so hokey it if he released it now, it could be a comedy.

Travel plays a big part in his life, and he's spent time in Africa, South and Central America, Europe, and New Zealand. This love of travel is reflected in where he sets his novels.

Jeff works hard at writing great beach reads that engage, enlighten and entertain the reader.

He lives in Calgary, Canada with his wife Celia.

Read more about Jeff on his website and sign up for his newsletter to receive exclusive updates and reader bonuses:

www.JeffBuick.com

Made in the USA
Middletown, DE
03 November 2019

77821208R00215